Waterborn

William McDonald-Newman

To Red.
For all the stories you never had a chance to tell.

Throw your soldiers into positions whence there is no escape, and they will prefer death to flight. If they will face death, there is nothing they may not achieve.

-Sun Tzu

Olivia Blacklock woke to the harsh ring of a piercing siren. It sliced through the muddled thickness in her head, clinical and uncaring. Her eyes blinked open, but the world she found didn't click. Her mind just couldn't make it fit.

The whole space thrummed, like a drum just before the final fade of a heavy beat. There was a surging sensation to it, like a car in motion or a plane taking off. Soft blue walls curved inwards, hemming the long hall that stretched to the right and left. Nearly a dozen unfamiliar faces crowded two long benches.

The surging movement stopped, pitching Olivia against the man next to her. He grunted, and then pushed her upright.

Wide eyed, Olivia's hand dove into her worn jacket, clutching for a knife.

It was gone.

They were all gone.

One pocket after another, empty. Even the razorblade in Olivia's collar was gone. Her breaths became shallow, bile spilling onto her tongue.

Barely a meter away, a section of the bowed wall slid open. Frigid air blasted in, filling her ears with a roar. The wind bit and chilled to the bone.

A tall figure stalked by, pausing in front of Olivia.

It was a… thing.

An oceanic blue-green and lithe, swathed in gray cloth, the Thing seemed to dance with every step. It took a man in an expensive suit by the shoulders and drew him to his feet. The man's mouth hung open, his eyes wide and shocked as he stared into the Thing's face. It raised a scaled hand and drew a shape on the man's right cheek.

A breath later, it spun and flung him out of the opening in the wall.

Olivia watched, her thoughts too scrambled, bouncing around her skull like angry bees. She watched his drop.

For a few seconds, he was visible. The first hundred meters or so. After that, he was out of sight. There was no sound of landing. No impact.

All Olivia heard was the scream; faint, fearful, small in the wind.

Two hands lifted Olivia by her jacket. Her head turned. She locked eyes with the Thing. White, all white. Staring back at her were two perfect, glistening, ivory stones planted where eyes should have been. A finger sketched across her cheek, warm in the wind's chill. She hadn't seen the design on the man, but she felt it now. A single spiraling line curling outward into the shape of a teardrop. The tail pointed upwards, towards her right eye.

With a satisfied nod, the Thing spun her around.

Wind dragged at Olivia's clothing, tugging towards the open door. Those cold, elemental claws seemed to dig and draw, pleading and fearsome. Outside, the sky was bright and blue, stretching off into a sunny eternity, studded with wisps of gray.

Two hands pressed against her back.

Olivia dug her heels into the floor. She teetered for a moment, fighting not to fall.

Behind her, the Thing grunted, a rolling, gravelly sound halfway to a hum. Then a palm slammed into her back, firm as a rounded stone, and she flew.

Olivia blinked, her eyes watering, fighting to see what was coming. For a fraction of a second, she saw it all. A range of towering mountains, peaks crumbling and blunted, ran in both directions, slopes sinking in steppes down to a too blue ocean. A skirt of woodlands ran along the line between mountain and sea, clinging tight against the water's lap.

In a blink it was a blur. Tears filled Olivia's eyes as the wind tore the moisture from them. She closed her eyelids. She was too high. People back in London had tried to jump from the bridges sometimes, but most weren't tall enough. Couple broken bones, usually, maybe a concussion. Suicide by bridge took a lot of down.

This? This was too high. There wouldn't be a body; there'd be a pasty splatter.

Maybe the sea would wash her away.

Olivia wondered how it'd gotten her here. The Thing. Kidnapping street kids was easy, but usually it was pervs or pimps. She'd cut a guy last week for getting handsy, but no one had tried to grab her yet. Rags and dirt usually kept the worst off. They didn't know what a kid might be carrying under all that, let alone look like. Too much expense. That, and Olivia was small. Some pervs paid more for kids, but they wanted pretty ones, not malnourished streeters.

It was a long fall.

Maybe that'd make the landing quicker.

Maybe she wouldn't even feel it.

One second she'd be another scummy streeter with too few meals in her belly, the next she'd be gone.

The teardrop on her cheek stung, hot, bits of its heat spreading beneath her skin.

Maybe whatever came next would be kinder. But probably not. She'd been to church once. For the food. Drugs had been a major topic. That and prostitution. And theft. She hadn't really listened. Drugs had just made things harder for her, and the pimps scared her. She'd kept quiet about her sticky fingers.

Sticky fingers didn't help at times like this. Neither did the knives she didn't have.

The ground had to be close. The air was thicker, wetter, rich with salt, and she could hear waves crashing.

Olivia opened her eyes again. Just to check.

There was the water. Filling her vision. So close.

She didn't want to die.

A furl of blue-green rose before her eyes, the curved surface leaping up at her.

Olivia's eyes slammed shut again. She was going to be eaten. That sucked. It'd be slower than a landing. Stomach acid and all. Not like she had a choice though. Maybe the fish would choke on her. Now that'd be-

She hit, but…

No teeth.

No impact.

Just softness.

Olivia opened her eyes again.

The water was there, around her, all blue and clear, stinging with salt. The pillowy texture faded as the tower of liquid sank back into the sea. It drew her down, her aquatic cushion melting into normal water. The crash left her adrift in a wash of salt and bubbles, below a sun-dappled surface.

Air.

She needed air.

Olivia screamed, silent, and nothing but bubbles pouring forth. She tried to follow them up.

Air, she demanded, willing herself towards the gleaming warmth of sunlight.

Around her, water surged again, thrusting her back towards the surface. She gasped a lungful of sweet oxygen. Another breath.

Something had caught her.

But abnormal water was not the main issue right now. Olivia had just survived being thrown from some weirdo's plane, yay, but now she was in the sea. This wasn't question time, this was 'desperately not drowning' time.

Glaring around, Olivia found the mountains. They weren't hard to find. She was about a hundred yards from the nearest sandy rim to their green skirt. From here, all that green looked comfortingly tree-like.

Swimming to shore wasn't too bad. Olivia remembered how to swim. She'd tried not to, but it'd hidden, spiderlike, in the bowels of her memory.

One hand in front of the other. Feet kicking. Breaths came in labored, heavy beats, but the panicked bursts and gasps were gone. The motions helped. No need to remember the rest if she didn't have to. Her clothes weighed her down, and she must've left a trail of dirt and grime, but she made it to the beach.

The waves were small, but they still buffeted Olivia as she stood, hands digging into the wet sand. Her shoes squelched as she stood. Clear of the lapping waves, her knees bent, numb. Kneeling, back to the sea, she caught her breath. She felt soreness begin to seep in. Too many muscles that she hadn't used enough. Or that she'd starved. All of her had been pretty starved a couple times. Soup kitchens ran out fast in winter.

Yanking off her shoes, Olivia upended them, pouring the seawater out. She glared at them as they dripped. Her feet would be wet for hours if she put them back on. Wet feet sucked. Torn up feet were worse though. Wringing out her socks was pointless. After a long, hot summer, they were thin, worn, and entirely gone in places. It was hotter here though. Too hot for her two shirts, hoodie, and jacket.

"Fuckin' hell," Olivia grumbled, pulling off her layers. She'd carry them. Might get cold at night. She put her shoes back on, socks and all.

Glancing around, Olivia took it all in.

The forested carpet at the foot of the mountains spread out around her, rocky and wooded. The trees were short, smaller than the ones in the parks back in London. Maybe ten meters tall at the extreme. They were thick, though, dense and gnarled, coating the stony ground with shadows. From what she'd seen above, it was a thin border that encircled the actual slope. It must get too rocky there for the trees.

Olivia had no idea how she'd gotten here, but the view she'd seen from above made this 'here' very distant from yesterday's 'here.' Giant mountain ranges popping through the ocean weren't very British. That and not seeing any UK-looking blobs in the distance. Or city-looking ones. Just mountains and water and islands. Even the trees were wrong.

So, that made this definitely far the hell away from London.

Which meant that Olivia needed new rules.

Old rules, like 'Stab Pervy Bastards Whenever Possible,' no longer applied. Well, unless some pervs showed up. She could add that rule back if that happened.

"Rule One…" Olivia said, but she trailed off.

Having no idea what Rule One should be made vocalizing it a problem. She licked her lips, thoughtful. They tasted like salt. Salt made people thirsty. That thought made her instantly aware of exactly how painfully thirsty she was.

"Rule One: Find The Water," Olivia declared. With that, she set off.

The woods were just as sucky as they'd looked. Between the slick rocks that coated the ground beyond the beach, and the stubborn trees that clung to every crack and seam, walking was rough.

A dozen yards in, Olivia slipped. Her hands slapped into the boulder she'd tried to climb, saving her skull, but her feet hit the roots that ran along the bottom of the rock with an abrupt jolt. She frowned and sat, massaging her ankles.

It was fine. Luckily.

Not being able to walk would mean no water.

Groaning, Olivia ran her hands through her hair and thought it through. The fall had been a rush, but now the adrenaline was settling. Reality rushed in, like a falling ceiling. God, she was screwed. No food. No water. No idea where she was. Shit, if she hadn't known how to swim she'd already be dead. Her eyes stung. Her vision swam, blurring.

Shit.

She didn't have time for this. Falling apart wouldn't help.

Olivia took a deep breath. Another. Her fingers clenched in her hair, yanking at her scalp. The pain pulled her back. She'd hated London anyway. No reason to miss that hellhole. This was fine. She just needed some stuff. She'd be ok. There were all those 'Reality' shows about people surviving in the wild. This was fine. Totally doable.

Tears wouldn't do shit.

Standing again, Olivia shifted her weight around, testing her ankles. They were fine. Not even sore. Lucky.

"Rule Two: Don't Climb The Big Rocks," Olivia said, making her way around the edge of the boulder. There was a cluster of smaller ones clenched between it and its neighbor in the ridgeline. A couple of crooked trees poked through the holes in the stone. She tested each step this time, putting a bit of weight on at first to make sure it'd hold.

Water filled more and more of Olivia's mind as her mouth grew dry. Drier, really. She wasn't hot, yet, but that was because of the wet clothes and shade.

On the other side of the boulders, the ground was higher, but level. Smaller rocks, gravel, pebbles, and sand filled the space between sprawling roots that mirrored widespread and leafy branches. It made the ground strange, dirt-like from shadows and bark, but as Olivia moved she could see the bare rock and sand appear beneath the interlaced tendrils. Overhead, the air hummed, chirps and creaks mingling with the rustling leaves. Ocean wind whistled through every few minutes, hushing the click and buzz of insects. A bird hopped along a root at her feet and plucked a pebble from the ground.

No, not a pebble, a bug, Olivia realized, chuckling as legs and a segmented torso appeared when the thing gave up on its camouflage.

But the chuckles died.

The bug reminded Olivia too much of herself. She thought about kicking the bird to save the bug, but she didn't. Life was life. Food chains and all that bullshit. She kept going. The base of the mountains couldn't be far now. She'd already been walking for a quarter of an hour or so.

Another quarter of an hour later, Olivia still hadn't reached the mountains. The woods were wider than they'd looked. But she was feeling a lot better about how far it was from the plane. Mainly because of the pancaked corpse she'd found.

It hadn't been in Olivia's path, but she'd followed the noise. Not the noise of an impact. It'd been the chittering and chirping that'd drawn her. Bugs and birds had been battling for the bits. She kept her distance. From the scraps of gray suit near the edges, it'd been the guy shoved out of the plane just before her.

"Yup," Olivia whispered under her breath, backing away from the bloody rodent feast, "Feeling really good about swimming now."

No matter what weirdness with the water, at least she hadn't become bird-food.

Olivia had backed off the mess and kept on going towards the mountains. They stretched on to her right and left, visible through the cracks in the leafy treetops. Fewer holes made it harder and harder to see the rocky ridge as it neared the horizon, and then disappeared entirely from view. The mountains didn't stop though. She'd gotten a good enough view during her fall to know that.

Weaving through the trees, Olivia finally reached the base of the mountains. Before her, the ground fell away, dropping three or four meters in a cascade of boulder and block. The trees stopped at the top, leaving the sandy stretch beyond sunbathed, and washed in a rush of cool, clean air. Spotted with rounded stones, the sand tapered for a dozen meters, down to a shallow stream of clearest blue. The stream ran parallel to the wooded rise at Olivia's feet, fed by the mountainside opposite her.

That was what made Olivia's jaw drop. The mountainside was unnatural. There was no earthy slope, no tree coated rock. Instead, it was like a stair, pool after pool of clear water gathering in tiny plateaus before leaking down into those below. The leaks glittered in the sun, falling droplets shining like jewels. The pool lips were studded with little spurs of land, little clusters of sand and rock and tree. It was like staring at the side of a flower, each layer of petals full of a dewy glisten and trickle, rising up and up towards the sky.

Here and there, cracks between the petals fell upon cracks on the tier below. These deep clefts stood out like shadows, crevices where a splashing drizzle echoed. Olivia could almost feel the colder air oozing from them, tucked among the sun-warmed pools. Most were small, barely a few steps across.

"Rule One," Olivia reminded herself, focusing on the stream. She made her way to the stream at the mountain's feet. She left her jacket and hoodie on a rock and knelt to drink.

Olivia jerked back, surprised. It was warm! Somewhere between cold and hella cold had been more what she'd expected. She drank anyway. It was good, clean, and tasteless in a way that she hadn't had in years. Since before London. Back when she'd been in the States. And had parents.

Snarling, Olivia weathered the memories as they washed over her. She was used to it, but that didn't make it easier. She kept drinking. It washed away the dry saltiness on her tongue. The odd warmth distracted her. The flashes of memory weren't the first things she'd distracted herself from today. Probably wouldn't be the last.

Turning her head, hands still holding another mouthful of warm water, Olivia glared into the sky. She turned, checking back over the woods. The plane was still there, hovering high above. It wasn't a plane though. She'd been pretty sure it wasn't, but the alternatives…

Easier to ignore it.

But now she'd looked.

The 'plane' was as lean and muscular as the Thing. Two outstretched limbs curved from each side, stretching like the triangular wings of a Manta Ray. The arms fluttered, undulating and spraying glittering, shining liquid outwards. The wings were evenly placed, each centered on one lightly rounded corner of the main body. Wider than it was long, the whole thing flexed with its wings, ripples of effort racing across its surface as each undulation rolled into the next.

Olivia shivered. It felt wrong. The closest thing she could compare it to would be some kind of sea monster. Faceless and hungry, it'd be the kind that'd surge through inky depths in a documentary. The problem was that this one wasn't half hidden by shadows. It glowed an almost blackened blue, shining as the sun twinkled from the droplets cascading from its limbs.

Back to the water, Olivia decided. She focused on taking another drink. Time for another Rule. Something to distract her from… everything.

Nat wasn't alright. She knew she wasn't, and she knew why. The nausea in her belly had started after finding the body in the woods. It didn't take a genius to put one and one together and find a two.

"Medical track my ass," Nat grumbled, maintaining her pace. Fresh water would be inland, somewhere near the mountains, not that she'd learned that from a class. Wilderness survival hadn't been included. Her family had camped, reluctantly. She remembered that anything near the beach would be tidal, and thus salty. Not to mention bacteria. After an entire course on virology and common bacterial infections last semester, she knew better than to even try. Clean and fresh, that's what she needed, and that meant a spring, which meant the mountains.

Leaning more heavily on her stick, Nat tried to settle the wobble in her stomach. Working in healthcare had been all about fixing this worry, about knowing how to take care of herself. Now here she was on the ass end of nowhere.

Suddenly, the edge of the woods came into view. Nat could hear running water. She was getting close. Hopefully the alien had been nice enough not to poison anything.

Ugh.

Alien.

Just thinking the word made Nat roll her eyes. She couldn't come up with another explanation though. One of her brothers was an aviation nut, and he'd never mentioned or shown her anything like that ship. Nervously, she glanced over her shoulder, eyeing the craft through the leaves. It pulled at her curiosity. It looked biological, like some creature from a sci-fi show that'd been 3D printed a hundred sizes too big and brought to life.

Water. Water first.

Nat kept going, watching her feet as she hopped from a low boulder to the sand. Hitting the ground, she rolled forward, spreading the impact. She smirked, as she rose to her feet again. Gymnastics lessons paying off, even half a decade later.

Then Nat took in the beach. First came the rock that wasn't just a rock. There was a lumped up hoodie and a denim jacket, worn and threadbare.

Then came the squeak.

Nat stared at the first living person she'd seen since being shoved out of the fish-craft. Nat didn't know if she'd squeaked, or the girl.

Barely five feet tall, the Asian girl was thin and wiry, oversized shirts and jeans hiding all but her face, hands, and tar-black hair. She knelt, but in a blink her torso shifted slightly. The change made her resting legs into coiled springs, twin wires ready to leap into flight. One of her hands dropped with a splash, clenching a handful of wet sand.

"Whoa!" Nat blurted, her hands rising, palms out. Her staff fell onto the sand. Her heart thumped in her chest.

The girl stared, wide eyed, her nostrils flaring.

"Whoa!" Nat repeated, quieter. "Calm down!" she added, mostly to the girl, but partially to herself.

The girl's eyes narrowed.

The water burbled, filling the silence.

"I'm not here to hurt you," Nat explained, as her breathing slowed. She tried for gentle, calming. Maybe the girl didn't speak English?

"I got dumped out of that thing," Nat added, gesturing at the fish-craft, "And I'm just looking for water." She nodded behind the girl, at the stream.

The girl didn't look away, her gaze odd, low.

Nat paused, realizing why the look felt so strange. The girl wasn't looking at her face, but at her torso. The girl's eyes were slightly unfocused, oriented on the center of Nat's mass.

"Listen, I just want some water," Nat said, stepping forward.

The girl stepped back, her foot splashing in the water. The hand she'd had in the sand pulled back, ready to throw, while the other flexed, grasping for something.

Nat froze, eyes wide and mouth agape.

The grasping gesture ended with those long, thin fingers closing on a pale blue shape. It looked like a knife. Only a few inches long, and thin, with a handle that melted, dribbling in and among the fingers.

Following the drips, Nat watched the last few fly up from the water's surface, defying gravity to reach the girls fist.

Gaping, Nat just stood there, shocked.

Sci-fi fish-ship was one thing, but making knives from anti-gravity water pushed Nat's ability to rationalize. There was only so much some dark-ops military group could be hiding, and ragged kids didn't usually run around with secret military tech.

The girl frowned, then looked at her hand. She blinked. Then blinked again.

"Ok, I'm getting that you don't speak English, but maybe if I keep saying friendly things you won't stab me?" Nat proposed, hopeful. It gave her something else to think about. She stared at the girl's face, trying not to look at the thing in her hand.

"Yeah, that sounds right," continued Nat, keeping her hands raised. "Nice and peaceful. No stabby, please. I'm a nice Canadian, if you know where that is. Probably do. Most people know about Canada. Well, most Earth people. Maybe you're an alien too. Man, that'd throw the scientific community a curveball. Yeah, found aliens, but they just look like us. Hollywood'll give themselves an award for being right all along."

The girl looked at her again. Her features were taut, skin drawn close to sharp bones by starvation and tension.

"Less talking? I can do that, no problem. Less talking coming right up," Nat agreed, nodding understandingly and acting as though zipping her mouth. "Mmmh?" she mumbled through her clamped lips, trying to smile and give two thumbs up. Her heart thudded louder in the relative silence.

Staying low, ready to leap, the girl eased out of the water and along the bank. Her eyes barely moved, watchful, and the knife didn't waver. Once she was several meters out from between Nat and the water, she nodded.

Confused, Nat pointed at the water then at herself, brows raised. She really wanted to verbalize the question, or just to ramble in general to fill the anxiety stoking silence, but that seemed like a bad idea.

The girl nodded. Her legs relaxed, coiled springs slowly easing as she straightened for the first time.

Doing her best to smile, Nat dipped her hands into the water, raising a handful of the clear liquid to her lips. Warm? Warm water… She glanced at the mountainside. The layered pools must act like solar heaters, raising the temperature of the water as it traveled down. She frowned. That explained the warm water, but it didn't explain how the hell this much water got that high in the first place.

The girl grunted, breaking through Nat's ponderings.

Grinning through gritted teeth, Nat drank down another few gulps and straightened. Not talking combined with the wacky geology was making her nerves even worse. Aliens and girls with wacky knives were bad enough. She looked at the girl. At some point while Nat had been drinking, she'd moved around to stand by Nat's stick.

The girl raised one eyebrow and jerked her chin at the mountains.

Nat pointed at her mouth, asking permission. It was annoying, but better than getting stabbed. Maybe if she could talk again then Scrawny McStabby would calm down. Not a bad nickname actually. For a moment, her smile became genuine.

Stabby nodded.

Releasing a comically exaggerated sigh, Nat tucked a lock of her own dark hair behind her ear. She put on her best smile and said, "I've got no idea where we are. I just got dumped out of a strange aircraft and then the water caught me. I came inland looking for fresh water. Since you're asking me where here is, I'm guessing you're not a local?"

Stabby's head tilted slightly, flickers of curiosity in her dark eyes. She nodded, fractionally.

Nat's smile widened. Either Stabby knew English or she was guessing. Either way, it was a start. It didn't help with the 'where are we' or 'what was that thing' issues, but those could wait. This may not be Canada, but surviving here wouldn't be a picnic.

"Can you hunt?" Nat queried, nodding to the woods.

Stabby stayed still.

"Fish?" Nat added, pointing at the water and then pantomiming eating.

Nothing.

"Great," Nat grumbled, turning and looking up the mountain. "Just great. I guess we'll have to go find some of the others and see if they can find us food."

Stabby twitched, her eyes flicking to the sides as though suddenly aware that her back was facing the way others would probably be coming from.

"Listen," Nat said, drawing Stabby's attention. "I'm Nat. I'm Canadian. I'd really like to not get stabbed, and some food would be nice too. Why don't we go and look for other survivors?"

The moment stretched. Then Stabby nodded. The pale blue blade in her hand liquidated, pouring through her fingers.

Groaning with relief, Nat looked up at the sky and mouthed 'Thank God.' When she looked back at Stabby, the girl was shifting her weight, eyes a bit wide now that she just had a handful of sand.

"Hey," Nat said, raising her palms again. "All good. We're ok. How about I lead the way. You walk behind me. We can just head down this river for a while and see if anyone else shows up. That ok?"

Stabby rolled her eyes and nodded.

"Yeah, you definitely speak English," Nat grumbled, looking in either direction. They looked about the same.

Kneeling, Stabby dropped the handful of sand and picked up Nat's stick. It was a bit tall on her, sticking up above her head, but it appeared to fit comfortably in her long-fingered hand.

"You keep an eye on that stick," Nat said, setting off to the right, along the stream. "Wouldn't want the dangerous Canadian to have a stick. Oh no, the Canadian might go bonkers and start using the stick to whack little girls on the head. Cannibalism is so common in Canada these days. Maybe it's because they're just spelled so similarly! I bet that's it."

Nat continued to talk, filling the silence as they wandered. It made her feel less nervous about being eaten by the underfed looking Stabby.

This. Bitch. Would. Not. Shut. Up.

Olivia contemplated trying to do the knife thing again. Then she could stab Nat the Chat. Just a little. Maybe she'd shut up then.

There were two reasons Olivia didn't.

One, the talking grated, uncomfortable and shocking after so long on her own, but it was a strangely cathartic pain.

Two, Olivia had no bloody clue how the hell to make the knife. She'd been scared, jumpy, and wanted a knife really, really badly. And there it'd been. It'd felt so odd in her hand; comfortable and light, like another finger stretching towards Nat the Chat.

The reminder made Olivia look Nat up and down again. Canadian, huh? Hadn't been many of those in London. Tourists, mainly. The woman was tall, her browned skin just light enough to make her bold, black hair and bright blue eyes stand out. The jeans she wore were tight, and her little leather jacket barely reached her waist. Her backside, well, it was curvy in a way that made it clear she'd never gone hungry.

Scowling, Olivia's hand tightened around the stick. It wasn't as good as a knife at deterring trouble, but it'd do. Sticks had more range, but knives were scarier. Problem with knives was that they let the baddie get close. Good for sneaky stabbing, bad if the other guy saw it coming.

The guy who'd sold Olivia her first knife on the street had made her wait while he told her a story about knife fights. He'd said that in a knife fight, the winner was the one who went to the hospital, but the loser got a coffin. She'd seen enough knife fights since to agree. As close as it took to stick someone with a blade, they could stick right back. The guy had tried to get in her pants in exchange for his advice. Turned out Olivia was better with a knife than he'd expected. She'd gotten a couple more knives out of it. And some watches. And her cash. It'd fed her for her first week. Then some asshole had beaten her and taken all but two of the knives. Hadn't been able to find them. After that, she'd slept with a knife in hand.

Something snapped to the right. Rocks crunched, pressed together by a foot. Olivia stopped, staying very still. She watched the trees out of the corner of her eye.

Nat the Chat kept walking.

Olivia hissed, dragging a breath between her tongue and teeth to catch the woman's attention.

"-The ship looked like nothing I've heard of. Gotta be some kind of extra terrestrial, but I don't get why they'd snag a bunch of people and dump them somewhere. Maybe this is an experiment? Like, they'll decide on whether we make good slaves based on how well we survive here. That'd be tricky. We'd have to kill ourselves early or we'd be condemning humanity. Damn. Dark. Hey, maybe they just thought we could use a new place to live. Global Warming and all that. Could be nice space-people," Nat continued.

Rolling her eyes, Olivia tucked herself a little further behind a tree. Half in the rocky rise and half in the sand, the tree's wide trunk was easy to fit behind. She felt a twinge of embarrassment about leaving Nat the Chat like bait, but she'd tried to warn her.

More rocks grated, the harsh scratching sound carrying over the stream's gurgle.

Staff in one hand, Olivia slid up the rock wall with her other three limbs. No loose rocks. Quiet as a mouse. The sand on her sneakers rasped as they ground into the stone, but it wouldn't be audible. At the top, she scanned the trees. Eyes relaxed, she waited, searching for bits of movement and colors that didn't fit.

"Stabby?" Nat squeaked, her pitch rising, the word scurrying into the woods.

"Uh, hi?" a man's voice returned, coming from somewhere to Olivia's left, almost between her and Nat.

Low to the ground, knees bent and staff pointed like a spear, Olivia crept towards the voice. Not attacking Nat on sight or trying to follow her was good, but it was a deep voice, the kind that came with a big muscly person. That was bad.

"Hi?" Nat said, still high and confused, but obviously rallying. "You drop out of the fish-thing too?"

"Yeah," he replied, chuckling with an awkward kind of embarrassment. "That was…"

"Crazy, right?" Nat said, laughing nervously. "Yeah. My theory is that this is an alien planet, but I'm still working on why we're here."

"I heard," he answered, audibly wincing. "I wasn't sure if you were friendly so…"

"You listened in?" Nat guessed, sighing. "Guess that's fair."

"Do you usually talk to yourself or is this a special occasion?" he said. The words were different, warmer, as though he'd decided that he liked her.

Olivia rolled her eyes and kept creeping forward. She had four years of experience on how 'friendly' and 'safe' were very different. Hell, most of her experience said that friendly was rarely, if ever, safe.

"No," Nat said, "I was talking to someone. She got thrown out of the plane too, but I don't know where she went."

Gritting her teeth, Olivia kept moving. The urge to express her exasperation was immense, but that would give away where she was.

"Oh! Maybe she wandered off? Can I help you look for her?" he offered, his crunching steps moving closer to the rocky drop-off.

"That'd be great!" Nat said.

Catching sight of Nat through the trees, Olivia saw her wide smile. She felt kind of bad for Nat. Trust like that got people hurt. Badly. Then she realized how much the woman hadn't had to go through. It took a lot of safety and comfort to keep a person that trusting. Yeah, she didn't feel bad for Nat anymore.

The man slid into sight between two trees, facing Nat. His face was obscured by a branch, but he was big. Six feet and change, with a stained white shirt, black slacks, and skin the color of dark amber.

Six feet. Bloody hell.

Good thing Olivia had the big stick. And was directly behind him.

"Do you remember when you last saw her?" the man asked. "Oh, and I'm Tybalt. Ty for short," he said, waving in a nervous, friendly way.

"Natalie, but call me Nat," the Chat said, smiling up at him. "I saw her… I guess five minutes ago? Something like that. She's really quiet."

"What's her name?" Ty asked, turning to peer into the woods.

Olivia flattened her back to a trunk. Her breath stopped. Her heart thrummed. Goddamn. Next time she heard someone sneaking up on them she'd just run and leave Nat to chat them to death. Shit.

"She didn't say," said Nat, mournful. "Really quiet kid. Maybe fifteen or sixteen-ish. Short."

"We can backtrack the way you came. She probably left a trail in the sand," Ty suggested, turning back to Nat and stepping down to test the footing on the rock wall.

Ducking around the tree, Olivia surged forward. In a second, she'd halved the distance. He was halfway down the wall, a few steps from the edge of the trees. She was nearly-

"Yo!" a woman shouted, her voice blaring through the trees behind Olivia. "I'm coming! Don't go anywhere! I'm on my way!"

Shocked, Olivia froze at the top of the drop-off and looked at Ty's back. His head was right there. She could clonk him. Easy.

"Stabby!" Nat said, her smile warped, a mingling of joy and confusion.

Ty rotated at the hips, his feet planted on stable stones. His eyes met Olivia's and went wide. Twenties, she guessed, taking in his bright green eyes, wide nose, and full lips. There were no lines there, no wear or worry, just like Nat. The sight made Olivia really, really want to hit him.

"Found you?" he said, offering her a shy half-smile. His hand rose, as though about to help her down to the beach.

"Why the fuck did those aliens think this was a good place to dump us?" the shouting voice blared, bouncing off the trees. "Hey, y'all still there? Give us a shout!"

"Over here!" Nat called back, grinning.

"Thanks!" the shouter declared.

"Need a hand?" Ty said, raising his hand another inch or so towards Olivia.

Rolling her eyes, Olivia stepped back towards a tree. She stopped with her back against the trunk. She glared at Ty, hidden from the oncoming shouter. These two morons might not be worried, but Olivia liked not being dead, and a little paranoia went a long way.

Ty frowned at her. He glanced beyond, towards the shouter, and smiled. "Hey!"

"Hey!" the newcomer said, drawing the word out. She ran forward, only halting when she was at the top of the rock wall. "Hiya, pretty people," she added, looking back and forth between the Ty and Nat. "I'm Bee."

"Ty," Ty offered, beaming at her.

"And I'm Nat," Nat said, biting her lip with a hint of worry. "Don't make any sudden moves."

"Why?" Bee asked, hands going to her waist, hip cocking. "You two got alien herpes already?"

Ty's mouth flopped open but no sound came out.

"No," Nat chuckled, cutting him off. "I just don't want Stabby hitting you with a stick."

Olivia rolled her eyes again. Morons. She was surrounded by morons. Hell must be like this, but with more fire and kinky shit.

"Stabby?" Bee queried, losing some of her pleased confidence.

Nat jerked her chin behind Bee.

The woman glanced back, expecting a joke.

Fuck it. Olivia raised her free hand and waved. No smile though.

Bee looked the same age as the others, late teens, early twenties, but her hair was a bright, bold green, laced with shocks of blue and black. It parted off-center, most of its mass tumbling down the right side of her head, stopping just short of her chin. The hair distracted from her fragile features and soft lips, bits of the dye on her scalp bleeding onto her pale skin. She was built pretty, with curves that would've gotten her killed or kidnapped where Olivia was from.

"What're you doing there?" Bee demanded, spinning on her heel to square off with Olivia.

"I think she was trying to sneak up on Ty," Nat explained, walking over to the rocks. "Probably worried he was a predator, a wolf or something."

Internally, Olivia noted that Nat was using 'predator' to refer to an animal, not a perv. Wild animals hadn't occurred to Olivia. Fuck. What would she do about them? She glanced at Ty. Maybe he could deal with the animals. If he got injured fighting a bear he wouldn't try anything. Two birds, one stone.

"What's your name?" Bee asked, bending to put her head at Olivia's level.

Internally, Olivia stifled the urge to whack her. Bee wasn't that much taller. Bitch.

"She doesn't talk," Nat supplied. "Hasn't said a word since I found her."

"Weird," Bee said, thoughtful. She looked at Nat, then Ty, then noticed the water. "Oh thank God! Water. Shit. I need a drink."

Ty offered her a hand.

Taking it, Bee shot him a wide smile, and stepped down. She stumbled, nearly knocking Ty over, but somehow hopped to the ground all right. Leaving Ty wobbling and staggered, Bee headed past Nat and down to the water.

"Thirsty?" Nat said, looking at Ty and gesturing towards the water.

Righting himself, barely, Ty nodded. He looked back at Olivia, visibly debating whether to offer her a hand too.

"She won't take it," Nat noted. "She can take care of herself."

Unbidden, a smile pulled at Olivia's lips. She snorted.

Ty's brows rose, surprised and intrigued.

Like that, Olivia's amusement was gone. Pushing off her tree, she went to the smooth side of the boulder and jumped down to the sand. The staff hit first, slowing her descent in case of hidden rocks. It was a bit like showing off. Kind of. Not really.

"It's warm, but this shit is cleaner than what I've got at school," Bee laughed, sitting back on her heels and looking at the water. Her chest heaved, breathless from the massive gulps of water she'd taken.

"Yeah," Nat agreed, looking up the mountainside. "It's coming down from up there. Must be naturally filtered through the earth on the way up."

"Pretty sure water doesn't flow that way," Bee countered, frowning back at her.

Olivia rolled her eyes and got her own drink.

So, there was Bee, the hot punk, Ty, the big 'helpful' guy, and Nat, the Chat, who apparently had a zillion siblings, was Canadian, a med student, and hated glue.

Three spoiled, black moneybags, and Olivia.

Yeah. They were all gonna die. Question was would she kill them out of annoyance, or would something big and hungry found them first?

Killing all of them wouldn't be too hard. Joey had killed bigger than the black guy, and the little girl was the only one with a weapon.

But did he need to kill them?

Bee, Ty, Nat, and Stabby.

Stabby. Joey smiled. Funny. Curious, too. Stabby. Did she have a knife? Knives were best. Easy to hide. Effective. Personal. Joey liked knives. Always had.

Stabby. Stabby had a knife. Or a shiv.

Joey's hand tightened, his calloused hands rubbing the rough bark of the stick he'd found. It'd taken nearly a quarter of an hour with a sharp rock, but he'd put a tip on it. Not as good as a knife though. Knives could cut and slice, perfect for skinning and carving. Putting holes in animals wouldn't do, not if he wanted a meal. Right now, he'd have to tear off pieces to cook.

Tear.

Joey shivered, disgusted. How uncivilized. If he was going to resort to cannibalism to survive, there was a right way and a wrong way.

On the other hand, it would be a week before starvation sapped his resolve, chewing away at his own body. Now that Joey knew where the fresh water was, there was no rush. Besides, it was lovely here.

Rolling onto his back, Joey smiled up at the sun, enjoying its warmth. So different from home. It'd been snowing back home yesterday, and now he was in a tropical paradise. It was almost as good a treat as being away from his parents.

Aliens.

That'd been Nat's theory.

Maybe. Joey certainly hadn't recognized the creature on the ship. Alien seemed more likely than fish people from under the sea, or faeries from the bowels of the earth. Cracking his eyes, he looked out over the treetops. He'd check the stars tonight. If this place were an alien planet, well, the stars would be different.

Joey shivered, curious and excited.

Alien.

He'd never had alien before.

"What?" Nat asked, thoroughly confused.

"I'm just saying it'd be easier, going forward, if we knew who was in charge," Ty said, doing his best to lean casually against a boulder. "Simplifies things."

"I'm so glad I'm not the only one!" Bee said, sucking down another gulp of water. She stood, turning to face the others with a majestic toss of her hair. "You're completely goddamn right. I didn't want to bring it up, but things would be a lot better if we voted now. That way, when we find the others, there won't be any cockups."

"Cockups over what?" Nat demanded, nonplussed, looking from one to the other. "About whether we want to live? It's kind of an easy yes or no situation. This isn't a game show with a bunch of wacky challenges we've got to compete in. We've got water, we need shelter, and we need food. Shit's pretty damn simple."

"Shit's never simple," groaned Bee, waving her arms exasperatedly. "There's always that one ass who wants extra food, and the brat who doesn't like to work, and the moron who really likes showing off that they know shit."

"I think that kind of thing will be fine," Ty said, shaking his head. "People can generally get along and figure stuff out. Look, we've already gotten over the shock of getting airdropped here. I'm worried about when we have to make a big choice. The minute we find out what the aliens brought us here for, or where to go, we'll fall apart. That could get us all killed."

"Ok, you're worried about morons," Nat said, gesturing to Bee. "You're worried about big decisions," she went on, gesturing to Ty. "I'd really like to have something to eat. I vote that we worry about food first."

A tongue clicked, sharp.

Nat's brows rose, inspecting the suddenly audible Stabby.

Once she had their attention, Stabby raised her hand to head height and nodded at Nat.

"Thanks," Nat said, tentative but grateful for the support.

"I'm good with that," Bee agreed, her smile returning. "I like food."

"Ok," Ty conceded, eyeing Stabby with a wary curiosity.

They stood there, waiting.

"Well?" Nat prompted. "Does anyone know where to find food on tropical islands?"

Ty bit his lip, thinking.

Stifling her frustration, Nat asked, "Anyone gone camping before? Fishing?"

"Never got the draw," Bee answered, shaking her head.

"What?" Ty said, frowning.

"One, no booze," Bee said, raising a finger in front of her face. "Two, no shower." Another finger. "No bed." Third finger. "That's three strikes. If I'm going to leave my place for more than twenty-four hours I want at least two out of those three."

Stabby snorted.

"I've got some bad news for you," Nat said, fighting to hold back laughter. If she started, she might end up crying. Her emotions were all over the place. At least the conversation was helping. At least she wasn't alone.

"Oh for three, Bee," Ty said. "The river might work as a bath though."

"Prefer hot tubs," Bee grumbled, eyeing the water.

"Food," Nat said, trying to get them back on track. "We need food. Ty?"

"I went fishing once, but I don't have any equipment," he said, shrugging, apologetic. "I've hunted too, but only a little and with guns."

"No guns, no fishing gear," Nat summarized, rubbing the bridge of her nose. "Got it. Thanks."

"We could eat bugs," Bee suggested.

"Bugs?" Nat repeated, her skin crawling.

"We don't know what's poisonous," Ty said, much to Nat's relief.

"Your face is poisonous," Bee growled, her face scrunching as she stuck her tongue out at him.

"No bugs," Nat said, her skin still doing its best imitation of a toddler's messy crawl.

Bee shrugged and crossed her arms.

Scanning their surroundings, Nat searched for something, anything. There had to be a way to get food. Fish was safest, hell, easiest, but they didn't have a pole or string or a hook or…

"Maybe we could sharpen Stabby's stick and spear a fish?" Nat suggested, flashing her friendliest smile in Stabby's direction.

The girl frowned.

Ty lifted a small rock from the wall where he was leaning. He ran a finger along one edge. "Plenty of sharp rocks. That'd be pretty easy, but who's going to do the spearing?"

Nat looked hopefully at Ty.

"I can try," he agreed, visibly trying to rally confidence.

"Perfect!" Nat said, pleased. Fish was good. Hell, anything other than bugs was fantastic. "Stabby, can we have the stick?"

Still frowning, Stabby looked pointedly at the woods.

"But that one's right here and it's so straight and perfect," Nat pleaded, walking over to her. "We can find you another stick. Please?"

"Hey! Stop bullying the kid," Bee said, shifting uneasily. "We can find another stick. No need to give her shit. She's gone through enough today."

"We've all gone through a lot today," Ty said.

"No shit, Sherlock, but she's a kid!" Bee growled.

"Shut up!" Nat shot over her shoulder, adding to Stabby, "Stick? Please?" Just in case something wasn't translating, she held a hand out towards the stick. That should help get the point across.

Stabby's eyes were thin, barely open at all, and her mouth white with pressure. She let go of her stick, letting it fall towards Nat's hand as she shifted back towards the boulders at the edge of the beach.

Smiling, relieved, Nat tossed the stick to Ty. "Get sharpening. Bee, you and I are going to try to build some kind of shelter."

"You use this word build," Bee replied, stretching the word out into an extra syllable and adding air quotes.

"Do you want to sleep on the sand?" Nat asked.

Bouncing on the balls of her feet, Bee's green locks bobbed, bits of blue and black showing through. "It's not that bad."

"It'll get cold after the sun goes down," Nat informed her, starting up the rock wall. "And who knows how many things live in the sand and come out at night."

Torn between annoyance and sudden concern about sand-bugs, Bee grumbled her way along in Nat's trail.

At the top of the semi-stair of stones between two boulders, Nat realized that Stabby had disappeared. Damn. Nothing to do about it now. If Stabby ran off, it wasn't Nat's fault. She wouldn't feel bad about it.

Nat couldn't quite manage to convince herself.

Distraction. That'd help.

Focused on the task, Nat set about finding something that'd add 'soft' to a ground that seemed entirely disinterested in the trait.

Ty woke up slowly. Really slowly. Falling asleep had been hard enough, so his subconscious was probably throwing up every roadblock it could. He wiped the crusty bits from his eyes. At least the noise was gone. Last night, after they'd settled in to sleep, the woods had woken up. Humming shouts and deep bellows had carried through the treetops, perforated with sharp cries and hissing barks. Freaky.

Shaking his head, Ty pushed the memories to the back of his mind. He sat up, blinking at the light. The girls were still asleep. He paused, looking at them. Bee's hair was different, colorful, but it was her expression that caught him. There was amusement, warm and bright, like a candle in the dark. It wasn't an actual smile, not even a full expression really, but there were hints; a tiny bend in her lips, a crinkle at the corners of her eyes.

Rubbing his face with his hands, Ty dragged his mind away from the woman he'd slept next to. He didn't like to curse, but this was one of the moments when he could relate to those that did. One night in the woods away from home and he was acting like a horny high schooler. He was better than that.

Ignoring the urge to check out what Nat looked like asleep, Ty stood and stepped down from the mound of rocks the girls had built to shore up their wood and leaf bed. It hadn't been comfortable, but it'd been better than the rock. He watched his footing, careful not to wake them. He'd managed to mess up the stick last night, so the first thing to do was find a new one. The damn thing had been too thin. The end had just snapped off whenever he got close to putting a point on it. He didn't even want to think of what Stabby was going to do when she found out.

First things first, Ty decided. Water. He needed to clean the taste of sleep from his mouth. The shelter wasn't far from the beach, so he'd need to stay quiet when he got to sharpening. Maybe he could find a better rock too.

At the top of the drop-off, Ty stopped. The beach looked a lot like it had last night. There were tracks and dents in the soft sand where they'd walked and broken bits of stick where he'd worked.

The spears were new though.

Four lengths of wood, a bit bent here and there, were sticking out of the sand. Each was about Ty's height, their ends shining in the morning sun, jagged and sharp.

"What the…" Ty mumbled, peering up and down the creek. Nothing. Back among the trees? Nothing. He made his way down the rock wall and over to the spears. He pulled one from the ground and hefted it. It was nice. Good weight, good length, very stabby.

Stabby.

Ty shook his head, smiling. In a video game, she'd be the one to protect; she'd be young, probably traumatized, lacking the skills to save herself, but with some gift that'd help the protagonist. He chuckled. Well, if he could figure out how to use them, she might have already revealed her protagonist helping superpower.

Kicking off his shoes, Ty waded into the stream. Near the middle, leaning against the weight of the current and wet up to his waist, he raised the spear and waited.

If Ty was going to really, really honest, he'd actually only gone fishing once. Probably a good thing Nat hadn't produced a fishing kit out of her back pocket. Spear fishing was better. He'd never actually done it, but there'd been a video game he'd loved that had a spear fishing bit. And he'd read a book about a kid learning to spear fish after a train wreck got him stuck in Canada, or something like that. At least this water wasn't cold. He shivered. Just the thought of spear fishing in icy water was bad.

A fish darted through the crystal clear water. It was barely visible, more a flicker of displacement, its pale brown scales tuned to the sand below.

Ty waited. In the game, going after the first fish had been an amateur move. The bigger fish came later.

Patience.

Deep breath in, deep breath out.

Long minutes later, Ty noticed something move out of the corner of his eye. A gentle turn of his head gave him a better view of the beach.

Small and quiet, Stabby looked back at him. Her hoodie shaded her head and face, its sleeves hugging her lean arms. The cuffs were stretched, pulled forward nearly to her fingertips, her thumbs emerging from crude holes to each side. She had one pinky up to her mouth, her teeth bared and tugging at a bit of nail. She raised one sarcastic brow. Then she flicked her eyes towards the water around his feet.

Getting the message, Ty returned his attention to the river. It wasn't that she scared him, no, he just wanted to fish. Yeah.

Another fish swam by, slower than the first.

Ty waited. He wanted bigger.

Eventually, bigger came along.

In a burst of motion, Ty jabbed the spear into the water, his stomach suddenly cavernous at the prospect of a meal. The wood punched into something, nearly slipping from his hand as it jerked to a stop.

Armored fish? What the…

Ty tried to hold still, waiting for the disturbed sand to resettle. He didn't dare move the spear before he knew what he'd caught. If he lifted the tip, it might swim off!

Eventually, the sand settled. Unsure of what he was seeing, Ty took a breath and ducked underwater, feeling around where the spear vanished into the sand to be sure. For the second time today, he related to people who cursed. He'd missed the fish. All he'd managed to stab was sand. Pulling the spear out, he spun it and checked the point. A bit blunted, but not bad. Could be worse.

Sighing, Ty planted his feet in the fine grains of the riverbed and readied himself again.

More waiting.

It took a quarter of an hour for the fish to come back.

No success. Just more sand.

Grinding his teeth, Ty waited.

Another quarter of an hour passed, though it felt like more. Patience was frustratingly hard to come by.

Another fish came. This time, Ty didn't wait for bigger, he just went for it.

Sand. For the third time.

Taking deep breaths, Ty left the spear and got out of the water. His fingers weren't wrinkled, but his toes were. No way to dry them but to wait. Flopping down onto the beach, he spread his arms and legs and stretched with a groan. His back popped, as did a few of his fingers and an elbow. Relaxing, he pressed his back into the cool sand. The sun was still low, not yet high enough to begin warming the bits of shattered rock.

"I used to get up late in the day," Ty said aloud, needing to say something into the silence, even if Stabby wouldn't reply. "Nine. Ten. Seeing sunrise was for the early birds. Guys who took morning classes. After I graduated high school, I decided I was done with the early morning thing. Hated it."

Nothing from Stabby. She was still watching the water. Or at least she seemed to be. Hard to tell with the hood.

"It's Thursday back on earth," Ty went on, thinking. "I have two classes this afternoon. Meeting with my advisor in the evening. Dinner. Was finally going to ask out Dina afterward."

Silence.

"I wonder who will miss me," Ty pondered, his thoughts thickening, leaping from one idea to the next. "Dad's too busy trying to design another mall, and mom's in the middle of election season. She'll probably be annoyed at having to dress for mourning. I had friends at school though, they'll miss me." Internally, Ty realized that the hope hadn't come out very hopeful. "Probably," he added, deciding it was better to admit it now. "We weren't really close. Some guys I knew from class. Couple from the Gamers' Club. I guess I'd be surprised if they actually went to my funeral."

Stabby grunted.

"What, don't think we'll get funerals?" Ty asked, propping himself up on his elbows. "It might take a while. Cops will open Missing Persons cases. They'll bury us eventually, though. I don't think we'll get back before that. No way."

The hood rotated and Stabby met Ty's eyes. Her gaze was flat, bored. She grunted again, nodding at the water.

"What?" Ty said, surprised.

She rolled her eyes, pointed at him, and then at the water.

"Fine, fine, fine, I'm going," said Ty, sighing and sitting up. His toes had just begun to dry. Back in the river, he trudged to where the spear still stuck into the air. Finding his footing in the sand, he set his heels into the depressions his weight had made before. Spear raised, glaring into the clear water, he waited.

A fish.

And he missed. For a fourth time. He could tell by feel now. Withdrawing the spear, he checked the tip. Blunt. Climbing out, he grabbed the second of the four Stabby had made. She didn't even look at him, just stared at the water as he passed. Back in place, he lifted his spear and held still.

Patience sucked. Boredom was starting to make Ty mad. He could feel a headache coming on.

This time the fish wasn't a brown; instead it was a gray, larger, with quills running along the spine of its fins.

Ty stayed still, holding until it was almost exactly in front of his spear. Then he rammed the stick down.

Sand. He could feel it. Nothing else. No fish.

To his right, something slapped against the beach.

Ty's head spun, trying to track the source of the sound.

There was the fish, right there, on the sand, glistening in the light. Its flailing tail twisted it this way and that, grains sticking to its slick scales.

"What…" Ty mumbled, staring.

Stabby lifted one foot and set it down on top of the fish, pinning it. In a flash, she brought her fist down on the fish's head. It stopped just short with a meaty crunch. The fish jerked, and then went still.

Blinking, Ty tried to get a better look at what was in Stabby's hand. It looked blue-ish? She pulled away and a thin blade coated in crimson emerged from the fish. Ty's mouth dropped open, his mouth trying to find the right words while his brain fumbled between jumbled thoughts.

Suddenly, the hand holding the knife flicked, flashing to one side. Blood splashed across the sand. Ty's eyes followed the red. When he looked back at her hand, the knife was gone. She stood, retrieved a rounded stone from the drop-off, and set it on the sand near where she'd been sitting. She lifted the fish, dipped it into the river, rinsing it of sand, and set it on the stone. Finally, she turned, gave him a look of bland interest, and sat.

Ty closed his mouth. Then he gulped, watching crimson streak the grey rock.

The silence stretched, fraying Ty's nerves.

Eventually, Stabby raised one eyebrow.

"Don't mind me," Ty mumbled, trying to focus on the water again. His thoughts were chaotic, ideas and guesses and questions fracturing and mingling like some kind of mental kaleidoscope on drugs.

Fish. Gotta get a fish. Ty oriented himself on that, organizing his thoughts around the seemingly simple task. Weird fish-levitating knife girls could come after he'd eaten something.

It took another quarter of an hour for a fish to come along. Ty went for it, but all he felt was sand.

Then there was another wet, sandy slap. Then a crunching, meaty thud. Then another.

Ty closed his eyes. Did he really want to look? A hero would look. Any lead in any book worth a damn would look. So he looked.

On the beach, not twenty feet from him, Stabby was rising to her feet, a fish in each hand. The first was still on the rock. She'd gotten two this time. She rinsed them and stalked towards the rock wall. At its foot, she paused, using her feet to roll a pair of stones free. Once she had them by the first fish's rock, she arrayed her catch. Liquid ran from them, blood and water wetting the stones, gleaming in the sun like the mountainside trickles.

"Uhm, I guess we should start a fire. You know, to cook those," Ty said, trying to regain some sense of normalcy. Wandering off to find pieces of wood would buy him time to think. Also to figure out quite why he was so shaken.

Stabby nodded, her expression giving no clues about what went on behind those slate-gray eyes.

"I'll go find some wood," Ty said, heading for the beach. He kept away from Stabby, doing his best to make it look accidental. On his way up the wall, he realized he still had the second spear in hand. Glancing back at Stabby, he shivered and kept going. The spear made him feel better.

Tugging her laces tight, Nat rose from the semi-soft, raised bed and trudged off to the river. Bee was still sleeping, somehow. The woman tossed and turned more than a washing machine. Rubbing the corners of her eyes, Nat thought wistfully of coffee. Coffee, her greatest addiction. Maybe there was a plant they could make into a tea so she could get a caffeine fix.

Coffee. Tea. Leaves.

Nat's stomach growled, cavernous and empty.

Shit.

Food. Water was the life threatening one, but the river covered that. They'd need food to survive now. Better shelter too. The stack of leaves and branches was a short-term solution. Nat had woken twice in the night and listened to insects and small creatures scurry. They hadn't climbed the little bedsides, but it wouldn't last. One would come investigating, then more, and then losing sleep would be the least of their worries. One venomous insect and they were dead. Hell, one accidently inhaled bug covered in alien bacteria and they might all be dead of this world's common cold equivalent. They didn't have any immunity to the diseases here. Fuck.

"Ok. Don't get sick. Be careful. That's all that can be done," Nat told herself, shoving the sudden inevitability to the back of her mind.

Food. Shelter. Then the other stuff.

The food question came with a rather neat answer, once Nat reached the beach. Three fish and one unconscious girl in a hoodie. The former looked extremely edible, as long as the latter didn't mind sharing.

"Stabby?" Nat asked, stepping from one rock to another as she worked her way down the stony ridge that lined the beach.

Nothing. The girl was curled around herself, balled up next to the fish. Her side was rising and falling, though, so she was breathing. Breathing boded well.

"Stabby," Nat said, sharper, almost hovering over her now. She didn't really want to get any closer, but a dead Stabby was bad. All of this was more than a lot, but Nat was holding it together. Watching someone die…

She'd taken too many med classes not to do something.

Gritting her teeth, Nat bent and pushed back Stabby's hood. She was pale, with dark crescents under her eyes. Sick was looking more and more likely. Well, too late now. Either Nat could try to help Stabby and find out what happened or she could leave, cross her fingers, and pray.

Nat wasn't the praying type, so it wasn't a hard choice.

Pulse. That'd tell her how Stabby's heart was doing. Nat slipped her hand down, two fingers pressing to the vein on the girl's neck.

"Fucking hell. Come on!" Nat hissed.

Stabby groaned, a shiver running down her back, despite the warm sand and sun. Her eyes shot open, gray irises nearly blue in the light.

Between one breath and the next, Nat felt something dig into her own neck.

"Whoa!" Nat said, slowly removing her hand from the girl's skin. "Let's take a second and talk about this. You looked like you were hurt. I wanted to help. That's it. No need to get stabby, Stabby. I'm just being Canadian. Well, and a med student. More the student bit really. Bit cliché to relate niceness to being Canadian, but I've always found it funny, ya know?"

Groaning again, Stabby rolled her eyes. The pointed weight at Nat's throat vanished.

Nat's right hand shot up, pressing against where Stabby had touched her neck. There was a cut. She could feel the blood between her fingers, wet and slick.

"I was just trying to help," Nat grumbled, straightening and stepping back.

Stabby sat up. She shook her head, trying to clear it, and rubbed the bridge of her nose.

"Who caught the fish?" Nat asked, remembering the food.

Stabby didn't reply.

"These yours?" Nat tried, walking over to the two spears sticking out of the beach. A third lay near them, but it didn't have a point on it.

Stabby nodded, watching Nat, a dangerous spark lighting in those gray eyes.

"Whoa," Nat said raising her hands, and stepping back. "Time out, ok? We're good. Backing up. Not messing with the spears. Got it. No problem. I'm just trying to figure out who to thank for breakfast."

Twisting, Stabby jerked her chin towards the woods.

"Ty?" Nat guessed.

Stabby nodded and pulled her hood up.

Frowning, Nat looked at Stabby. Then she squinted at the sun. Then back at Stabby. Probably trying not to get burnt. Nat's skin was already warming, and Stabby was a lot paler. Shading her eyes with one hand, Nat looked up again and tried to guess the time. Late morning. Halfway to noon, if noon was when the sun came directly overhead. Damn. Now would be a great time to know how to make a sundial.

"Ok, so you made the spears, Ty killed the fish, and he went to get wood?" Nat asked.

Another nod.

"Great. So now we're waiting for tall dark and handsome to get his pretty butt back here unscathed so that we can find out if anyone knows how to start a fire so we can avoid starving. Great!" Nat threw her hands in the air, her voice loud enough to bounce back off the rocks and pools of the mountainside.

Behind her, Stabby chuckled.

The sound made Nat smile. It was nice. Being hungry and unable to eat wasn't nice of course, but Stabby's laugh was. There was punch to it, less an expression of humor than an almost palpable force.

Looking away, Nat tried to hide her reaction. Stabby probably wasn't the laughing type, and making a deal of it would just make her, well, stabby.

The change of perspective brought Nat's gaze to the water. Water currently occupied by a trio of very large fish. They shot past, their cloudy-blue scales standing out against the sandy bottom. Back and forth, almost prowling the clear stream.

"Uh," Nat mumbled, squinting, trying to get a better look.

One paused, momentum stopping abruptly as its head twisted towards Nat. Two eyes looked up at her, deep and dark, set high on an angular, jagged face split by a row of spines that continued along its back.

Nat backed away from the water's edge. Being three steps from the water didn't feel nearly far enough. "Hey, Stabby, can I borrow a spear?"

Nothing.

"Stabby?" Nat said again, still watching the thing in the water. A second member of the trio stopped, turning to face her alongside the first.

Something tapped Nat's knuckles. She flinched, shying away, but it was one of the spears. Taking it, she glanced back and saw Stabby. The girl let go of the spear, hefting a second one. The bark was rough under Nat's fingers. The wood was heavy too, dense and strong, which made her feel a bit better when the third fish came to look at her.

"Let's back up nice and slow," Nat said, trying to sound less worried than she was. They were fish. Worrying made no sense. Why should they be worried about some fish? Who on earth worried about some curious fish?

But this wasn't Earth.

"Don't make me spear you," Nat warned back up, her feet dragging across the sand. They were six steps from the water now, maybe ten yards from the fish.

On lighter feet, Stabby did the same, the tip of her spear never wavering. Nat's wasn't nearly so still. She kept changing targets; unsure about which fish she was more worried about.

"Goddamn fish-people kidnapping us in screwy fish-planes and now we're on some damned island being watching by shitting fish-fish!" Nat whispered. "What bull-"

Nat's dragging right heel hit rock. Staggering, she tried to get her other leg under her. It didn't work. She pitched backwards.

All three fish shot forward, surging through the water and charging across the sand.

Eyes wide, Nat tried to process what she was seeing. It was too weird, even with the worry already in her head. Sand flew around them, sprayed by the clawing, shoving motions of their thick fins. Fins akin to gators' legs churned, webbed flesh stretching out in front and behind, almost hiding the bony, clawed limb at the center.

Nat screamed, scrabbling to get away, her fingers dragging at the sand. Her right foot was numb, so she used the other to kick sand at the oncoming fish-monsters. The spear was gone. She'd dropped it in the fall.

Rushing forward, Stabby rammed her spear into the frontrunner. The thing hissed and bucked, try to writhe off its skewer.

The other two kept coming. One turned towards Stabby, but Nat's mind was on the fish still headed for her.

Years of med school, years of undergrad, all the bullshit of high school and middle school, and Nat was going to die on some strange world, murdered by a fish.

Fuck. That.

Twisting around, Nat coiled her body and cocked back her right arm. A second later, the fish was there, jaws swinging wide. Her fist shot out, meeting it with a sickening crunch. A ripple rolled along the fish's body, like a miniature earthquake that only touched its flesh. The fish collapsed, its face a compacted mess of blood and scales and bone, rents open and bleeding like zebra stripes across its back.

Flashes of pain jabbed through the meat of Nat's fingers, bringing tears to her eyes as her jaw dropped. Dazed, surreal, she saw teeth, broken from the fish's mouth, embedded in her fingers. She kept her hand in a fist. If she flexed her fingers, it might drive the teeth deeper. Blood began dribbling from the wounds, running down her wrist and arm. Pain throbbed through her brain like a strobe.

Behind Nat, rocks tumbled loose from the wall, cracking as they cascaded. Footsteps thudded into the sand, moving closer. She curled tighter around her hand, trying to settle the massive rush of adrenaline and relief and pain and shock.

"Where?" Ty blurted, his hands pushing her shoulders up and back.

"Hand," Nat hissed, clutching the limb.

"Uh, crap, uhm… We need to clean it, make sure there isn't anything in the wound," he said, dithering.

"Water," Nat reminded him, a sob wracking her.

"Got it," Ty replied, his arms settling under her knees and lower back. Then he lifted, plucking her from the ground.

Seconds later, warm water splashed across her back, barely preceding Ty's rapid descent into the stream. He knelt over Nat, setting her on the shallow riverbed. He reached for her injured hand.

"Wait!" Nat gasped, holding her hand by the wrist and struggling to keep it from him.

"What?" Ty asked, his face afraid, full of worry and concern as blood spilled into the water at her elbow.

"If I say stop, you fucking stop, clear?" Nat hissed, trying to see him through fresh tears.

"Of course," he replied, lowering her arm into the water.

Pain blossomed as the water hit her fingers. Nat began to drown in it all. Too much. Too much.

It wasn't the first time Bee had woken to screams, though she preferred the fun kind. This definitely wasn't the fun kind. Hell, even if it did sound like the fun kind, she wouldn't believe her ears out here in this shitty mess of tropics and wilderness.

Scrambling out of the shelter, Bee yanked on her shoes. Hopping in the direction of the beach, she tugged the second one into place. It slid on, finally. She sprinted off as another scream echoed through the trees.

Bee babbled as she ran, curses hissing between her gritted teeth.

Skidding to a stop at the top of the drop-off, Bee's eyes went wide. Nat was in the water; Ty crouched over her, one of her hands cradled in both of his. Stabby was halfway between Bee and the water, something long and green latched onto her leg, blood spewing from a gash on its back. A second fish flopped on the sand, a spear through its head, and a third lay on its side, twitching and headless.

Stabby wasn't moving.

"Nat!" Ty blurted, his voice high as Nat's head lolled to the side.

"I'm coming!" Bee said, barreling down the wall. She took off across the sand, weaving between the fish, and splashed into the water at Nat's side.

"One of the fish got her hand," Ty said, desperate, his left hand holding Nat's wrist, his right her head. "I think she fainted from the pain."

"Lower it, I'll check," Bee ordered. There was so much blood. Flaps of skin hung loose, and bits of white poked through. Nausea settled on her, like a hot blanket. The taste of sick filled the back of her throat.

Ty lowered the hand into the water. Scarlet flowed outwards, dragged away by the current. Freed from the bloody shroud, torn skin fluttered around the jagged roots of broken teeth.

Swallowing, Bee tried to counter the rising vomit in her throat. Using one hand to hold the finger, the other to pull a tooth, she started at the thumb.

The first finger sucked. It had to be done, though, and that kept her going. If Nat woke, this would be even worse. It had to be done now, and getting sick wouldn't help anyone.

The second only had two teeth in it. Easy. Bee forced herself to smile, working to keep the task as abstract as possible. Like a puzzle. Like a game. Definitely not flesh and blood she was pulling teeth from, no, of course not!

The third one was horrible. More than half a dozen teeth that Bee could see. The second one grated, rubbing against bone.

Spinning, Bee heaved, what little there was in her stomach spurting into the water. It was mostly liquid, acid and water, and wandered away on the current. She rinsed her mouth, spitting out most of the sticky puke, then turned back to Nat and Ty.

"You ok?" Ty asked, eyeing her. He didn't look good himself.

"Fuck no," Bee said, her voice hollow, faint. "We need to finish. Rinse again."

He lowered the hand, shaking it slightly to increase the force of the water against it. Lifting it again, he looked away, lips pursed.

Gritting her teeth, Bee kept going. She dry heaved a half dozen more times before it was done, but she did it. When there were no more teeth poking out, and none that she could find by feeling around the wounds, she nodded to Ty. "Done," she whispered, sinking into her seat on the riverbed.

"Should we leave her in the water? Give it more time to wash clean?" Ty asked, frowning.

"I've got no fucking clue," Bee said, rubbing her eyes with the heels of her hands. Shit. She'd really just done that. She'd never get rid of those memories. She needed a drink. Several.

"Can you hold her? I need to check Stabby," Ty said, glancing at the prone girl on the beach.

"Yeah, go," replied Bee, taking the woman by head and hand. She looked better already, the bloodless pallor fading, and her hand wasn't bleeding as much.

Ty made his way out of the water and over to Stabby. Rotating to watch, Bee settled Nat's head against her shoulder. She still didn't know what the hell had happened to them. Shit. Nat's hand would probably get infected out here. Maybe they'd have to cauterize it or something.

A sound like a knife through meat came from Ty and Stabby, pulling Bee's attention back to the moment. The man tossed aside the massive fish that'd been latched to the girl's leg. He gathered Stabby into his arms and carried her to the water. Squatting next to Bee and Nat, he tugged at the blood-soaked pant leg.

"You see anything stuck in there?" Ty asked, using his grip on Stabby's knee to display the damaged calf. He was on the wrong side of her to see it clearly.

Shooting the big man an incredulous look, Bee shifted Nat a little to one side and examined Stabby's leg. Water had plastered the denim to her skin, but not in the same place as when she'd been bitten, so only half the bite was visible. It was bleeding, badly, but Bee couldn't see any teeth. Seeing wasn't enough though, someone needed to feel around and be sure. Looking up at Ty, she considered telling him to do it, but she'd already done it once. She'd have a better chance of finding things.

"Hold her still," Bee ordered, wrapping her left arm around Nat's shoulders to hold her in place.

When Ty nodded that he had a good grip, Bee reached for the wound. There was more flesh in the girl's leg than in Nat's hand, so she didn't have to worry about thinking bone was tooth, but it felt just as sickening, wrong. She heaved, her hand freezing, her face twisting towards the open water. A dribble of stomach acid splashed into the bloody water.

Bee spat out what was left in her mouth and continued. Minutes ticked by before she was sure. She nodded. Ty's grip relaxed, allowing Stabby's leg to sink into the water.

"What do we do now?" Bee asked. She knew that neither of them had a clue. If they had, they'd already be doing it, but she had to ask.

"Bandages," Ty decided, nodding reassurance to himself. "We need to bandage their wounds. Keep them hydrated till they wake up."

"The camp's too far," Bee said, scanning the beach. "We need to keep them here, where their clothes can dry in the sun."

"Good idea," Ty said, nodding again, his dazed worry dwindling. "I can put something together if…"

"If I hold onto them?" Bee grumbled, rolling her eyes. "We can just put them on the beach till we've got something."

"I don't know if their wounds are clean yet," Ty countered, shooting a look at Nat's hand. "And if we take them out to dry then they'll get cold, and we'll have to put them back in again to wash away the sand."

"Fine," Bee conceded. She didn't agree with him, but she didn't want to argue. She wanted a drink. Several. And a good smoke. And coffee. Gods, anything sane and normal would be great.

Depositing Stabby's head on Bee's free shoulder, Ty climbed out of the water again and jogged to the rock wall.

Twitching and wiggling around, Bee eventually found a comfortable position. The water was up to her armpits, but it was enough to make Nat and Stabby feel light at first. Time wore on and their weight grew. Ty was rolling rocks down from the wall; building a raised platform like the one they'd slept on last night. The problem was that it was so damn slow. Frustration reared, fed by nausea and exhaustion and hunger and the various semi-addictions that she really preferred to continue enjoying. Watching made her notice every misstep, every wrongly placed rock, and every slight delay as he stopped for a breath.

Bee closed her eyes. Inhaling through her nose, she slowly filled her lungs. Meditation. Good shit. Frustrating in its own right, but meditation frustration would make her feel better about the piss poor job Sad-Sack McBossy was doing. She sat, she breathed, and she hoped that Nat and Stabby didn't die. Getting left to survive solo with Ty might end up with cannibalism, and apparently she didn't have the stomach for that.

Pausing on a boulder at the forest's foot, Zed stilled, listening. There hadn't been any more screams, but she was pretty sure this was the right direction. The mountainside messed with sound, so the screamer could be up there. She hoped they weren't though. She'd gotten a good look at some of the things that lived in those pools and she didn't want to do it again. If someone had been dumb enough to get attacked there, she'd be lucky to find blood, maybe some bones.

So, they had to be near the base of the range. Somewhere along the freshwater, where the pool-dwellers could reach, but not the big ones.

With a sigh, Zed shifted her grip on her spear and set off again. Her drill sergeant would be proud, the butt-headed bastard. Zed hadn't run so much since she'd finished Basic Training. Not having to carry fifty pounds of gear was nice.

A long, loping jog carried her over the even gravel, just back from the beachside boulder wall. Her boots were heavy, steel toed and rubber soled, but she kept them on, especially when running. Too many things hid in shoes in the night, and too many other things infected the slightest cut on a bare foot.

Time passed, a blur of calm, happy adrenaline. Zed loved running, and the steady, thrilling excitement of this wild world had yet to ease. There was so much to see, so much to try. She needed a team first though; she couldn't try it all on her own. People to watch her back.

Zed smiled. A team. Definitely necessary. Especially if she was going to go hunting for Big Fish.

Ahead, the wall swung left, curving out from the forest to follow the gentle curve of the river. Zed cut through the copse that sat on the outcropping, her thudding steps crunching along.

Someone squeaked. A figure slipped from behind a tree, tumbling from sight down the wall.

Leaning into her run, Zed accelerated, curious. Were they hurt or were they following the screams too?

At the edge of the trees, Zed angled up the largest boulder, leaning back to drain away her momentum as she got a view of the beach below.

The figure was at the bottom, sprawled on his back. He was thin, all long muscle under tight jeans and a plain t-shirt, with brown hair springing like weeds from his scalp, just short of shaggy. Boyish, maybe in his late teens, he looked up at her from beneath delicate glasses with thin, rounded frames.

"Who the hell're you?" a woman demanded, her voice hard and thick with fear and fire.

The call drew Zed's attention to the people further down the beach, a foursome that had clearly been the source of the screaming. One lay on a low bed of stacked stones, another was being carried to the bed by a large black man, while the fourth, the speaker, appeared to be washing blood from her clothes.

"Hi!" Zed replied, waving happily at them. "I'm Zed. Heard the screaming, so I came to see if anyone else survived the drop."

"Well, uh, we did," replied the large man, looking warily at her as he set his burden on the stone bed.

"Names?" Zed queried, grinning as she waved an inquisitive hand at them.

"I'm Ty," the large man replied, a friendly smile tugging at his lips.

"Bee," the woman added, moving onto the dry sand. Most of the blood had washed away, but her baby blue shirt had a muddied dimness to it.

"And you are?" Zed asked, turning a bright smile on the man in the sand. He'd been doing a good job of being quiet and still and forgettable, but he was out in the open, sandwiched between Zed and the foursome. Not optimal hiding territory.

"I'm Joey, Joey Greer," he answered, his mouth curling into an abashed smile.

"Great! We can meet the sleepers when they wake up. Now, are those fish edible?" Zed queried, rising to her tiptoes to peer with exaggerated interest at the dead creatures at the foot of the stone bed.

"I guess so?" Ty hazarded.

Midway through attempting to press the water from her short hair, Bee made a nonplussed face.

"Perfect!" Zed said, hopping from one stone to another as she descended from the forest's wall. "Let's get a fire going and eat. Then we can chat about why Joey was snooping, why Bee's covered in blood, why Ty has a stone bed, and what happened to them," she said, nodding towards the unconscious duo as she lifted Joey to his feet. "Good?" she asked him, holding her wide smile in place. He was taller than her, but only by an inch or so, and that might've been a difference of hair volume. Ty though, ha! When she turned and pushed Joey with jocular fervor in the direction of the others, it was clear that Ty was the tallest of them, and damn well built at that. Six and a half feet was nice. Just short of when people started looking weird, in her experience.

Joey chuckled, an odd, off sound. "Sounds great. Thanks for helping me out there. Shy, you know? Bit of a scary couple days."

"Happy to give you a shove in the right direction," Zed returned, patting his arm. She wasn't sure if she bought that. No, she definitely didn't, but it was a pretty fast recovery if he'd been planning something bad. Most people didn't lie that fast.

"Glad you found us," Ty said, wiping his hands off on his pants and offering Joey a handshake.

"Yeah, that," Bee agreed, standoffish as she lingered near the water.

"Peace?" Zed offered, letting her spear drop to the sand, her palms pointed out. "Sorry for the surprise, but I heard screaming…"

Silence stretched for a moment, then Bee nodded. "Chill. We could use the help anyway. Neither of us knows first aid."

"Or how to start a fire," Ty added.

"I can do first aid," Zed said, nodding.

"And I can get a fire started," Joey offered.

"Say what now?" Bee snarked, eyeing him with disbelief.

"Boy Scout plus glasses," Joey said, blushing as he tapped his frames. "Fire coming right up."

"Say that again but with more words?" Bee asked.

"Little magnifying glasses," Joey explained. "Just add sun."

Ty glanced skyward. "Thank God. I think I'm starting to forget what food tastes like."

"Ty, why don't you grab some wood while Bee helps me," Zed suggested, beaming and happy at how quickly her newfound team was gelling.

Nodding, he gave her a wide grin and headed up the wall. While Joey went over to the dead fish, Bee followed Zed to the stone bed.

Leaning down over her patients, Zed looked them over. She sat and started with the obvious. "Names?" she queried, nodding at the two unconscious women.

"Nat's the Canadian model that decided she wanted to be a doctor," Bee supplied. "And the Asian chipmunk with murder on the mind is Stabby."

"Chipmunk?" Zed asked, confused.

"She's small," Bee explained.

"No, I mean like the cartoon?" Zed clarified, smiling.

"They're actual animals," returned Bee, defensive. She crossed her arms; standing beside the bed, just close enough to loom protectively.

"Oh. Good to know," Zed said, filing that fact away under 'unnecessary realizations' and Bee under 'easily offended.' She pulled the leg of Stabby's jeans up, trying to get a look at the bloodied mess.

"She going to be ok?" Bee asked, gruff.

"Can you get me some water?" Zed returned, not looking up. Once the woman was halfway to the beach, Zed gently wiped away the mix of blood and water that coated the wound. She needed to see what was wrong under it all. The problem with that goal was immediately obvious. The skin was pristine, tanned and dirty maybe, but no gaping wounds. She kept wiping, trying to find a source for the blood that matted the girl's leg and jeans.

Nothing.

Switching to the other woman, Nat, Zed plucked her hand from the table and checked that. Nothing. No explanation of where the blood had come from.

"Huh," Zed grunted, impressed.

Had it been a trick? But then Bee wouldn't have left her on her own to prove that they weren't injured. Bee and Ty had believed that these two were hurt. With all the blood, maybe they hadn't checked for wounds. Fish blood and human blood looked similar…

But they'd gone into the water. That would've washed it all off, if Nat and Stabby had covered themselves in animal blood. Too many questions.

"What-" Bee blurted, her voice coming from just behind Zed's shoulder.

Zed spun, her ponytail slapping against her cheek as she locked onto the woman. Shock, surprise, relief, all raced across a dark skinned face. Bee's wet and flopping locks of green and blue and black made the emotions feel younger, exposed, like seeing a tiger soaked and embarrassed. It felt off. Private.

"What happened?" Bee asked, eyes never leaving Nat's hand. The other expressions faded, replaced by something curious, maybe even hopeful.

"Not sure," Zed said, shrugging. "I wiped off the blood. That's it."

"There's nothing?" Bee pushed, her gaze switching to Zed's face, hunger in her eyes.

Taking Nat's wrist, Zed offered the hand.

Shifting to stand beside Zed, Bee poured the water from her cupped hands onto Nat's knuckles. Blood slid away, clots and sand dribbling onto the rocks below, leaving bare, smooth skin.

"Fuck me," Bee muttered, numb.

"No thanks," Zed joked, smirking. It made her feel better. Familiar territory.

"Not like that, Blondie," Bee retorted in a forced grumble. "Shit. It's all gone."

Tilting her head, Zed asked, "Are you sure she was hurt?"

Bee winced. "Yeah. I pulled about a zillion fish-teeth out of that hand."

Zed nodded at Stabby. "What about her?"

Another wince. Bee looked like she was going to be sick. "I had to feel around her bite to make sure there weren't any teeth."

"Miracle?" Zed suggested.

Bee snorted, the curious hunger coming back. "Magic?" she countered. "I don't think Stabby's any god's type."

"Polytheist?" Zed queried, her eyes narrowing, honing in on the woman before her.

"You first," Bee volleyed back.

"I like guns," Zed answered, smiling at the quickness of the retorts. "And challenges. Haven't made a call on God yet."

"Rebel from a monotheist family," Bee guessed, chuckling. "Same here, but with booze and fun."

"Muslim?" Zed wondered.

"Nah, homegrown 'Merican Christian," Bee explained, groaning at the memory and standing upright. She twisted, popping her back. "So, magic?"

"What's next, Hogwarts?" Zed said.

"No, lunch, hopefully," Bee said, gesturing over her shoulder towards Joey. "Apparently he really does know how to start a fire."

Glancing past her, Zed could see Joey, kneeling beside a small fire he'd made near the fish. Stones encircled the broken sticks he'd somehow managed to light. He was wiping moisture from his glasses, eyes never leaving the crackling sticks.

"Handy," Zed noted.

"Yeah, if he pisses me off and I kill him we can keep his lenses," Bee added, all bland disinterest.

"Excessive?"

"How'd you guess my middle name?" Bee demanded, peering querulously at her. Then she winked, cackled, and headed towards the water.

"What're you doing?" Zed asked, confused by the sudden switch.

"Getting more water, doofus," Bee called back. "Waking up bloody sucks."

Zed rolled her eyes, stood, and followed. Might as well help, and Joey seemed both intent and perfectly capable of handling the food situation.

Waking up on Wacko Mystery Island was just as unpleasant the third time.

It also thoroughly reminded Olivia of Rule One: Find the Fucking Water. Her throat was parched. Sitting up, she blinked furiously. The movement made pain burn through her hips and shoulder, as well as her neck. She checked what the hell she'd been left to sleep on.

Rocks.

A bunch of goddamn rocks.

Morons.

Standing, Olivia headed for the water. At the stream, she knelt and drank.

It was late in the day, nearly dark. Someone had started a fire between the morons' 'bed' and the water, but it'd burned down to the embers. Scattered sticks lay near it, little piles of delicate bones and blackened scales alongside them. At the top of the boulder wall, a second bed had been made. It looked like Nat and Bee's from last night, but lower and wider. From the heads Olivia could see, more people had shown up. Bee's green and black and blue drifted in the breeze, Ty's scalp was like a dark stone, but the other two were new. She didn't recognize the fluff of brown curls, or the ethereal blonde ponytail.

The bones and scales must be from the fish. Olivia felt a bit pissed that Ty and Bee hadn't left any for her, but she wasn't surprised. It did surprise her that they hadn't left some for Nat. The black woman was still on the 'bed' on the beach, snoring. The sun hit her face and made it almost glow.

Worried, Olivia reached up and felt her cheeks. Nothing. Good. Her hood must've been up while she'd been out; otherwise her skin would already be burnt. She felt her leg, where the wannabe crocodile had bitten her. Just holes in the denim.

Olivia smirked. No sunburn, no wound. All good news, except for the lack of food, and she knew how to fix that. With a spin, she faced the center of the stream. She reached for the river with one hand, fingers spread. The water slipped into her senses, like another limb. It felt comfortable, if heavy.

Waiting wasn't too bad. Tiring. But most things were, if you did them long enough. It stretched her, like trying to identify swim strokes by sound while being tickled. Her head began to sting as minutes passed. The weight grew, bearing down on her. This had been easier with Ty in the water. All she'd had to do was snatch when his body language said there was fish. No waiting. The memory made her smile.

Then a pair of fish slipped within her touch, off to the right. Olivia waited.

They swam further into her stretch of river-sense.

Two meters in.

Three.

They moved away, back the way they'd come.

Turning again, they shot back, moving in front of Olivia. She closed her outstretched hand, twisted, and pulled. She imagined catching the fish that way, imagined snatching them from the blue.

Two slaps came from behind her.

Olivia whirled and pinned the one nearest the water with her foot. Her hand rose, she wanted a knife, demanded it, and stabbed the fish behind the head. A moment later, the second one joined the first.

Olivia paused, the dead fish flopping before her, blood pooling. The knife in her hand was blue, solid, and felt less like a blade than an extension of her hand, like another finger. It sounded dumb, even in her head. People could get good with blades, hell, some had a natural talent with sharp shit, but they were never part of you. This felt like it was her. She knew she could bend it, change it, despite its apparent permanence.

Instead, Olivia let go. She stopped wanting it. She didn't need it.

The water dribbled down her fingers and onto the beach.

Ignoring the part of herself that examined events like this and said things like 'what the hell,' Olivia picked up the two fish and made her way to the fire. A stack of spare branches had been laid half a meter from the coals, so she used some to get the fire going again. It didn't take long. The arrival of new wood knocked ash from the embers. By the time she'd spitted the two fish on sharpened sticks, the fire was crackling again. Someone had staked a Y shaped branch on either side of the stones circling the fire, so she set her dinner on them and waited.

The fire caught her eye. Tongues of red licked across scales, reminding her of bad nights. These tongues left blackened scars, not spittle. She wasn't sure which was worse.

Looking away wasn't an option. It occurred to Olivia, but it wasn't an option. She'd survived. That's what mattered. If she forgot it, any of it, then it might happen again. Rules needed reasons to exist, or they faded.

Olivia wondered how many things she'd survive before she learned this world's Rules. The tears came again, brimming and blurring the fish and the fire. Her hands slid under her hoodie, clutching her hair near the base and yanking. Fuck! It hurt, but she didn't speak. Might wake someone, and these morons were less interested in helping her than the gangs had been. That'd been a rough winter. Warmer though. And fewer beatings, mostly. They'd nearly killed her at the end. Hoarding her share made her a juicy target. Juicier. One of the guys had claimed she'd been holding out on the boss. After that… Well, it hadn't been anything new. She'd lived.

A bit of prodding proved that the fish was looking pretty edible. Not that Olivia was picky. Food was food, and people ate raw fish all the time back on earth. Expensive raw fish.

Lifting one spit from the fire, Olivia blew on it, cooling it as she picked out a smaller bit of wood to pull the skin off with. She found one. It came free after a few tugs. The meat was pretty thin, but it was long and she had two. Using her fingers, she tugged bits free of the bone and began to scarf it down. Not bad. Bit hot, but it filled the gaping hole that'd once been her stomach.

The first one was gone in under two minutes. Olivia took her time with the second. By now the fire was lively, blackened sticks and rich, ruby embers feeding tall flames. She tossed the old bones and skin in the fire, enjoying the crack and sizzle as they scorched. After a few minutes, she did the same to the skins the others had left, but she kept their bones. Some of them. Most were too small, too thin, or a bad shape. A few were long and sharp, so she kept them, hiding them in pockets and hidden seams. Those fuckers on the ship had taken her tools. The bones would work till she found better.

Someone coughed. Close.

No jumping. No sudden start. Stabby looked up from the fire.

The blonde looked back at her, ponytail bouncing in the wind. Her face was tanned by long days in the sun, and one brow was dark where a scar cut across it. A petite nose and pouting mouth gave her a light, young feel, helped by her half smile and the glitter of mischief in her eyes.

Olivia waited. Coughs didn't merit responses. Maybe Blondie had a cold. Or alien plague.

"I'm Zed," the woman offered, her half smile growing as she stepped closer to the fire. "I got here while you were out. Bee and Ty asked me to check your leg, but it looked like you were fine."

Yup. Made sense. Olivia didn't have anything to add to that, other than that they should've left her some food.

"We were going to leave some fish for you, but it would've gone bad in about an hour at this heat," Zed explained, glancing at the sun on the horizon. "Guess that makes that east."

Olivia blinked. Huh. The sun was setting over the ocean they'd been dumped in. That meant the mountain range ran almost exactly north-south. Convenient.

"Thinking about going west?" Zed queried, flopping down onto the sand on the other side of the fire.

Snorting, Olivia shook her head. Mountain climbing was a no.

"Fish get bigger up that way," Zed continued.

Olivia shot the woman a look she hoped would illustrate the level of stupidity Blondie was sinking to. Bigger fish than the baby crocs was more fish than she felt like taking a stab at. Especially if the meat didn't keep.

"I guess you don't really need the fun," Zed sighed, blithely gazing off down the river. "How's the magic business?"

Nothing. Give her nothing, Olivia told herself. Stuck up bimbo.

"You can hear me, you can understand me, and you speak English," Zed said, tilting her head as she examined Olivia across the fire. "You trying to come off as tough shit?"

Olivia grinned. Blondie got jokes. She was tough shit. No need to prove anything.

"Just looking for buttons?" Zed guessed, her tone halfway to laughter.

Raising one brow, Olivia silently made it clear that she didn't have to look.

"Ouch." Zed chuckled, nibbling her thumbnail. "Ok. Different tactic: I'm Betzaid Al-Hakim, recently of the Israeli Defense Force, Armored Corps, 500th Brigade, and disappointing daughter disinterested in marriage, children, and men in general."

Sharing without the bullshit. That was new. Not lying was nice too.

Olivia nodded, thinking.

"Olivia Blacklock, London vagrant, ex-everything else," Olivia said, eventually.

"Like?"

"Student, daughter, athlete, person."

"Rough," Zed said.

Olivia waited. Nothing to say. And people usually filled silences. Sure enough…

"You were the first one out the door."

"Second," Olivia noted, remembering the man in the suit.

"Did you have magic before?"

"Nope."

"How does it work?"

Olivia shrugged.

Zed rolled her eyes. "Thanks."

"Do you want something?" Olivia offered, relenting. She was bored. And the woman made her smile.

"You to tell me how you do magic?" Zed retorted, shooting her a sarcastic look.

"Simpler."

"To go home?" Zed said, her brows furrowing with the beginnings of confusion.

"Simpler. A tool."

"A knife," Zed said.

"Hold out your hand. Want it," Olivia directed.

Zed raised one hand and stared at it. Nothing.

"Works for me," Olivia said.

The look Zed gave her was withering.

Olivia shrugged.

"I'll practice," Zed said, dry and disbelieving.

Nodding, Olivia raised her own hand, willed a knife from nowhere, and rolled it between her fingers. She had no idea how it worked, other than it made her eyes flutter with the sudden need for a nap, but it worked.

Zed was silent for a long moment. Blinked. Blinked again.

The blade twirled, flipping between Olivia's digits.

"Nifty," the blond declared, half-frowning with thought.

"Don't break anything," Olivia warned.

Rolling her eyes, Zed smiled and asked, "Don't they teach children to respect their elders in the UK?"

"Age?"

"Twenty."

"Not an elder."

"Bullshit," Zed said, looking Olivia up and down. "You aren't eighteen, let alone twenty, Stabby."

"Religious?"

"Why?" Zed asked, curious, her head tilting to one side.

"Because you act like you want to be holey," Olivia answered, deadpan.

Zed frowned. "Wait… was that a joke?"

One thin eyebrow rose on the right side of Olivia's face. The woman didn't seem like one of the morons.

Chuckling, Zed returned, "I was raised Muslim, but my family was a little pissed when I left to join the army."

"How bad?" Olivia asked, wincing. She knew what it was like to lose everyone, but to be voluntarily lost…

"I tried to visit home after my first year. I had a few days of Leave. My older brother nearly attacked me with a bat. My dad had a gun. I saw my mom in a market once, but I didn't go near her."

"Watched," Olivia guessed.

Zed nodded. "My mother was worse than my dad. I probably screwed them socially by leaving. If she'd had the gun when I went home, I might not have come back to do my second year."

Quirking her head, Olivia asked her next question without a word.

"Two years is standard for female service members in the Israeli Defense Force," Zed answered, her eyes shifting to the fire. "I had a combat role, which meant that I got an extra four months. That's what I had left before this."

"Plan?" Olivia prompted.

"I was thinking of moving to Hollywood and seeing if they had any badass Amazons roles for me. Gal Gadot but Blonde et cetera," joked Zed, her lopsided grin casting shadows across her tanned cheeks. "Either that or finding some soulless private army that needed a pair of hands that didn't have a dick's ego attached."

"Why?"

"Because I couldn't go home?" Zed offered, smirking proudly, as though relishing the rush of memories.

Olivia shook her head. She'd known the woman for five minutes and that didn't fit.

Sitting up, Zed rested her arms on her raised knees. Her fingers weaved together, dancing in the flicker of flame. "I got addicted to the rush. I liked shooting at people. Being shot at wasn't as nice, but I didn't qualify as a sniper."

"Boredom, maybe," Olivia muttered, thinking.

The blonde was sharp. She'd wrapped her head around magic and super-fish and this place pretty damn quick, and on her own. There wasn't hesitation when she thought, just a smooth run of fresh ideas. She was brave, easily bored too, but that wasn't the drive.

"Loneliness," Olivia decided.

Zed's smirk twisted, suddenly edging towards mean. "Me? Or are you projecting?"

Nothing. Not a word. Olivia didn't have to answer shit. She wasn't projecting, she was recognizing, but maybe talking wasn't worth it.

"Orphaned, left on the streets. Must've sucked," Zed fired at her.

Nothing.

"Surprised you didn't get picked up by a pimp. I heard London was big on that kind of stuff. Little Asian girls are a whole thing, aren't they?"

Nothing.

"Maybe they didn't want you either," Zed pushed, her expression thoughtful, clinical. "Or maybe you caught something before your parents called it quits."

Nothing still. Olivia measured the time between her blinks, her breaths. She'd heard it before. Wasn't exactly a creative angle. Back before her life had gone to shit, one of her favorite TV characters had said something about making weakness into armor, that way no one could ever use it as a weapon. The punch-line she'd gotten was that she couldn't kill everyone who gave her shit. Not right away. Sometimes not ever. Not every weakness could be armor. Like, being alone, for example. Sure, it made her hard to find when trouble came looking for her, but that just meant that she got an extra helping of random trouble. And random trouble felt twice as unjust, for some reason.

"Dumbass," Zed said as she stood, almost spitting the word across the fire. Then she turned and left, heading off down the beach.

Watching her go, Olivia let one particularly sharp chunk of fishbone slip between her fingers. Its wider end caught when she clenched her fist, leaving the sharp tip pointing outwards, like a punch-dagger. Twenty seconds. She could stand, run over, and stab the blonde. But the woman might hear it coming. Or Olivia might miss her kidney. She could go for the spine instead, but the fishbone would snap if it clipped vertebrae. Base of the skull might be easier. That way, Zed wouldn't have a chance to turn around and try to kill her back. Again, there was the vertebra problem.

Two years as a soldier, huh? Olivia wasn't going to risk the woman getting a chance to retaliate. She just sat, waited, and watched.

Once Zed was out of sight, Olivia tucked the fishbone away, hiding it and the others in pockets and seams. Once she was done, it was time to practice. Fishing was too tiring to do often, but the knife thing would do.

For a moment, Olivia wondered if she wanted to try a different type of knife. In her head, she imagined the various shapes. One, a massive

American hunting knife, the kind a Hollywood baddie would wave around to make it clear he was bad, came to mind. The thought slipped forward, smooth and simple.

Suddenly, her hand itched, the skin pinching, tugging.

Olivia's eyes flew open. The giant knife sat on her palm, warm to the touch. The itch had been the water reforming. Huh.

That told her four things.

One: that her creations weren't solid, they changed when she thought of something else.

Two: that the water was from the river behind her, thus the warmth.

Three: that if she got distracted, her knife would vanish.

And four: she could make other things.

Four was the big one.

Curious, Olivia made the bit of water into a stick, little twigs and leaves sticking from it, and poked a hot coal with it. It sizzled, hissing. Portions of the coal blackened, dying on contact. So, still water, just shaped.

"Can I…" Olivia muttered, trailing off as she flicked her wrist, launching the stick-like handful of water towards the rock wall. It flew, arcing through the air, clacked off the stone, and fell to the ground. She could feel it, more than a dozen meters away, hidden by the sand. With a thought, she let go. The solid, hard feeling melted away into nothingness.

Huh. Magic water could be shaped, thrown, and reshaped, as long as she didn't forget to hold it together. Handy. Not so useful if she needed to sleep, but otherwise…

On the bed at the top of the wall, Bee sat up, watching.

Olivia waited as the woman slipped quietly from the bed and made her way down to the beach.

Olivia raised an inquisitive brow. How long had Bee waited before getting up?

"Long enough," Bee said, answering the unspoken. She glanced back at where the knife had hit stone.

Olivia grunted, noncommittal. She should've stayed mute.

"Zed was an asshole," Bee added, sitting down with her back towards the wall. "But you did hit her where it hurt."

Nothing.

"You really twenty?" Bee asked, shifting abruptly from sympathetic to curious.

A tiny smile tugged at Olivia's lips. Her head shook before she could stifle the urge.

"Older?" Bee laughed, amusement making her eyes spark.

Another head shake.

Bee smirked. "Younger?"

Olivia nodded. "Nineteen."

"Not that much younger," Bee scoffed.

"Exactly."

"You know, we're the same age," Bee informed her, rocking in place.

"I do now," Olivia returned.

Bee's smile softened. Silence stretched for a moment, then she went on, "What's London like?"

"Cold, hot, wet, dry, rich, poor, chaotic, orderly, English, British, and urban," Olivia answered, one eyebrow rising.

"Fair enough," Bee half-apologized, looking away. It'd been a dumb thing to ask.

"Where're you from?" Olivia offered.

"Wisconsin," Bee said, her eyes going a bit distant. "Grew up in Madison, but I've been in Massachusetts for school. Little liberal arts college."

"Must be smart," noted Olivia, unsure what else to say. College had stopped being her future a long time ago. Somewhere between her mom dying and her coach refusing to take her in. She'd known why. People would've gotten curious, and then they'd have realized that he slept with half the parents, not to mention a few team members. Asshole.

"Not really," Bee replied, chuckling. "I said I went there, not that I was doing well."

"Dumb or distracted?"

"Ouch!" Bee said, exaggerating a wince. "You sound like my sister."

Olivia waited. Most people weren't good with silences, but Bee seemed to have a particular weakness for filling them.

"Are you going to miss anything?" Bee said, clearly trying to avoid thinking of her family.

"Beef," Olivia answered without hesitation. "You?"

"Oh, that's hard," Bee delayed, thinking. Her smile came back. "Chocolate. Fondue. Bananas. Croissants. Tequila."

"Tequila?"

"Painkiller and stress relief," Bee grumbled, glaring at the jungle behind her. "Till we know which leaves make the happy smoke, alcohol would be nice."

"Party girl," Olivia stated, half-smiling at the odd, unfiltered person across the fire.

"Certainly didn't help my grades." Bee snorted. "Got distracted by all the people. Pretty and otherwise. Drinking, sex, both fun, but dancing, exhausted midnight conversations, the drunken ramblings of a passionate philosopher or a pre-med on more drugs than most surgery patients, that's what I loved."

"Eloquent."

"Took a couple writing courses my first semester," Bee explained, winking. "Figured it'd help with surviving the rest of it."

"What do you think of all this?" Olivia queried. If they kept talking about college, she might end up stabbing Bee. She wanted to know Bee, but that part of the girl's past stung.

"I think that guy in the ship was fucking creepy," Bee replied, watching the fire. "I think these marks on our cheeks mean something, but that none of us want to think about them." She reached up and ran her fingers across the design on her cheek. It was the same as Olivia's. Spirals, the outer arm ending in a teardrop flare that hung from the right side. The shapes were all a vibrant cerulean; blue as the ocean, despite whatever melanin it sat on.

"Why give us all the same tattoo?" Olivia wondered aloud.

"Maybe they're more like brands, like for cows."

"Put cows next to barracuda-crocs?"

"Fair point. No clue then."

Olivia sighed. Fat lot of help that was.

"So… magic," Bee bulled on, leaping topics again.

"Didn't catch that part?"

"I did, I just didn't get it," Bee explained, rolling her eyes. "You just want it?"

"Works for me."

"Prove it."

Olivia snorted.

"Liar."

"Been called worse," Olivia noted.

"Come on," Bee groaned, smiling with excitement. "That thing you threw at the wall was magic, right?"

Nothing.

"I already know you can, so why not?"

Olivia thought about it. It was tiring, but not terrible. And she was curious about trying something bigger. Two birds, one stone. They might all be dead in twenty-four hours, so it seemed silly not to try. What to make… She already knew how to make a knife. A simple shape wasn't enough of a test, but too many moving parts might cause problems.

Something beautiful, Olivia decided, something that would balance the bad memories and painful Rules.

Olivia imagined a tendril of water floating past her shoulder, halfway between some kind of anti-gravity snake and a wisp of smoke. It coiled around her hand, ringing it, making her fist into a tiny Saturn lit by the fire. The water glowed, red and orange gleams riding the flow.

Smiling, Olivia fractured the spinning halo, breaking it so that slim limbs radiated outwards. Scarlet skimmed their slithering surface, bright as it became a sunray crown. It hung there, orbiting her hand, light dancing across its surface.

It didn't sting like feeling the river had, but it felt odd, as though some bit of Olivia was stretching, flexing. Like swim practice after a long, relaxing weekend of laziness.

The image in Olivia's head shifted, the hoop and rays streaming together in front of her fist. A rough disk came out of the mess, its surface uneven and bouncing, wavelike. A figure rose at the center, arms shooting forward, dragging at the dips and rises, feet kicking.

Olivia remembered what she'd looked like back then, and that was it. A single stray memory, and there she was, in miniature, doing what she'd done best.

It brought back a lot of other memories. Mother crying, hands shaking as she tried to find a bottle of pills. A coach, leering as the team captain played with his tie. A teammate smirking as new hazing rituals raced through her mind. Mother again, blank and empty now. A teacher's pitying hesitation, yet another failed test in hand. A principle trying to smile as a 'could've-been' athlete was expelled. A banker apologizing, saddened to inform her that there wasn't any account under that name. A landlord handing over the last notice for eviction, giving her looks like the coach that'd booted her from the team 'because of her grades.' Perv.

The swimmer was long gone; a mash of faces and gesturing limbs and half formed surroundings hung in its place. A dozen snapshots tried to play out all at once in the same bit of air.

Olivia's fist clenched. It washed away. The memories burst like bubbles. The water splashed across the stones at the fire's edge with an angry hiss. She wasn't sure whether stifling the memories cancelled the magic or if the magic stifled the memories. Either way, it was gone. She was fine.

"Wow," Bee said, her eyes wide and fascinated. "That's new."

"Magic," Olivia noted, wiggling her fingers in as mysterious a fashion as she could manage. It hid the shaking.

"No shit, Sherlock," Bee returned, chuckling again. The interest in her expression didn't wane. "So, just want it?"

Olivia nodded.

There was a tremble in Bee's hands, an excited glint in her eyes as she raised her hands in front of her. Then she frowned, glaring at a point in the air over her palms.

She kept glaring.

And glaring.

"It's not working," Bee groaned, dropping her hands.

"What're you trying to make?" Olivia asked, smiling at the way Bee's nose scrunched when she gave up.

"A book," Bee said.

"Try simpler."

"Like?" Bee queried, rolling her eyes. Apparently books seemed pretty simple already.

"A cup."

Sighing at her immense suffering, Bee raised her hands once more. She glared. This time, it sort of worked. Flickers coalesced in the air, streaming together and globbing into an uneven and wobbly shape in front of her eyes. It wasn't solid, and it was more like a small bowl than a cup, but it was close.

"Well, that's total shit," Bee grumbled, her lips pursing as glare became frown. "Wait…" she added, her tone shifting, higher. "Wait- I… is that-"

"Magic?" Olivia said.

"Is it - What I mean is - Wait, did you…" Bee mumbled, thoughts barely reaching her mouth before being eclipsed by the next.

"Oh, no," Olivia joked, raising one amused brow, "I definitely made that shitty wannabe cup just to trick you into thinking you could do magic."

"Shut up!" Bee blurted, smiling now, the cup cradled in her hands. "Less sass, more Giles."

"Who?"

"It's a TV show thing," Bee explained, her eyes rolling. "You ever seen Buffy?"

Olivia shook her head.

"Seriously? Where've you been? Under a rock?"

Patient, Olivia raised one much exercised eyebrow. She'd done more talking on this island than she had in the last week. Thank goodness her face was used to doing most of the work. It'd need to step in when her voice died from overuse.

"I mean, before you were homeless, you gotta have watched TV, right?"

Olivia shook her head. "Athlete."

"What the fuck kinda athlete doesn't even watch TV?" Bee demanded, leaning forward with absolute disbelief.

"Swimmer."

"You must've been ridiculous," Bee chuckled, eying her.

"Wanted to be an Olympian," Olivia elaborated. Part of her wanted to share. She'd never talked about it, not after her coach kicked her onto the streets. But this was a new world. Maybe it'd be easier.

"You seem a little short for an Olympian," Bee joked.

"And you're no Leia," Olivia said.

"See? You've seen TV!"

"Star Wars is different. My parents used to leave the original trilogy running to get me to fall asleep."

"Nerd," Bee snorted, smirking.

"Not much of anything anymore, remember?"

"Once a nerd, always a nerd," Bee said. "Being homeless doesn't change that."

"You better hope so," Olivia said, smiling. "Now we're all homeless together."

Bee laughed, her voice bouncing off the rising pools of the mountainside. "Listen, if Blonde and Bitchy gives you more grief, let me know."

"So you can nerd her to death?" Olivia queried, sarcasm thick enough to drip.

"No, I did two years of Martial Arts and Self Defense at school. Just sic me on her," Bee explained, flexing one bicep and kissing it appreciatively. Then she winked.

"Oh yeah, I feel so much better now," Olivia said, poking the fire with a stick. It was nice of her to offer, but two years of Army versus two years of not Army would be a short fight.

"You should. It's your job to live up to your name while I have her distracted."

Olivia frowned. Live up to… Stabby? Oh. Ok, that wasn't bad. "Thanks," she said, shooting the dark woman a small smile.

"Just don't be late. If Blondie kills me then my sister's gonna spend eternity teasing me about it," Bee grumbled.

"What's that like?" Olivia asked, curious.

"Sisters? Like having a best friend who's an asshole," Bee said. She paused, thinking. "It's like having someone who's always in your corner, even when they don't get it, but knowing that some of the worst fights you'll ever have will be with them. They're the best and the worst."

"Brothers?"

"No idea. Probably the same but smellier," Bee said, bland. "And with more dangly bits."

"Dangly bits?" Olivia returned, trying not to crack up at that particular bit of slang. She'd heard a lot of euphemisms, but that one was still funny.

"Yeah, you know, a one eyed wonder worm," Bee went on, carefully disingenuous.

Olivia pursed her lips, fighting laughter. That was new.

"High pressure vein cane?"

A cough of humor slipped through.

"Personal favorite: Pride Rock."

"I'm never going to be able to see that movie the same way again," Olivia whispered, quelling the urge to burst out laughing.

"You're welcome," Bee said, tipping a non-existent hat.

"You wanted someone in charge," Olivia said, thinking back to yesterday's chat. Ty and Bee. It'd be interesting to see who got frustrated and got on the other's case first. "Was that Pride Rock related?"

Bee tapped the side of her nose. "Nail on the head. Guys get pushy about that shit."

"Still worried?"

"Damn right I am," Bee scoffed, looking over her shoulder at the sleeping bodies. "Ty's a big dude who's already wanting to be in charge, and the new guy's too quiet."

"New guy?"

"Joey. He and Zed came in while you were out. He started the fire and butchered our fish," Bee explained. "Oh, sorry we didn't leave you anything. It spoils pretty fast, apparently."

"It's fine," Olivia said, shrugging it off. It was nice of her to mention it. "Joey. Quiet?"

"Yeah," Bee confirmed, turning and pointing at the puff of scruffy brown hair visible on the raised bed. "That's him. Thin, medium height, glasses. Looks ok, but he hasn't said a lot yet."

"You don't like guys," Olivia stated.

"Stay on topic. I don't like them in charge," Bee said, shifting to face the fire again. "And telling them they can't be is a great way to find out who shouldn't be."

"Intricate."

"Clever," Bee countered, tapping the side of her head. "If someone fights to be in charge, they're usually an ass that gets off on it. Bad news. If they're chill and go with someone who might be a worse choice in their opinion, then that's a decent human. Girls can be the same way, but Nat's chill and you weren't interested."

"And Zed?"

"I have a thing about authority," Bee deadpanned. "It gives me the violent urge to say things like 'fight me' and 'fuck off.'"

"Maybe not Zed then," Olivia agreed, covering her mouth with a hand to hide her smile.

"Probably best," Bee concurred. "So, what're you going to do with your night? We've kind of FUBAR'ed the 'sleeping at night' possibility."

"Practice," Olivia said, thinking over her options and ignoring the unknown acronym. "It's tiring, so I might be able to sleep tonight after all."

"Ha! Explains my sudden urge to nap," Bee joked, tossing the wobbly cup from one hand to the other. On the third toss, it popped, splashing across her hand. "Whoops."

"They don't last."

"No shit, Sherlock," Bee said, shaking the water from her hand with a bemused smile. "Oh! I wanted to ask if you knew why those toothy bastards showed up."

"Maybe they just go up and down. Hunting," Olivia suggested, glancing back at the river. It was a fair question, and one she should've thought of before she went fishing. Dumbass.

"What happened before they showed up?"

"Ty was in the river, spearfishing. I yanked some fish out when he missed, stabbed them, and put them on rocks," Olivia explained, gesturing at the stones near the fire. Blood still crusted their outer surface.

"Did you stab them in the water?"

"No, but I rinsed them off afterwards," Olivia said, thinking. "The Crocs might've followed the blood."

"Like sharks. Makes sense to me. 'Crocs' is better than 'toothy bastards' too."

"Whatever," Olivia mumbled, frustrated. First she forgot to check for killer fish, then she needed help to figure out why they'd ever shown up. All the sun must've fried her brain. Too long out here and she'd be asking what two plus two made.

"It wasn't your fault," Bee said, her tone softer, comforting.

"Fuck off," Olivia growled, rising to her feet. "I'm gonna go sleep."

"See ya, Stabby," Bee replied. The softness was gone, replaced by an odd thoughtfulness.

Olivia didn't say anything. She walked away. Fucking assholes trying to understand her, trying to fit her in their neat little boxes with neat little shit labels. Shoving a chunk of fishbone through Bee's ear would be satisfying, but the fallout would suck. Bee would help with Zed, and that meant that Olivia wouldn't have to watch her back. Well, watch it more than usual. Better to keep things as they were.

Heading down the beach, in the direction opposite the one Zed had taken, Olivia kept her eyes peeled. Nat and the others had slept on rocks and sticks and leaves. She'd take a branch over that any day. She hadn't been in any woods bigger than Hyde Park, or Regent's, since moving to the UK, but sleeping in branches had been a childhood pastime. It'd come in handy a couple times in London. Not all the parks were patrolled, and cops rarely checked the trees.

The trees here were squatter, thicker, and more uneven. That meant easier to climb and less risky to fall from. Better than pavement any day, as long as the bugs kept to themselves. The insects Olivia had seen stayed on the rocky ground, fearful of the birds in the branches. Worked for her. None of the featherbrains had come after her, and she'd seen nothing bigger than a songbird.

Skipping from one rough wall-stone to another, Olivia scaled the beach's rim and angled back the way she'd come. Once she could just see the campfire and Bee on the sand below, she went tree hunting. Didn't take long, they were all pretty good. Once up on a suitably wide and relatively even limb, she checked the view. She could make out most of the beach without being visible. Good.

Half asleep already, Olivia drew a few drops of moisture to her hand and spun them. They circled her fingertips, like clear moons. Sleep beckoned with each circuit. Energy fueled magic, huh? And magic had limits. Nice logical ones, sort of. It would make sense if it worked like a muscle, growing with use, but with an upper limit. That's what logical magic had worked like in books anyway.

"Fine fucking time for this shit to show up," Olivia whispered, spinning the drops faster and faster. Sleep would be a blessing. Rest would make her less pissed.

Magic. Four years of her life spent living in hell, and now this. Magic. Aliens. Random assholes. Big Croco-Fish trying to earn a 'Man-Eater' certification.

Bullshit.

Olivia had decided a long time ago that the world wasn't fair. Reality had kicked in sometime between her mom's first and third near overdose. The fourth one, the one Olivia hadn't been home for, had been the clincher. Coach, the principle, everyone else, they'd been par for the course. No help.

Moments like this, when some part of Olivia forgot that reality didn't give a shit, made her wonder whether it would've been better if her mom had died earlier, or later. If Olivia had saved her another dozen, two dozen times, maybe she could've graduated. Or gotten to the Olympics, somehow.

But that was bullshit. Olivia's mother had spent every dollar they had before her overdose. She wouldn't have been able to afford another round of her menagerie of chemical cocktails.

No.

Graduation. The Olympics. Olivia's future. That'd all died long before her mother decided to try a few more red pills than usual, just for funzies.

Magic couldn't bring any of that back. It couldn't have done shit to stop them either. It was another tool, just better.

The Rules were different, but the Goal hadn't changed; survive. First and foremost, make it to tomorrow. Magic would make that doable on this little slice of hellish paradise.

"Hell or paradise," Olivia wondered, drifting off.

The droplets fell, vanishing on the rocks below.

Exhaustion, like a weighted cloud.

Finally.

Napping without an alarm clock was going to be a problem. Ty could tell this from the distinct lack of sunlight. It'd been around midday when he'd collapsed onto the hastily thrown together bed and dozed off. A few hours of daylight before dark would've been really nice. Light kind of came in handy for just about everything out here. Worse, he didn't know how long after sunset it was.

Ty sat up, rubbed his eyes, and peered at the beach below. He was the last one up, which explained the empty bed beside him. Bee, Joey, and Nat were sitting by the fire. Their voices were low, hums hidden between the rustle of leaves and the crackle of flames. The river was quieter, a gentle under-note that blurred the edges of what few words drifted on the wind.

Falling back to sleep was out, and it was cold. Ty rubbed his bare arms, finally noticing the first hints of chill settling in. Fire. Fire was optimal.

So many rocks had been pulled from the wall that the larger ones made a stair-like shape. The steps were high, easier to go down than up, but workable. It was less treacherous than before, which was good. Falling and looking like an idiot was a good way to ruin a day.

"Evening, Sleepyhead," Nat called, waving.

"Hey," he said, shooting her a smile. "How long was I asleep?"

"Most of the day," Bee answered, poking at the fire with a stick. Sparks flew as she resettled things. "Sun went down a few hours ago."

"Wow," Ty said. He forced a chuckle, trying to add a bit of humor to the moment. "Guess fishing was harder than I thought."

Bee smiled, still watching the fire. "Oh yeah? How was that?"

"Fishing?"

Bee nodded.

"I'm gonna go find some more wood," Nat noted, standing up.

"Are you sure you should-" Ty began, glancing worriedly at her hand. She'd been bloody and beaten only hours ago.

"She's fine. Wood would be great, Nat. Ty, sit," Bee directed, pointing her poker at the spot Nat had vacated. The tip of the stick glowed.

Ty frowned, confused by the sight of Nat's perfectly fine hand. "What-"

"Magic," Nat answered, cutting him off. "Sit. Bee will talk you through her theory. Right, Bee?"

"First I'd love to hear about Ty's fishing expertise," Bee said, blowing gently on her stick's glowing end. The ember flared, a wisp of smoke curling in the firelight.

"My what?" Ty asked, even more confused. Magic, mysteriously healing wounds, Bee's attitude, time wonkiness; he really should've just gone back to sleep.

"I'll go get some wood," Nat stated, heading for the wall.

"I'll help," Joey offered, getting up and following her.

"Thanks," she tossed back as they headed off.

Which left Ty standing by the fire with a seated and serious looking Bee.

"Sit," Bee directed, yanking Ty's attention back.

"Ok," Ty said, easing himself down beside the fire, careful to keep the river in view. "So, what's up?"

"Fishing?" Bee queried, watching him over her stick.

"Again? I just did that this morning," Ty joked, trying to get her to laugh. He had a bad feeling about this.

"Did you?" she queried, bland. "How many did you catch?"

"Oh!" Ty blurted, smiling with relief as he figured it out. "Stabby helped. She was really good."

"Did-all-the-work type good?"

"It was a group effort," Ty said, frowning. He hadn't meant to not mention that Stabby had gotten the fish, but it'd just been... too weird.

"Group effort," Bee repeated, not buying it. "Huh."

"I found the fish, and she..."

"Did everything else?" Bee supplied.

"She used magic to pull them out of the water," Ty explained. "Dropping the 'magic is real' bomb while everyone was still freaking out over Nat and Stabby's wounds didn't seem like a good idea. So I didn't mention it."

"Huh," Bee grunted, frowning. "Ok. Fair point."

"Thank you."

"I still don't like you."

"You don't even know me," Ty returned. "And why do you think that matters? We're all here. We all want to survive this. Picking fights is wasteful."

Bee's frown faded, replaced by a cold expressionlessness. "Your face is wasteful."

"Your mom's wasteful," Ty tossed back, unsure whether the sudden onset of middle school insults was a good sign.

"You're not wrong," Bee said, cackling. "Hates recycling and never keeps leftovers. Better than your mom though. After I-"

"Can you not?" Ty interjected, wincing. "My mom's dead."

"Oh shit," Bee said, her face falling. "I'm sorry, I didn't mean-"

"Just kidding!" Ty laughed, pointing at her sad expression. "Gotcha!"

"Asshole!" Bee shouted, snatching an untouched stick from the ground and launching it at him.

Ducking away, Ty let it bounce off his shoulder. He didn't stop laughing.

"Prick," Bee muttered, trying to glare at him. Her face kept trying to smile, so the glare lost some menace. "Sass is my division, your job can be lifting shit or something."

"You trying to flirt with me?" Ty queried, surprised. The thought hadn't occurred to him till now.

"Trust me, if I were flirting with you things would be hella more awkward," Bee snorted, rolling her eyes and turning back to the fire.

"Not your area of expertise?" Ty guessed.

"Oh no," Bee declared, waving her hand with sudden and dramatic overconfidence. "I'm the mistress of flirting. I like to flirt people into bed all the time. That's my thing. I flirt, have some fun, and then hit a nice pub for a shot of tequila before starting over. I like to get three in on Friday, four on Saturday, take Sunday off, and then go for one or two during the week. Classes slow things down."

"Yeah, me neither," Ty said, chuckling.

"You saying you don't believe me?" Bee asked, facing him. The firelight lit her face from below, casting stark shadows around her eyes, the barest glimmer of the iris glinting through.

"What answer doesn't get me killed in my sleep?" Ty returned.

"Sounds messy," Bee said. "Maybe I'll just lure a Croc out to eat you."

"Croc?"

"The things that came after Stabby and Nat," Bee explained. "Stabby calls them Crocs."

"Like the shoes?" Ty asked, trying not to reel at the revelation that Stabby could talk.

"No, like Crocodiles, asshole," Bee corrected, shooting him a half-amused look.

"So, what's your magic theory?" Ty went on, leaping for a safer topic. "Can we all learn how to do it?"

"I think so," Bee answered, thoughtful. "Stabby showed-"

Across the fire, on the other side of the stream, water billowed outwards. It splashed from the stone rim of the lowest pool, barely preceding the massive, shadowy body that'd propelled it. The thing surged, dropping into the stream with a deep, echoing smack. The sound crashed against the tree line, hitting just ahead of the wave that swamped half the beach. The wave's curling lip hit the fire, sending up a roaring hiss and a cloud of smoke and steam.

Ty scrambled backward, his fingers and heels digging into the sand. Bee was a half beat behind. His scramble turned into a frantic rush to his feet, anything to get away. His eyes flicked back, drawn to the thing.

It was big. The Crocs had looked like meter long death-fish with reptilian limbs. Comparing them to this was like comparing an iguana to a Komodo dragon. This thing was at least three or four times as long, and beefier, with thick ridges along its length, and four pearly tusks protruding from around its mouth.

Tearing his eyes away, Ty dug in his feet and took off at a dead sprint. He almost ran into the wall, but managed to slow his momentum enough to turn it into a jump.

A scream filled his ears halfway up.

Bee's scream.

It wasn't a frightened scream. More like a cocktail of frustration, pain, and impatience. Her right ankle was bent in such a way that Ty's stomach rolled at the sight. She was kneeling on her other leg, a rock in each hand, looking back at the beast.

It surged forward, clawed limbs furrowing the river's bottom, more waves rising as its bulk drove forward.

With a fortifying breath, Ty leapt down and raced back the way he'd come. There wasn't much thought behind the action. Heroes saved their friends. Simple. Yes, whether she was a friend was kind of in question, but heroes also saved pretty girls.

Either way, it was hero time.

On the far side of the waning rush of steam from the quenched campfire, the monster's tearing steps launched it onto the beach. Thick as a tree trunk, its body hung in the air with unearthly stillness as its legs pounded. Prominent eyes sat high and forward on its head, straddling the thick brow that ran up from a wide, tusked maw.

Both glistening orbs stared at Bee, a filmy blackness sweeping down to block a spray of sand. Between its own monstrousness and the shadowy moonlight, it wasn't a pleasant sight.

"Drop!" Ty said, grabbing Bee under her arms and lifting her into the air. She let go of the rocks, squeaking with surprise as he swung her onto his shoulder. She didn't weigh much, but it slowed his turn.

"Screw you!" Bee shouted, the declaration somewhere between reflex and war cry.

The sand dragged at Ty's feet, forcing him to push harder for each step. Bee's broken foot hung in front of him, a reminder of how bad the next step could be. He kept running. The wall was getting closer, looming ahead.

"Shit-head!" Bee said, but this time there was violence in it, a caustic displeasure.

Out of nowhere, Bee's weight drove into Ty's shoulder, twisting him. His free hand flew out, hitting a blessedly rock-free bit of sand.

The monster shrieked, a high, keening outcry.

Bee screamed. Her broken ankle had been driven into the sand. Her free leg spasmed, pushing her back towards the beast. Trying to keep his grip on her, Ty rolled onto his back.

Tusked, scaled, and toothy, the fish-creature stared back. It was right there. Two, three steps away.

It hissed, its single eye wary, locked on Bee's flailing. The other eye was milky, leaking pale liquid from where a trio of glassy spikes pun.

"Fuck you!" Bee shouted again, throwing a punch towards the fish. A trio of glassy slivers shot out, but the monster's head turned. All three hit scaled, bony brow and shattered.

Three thoughts flashed through Ty's mind.

One; Bee must've put the three spikes in the thing's eye.

Two; snacks fighting back weren't going to make it smile and walk away.

And three; why wasn't he running yet?

Scrambling to his feet, Ty scooped Bee into his arms and took off up the wall. The steps were tall, but she was light and he had long legs. Teeth snapped near his heels. The grate of tusk and stone echoed in his ears.

Ty's feet settled on the top of the wall with a gravelly crunch. Relief flooded his system, adding to the sizzle of adrenaline. His heart pounded in his ears like a drum.

"Put me down!" Bee demanded, shouting bare inches from his right ear.

Alacrity born of fear pulled Ty's arms away before he had time to process what would come next.

Bee's eyes went wide. Then she dropped, her hands clutching at Ty's shirt as she tumbled to the ground. She howled, her bad ankle once again hitting hard resistance. When she landed, she had his shirt in her hand, but Ty didn't notice the cold night air. He was busy staring down the wall at the fish-thing.

"What the fuck happened?" Nat demanded, breathless as she burst from the woods.

"Big fish?" Ty offered, still trying to sort out exactly what his internal chemistry was doing. Part of him was very happy staying up here, another wanted to try running another few miles, just in case, and some bit was requesting a full frontal charge on the monstrosity.

Joey slipped from the woods, his pale arms wiry with corded muscle. He grunted at the sight of the thing.

"Is it gonna come up here?" Nat asked, her chest heaving, eyes wide as saucers.

"I don't think it can climb well," Joey said. "See those short limbs? Made for sprinting out of water, if it has to leave water at all. Like the Crocs."

The super-Croc was silent, staring up at them. Its mouth hung open by a fraction, thick, uneven teeth showing through.

"Well then how did it get up into the pools?" Ty countered, waving at the mountainside. He was really ready to embrace a 'run away' plan.

Joey frowned. "Huh."

"We need to-" Ty began, but a sharp whistle cut him off.

Stabby was a couple dozen meters down the wall, crouched on top of a boulder. She pointed at the fish then drew her thumb across her throat.

"What?" Nat said, confused.

"I think she thinks we should kill it?" Ty muttered.

"Like it. Makes sense," Joey agreed. "I'm in."

"What?" Nat barked, rounding on him.

"For glory," Ty concurred, his chest swelling. It sounded dumb now that he'd said it, but it'd been great in a movie. He'd try something else next time. Point was, it could climb. Run or fight.

"What?" Nat barked again, glaring at him.

"Take care of Bee," Ty directed, rolling his shoulders. "We got this fishy." It sounded way more badass than his first line. Somewhere between the rush of looking like a hero and the adrenaline, the whole frontal charge argument was definitely winning.

"She's out cold," Nat informed him, waving at her. "You're gonna be a lot worse!"

"This would really work better if we had those spears," Joey noted, nodding towards the spears sticking out of the wet sand just to the left of the monster's churned path.

"Stones will have to work," replied Ty, already searching for a good, sharp rock.

"Agreed," Joey said. He plucked up a smooth, rounded one bigger than his fist.

"Morons," Nat growled. She still knelt for a rock.

Ty's brow furrowed, surprised. "What're you doing?"

"Keeping you two dinguses from getting your asses munched," Nat retorted. She found a chunk of broken rock with a long rough edge and stood. "Thank me later."

"But you're the medic!" Ty argued, frowning at her. "And…" Realizing where the second sentence would've gone, he chose not to finish it.

"And?" Nat repeated, glaring.

"Nothing. Nothing at all," Ty blurted, giving up. Being labeled as sexist wasn't very heroic, but women should really let themselves be protected. Especially the ones that were supposed to be suitably impressed by the upcoming heroics. And Bee was unconscious!

"Good," Nat declared, gazing down at the beastie with distaste. "So, what's the plan?"

"Keep talking so that this thing doesn't notice Stabby?" Joey suggested, bland. He nodded out at the beach.

Ty looked. His jaw dropped.

The monster was still watching them, eyes leaping from speaker to speaker. Something was moving on the beach behind it. A shade flitted. It slipped from sandy mound to unearthed boulder, always in the shadow of the detritus. It'd snuck close, bare meters from the monster's tail.

"She's pretty good," Joey continued.

Ty fought to find words.

"She's going to get herself killed!" Nat hissed, waving angrily.

Joey's brows rose. "Distracting her won't help."

Freezing, Nat's teeth audibly ground.

"We've got to do something," Ty said, moving closer to the edge of the wall.

"We're already doing it," Joey noted. "Unless you'd like to become an edible distraction rather than an auditory one?"

"What?" Ty asked, confused.

"It might work. You might change your mind at the last minute though. I guess I could shove you if need be," Joey conceded. "It seems like a waste though. Chatting seems to be just fine."

"What is wrong with you?" Ty demanded, staring at the shorter, thinner, white, and altogether strange man.

"Did you hit your head?" Joey returned, looking back at him with a pristinely calm expression. "You keep getting surprised by the simplest things."

"I still want to know what the hell Stabby is doing out there!" Nat hissed, waving at the mobile shadow.

"Hunting?" Joey guessed.

"Getting herself killed!" Ty countered, still trying to understand why the little maniac was doing this.

"Oh look," Joey added, smiling slightly, "She's got a spear."

Nat and Ty stared.

She had. She'd also moved to stand at the center of the messy trail the monster had left in its wake.

"What-" Nat whispered.

Crazy. Pure and simple. Otherwise, why the bloody hell was Olivia standing here?

The tusky dino twitched. Its tail flicked back and forth across the sand, like a giant, scaled broom.

Any second, it could turn and see Olivia. Every moment she waited was a risk.

Time to do this thing.

"Hey!" Olivia shouted, rising from her crouch. The sand at her feet was uneven and wet, but she wouldn't fall. She didn't want to, and she could feel something connecting her legs to the sand. She wouldn't fall.

Tusky spun, tail whipping about as its thick limbs thudded into the beach. One bulbous eye settled on her. A black membrane slid across its surface, like a reptilian double take.

Then it charged.

Olivia could feel its steps through the ground. It had to be at least a ton, and it was fast. Like the rabid progeny of a heat seeking missile and an alligator, it came, tail whipping and limbs akimbo with every ounce of strength it had.

The Goal was the same, Olivia reminded herself. Make it to tomorrow. See tomorrow. Breathe tomorrow.

Copying what she'd done with the knife, Olivia saw a spear of pale ice spread across her palm, awful saw-blade tips shooting in either direction. Tiny streams of moisture shot from the ground, spraying bits of sand. The water hardened as it rose, landing cold and hard in her fist.

Olivia punched the spear at Tusky's face, those moonlit edges grasping for scales to tear and flesh to rend.

Tusky balked, flinching away. Olivia's spike tore across the monster's left shoulder. Hide tore, starlight giving inky blood an eerie sheen.

Charging past, Tusky headed back towards the beach and the quenched campfire.

A numbing exhaustion rolled up Olivia, starting at her toes and blossoming to a staggering chill in the back of her head. She fought to keep her eyes open. Not now. Not yet. This wasn't done! She held the spear in her head, forcing it to stay real.

Olivia spun, tracking Tusky as best she could. Cold ran up her arms, shivers echoing back from her spine. There'd be another charge. It was coming. She just had to be standing when it did.

Turning at the mess of what'd been the campfire, Tusky paused. Its right arm swung under and up as it lunged. Sand and fire-warmed stones sprayed across the beach.

Cold and dizzy, Olivia dove for a sandy bowl that the beast's foot had gouged. Maybe that would be enough.

"Hey!" shouted Ty's voice, closer than she'd expected.

A deep thud came from the direction of Tusky. It growled at the second. It hissed as a third came.

Glancing up from her little foxhole, Olivia saw Ty, Nat, and Joey lift fresh stones. The three were scattered between Olivia and the wall.

"Hey, you, Ugly!" Ty shouted, waving his free arm as he headed to the side. "Over here!"

"You alright?" Nat queried, darting close to offer Olivia a hand.

Olivia nodded, stood, and nearly fell. Her knees were weak. Her muscles were trembling. Damn magic.

"Any tips?" Nat asked, hints of fear slipping into the words.

Magic. She wanted to know how to do magic. Olivia shot her a thin grin. "Want it."

There was enough moonlight for Nat's incredulity to be visible, but she didn't ask again. Instead she turned and threw her rock, then went looking for another.

Tusky barely noticed the oversized pebble. Its eye danced among the four of them, wary. That thick trunk of a body hung low now, dragging across the sand as it backed away.

Shit. Olivia knew that look. Pointing a knife at someone starving was the same. Caught between two threats, most creatures didn't take long to pick. Right now, this one was choosing between starvation and the chance they'd take its other eye.

"Big Fish!" Zed shouted, racing past in a blur of limbs and blonde hair. Her ponytail was gone, leaving long locks free to trail behind her. She had a wooden spear in each hand, one held to her side like a lance, the other high and drawn back, like a scorpion's tail.

Tusky hissed and slammed its tail. The ground shook. Its body rose inches above the sand from the sudden force. Then those four limbs dug deep. Between one breath and the next, that mass of scales and teeth and tusks shot forward.

Springing from the beach, Zed flew left and up. Momentum carried her forward, over Tusky's reaching, gaping mouth. Its jaws clicked closed a whisper away from her.

Almost doubling over, Tusky whirled to follow Zed's path. The blonde landed, rolled, and shot to her feet. She faced the monster, a single spear at waist height.

Wait. Only one spear?

Olivia's eyes shot back along Zed's progress. She saw the other spear sticking from the shadowed beach just as Tusky charged into it. There was a thud, squelching and wet, like a dull knife through raw meat.

The massive lizard shrieked, high and echoing. The spear-tip stuck from Tusky's back, a mangled chunk of wood pointing to the sky. Slowed by the turn, stunned by the sudden impaling, Tusky sank low. Desperate, gargling breaths bubbled from its throat.

"We killed it," Ty said, somewhere between exhilarated and shocked.

Nat grunted and went for another stone. "Not dead yet."

"The spear went through one of its lungs," Joey said, walking closer to the monster. "It should drown in its own liquids in under a minute."

"We won!" Zed shouted, jumping up and punching the air. "Hells yes!"

"I'm going to check on Bee," said Nat, taking off towards the wall, rock in hand.

"Is she ok?" Zed called, peering over the quivering and quaking body of the dying monster.

"Her foot got messed up when this thing attacked," Ty explained, moving nearer.

"Messed up?" Zed repeated, clearly unimpressed by Ty's attention to detail.

"Her foot hit a rock in the sand and twisted. I didn't see if it was sprained or broken, but it wasn't at a good angle and it got hit twice afterwards."

"Huh," Zed said, frowning. "Suboptimal. Leg injuries are bad news. Yo, Stabby?"

Propping herself on the mound of sand she'd hid behind, Olivia stood. It didn't change her view much, but it made her feel less intimidated by Zed and the massive soon-to-be corpse between them. It also kept her from falling over. "What?"

Ty stared, his eyes big and bright in the moonlight.

Joey barely glanced at her, calm as could be, and brushed some sand from his pants.

"Can you heal Bee's leg?" Zed queried.

Olivia shrugged.

"Yes or no?" Zed pushed.

"Dunno."

"Can you try?" Ty asked, his voice full of an odd lurch, a kind of guilt and frustration.

Nothing. Olivia didn't owe him shit. Didn't owe any of them shit, really. He didn't hold her eyes.

The monster wheezed, wet coughing sounds emerging from the depths of its toothy mouth.

"Well?" Zed asked again, moving closer to Tusky.

Olivia's eyes narrowed. What a tosser. Standing over her kill. Trying to look powerful.

Screw her.

They could figure this shit show out for themselves.

Ignoring the cold in her bones, the tremble in her legs, Olivia walked steadily across the beach. She went to the low, stone bed, lay down, and fell asleep before she could count to three.

Daylight made the night's attacker even more unearthly. Its mouth was a lot like a shark's, all rows of saw-blade teeth, studded with tusks that would've looked comfortable on a Hippo. The body was shaped like a crocodile's, but the skin was wrong. Bones stood out in ridges beneath the taught hide, giving it a ribbed, almost armored look.

It was a weird mix of barracuda and crocodile, with just enough of a hippo to make it seem excessively excessive.

Nat eyed the stream. There was a risk to it now. An unspoken threat. She didn't like that. Aliens and weird islands that didn't get how geology worked were one thing, but deadly, bastardized versions of Earth's 'Most Likely to Eat Your Face' was sucky in a whole new way.

"Fuck it," Nat muttered. She stomped over to the water and drank. She gulped it down, finally relaxing as it salved her parched and painful throat.

"Long night," Ty said, coming up beside her. He squatted and took a long drink of his own.

"Too true." Nat sighed. "You sleep?"

"A little," Ty replied. "You didn't?"

"Not a wink. I kept imagining if another one came out of the river."

Ty grunted and looked up the mountainside. "Think there are more of them up there?"

"I wish I didn't," Nat said, doing her best not to glance up. "If we're lucky, they're solitary, that way the others won't come looking until this one's scent markers are long gone."

"Fish using scent markers?" Ty asked.

"Good point," Nat said, blinking at the water in her palms. "What do fish use to mark territory?"

"Hopefully something that takes even longer to wear off than scent," Ty joked, shaking his head.

Nat hummed her agreement. Another sip. She could tell he wanted something, but she wasn't going to ask.

"When your hand got injured…" Ty began.

Nat waited.

"When you got hurt, how did you get better?" Ty asked, stumbling.

"No idea."

"Magic?"

"Probably," Nat said. She shrugged. "Nothing I did. Stabby's the magic one."

"And Bee."

"Bee?" Nat repeated, surprised.

"That thing's eye? That was her. Stabby didn't show up till later."

Nat nodded. Made sense. Somehow, she hadn't made the connection. Magic was still a bit of a hang-up.

"You were pre-med?"

"Yeah."

"Lots of science courses?"

"Yes?" Nat said, twisting it into a question. What was his point?

Ty chuckled. "Must be hard for you. Magic. Kind of pokes holes in your field."

"No, it doesn't," Nat disagreed, shaking her head. Annoyance flared pursed her lips. People didn't get to talk shit about medicine in general, and her life was off limits to trash talkers. "What do you do in school?"

"Let's just say I'm a little better prepared than you are," Ty explained. He stared off at the mountain's heights, pride writ large in the self-satisfied curve of his smirk.

"Majored in Applied Magical Theory, Mage Systems, and Supernatural Species, huh? Maybe a minor in Wilderness Magic or Xeno-Ecology?"

"I mean, not exactly," Ty backpedaled, his smile faltering.

"Ah, so maybe Political Science? Theater? Philosophy?"

"No?"

"So you don't have any helpful magical expertise, no scientific know-how, you can't help us organize, can't keep us inspired and entertained, and can't help us through any potential moral quandaries. What were you saying you were good for?" Nat asked. Sure, it was mean, but she was tired and he had shot first.

Ty didn't reply.

"So, what were you studying?"

"I was a Lit major. Mostly British, with some American Classics," Ty admitted.

"There a lot of magic in that?"

"No, but I read Harry Potter about twenty seven times."

Nat snorted. "I don't think knowing what house you fit in will be helpful." She walked back towards the wall, careful to not stomp.

"Hey!" Ty said, jogging a few steps to catch up. "That's uncalled for. There was a lot of other fiction about magic, so maybe someone got something right. That could be a big help to us."

"Or those preconceptions might fuck us over," Nat countered. "Hard to say, with both of our magical types unconscious. Even if they were, they both don't like you."

"Bee and I figured things out," Ty scoffed, his smile returning.

Nat laughed. "You talked over how you dropped her on her broken ankle? Those were some unhappy screams."

"Ok, so she might be a little annoyed."

"And Stabby?"

"Might consider me fish bait," Ty grumbled. "But this could still be helpful! Knowing how things work is the best way to plan ahead. Otherwise we're just blundering around in the dark."

"You're assuming Bee knows enough for you to even guess at which piece of theoretically helpful writing is applicable," Nat pointed out. "I say Bee because it seems safe to say that Stabby won't tell you shit."

"Fine," Ty sighed, shaking his head. "So maybe it wasn't a great idea."

"At least not for the moment," Nat added.

"I'll keep it on the back burner and get back to gathering firewood."

"Hey," Nat said, catching his arm and pulling him to a stop. "You were a jerk about my area of study, so I shot back. What you know may not be handy till later, but don't get salty. We may spend the rest of our lives out here, and wandering off alone sounds like a good way to become croc food."

"So we're calling all the fishies crocs?" Ty asked, switching topics before he got more frustrated.

"No idea," Nat said, taking a deep breath and not looking at it. "Maybe Stabby will come up with something."

"Her talking is weird."

"Not as weird as magic," Nat replied. She continued towards the wall.

This time, Ty didn't follow.

The steps were a bit tall, each about the height of a coffee table as compared to the one below. It was enough to make going up slow and laborious. Better that than a monster accessible ramp. At the top, she made her way over to the stone bed, its surface green with leaves.

Bee was awake, rubbing her face with both hands. Her eyes were tightly closed against the rising sun. Her hair was a mess, already knotting, the green and blue dyes fading to black.

"Good morning," Nat said, sitting down next to her. "How's your leg?"

Bee groaned. "I think someone must've amputated it, then found the most villainous demon in hell to torture its phantom just so that I could get a feel for what's coming."

"Big fan of hell?" Nat joked, feeling for swelling around Bee's ankle.

"I figure it's the most likely outcome for me," Bee answered, settling one arm across her face. "Most religions have something like it, and I've never heard of a heaven for drinkers, druggies, troublemakers, and generally pissy people."

Nat shook her head, not sure whether to laugh or frown. "Glad you've got such a positive self image."

"Depends on the moment," Bee chuckled. It was a harsh, thick sound, like a grater against ginger. "Better to keep it real. Hell, maybe it's all bullshit and we all just get to catch up on sleep when we die."

"Wouldn't you get bored?" Nat said absently, distracted by the way Bee had just shifted her broken ankle without so much as a wince.

Bee snorted. "The worst shit that's happened to me has been while I was awake. It's never hurt my sleep."

"Is that a good thing or a bad thing?" Nat asked, curious at the way she'd said it. She poked Bee's shin.

"That's the trick. I thought it was good, but not having nightmares makes you wonder. When something bad happens but your dreams stay pearly, it's a bit like finding out you're already a bit evil. Or psychopathic. It's hard to tell."

"Uh, Bee?" Nat said, poking the wrapping that protected Bee's break.

"Yeah?" Bee replied, raising her arm just enough to see Nat's face. "Sup?"

Nat poked the ankle again. "Can you feel that?"

"Feel what?"

Blinking, Nat thought through the situation. She was jabbing a finger into what had been a broken joint and Bee wasn't just unhurt, she couldn't feel it at all. "Did someone wake you up while I was on the beach?"

Bee nodded, blithely unconcerned. "Yeah, Joey came by."

Oh shit. Nat stifled a rush of worry.

"Did he give you something to drink or eat?"

"He did," Bee confirmed, smiling. "He gave me a leaf or something. Tasted kind of like mint, but wetter."

"Did he say why?" Nat queried, fighting back the urge to go and strangle the undersized beanstalk. If she strangled him she'd have to bring him back to interrogate him about where he'd found a painkiller.

"He said I needed something to eat and that it'd help me feel better." Bee shrugged. "I figured he'd shove off and let me sleep if I ate it, so I did."

"Do you remember which way he went?"

"That way," Bee declared, raising one arm and pointing down the wall. "I think."

"If he comes back, tell him to come talk to me," Nat said as she stood.

"Aye-aye, mon capitan!" Bee confirmed, using her pointing arm to give a lopsided and jocular salute.

Nat left before she did anything that might reduce Bee's recovery, like slapping her upside the head and telling her in no uncertain terms to never eat unidentified plants on alien planets. It seemed basic, but apparently the American had less sense than two snails in heat.

And Joey!

Why the hell had Joey wandered in and given her some leaves? Who the hell just finds random leaves that taste like wet mint and make someone high enough to not notice their fucking broken ankle?

That was a lot of high. A lot. Medical grade, but faster, from the sounds of it. Most painkillers were slow acting, but that had numbed Bee in under a minute. That had to be addictive. Really addictive.

Stopping at the top of the makeshift stair, Nat scanned the trees. There were a lot of unknowns in there, even before eating the greenery became a factor. She headed down to the beach. Hopefully Stabby would have a few answers. At the very least, she'd distract Nat from the need to find Joey and shake him.

Sitting down on the stone next to Stabby, Nat took a moment and looked at her. Just looked. Bee had been ok, with only her hair and injury giving away how long she'd been out here. There was none of that illusion in Stabby. Her layered jackets and hoodie were torn and dirt stained, with stray leaves here and there. Her jeans were torn around her knee, colored by browned bloodstains. The cuffs of her hoodie peaked out around her wrists, bits of blood hanging to the threadbare hems.

Stabby shifted, her head rotating just enough for her to look at Nat. The spiraling teardrop on her cheek gleamed blue in the morning light, adding color to a face otherwise dominated by cold gray eyes.

"I want to talk to you about magic," Nat said, staying very still.

With a noncommittal grunt, Stabby rolled away and slipped off the edge of the stone bed. Her feet hit the sand, steadying her as she stretched, catlike. Her arms spread wide, bending backwards as her spine flexed. Joints popped and Stabby hummed.

"You've already talked to nearly everyone else," Nat said, smiling her most disarming smile, "Might as well talk to me too."

Stabby raised one eyebrow, unconvinced.

"You and I got over that attack really fast," Nat explained.

Stabby shrugged.

"Listen," Nat continued, rolling her eyes. "I'm not the magic one. I don't magic, and we know you do. A magic thing happened. That means you're the one that did it. I need you to do it again, before Joey turns Bee into a test rat for the local fauna."

Nothing. The girl just stood there, unmoved.

"I tell you what," Nat growled, racking her brain for options. She just wanted to fix her damn patient. This twerp had a solution and she wasn't being helpful! "If we stick together, we can make it through this. Maybe you don't get that, but I do. You fix Bee and I'll owe you. Favors are a big part of honor, and that's what keeps people alive in the wild, right? You can hold it over my head all you want. Even if you don't respect the rest of us, you can respect the value you can potentially get from me. You in?"

"You talk a lot."

Ok. That was the last straw. Ty was getting rude, Joey was poisoning her patient, Bee was a numbskull, and now Stabby was being a total prick. Nat was pissed.

"And you don't talk enough!" Nat burst out, nearly shouting. She stood, hands clenched into fists as the settled on her hips. "I don't fucking get any of this magic bullshit, but I do get that Bee's lying up there, screwed, and you're down here, fine and dandy! I want to fix her, and that means you need to step up. So, what does it take to make you get that we need each other?"

Silence stretched for a moment. The river lapped at the sand. The breeze played among the leaves. The trickling of one pool into the next was a gentle chorus from the mountainside.

"Put her in the water," Stabby said.

"Why?" Nat asked, her brows shooting together.

"That's what she did with us."

With that, Stabby headed off towards the stream.

Watching her receding back, Nat shouted, "Ty!"

"What?" Ty called back from somewhere near the monster corpse.

"Help me move Bee!" Nat growled, heading over to the wall.

"Why?"

"So we can heal her!"

"With water?"

"Shut up and help!"

"No need to be a dick about it," Ty grumbled, barely audible as he appeared around the scaled body. His step had a stomp to it, a hint of annoyed displeasure as he followed her to the wall, up the stair, and over to the stone bed.

Nat really wanted to hit him, but she didn't, through some miracle.

"Yo, it's the squad! Whaddup, squad?" Bee said, rolling over to watch them, her chin propped on a round stone. "Heard I'm water bound. Is it my birthday, or did someone send me a bathing-hotties-o-gram?"

"A what?" Ty said, confused.

"Like a kiss-o-gram," Bee explained, beaming. "But with more than one and more bathing and less kissing."

"So not at all like a kiss-o-gram," Nat added.

Bee pouted. "It was funny till he made me explain it."

"What a party pooper," Nat commiserated, trying to smile despite the returning desire to hit someone. Repeatedly. Maybe Joey. "Ty?"

"Yes?" he answered, busy deciphering Bee's humor.

"Pick her up, please."

Ty looked at Bee.

Bee rolled onto her back and peered up at him. "You're tall. Have you always been that tall or have I shrunk?"

Looking at Nat, Ty frowned and mouthed, "Is she high?"

"You. Bee. Water," Nat said, sticking to the essentials.

"Ok," Ty conceded. He shrugged and picked Bee up, his thick arms ginger and tentative.

Jogging ahead, Nat tried her best to back down the stairs in front of them. If Ty dropped Bee then things would be bad, regardless of Joey's turbo-painkiller. Leaves wouldn't do shit for broken necks or cracked skulls.

"Careful!" Nat warned, eyes wide as Ty nearly missed the second to last stone.

"It's fine," he huffed back, rolling his eyes and jumping to the ground.

"Just keep in mind that the six of us may be the only humans any of us ever see again," Nat growled, making her way across the beach.

Ty didn't reply.

When Nat looked back, his face was thoughtful. Yeah. She hadn't really thought that one through either. Scary.

"I guess the aliens might show up again," Nat admitted, her thoughts flying. "But they didn't seem relatable. Others might be nice though. Less murder-y. Maybe that one just watched too many Survivor reruns. The next one might be not awful. Might even be able to speak English. Well, probably not. English would be a stretch. Charades could work though. Hard to really get to know someone, but we could figure out how to ask to not be thrown out of planes and fed to crocs and super-gators."

Ty grunted, hoisting Bee a bit higher in his arms.

"Anyone ever told you that you talk a lot?" Bee asked, sighing as she rested her head against Ty's chest.

"Never," Nat replied.

Stabby sat at the water's edge, her feet outstretched to soak in the lapping waves.

Glancing down at the petite woman, Nat slowed to a stop beside her.

"Well," Nat said, squinting as she tried to find the faintest hint of discoloration in the water. "I guess it comes up sometimes. I've never understood why it's a bad thing. If people didn't want me to talk so much they should just talk more."

"Is that conversational blackmail?" Bee wondered.

Kneeling, Ty lowered Bee into the water.

"Nope," Nat answered, looking at the side of Stabby's hood, "It's called logic."

Stabby didn't do anything.

Ty sat. The water lapped against his side, wetness rising up his shirt.

One of Bee's arms was pinned against Ty's chest, but her free one wandered in the river. A stick drifted by and she slapped at it. Then she giggled.

Swallowing her frustration, Nat waited. If Stabby was waiting for her to beg, she was in for a surprise. The morning was still young, but Nat was pissed enough for a whole week. Stabby was going to get an earful if she didn't do something.

So Nat waited.

And waited.

After a few minutes, Ty shifted in his seat on the riverbed. "So, uh, what're we waiting for?"

Nat frowned at him, grunted, and looked at Stabby.

Nothing.

Grunting again, rather pointedly, Nat rocked forward on the balls of her feet. She couldn't see around the hood. Damn piece of cloth.

Ty adjusted again.

"Ok," Nat said, glancing skyward and fighting for patience. "Stabby?"

Stabby grunted questioningly.

"You going to do your thing?" Nat queried, waving towards Bee.

"What thing?"

"Magic!" Nat snapped, her nerves fraying.

"I don't heal things," Stabby corrected.

Nat nearly screamed. "Then why the hell are we dunking her in the river?"

"Because it worked on us."

"Wha-"

"She's right!" Ty interrupted excitedly, glancing down at Bee's glazed face. "We put you in the water to clean your bites. That might've been what healed you! This river could be magical, and that's why Stabby has magic now!"

"What river have you ever heard of that does that?" Nat scoffed.

"There are healing pools and springs in a lot of myths," Ty said, his tone shifting, his eyes going a bit distant. "In Irish mythology especially, though many water gods worldwide also had regenerative abilities."

"What river that you've actually been to," Nat corrected herself.

"What alien planets did you go to before this one?" he returned.

Nat frowned. She didn't like it, but he had half a point. "So we're just going to stand here and wait for the water to fix her?"

"You could help," Stabby suggested.

Nat growled, stamped around the shorter woman and glared under her hood. "How?"

"Get in and want it."

"The hell does that mean?"

Stabby didn't answer. Instead she looked over at Bee and raised one eyebrow.

"Shit," Nat sighed. She went to sit beside Bee and Ty. As Nat lowered herself into the water, Zed came up to stand near Stabby. Joey was on the wall behind them. She considered glaring at him too, but decided against it. The look wouldn't be as withering at this range.

Taking Bee's drifting hand in one of hers, Nat settled her other on the woman's forehead. She was sitting cross-legged in the water, mirroring Ty, knee to knee with him.

"How does this work?" Nat asked, wincing as she made the mistake of actually thinking through what she was doing. Magic. Jesus.

"What do you want?" Stabby said.

Nat smothered her need to point out that Stabby hadn't answered the question. She also had an ongoing deep desire to smack Stabby, but that wasn't as immediate an urge. "I want Bee to be ok," she said instead.

"Good. Look at her. Want that. Imagine it happening."

An eye roll nearly overtook her, but Nat buckled down and tried. Magic was real, that'd been proven. Stabby could do magic. Not listening to her right now would be moronic. Besides, if it didn't work Nat could hold it over the woman and make her do it.

Win-win.

With that in mind, Nat narrowed her attention, zeroing in on the task at hand. She thought of Bee's ankle. She imagined a clean, healthy joint. It fell into place, like a puzzle piece. Easy.

Nat shifted in her seat, settling deeper into the soft sand.

Smiling, beaming, Nat imagined a time-lapse of it all. Memories of bone-models and flashes of the sassy American raced through her head. She imagined the broken ankle repairing; saw it happening. Muscles knit, bone regrew, and swelling shrank.

Holding it together felt like holding a weight overhead, the pressing, deadening pull of gravity growing to a distraction. Nat kept going, visualizing a 'fast-forward' button and hitting it. She couldn't stop. It was all in her head, and if she couldn't focus for a few minutes then why had she ever even considered being a surgeon?

The weight increased, stinging now.

Then it began to burn. Lightly at first, but sank deeper with every breath.

After another few torturous seconds, the weight drove down. Then it was done. Gone. The ankle was all right, whole and well.

Nat gasped. Her eyes opened then fluttered, dry. Too dry. The muscles in her back clenched, yanking her upright, ramrod straight. Too straight. For a moment, she saw Ty's surprised expression, Zee's blinking face. Then Nat toppled into the water.

Warmth flooded her, pouring into her open mouth. Bubbles flew upward. They shot before her eyes and made the singular cloud bob and weave. Her eyes stung, that dryness lingering as the river filled her vision. Her back kept bending, one long backwards curl.

For a split second, Nat relaxed, muscles falling quiet.

Another spasm hit, but this time it was her legs. Suddenly stiff limbs thrust her deeper into the stream.

The glassy water did nothing to obstruct the light, but the too blue sky felt distant. A gasp of pain and surprise became another flurry of bubbles.

Figures appeared, blocking out the golden sun. Hands grabbed her. They pulled, yanking her up.

So slow. Too slow. The water was heavy, grasping.

Nat gasped again, drawing deep from her lungs as fear fueled adrenaline pumped through her veins. Chest tight, mouth agape and waterlogged, she waited for the cough. The first sputter of drowning.

But… It didn't come. The hands pulled, their progress so slow as to be unnoticeable, but the sputter, the choke, never came.

Nat had sucked down water, she knew that. Knew it. She had felt the warmth rush down her throat. She could feel the water still there, all the way down to her chest. But she wasn't drowning. Her lungs weren't screaming. The feeling of waiting, snapping pain in her muscles was gone. She relaxed, shocked, finally letting go of the desperate, clawing, demand for respite.

The water's weight vanished, like a mass thinning between Nat and the sky. Between one blink and the next, she jetted upward, those hands suddenly pulling with no force to counter them.

Scrambling to all fours, Nat coughed, splattering river-water across the shallows. She sat back, blinking.

Stabby stood over her, her feet still planted on dry sand. Kneeling beside the Asian woman, Bee's expression was dazed, but worry shone through. Ty and Zed stood in the river half a dozen steps back, waist deep and ashen.

Wiping the water from her eyes, Nat gave Bee a smile. "You ok?"

Bee blinked, confused. "Me?"

"She's not the one that tried to drown herself," Ty said, his voice thick with frustration.

"I was fine!" Nat said. The sooner she could blank that memory out, the better.

"The water held you down," Zed noted. Her frown made her disbelief in Nat's 'fineness' clear.

"My shirt must've gotten snagged on something," Nat countered. She waved a hand at the riverbed. "It just took a bit for it to tear."

"For someone that just healed a broken ankle you're a bit of a dumbass," Joey noted, coming to a stop beside Stabby.

"Don't forget breathing underwater," Stabby added.

"Did she?" Joey queried, his brows rising fractionally.

"She should've been out of breath after that long," Stabby said. There was a glimmer in her gray eyes, a spark of curiosity.

"Magic ice, magic healing, now magic underwater breathing," Zed listed, chuckling. "At least this one makes more sense than the rest." She patted Nat's shoulder and offered her a hand.

Taking it, Nat stood. "I guess so."

"Next time warn us?" Ty said, sloshing up to her other side. "I'd rather not have a heart attack. We're going to need all of us to make it through this."

Nat smiled. Maybe he believed, maybe he was parroting, but either way it was what they all needed to remember, and having someone other than her saying it was good.

"I'm hungry," Joey said, deadpan. "Why don't we get some food? We can talk afterward."

"Food sounds great," Bee agreed. Her smile was blissful, wide, and probably more than a little high. "I'm famished."

"Same," Nat concurred, realizing that her stomach was painfully empty in a way that it hadn't before. Bee could get over the damn leaves on her own.

"What're we eating?" Bee asked.

"I found some plants-" Joey began.

Nat leapt to her feet, hand raised at Joey to shut him up. "No. Benefit of the doubt on what you gave Bee, but no one eats any more alien plants until we figure out what's safe."

Joey raised one eyebrow. "How?"

"We'll figure something out," Nat declared, dismissing the question for later. "We stick to meat for now."

Zed nodded at the scaled beastie. "That monster looks cookable. It's been sitting for a while though."

"You're not supposed to eat meat that's been left out for more than a couple hours," Nat said sadly. It was a lot of meat to let go to waste.

"A little cooking and it'll be fine!" Bee said.

Nat shook her head. "It kills off some bacteria, but not the toxins they've produced. We need fresh."

"Who likes fishing?" Joey said, smiling around.

"Fishing is Stabby's thing," Ty answered, nodding to her.

Looking up at the woman on the beach, Nat tilted her head to the side. She could just see her eyes under the rim of the hoodie. "You up for fishing?"

"Just toss some bits in," Stabby replied.

"Bits?" Nat returned, confused.

"Of the monster," Zed said. "Smart."

"Should've thought of that," Ty mumbled, kicking at one of the stones on the riverbed.

Joey smiled and looked back at the carcass with a pleased expression. "Think we can keep some of the bones?"

"What for?" Bee asked.

"Weapons. Tools. Whatever," Zed said. "We'll keep whatever we can use. Too bad we can't tan the hide and make clothes or blankets or something."

"No salt. No lime. Other things too," Joey sighed, thinking out loud.

"What he said," Zed agreed. "Knows his shit."

"My parents were Park Rangers," Joey explained, shooting her a cool smile.

"Hunt?"

"Yup."

"Bow?"

Joey shook his head. "Nothing I can recreate with what we have here."

"Ok, I need to nap, and I'm betting Bee does too," Nat interjected. "Stabby, you're in charge of fishing up lunch. Joey, Zed, and Ty, you're helping."

"Aye-aye, captain," Bee snorted, but her smile was grateful, not sarcastic.

With that, Nat helped Bee to the wall. Halfway up, she looked back. The others were starting on the corpse. Hopefully nothing went wrong, but if it did at least she and Bee were on the wall, nice and safe.

Nat lay down on the leafy bed. Bee curled beside her. The overhanging branches hid them from the sun, offering only the dappled spots of brightness that sparked the eye and etched bits of reality into the mind. Wiggling, she settled more comfortably into the curve of the rocks below the bedding. The movement brought her back up against Bee's.

Nat froze, nerves tingling oddly.

The other women barely moved. For a moment, they breathed, long and slow.

The contact was nice. Even with the warmth of the day, Nat didn't mind the heat of Bee's back. It was comforting. Part of her felt like she should say something, but that risked ruining it. So she didn't. Neither did Bee. They just lay there, barely touching, and gradually fell away.

Olivia didn't like corpses. Most people didn't, but her dislike was a bit more personal. Her mother had made a habit out of looking indiscernible from dead. No matter how many times Olivia came home to that, she'd never gotten over that sudden cold tightness in her chest at the sight. Most of the time her mom had woken up. Vomiting. Hospital. CPR. One way or another she'd come back.

Not every time though. Not the last time.

There'd been other corpses later on. London had been lovely when Olivia had money and a place to live, but it had gotten harder to remember that pretty veneer with each pair of glazed, crazed, raging, or dead eyes.

Dismembering this monster brought back some of those memories.

Zed and Ty grunted, hefted a leg between them, and headed for the water. It was easier to debone the meat down there. The blood was already pooling on the sand here, and the stink was getting bad.

With a twist, Olivia popped another fang from the beast's mouth. It went with the others in her pocket, still dripping. The blood would wash out later. Cleaning them first would mean either trekking to the water or magic, and both seemed a waste. It was just a pocket. She yanked another tooth. They were long, maybe four inches on average, with long roots and saw-blade edges. The tusks were bigger, but she hadn't pulled any of those yet. Ty stood a better chance.

A meaty thunk from further down the body echoed across the beach, followed by the splatter of something wet. Glancing around the side of the monster's head, Olivia watched Joey lean back, gauge his next swing, and bring down a sharpened blade of pale ice. Seeing it was odd, like seeing her hand on another person's arm. She could feel the ice fighting to stay together, drawing from her to hold its shape.

"Careful," she noted.

"I am," Joey returned, nodding without looking up from his target. "Is it getting hard?" he added.

"Not yet," Olivia lied. It wasn't that bad, except when it skated off bone. Then she could almost feel her muscles twitch at the sudden drain.

"Thanks again," Joey said, slipping the blade between two ribs and dragging it out and down. The cut freed a stretch of scale that hung in his other hand. "Why do you think you're lasting so long?"

"Practice," Olivia guessed. Probably wasn't far off, but practice usually took longer to show results. She could just be good at it. But she wouldn't say that.

"I'll start practicing," Joey said. He grabbed a rib and tugged on it. No movement. "Handy."

"Very," Olivia agreed, returning to the teeth.

It was probably a mistake to teach them all how to use magic, but she'd only shown them how to make knives. Simple. They'd have figured it out soon anyway.

It definitely wasn't because she might need them to survive. Nope.

Zed had taken the longest to get it, but her knife had lasted for nearly ten minutes. Ty's had only gone for about five, and Joey's had crumbled after a minute. She'd expected Joey to get pissed at being last. Macho bullshit and all that, but he hadn't. He'd just looked at it, frowned, nodded, and asked to use hers.

Olivia had nearly stabbed him for asking, but then she'd realized that it was safe. She could melt the knife whenever. Besides, the extra work would tire him out. She smiled, wrapped her rag-wrapped digits around another tooth, and yanked. This one was on the upper jaw.

Another tingle of lost strength ran down Olivia's spine. It came a fraction of a second before the sound of ice hitting metal.

"Stabby," Joey said, the word slow, considering.

Tooth forgotten, Olivia stood and dodged around the open maw.

Icy machete at his side, Joey stared at a blue-green ball tucked between the monster's shoulder blades. It stood out among all the red blood and bits of pale bone. She froze.

"Tracking tag?" Joey said.

"Ty! Zed!" Olivia called. They'd have a better idea of what to make of this.

"What?" Zed said, hushed in an attempt not to wake Nat and Bee. The pair had only been out for a half hour or so.

Olivia didn't answer. She didn't look over the monster's back to make eye contact. Giving orders might piss Zed off, asking showed weakness, and silence would make her curious.

Sure enough, about thirty seconds later, Zed and Ty made their way up to the other side of the thing. Once they were close, it didn't take long. Joey's gaze might as well have been a big neon sign saying 'Wacky Shit This Way.'

"Tracker?" Zed guessed.

"That's what I said," Joey agreed, a bit stiffly, distracted.

Ty shook his head. "Might be some kind of mind control thing. That way someone could pilot these things like toys."

"Dork," Zed chuckled.

"Alien planet, kidnapped by fish-people, attacked by alien turbo-crocs of various sizes, need I go on?" Ty queried, looking down at her. He wasn't that much taller, but it was enough to be noticeable.

"Shut up. I wasn't disagreeing," Zed grumbled around a smile. "Nerd."

"Oh," Ty said, reassessing. "Then yes, I resemble that remark."

"Can we focus on the alien tech in the monstrous fish-bear on the alien planet?" Joey requested.

Olivia nodded her agreement. Blondie and big-boy could flirt some other time.

They all stood there, waiting, silent, as several slow minutes drifted by.

Ty shifted his weight from one foot to the other. "We should probably take it out."

"Yeah, that sounds really safe," added Zed, rolling her eyes.

"Well, what's your plan?" Ty jabbed back.

Joey and Olivia looked at each other. He raised one eyebrow. A silent 'you want to?'

"We could do something a little less moronic," Zed declared, hands on her hips as she turned to face Ty.

Olivia raised an eyebrow, throwing a silent 'you do it' back at Joey. His brow rose a little further and he glanced at the orb. He really wanted her to do it.

"You'll owe me," noted Olivia, barely above a whisper. Zed and Ty didn't notice. They were busy arguing.

Joey paused, then nodded.

Bending at the waist, Olivia reached out, plucked the orb from the mess of meat, and stood upright again. Nothing happened. The arguers turned to look at her. Ty was wide eyed. Zed looked vaguely impressed.

"So, not dead?" Joey asked.

Olivia shot him a scathing look.

"Just checking."

Zed chuckled. "If it isn't attacking you on contact, maybe it's meant to be removable?"

"Or they just didn't bother to build in a defense mechanism," Ty said.

"If they can make space ships I think putting a super-Taser in a golf ball wouldn't be a challenge," Joey countered.

"What he said," Zed said, watching as Olivia wiped the last bits of blood from the ball. "I'm gonna operate under the assumption that it's meant to be extracted. That means either we're supposed to find it, or someone else is."

"Maybe we were supposed to be fish food," Joey suggested, nodding down at the massive beast.

"If so, it's still meant to be collected by somebody," Zed said, frowning as she pondered it. "That makes it valuable. Maybe not usable, but valuable."

"Like a trophy," Ty said, catching up. "Antlers, a dragon's tooth, rabbit's foot, that sort of thing."

"Which would make it a bargaining chip for us," Zed declared, her eyes narrowing. "Not a lot, but something. It also tells us that this isn't wilderness, this is more like a national park."

"Maybe," Joey said, frowning. "It could also be a way of controlling an invasive species or monitoring a dying one."

"What if we're meant to find it?" Ty asked, changing tacks. "What if it's like a message in a bottle."

Zed snorted. "Telling us all the things they forgot to mention when they had us all neat and orderly in the plane?"

Ty shrugged. "Maybe we had to kill one of these to prove we were worth telling anything."

Pausing, Olivia squeezed the ball in her hands. It was the size of a golf ball, rough and porous. It felt almost spongy, but metallic. A sponge…

"Huh," Olivia grunted, thinking. She glanced at the stream. Then back at the could-be-sponge. Curious, she slipped around the carcass and headed towards the water.

The others went quiet, then jogged to catch up.

"What're you doing?" Zed queried.

Olivia ignored her. She didn't feel much of an obligation to be nice at the best of times, and she was busy at the moment.

"What. Are. You. Doing," Zed snapped. She punctuated the last word by wrapping her fingers around Olivia's bicep.

Sirens went off as bursts of white flashed across Olivia's vision. Her free hand flashed to her jacket, then jabbed a chunk of fishbone into Zed's hand.

Zed yelped, yanking her hand back.

The bone, thin and fishy, snapped in half.

Hands darting for fresh bones, Olivia crouched low. The ball hit the ground at her feet. Instinct kept her loose, every muscle a hair away from action.

Zed backed away, her bloody left hand pressed to her belly. Her right was up and curled into a fist. The corners of her mouth curled upwards, but her jaw was clenched. There was fire there, a rage that begged to fight, but there was pain gnawing at it.

Olivia knew the look. There was an all too familiar violence in it.

"Does picking a fight make you feel less lonely?" Olivia asked, knowing it would piss the woman off. Better pissed than thinking.

Olivia's own mind was a mess, frothing with light and fear and memories of dark alleys and boarded up rooms and dilapidated mattresses, stinking of trash and mold and sick. If Zed wasn't just as distracted, Olivia was fucked.

Tanned skin drew taught across Zed's bare arms, her jeans doing the same as strong legs tensed. Her jaw stayed clenched, but her smile faded. Swinging one leg forward, she swept a little wash of sand away from the beach's surface. Looking for rocks, anything that might injure her footwork or become a weapon.

"What are you doing?" Ty demanded, aghast.

"Shut up!" Zed growled.

Olivia thought through her options. Joey wasn't an ally. Neither was Ty. She had the fangs, some bones, and a lot of rage. But Zed had at least a quarter meter on her, not to mention a history of regular meals and exercise.

Not good.

If Olivia fought now and made Zed work for it, then Zed might not be so quick to come after her next time. That's how bullies worked. Better to lay down the line and get beaten for it than get walked on. She'd heal.

"I'm gonna kill you," Zed noted.

There went the healing option, Olivia thought to herself. Too bad. It wasn't a bad plan up to that.

"No one's getting killed," Joey said, sidling up on Olivia's right. He wasn't between her and Zed, but he held a large chunk of recently rinsed super-croc femur. The bulky ends made it a pretty impressive club. "We need each other."

That shook Olivia. Not because Joey had taken her side. What shook her was that he'd backed her up out of self-preservation. Screw altruism, she'd take good old self-interest any day. Way more comprehensible. Comforting, even.

"One stick-thin white boy with a bone and a wannabe Asian schoolgirl-witch cliché," Zed said, looking at them with an air of pissed off amusement. "I'm trembling in my boots."

Behind Zed, Ty stepped forward. He loomed behind her, barely a meter away. "Cool it, Zed," he said, his voice low and even. "We're all on the same team here."

Zed took a deep breath. Two. Then she smiled. It was thin, tense, and her eyes still gleamed with rage, but it was a smile. "You're right. All for one and one for all. Got it."

Olivia blinked. That definitely wasn't how she'd expected that to go. Not being dead was really nice though. She felt a bit embarrassed at how she'd been considering which way to run, even after Joey's offer. Nothing personal. He was less likely to get killed than Olivia was. Even if he were killed, at least Olivia would still be alive. The Rules might be different, but the Goal was still seeing tomorrow.

Olivia had been watching Zed's center mass, but she looked up as the pressure eased. Their eyes met. There was a bit of something in Zed's smile, and hiding around the rage in the woman's eyes, but Olivia didn't recognize it. Maybe it was a soldier thing.

Zed nodded.

Olivia mimicked the gesture. Apologizing for stabbing Zed's hand wasn't going to happen. She'd heal, magically or otherwise.

"Ball?" Joey said, wry and dry.

Remembering her plan, Olivia plucked the little metal ball from the ground and set off for the river again. The water flowed around her bare toes, soaking the legs of her jeans. She turned ninety degrees, so that they could watch, and plunged her ball bearing right hand into the clear water.

It'd felt like a sponge. That'd been the clue.

As it hit the surface it swelled beneath Olivia's fingers, as though sucking in a massive breath. Water rushed between her digits, fighting to reach the ball's porous exterior. It began to turn in her hand, as though a button had been pushed.

Olivia flinched, surprised by the sudden movement of water and ball. She let go.

Bobbing to the streams surface, light unspooled from the top of the ball. Thin streams and ribbons of color wound outwards, like snakes swimming through the air. They flowered into three equal hexagons, each numbered and roughly the size of a head. One through three.

Blinking, stunned, Olivia tried to process it. There was something surreal about the ball and its colors. Around her, nothing had changed. The world, the sun's warmth, the water's bubble and lap, the rustle of trees, even the salty breeze; all the same as a moment ago. But there it was, a weird sponge-ball wafting holograms into the air, like a bear walking through Piccadilly Square.

Curious, Olivia lifted her foot and dropped it again, making a small splash. The wake spread, butting against the orb. It bounced, as did the image above.

"I'm definitely getting menu vibes," Zed suggested, forced calm and interest in every word. "What do you think? I'm feeling three."

"What, like murdering the wildlife earns us a spin on the holographic lottery?" Ty scoffed.

Joey shrugged. "That'd make sense if this is meant to be a trophy or a prize."

"I still think it's a message. The numbers are probably the order we're supposed to read them in," Ty countered, stepping forward to stare intently at the hologram.

"Doesn't matter," Olivia muttered. If it was the order they should be opened in then they needed to start with 'one.' If it was a lottery then there was no more risk to picking 'one' than any other number. She felt tired just thinking about how long it'd take for them to pick 'one.'

Besides, she was still pissed at Zed, and Zed didn't want to pick 'one.'

Win-win.

Olivia looked at Joey again. The moment reminded her of when Zed and Ty were arguing about the ball when it was still in the corpse.

The corners of Joey's mouth curled and he nodded.

She stepped forward and waved one hand through the hex with the 'one' on it.

For a second, the shape turned a blank blue, and then it spun, sucking in the other two. The blob flattened and stretched into another hex, this one numberless and flat to the water. On it, two bars of green bordered a weaving row of gray and blue that ran from the edge nearest Olivia to the far side. All of it was faintly translucent, like painted gossamer.

Bending close, Olivia stared. From close up she could make out the details. The gray bits were mountains, the green trees. It was hard to find single trees or any but the larger pools without losing focus and catching the stream below instead.

Suddenly, Zed leaned in, poring over the shape from the other side.

Olivia flinched away, nearly taking a step back.

Zed beamed, her eyes on the hologram. She laughed. "It's a map!"

"Really?" Ty asked, splashing through the water to get his own look.

"No, she's definitely kidding," Joey said, dry and sarcastic as he came over.

A blue-white glimmer grew to shine at the center of the map.

"I think we've found ourselves," Zed said with a half-hearted chuckle. "That checks out with what I saw upriver, and where the nearest route to the ocean is."

Olivia grunted. Alien GPS mapping, but with no sign of satellites, signal, or delay. Wonderful.

"Next number?" Ty suggested, excited.

"Yeah," Zed said. "We need context for this."

"Agreed," Joey added.

"How do we get to Number Two-" Zed began. She went silent as the image spun, rising from disc to large orb. The round shape slowed, pits folding and flowing inwards until a face hovered before them.

All bone and muscle, with arrays of blue-green diamonds covering every bit of skin, the face looked smooth and hard. The diamond scales ran back from thin lips and a flattened nose to a pair of spiraling horns. They reared back, curling down before coming forward again, like a ram's. Their tips were near the chin, each delicate point sleeved in something like the spongy metal orb.

Olivia locked onto its eyes.

Perfectly uniform circles of pearly white. The rest had been more of a blur, harder to bring to mind after the fall, but the eyes were just as she remembered them.

Then she noticed the tattoos.

The face was similar, the eyes were the same, but the tattoos were all wrong.

This one had half a dozen lines running outwards from its eye sockets, stretching nearly to the roots of its horns. On the outer edges, where the twelve radiating lines grew far enough apart, droplets speckled the open space, like tears falling in every direction from those eyes. It wasn't just the tattoo's design that made it proof that this wasn't the being that had thrown them out. That was the fact that the tattoos pulsed with blackness, as dark as its eyes were pale. She would have remembered tattoos like those.

The face moved, tilting ever so slightly to one side. Its mouth opened, baring an array of teeth that looked shockingly blunt. She'd expected croc style saws, but instead they looked almost human. Thin, scaly lips curved upwards, giving them a small smile.

"My name is Blue-Sight, Fifth Holy of the Green-Walker Range," it said, its voice somehow silken smooth and just short of sibilant. "And for those of you wondering, I'm a male." It smiled again. "I have embedded this message in all the maps in your section of the Range so that you could have an idea of what is happening. I am not a Ranger, nor a Ritualist, but I have special dispensation to give you the basics. You have the right to know that much after killing a Kaskan. Say 'Ready' when you wish the message to continue."

With that, he froze in place, a slight smile on his lips as he stared at the beach. The four of them had moved around, towards the way he'd been facing, none directly in front of him.

"Wow," Ty said, barely more than a whisper.

"Aliens speak English," Joey noted with interest. "And are religious."

"Like civilized people," Zed added. "Except for the English bit."

"You speak English," Ty threw back.

Zed smirked. "I didn't say I was civilized."

Olivia rolled her eyes. The woman had either said the line a lot before or had practiced it.

"We should go wake up Bee and Nat," Joey said.

Olivia nodded. "And check for crocs."

"Can you do that?" Zed asked, brows rising.

Another nod. "I'll check. You go get the others."

Nothing happened for a second. Then Zed went. No comment.

"You trying to piss her off?" Ty asked, shaking his head.

Olivia ignored that.

"Keep it up," Joey said. "She needs a clean chain of command. You giving her shit and us backing you up might be close enough."

"Wait, no!" Ty denied, frowning. "Stabby's not in charge. No one is in charge. We talked about it."

"Why do you want to be in charge?" Joey asked, meeting Ty's eyes.

"Uh, because…" Ty trailed off. Then he rallied. "Because I'm the only one here who has a feel for the kind of Sci-Fi stuff we're going to run into."

"And?"

"And I know how small unit tactics work, how to wage war, survive in the wilderness," Ty added, pride slipping through. "Plus, I'm a good diplomat, highly intelligent, and have an excellent handle on game theory, psychology, and group dynamics."

Joey raised a hand, one finger up. "Zed knows how to fight, train, and work as a team." A second finger shot up. "I've yet to see you do anything particularly helpful to our survival besides lifting." Another finger. "You've already disproven most of the rest."

Olivia snorted. Funny and true. Nice mix.

"I think you're useful," Joey added, forestalling Ty's response with an open palm. "I think we need you, but you need to get that you don't have to be the best. Being the best at something is good, but being strong, or fast, or positive, or supporting might be more useful here."

Ty glowered, but didn't reply.

"You want to be in charge because you want to be in charge? Fine. Earn it. Learn and prove you deserve to tell us what to do, but so far, I'm in Stabby's corner," Joey explained.

Olivia twitched involuntarily. That was a lot to process all at once. The shit about Ty had all been pretty predictable, and adding the offer of a carrot at the end had been sweet, but Joey being in her corner was something else. It felt as out-there as the little spinning space-ball in the water.

"Does she even want to be in charge?" Ty asked, still addressing Joey. "And why her? She's picking fights and stabbing people! That's her whole shtick!"

"Isn't not wanting to lead one of the main qualifiers?" Joey asked, frowning in faux-thought. "So far she's fed us, protected us, led us, been a hard ass, and solved the alien mystery ball."

"He called it a map," Olivia noted, jerking her chin at the large, hovering face.

"Yeah, that," Joey concurred.

"Ok, I'll admit that Stabby's done a lot," Ty conceded, "But maybe we should hold off on deciding this until we're all here."

"I'm not deciding anything," Joey said, coolly amused. "I'm just telling you what I think."

"Olivia," Olivia noted. She wasn't sure why she'd stuck with Stabby so long, but Zed already knew, so why not.

Ty frowned, confused. "Olivia?"

"It's her name, dummy," Joey sighed. "And you should stick with Stabby. Scarier. Take it from someone named Joey."

Olivia chuckled. "We just got a voicemail from a guy named Blue-Sight. He seemed pretty scary."

"You're a few horns, some scales, at least a foot of height, and a lot of alien DNA behind in the initial scary impression meter," Joey replied.

"Who is?" Nat asked, walking up to them. "Zed filled us in."

"Yeah, and I'm still deciding if I really wanna know what Horny McShitface's voice sounds like," Bee grumbled, following her over.

"It's actually quite pleasant," Joey noted.

Bee looked at him for a long second. Then, deadpan, said, "I cannot find the words to describe how reassured that makes me feel."

Ty and Zed burst out laughing, and Nat was right behind them. Olivia stifled hers and tried to hide it as a cough. She owed him after all.

Joey just stood there and watched with a cool smile.

"Ok, let's see what he's got to tell us," Nat said, once the laughter had died down.

In the fraction of a second after she said it, Joey nudged Olivia. She controlled the urge to stab him. "Ready," she declared.

The stillness of the Blue-Sight's floating smile broke.

"Welcome to the Second Range-World of the Pacifist Vinna. Translation, this was our second colony, built after we, the Pacifists, left our home. Oh, and Vinna is the name of my species, in case that wasn't clear."

The face shifted, angling slightly to the side, as though thinking through what he should say next. "You were chosen because you all have Current in your blood. Or, magic in your genes, if you'd prefer. You're all young, in good health, and have Current, so we brought you here for a Rite of Passage. A sample group. The first stage is killing a Kaskan, so good job on that."

A hand rippled into existence in front of the face, clawed and webbed and scaled, with one thumb pointed upwards. Then it faded.

"By now you should have a feeling for your Current and you've killed. Hopefully, you've bonded as a team too. You'll need all of that. The next stage of the Rite is to defeat a camp of humanoids armed with knives and bows. They know you're coming, but not when. Their leader will be carrying a map to your next target. I suggest you keep their weapons and whatever else you need, because the next group will be better armed and more prepared. That pattern will continue until you finish the Rite. Say 'Ready' when you're prepared for me to continue."

Silence.

"What. The. Fuck," Bee hissed, barely above a whisper. "It's like Reality TV, but more deadly and less greedy."

"They could be filming it all," Joey pointed out.

"Nah," Ty muttered, thoughtful. "He said 'Rite,' and I've never heard that word used for something that isn't holy, and usually pretty private."

"I'm going to vote in favor of Ty's version because it's way less stressful than suddenly being on some kind of intergalactic Hunger Games: Team Edition," Nat said, rubbing her face. "Jesus."

"If it is, at least it's not airing in our neighborhood," Ty said. "We're a bit on the wrong side of the universe."

"Why me?" Nat muttered, glaring up at the sky.

"Current, young, healthy," Zed listed off. "Weren't you listening?"

"I will pour water on your face while you sleep," Nat threatened.

Zed frowned. "Good point. I do need to wash my hair."

"We good?" Olivia asked, enjoying a momentary smile. Knowing what was happening would make them all feel better eventually, but the humor helped with the shock. Humor was good. That's how a lot of London's streeters survived, but right now they needed to get through the message.

A chorus of affirmative grunts went around.

"Ready," Olivia said.

"Good," Blue-Sight said, nodding. "In summary: you need to kill a camp full of aliens that aren't Vinna, use the map you find to get to the next target, and not get killed. Current is powerful, but it cannot carry you back from death. If you need any of this repeated, reopen this file. File One will now display the target camp's location. File Three has a basic layout of what your opponents look, fight like, and are armed with. Six blessings."

With that, the face stilled, shrank, and spun back into a disc. After a second it split into three numbered hexes again.

"Huh," Zed grunted. "He didn't say what'd happen when we win."

"We get to go home?" Bee suggested.

Olivia looked at her, skeptical.

Bee winced at the reiterated unlikelihood of going home.

"Well, not following instructions will get us killed a lot faster," said Ty. He sighed and scratched the back of his head. "If this is a religious thing, us deviating would be an insult."

"I think kidnapping was a pretty big insult," Nat grumbled.

"Not from their perspective," Ty countered. "And they're the ones with the guns."

Zed laughed. "The Man in the Tank Will Prevail."

"Motto?" Joey guessed.

"Of the Israeli Defense Force's Armored Corps," Zed explained. "We play their way until we get tanks," she added, back on topic.

"Seconded," Olivia said.

"Same," Joey agreed, Ty on his heels.

"Makes sense," Nat said, nodding her ascent.

"Fucking hell," Bee muttered, using both hands to scratch her scalp, burrowing through her mess of green and black hair. "Fine. Let's do it."

"Good, first we do something about your hair," Nat said, swatting Bee's hands down. "And mine. Probably Zed's too."

"Do what?" Zed said, looking up from the map. She'd already moved on to studying the stretch of river and forest between the green dot and the red one.

"We need to cut our hair," Nat explained, thumbing at Bee. "It's going to get harder and harder to deal with, so we might as well go short now."

"You're right," Zed said, looking at Bee's tangled locks. She reached up and felt her ponytail. "My hair tie is almost dead anyway."

"And we have no idea of knowing what kind of local insects like to live in hair," Nat pointed out. Her hand flexed with the barely suppressed urge to check for new residents.

Zed looked at Olivia.

Olivia grunted questioningly back.

"Magic knives are sharper than whatever bits of broken bone we can sharpen up," Zed explained.

"Current is sharper," Joey corrected. "Might as well get used to the lingo now."

Zed nodded, but didn't break eye contact.

"You'll have to trust me," Olivia said, figuring that'd be the deal breaker.

Bee rolled her eyes. "It's just a haircut."

"Risk accepted," said Zed, a tiny grin appearing on her face.

Nat nodded. "As long as you don't scalp me, we're good."

Olivia gestured down at the water around her feet. "Take a seat."

"I'll get a stone to sit on," Bee said. She headed towards the stone bed further up the beach. Nat followed her.

With a shrug, Zed sat down in front of the orb. The ball was within reach and she was up to her bellybutton in the water. She placed a tentative hand on the map and pulled down. The map shifted, lowering to the water's surface. "Perfect," she declared, grin widening. "Ok, haircut?"

Olivia didn't reply. She wasn't sure what to say. Haircuts put sharp things right near the face, neck, back, and a lot of major organs. It was a good way to get dead, really. Even a rock or a big fist could kill someone if it hit the back of the head just right.

Zed was offering trust, even after their near-fight. Glancing around the woman's shoulder, Olivia could see blood swirling into the water, leaking from Zed's punctured hand. That was a lot of hurt to not be reacting to.

With a deep breath, Olivia willed water to her hand, made it sharp, and began to cut away the long strands of ethereal gold that hung from Zed's skull. Each cut became a flick, a gentle roll of the wrist that sent blade through gold without slowing. Between the swings her other hand gathered a new grip on long locks, readying them for harvest. Flick, gather, flick, gather. In less than a minute, it was all gone. Lengths of yellow drifted downstream. Zed's head was shaven, but there was about an inch of hair left, a kind of haloed shine given form.

"Done," Olivia said.

Feeling it with both hands, Zed nodded. "Thank you."

Using both hands, Olivia cupped some water and used it to wash away the loose hair. Coming around to kneel in front of Zed, Olivia said, "Hand."

Zed offered it, as though about to shake. Blood and water dripped from her palm. The bit of fishbone was gone, but the hole was still there, mostly. Skin had begun to knit back together.

Gently, Olivia took the hand by the pinkie and pointer and turned it palm up.

"I've been trying to heal it," Zed whispered.

Olivia didn't ask if it hurt. Dumb question. Of course it did. Instead, she dipped the hand into the river and focused. She extended into the water, reaching through it and into the wound. At first she tried to stop the pain, to dull it, then to heal the muscle. How to do that, she had no idea. So she wanted it, pushed the hand to be fine, to be better. It didn't have to be perfect. It was one thing to have a cut on either side, another to have a hole between them.

After a few seconds, Zed's breathing eased, slowing ever so slightly.

"Better?" Olivia asked.

"Pain's gone."

"You'll need to wait for the rest," Olivia said. She let go of the blonde's hand. "I need to make sure I can do the haircuts."

Zed nodded, distant. "I'll keep checking our route."

"How far?" Olivia asked, curious. It was hard to gauge distance out here, and Zed seemed to have done more exploring. Looking at the map would mean more to the soldier than it would to her.

"Maybe a week."

Nodding, Olivia stood and waited for the others.

A week. Might even be a boring one, now that Joey had Olivia's back and Zed seemed to have moved on.

This whole 'running' thing sucked, royally.

"Yo," Bee gasped, sucking in air. "Why," gasp, "Are we," gasp, "Running," gasp, "Again?"

"So that we're ready when we get to the enemy," Zed explained, spinning to jog backwards. The beach beyond her was smooth and golden, pristine.

This morning's run had been on the beach too, but all the walking between had been on the top of the wall. Safer, had been the explanation. Being up there meant less chance of being attacked by a croc or a 'Kaskan,' as Blue-Sight McShitface had called the big ones. The beach was safe enough at a run, according to Zed, but high ground was better for walking.

"Yeah, I got the exercising thing," Bee noted, nodding, sweat falling from her chin. "But wouldn't it be better if we didn't die from excessive readiness?"

Zed laughed. "My Training Officer used to say, 'Difficult in Training, Easy in Combat.' Pissed me off, but it saved my life."

"Another motto?" Joey queried, straight-faced and undaunted by the day's jaunt. "I thought one was the usual amount."

"I think soldiers collect them, like scars and bad pickup lines," Nat shot back.

Out of the corner of her eye, Bee saw Olivia angling towards the river and scooping up a handful of water.

"Water break!" Zed called.

"Thank the goddess!" Bee declared. She dropped to her hands and knees.

"I said water, not sleeping," Zed added, loudly.

"Yeah, yeah, not deaf yet," Bee huffed, crawling towards the river.

The others were already there. Ty dove in, as he had every time. He was overheating even more than Bee was, so the lukewarm temperature felt cool. Afterwards, the evaporating moisture was even cooler. Everyone else was drinking normally, though Stabby had her hood up and hiding half her face.

"So why do we stop whenever she gets thirsty?" Bee queried, addressing Zed as she thumbed at Stabby.

The woman smiled and finished her drink. "Because she's the smallest, lightest, most heavily dressed, and stops only when she really needs to. If she stops, we stop."

"Why not go by who's in the worst shape?" Nat asked, one hand running across her fuzzy scalp as her brows rose, interested.

"Because then that person will lag more and more. Pushing them to keep up makes them catch up."

Nat frowned. "Not exactly kind."

"Efficient," Joey noted, carefully untying his shoes from his belt loops.

"We done running?" Bee asked, picking up on the motion. Running barefoot was beach time; shoes meant they were headed back to the wall.

"Yup," Zed confirmed, grinning. "It's getting late. We can walk a bit more before we stop. Then Stabby will catch a couple fish while the rest of us get a fire and bed set up."

"Oh good, more walking, just what the doctor ordered," Bee chuckled between sips.

"Don't worry, all this running has us ahead of schedule. Once we get about halfway we can stop for a day or three and do some combat training. Not a lot, but something."

"What kind of training?" Nat queried.

"More than the Self-Defense course you took," Zed tossed back, her lips curling into a full smile.

"Oh, how clever," Nat grumbled sarcastically, unbothered.

Zed rolled her eyes, snorted, and explained. "Probably some hand to hand techniques, a bit of unit tactics, and some silent signals. If we can, I also want us to practice using Current to stab things under pressure."

Almost absently, Stabby nodded her agreement, audibly swirling a mouthful of water through her teeth.

"Sounds good," Joey said. "What do we want to do about gear?"

"We'll practice with the clubs too, but I think magic - I mean Current - will be more useful," Zed answered.

Stabby shook her head. "Clubs."

"What she said," Joey added, jerking his chin towards the shorter woman. "We aren't comfortable with Current. Clubs will come easier."

"Clubs it is," Zed gave in. "Shall we get going?"

"Oh sweet Jesus," Bee hissed, standing. "Must we?"

"We must," Zed said. She laced her arm through Bee's. "Come on! It's not that bad. Another mile or two and we can call it a day."

"No, another mile or two and then we all have to go wood hunting and pile up rocks," Bee corrected, glaring suspicion at her. They were eye to eye, almost the same height, but Army Girl felt larger. Probably all the muscles. Lots of nice muscles.

"At least you're not having to do pushups every time you talk back," Zed chuckled, her eyes going distant as she semi-dragged Bee onto the beach. "Basic would kick the shit out of you in no time."

"Is that, like, maybe why I never, like, joined the army?" Bee said, lightening her voice and adding a disingenuous giggle to her sarcastic retort.

Freezing in place, Zed stared at her.

"What?" Bee asked, reverting to her normal, cynical tones.

"Don't do that."

"Why?"

"Because I nearly ordered you to do pushups out of pure reflex," Zed warned, eyes sparkling.

"Well, you'll have to, like, corral that little urge, like, yeah?" Bee returned, smirking.

Zed's mouth opened, but Nat cut in. "We're not in the army, but that doesn't mean you get to be a dick, Bumble."

"Annoying," Zed said, smiling. "I like the new nickname."

"Now who's being a dick?" Bee said. She rolled her eyes. Nat's interference was highly unappreciated. She was neither clumsy nor like a bumblebee, thank you.

"It won't be a regular thing, Bee," Nat continued, patting her free shoulder. "Just when you act like a jerk to the one making sure we don't get killed."

"Or a jerk in general," Zed suggested, spinning and tugging Bee off down the beach in the direction they'd been running.

"We'll see," Nat said, keeping even with them. "Can't overuse it."

"Brings up a good question. Do we want to all keep our current nicknames?" Ty asked.

No one else leapt at the question, so it struck Bee that she should be giving it some thought. New nickname. She considered it for a long moment. Bee wasn't bad. Better than some things she'd been called over the years. Eh. A badass one might be fun, but it also didn't seem worth the effort. Nerdy nickname would be cool, but they probably wouldn't get the joke. Less fun when no one else got the laugh. She'd stay.

"Name's Olivia," Stabby said, breaking through the silence.

"Do you want us to call you that?" Zed replied.

"Stick with Stabby. Or Stabs. Or Olivia. Whatever," she said.

Relatively speaking, finding out the smallest member of their little band had an actual name wasn't much of a surprise for Bee. The others didn't look surprised at the news, other than Nat. Nat's mouth was opening and closing like a fish out of water.

"Hush," Bee whispered with as much drama as she could manage, gently lifting Nat's jaw until her mouth was closed. She placed a finger across the woman's lips. "All will be well. Run now, get annoyed about not knowing names later."

"Run? I was going to shift to walking, but if you insist," Zed said, nearly cackling as she shifted into a slow jog, dragging Bee by their still interwoven arms.

"No! Save me! Help me escape this hell!" Bee faux-pleaded.

A roll of Ty's shoulders unleashed a fury of pops and cracks. Ouch. It was looser post-pops, but it hurt a bit. Three days of running had put pain in his legs, for sure, but today's combat training had barely begun. He could already tell he'd feel it tomorrow.

"Ok, that's the warm-ups," Zed said. She beamed at them as she strolled down the line.

With their backs to the wall, the five of them looked out at Zed, her face framed by mountainside and river. This place looked nearly identical to where they'd been when they'd fought the Kaskan, but this bend was deeper, the wall a cozy barrier around them.

Ty straightened and set his hands at his sides. Getting offended at Joey and Olivia's jabs back before the run had been dumb. They'd been rude, but there'd been a point. Really, it was the point that made it hurt. That was his fault. Back home, he'd been good. His stories, his knowledge, had made him somebody. Here, not so much.

On the other hand, what Zed offered gave him another shot.

"Ok, so that? That's what we need to do every night before we go to sleep. That way we'll maintain muscle mass, got it?" Zed said, looking at each of them.

Ty nodded, focusing on himself and Zed.

"Push-ups, sit-ups, squats," she listed. "On top of our runs, we should be pretty ok. We're leaning on the running side, but that'll help boost cardio."

"Convincing us or yourself?" Nat asked, her voice warmed by a laugh.

Zed rolled her eyes. "Both? I was trained to do, not teach. This is trickier than it looks."

"And we don't have the gear you're used to," Nat guessed.

"At least I'm kind of used to the ground," Zed snorted, stamping on the sand. "I'll figure it out and we'll take it slow. Everyone does half an hour to an hour of exercise every night, at your own speed. Do as much as you can. If things hurt more than usual, ask Nat to take a look."

"Thanks," Nat snorted.

Zed raised an eyebrow. "Complaining?"

Nat groaned. "No, mom!"

Laughter. Ty laughed too, though it was annoying. Of course Nat would be healing, that was her shtick. His focus was on the tactics that Zed hadn't gotten to yet. If Ty played his cards right, he'd have a shot at being their tank. Front line, with maximum chance for heroism. That's what he wanted. He was going to earn it. They'd have a hard time harshing on him once he'd saved their bacon.

"Let's get started on fighting techniques," Zed said, gesturing for them to circle up. "I'm going to start with the idea, then a couple moves, then we'll practice."

Nods from everyone.

"Concept is this," Zed began, her voice harsher, sharper. "Don't stop. Don't hesitate. If you get into a fight, hit them. Hit them and keep hitting them until they can never hit you back. Aggression wins. Everything else sums up to that."

"Priority one: Hit them in the softest bits. The file says our targets basically look like us, but taller and thinner. Like basketball players, sort of. That means that their genitals, feet, tendons, and knees will all be easily available. It also means longer reach, so get in close before they can get you."

"Priority two: Don't stop. Keep going till they can't possibly hit you."

"Priority three: Attack first. Failing that, attack before they can get you a second time."

"Priority four: Improvise. If there's anything you can use as a weapon nearby, use it. We may need all the Current we can get to heal up, but don't hesitate to use it to save yourself. You've got to be alive before you can help anyone else."

"Priority five: Keep it simple and repeat. Don't overthink how to hit them. Just hit. If you hit them and it works, keep doing it. If starts working less then switch to hitting them elsewhere."

"Ok," Zed said, her eyes meeting everyone's in turn. "That's about as basic as I can make it. We good?"

Nat frowned, Bee looked a bit sick, and Joey looked as calm as ever, but Ty's stomach did a little flip when he saw Olivia's face. She was smiling. It wasn't a cruel smile, not even a big smile; it was the smile of a child on Christmas morning. The look of someone who'd figured something out, or found a much needed answer.

"Great, let's start with kicks, a couple punches, and not breaking whenever you fall over," Zed said, her smile wide and gleeful, full of memories and excitement.

Ty grinned and flexed his hands. He'd played enough videogames and read enough books to know the basics; he'd just never really tried to do them. This'd be a cinch. He'd seen it, heard it explained, now it was just copying.

Strolling down the line of moving bodies, Zed frowned. All of this was giving her a lot of fresh respect and appreciation for her Training Officer. No, not more… Perhaps different was more accurate.

It was one thing to respect a superior officer, and to respect someone who could train a person to kill, but this was respect for how she'd handled herself. Knowing what to teach someone and teaching well were two different things. Zed was finding that out firsthand.

Right now, the examples of this problem were among the quintet of punching people before her. As Zed paced, she counted off punches, slowly speeding the motions along.

Stabby wasn't having issues learning, but Zed still felt a little spike of anger when she looked at the shorter woman. Nothing Zed could do about that, other than be glad that Stabby's talent kept them from having to interact. Joey was also catching on pretty quick. He'd taken some kind of martial art before. Maybe Karate, or Taekwondo. His stance was solid and he already knew most of the moves. Surprisingly, self-defense hadn't been a bad base for Nat. She wasn't as quick as Joey, but she was athletic and working to catch up.

The real problems were Ty and Bee. Different problems, though.

Ty was big, strong, and had very little experience doing much with either asset. He kept hunching, as though trying to look smaller, and his punches had no control behind them. Kicks came out wrong too, forceless and inflexible. The flexibility wasn't terrible. Most of the kicks she was teaching aimed below the waist, mainly because anything higher was asking for a leg-catch or a trip. Plus high kicks went against 'Keep It Simple.' Ty needed practice. He needed to find a rhythm for putting force behind movement.

Zed paused and watched Bee. They were about the same height, and nearly the same age, but the African-American was thinner, inflexible, unused to any of these movements, and didn't have much sense of where her body was. Again, it was largely a practice issue, but they didn't have time.

"Here," Zed offered, catching Bee's eye. She raised her hand, palm out, at head level. "Punch my palm."

Bee did, breaking from the rhythm of Zed's prior counting.

"Good," Zed said, nodding. She pushed her fist a few inches closer. "Now punch through. Try to get to where you ended before.

Bee tried, but it came out short. She was changing her range to fit the new target. A frown formed on her face as she realized the problem.

"Again," Zed said, smiling. It was a common issue. It was about changing focus. Most people aimed at the point they thought their fist would impact, not beyond it.

After a few punches, Bee was improving. Slowly. That was how reflex and muscle memory worked.

Glancing away, Zed watched the others to ease some of the stress on Bee. Sweat was starting to roll down faces again. Most of it had evaporated when everyone had jumped in the stream during the lunch break. The day was nearly over. After this, they'd do a bit of magic - no, Current - practice, and then call it done.

Current. The word rolled through Zed's mind. It made her wonder about the Vinna mentality. Their ships looked like fish, they looked like they were fresh from Atlantis, and their maps worked on water. It wasn't a stretch to expect them to call supernatural abilities 'Current,' but were all abilities the same? And how much was talent? Stabby could hold a knife together for longer than anyone else. No way of knowing if that was innate, or if the Vinna done something to her. Or maybe her brain was different.

No way of knowing. For now. Once they all got practicing, the 'talent' theory would get tested. Maybe she'd just started earlier.

Glancing over, Zed checked on Stabby. 'Olivia' didn't feel right. It wasn't lethal enough. The girl felt sharp, like an edge with no safe handle. When they'd talked, Zed had gotten cut. Same thing when she'd grabbed her arm, though that'd been more literal. Both times had been Zed's fault. She should've known better, but that didn't ease the flash of annoyance.

Back in the Defense Force, a Training Officer would pick out people like Stabby and grind them down. Push-ups, sit-ups, whatever it took to wear them down until they listened, learnt, and figured out that they needed the people around them. Zed couldn't do that.

For one, it wasn't Zed's area of expertise.

For another, if Zed tried then Nat and Bee would go bleeding heart over it and try to save Stabby. Them, plus Joey, would be a major issue, even if Ty stayed out of it.

Zed winced as she settled on a solution. They'd have to talk. Work out the problem verbally. It'd suck, but it was better than Stabby getting someone killed because she was busy watching out for herself.

No time like the present.

"Keep going," Zed said, stepping back from Bee. "I need to talk to Stabby for a bit."

Stabby froze, face hidden behind her hood.

Joey's eyes darted between them.

"Just a talk," Zed repeated, smiling peacefully as she headed down the beach. Protective bastard.

From the soft ruffle of denim against denim, Stabby was following.

Zed kept going for nearly a hundred meters, out of the deep bend in the river that they'd set up in. Once the others were out of sight, she stopped and turned. The mountains' splashes were loud enough to keep them from being overheard, unless someone started shouting.

Stabby slowed, pausing with several generous meters between them.

"We both know I can't treat you like a soldier," Zed stated, working her way through the problem. "I can't treat anyone here like that, but that could be a problem."

The sun hand sunk below the pooled mountainside, but the clouds glowed with pinks and golds. The colors washed across Stabby's face as she pulled back her hood, highlighting a sharp nose and hollow cheeks. Her skin was smooth and just beginning to brown, making the gray of her eyes strange and pale. One brow rose, questioning.

Zed rallied, trying to stay on track. "We all need to prioritize each other. We all need to want to get each other through this. Usually, officers break down recruits then build them up again. That way everyone is part of the whole. They've all gone through it, they've all been trained to cover each other, and everyone knows that they need to do their job while everyone else does theirs. You trust your guys to cover your back as much as they trust you to cover theirs."

Stabby grunted.

"Nat, Bee, Ty, they're all team players. Joey too, as you've proven. My question is if you're going to have our backs."

For several breaths, Stabby pondered that. Then she asked, "Are you still pissed that I knew you were lonely, not just bored?"

Zed's fists clenched. It was the kind of shit she'd never shared. Enlisting had helped, but there was still a distance to that. The wound had stayed, deep and painful, but with a thin scab to hide it. It hadn't gotten worse, but it hadn't healed.

"Hurts," Stabby noted. "Least people knew your name."

Thoughts raced through Zed's head. Her hands loosened. Ouch. She hadn't seen it. Stabby had said she was an ex-athlete, ex-student, ex-daughter, and ex-person. Shit.

Zed had been so focused on figuring out about magic that she'd only skimmed the rest. The first two weren't terrible, but ex-daughter sounded bad. Ex-person was worse. Dehumanization was part of standard military practice. Recruits went through it before they were rebuilt into soldiers. Stabby hadn't been in an army, hadn't been part of anything. She'd been torn apart without anything to rebuild around.

Zed frowned. "I didn't listen."

"Still honest," Stabby returned with a slight smile.

"I didn't understand how much you'd lost. I'm sorry for not thinking it through," Zed apologized, looking at the ground. She'd screwed up. She'd focused on the info she wanted and getting pissed, not on who Stabby was. Olivia was.

Olivia nodded. "It's done. Still pissed?"

Straightening, Zed met the shorter woman's eyes. She could feel a sting of shame run down her spine. "No." She wasn't mad, at least not at Olivia. Zed was going to send her temper a strongly worded letter, though.

"Use me as bait," Olivia said, glancing towards the river.

Zed blinked, confused. "What?"

"I'll trust you to bust me out, you'll trust me to distract them," Olivia explained. "Proves something to both of us and gets the job done."

"Is it worth asking if you're sure?" Zed said, forcing a chuckle. Bait could make things a lot less deadly for the rest of them, but they had no idea what the aliens would do to her. They might just shoot her on sight.

Maybe she'd been very wrong about Olivia.

Olivia snorted. "Just don't make me rescue myself."

A smile tugged at Zed's lips.

"What?"

"Nothing."

Olivia shot Zed a disbelieving look.

"One of the training games my unit played," Zed explained. "Capture the Flag, but with our Commanding Officers as the flags. It was supposed to teach us how to work without them. He said the same thing you just did before he left."

The skin around Olivia's eyes crinkled, her mouth curving into a smile. "You comparing me to your ex-boss?"

"We'll see," Zed replied, walking in a slow circle, taking in the world around them. "Depends on how this fight goes."

"Glad we figured shit out," Olivia admitted. "Back to practice?"

"How much of this have you done before?" Zed said, voicing her earlier curiosity.

"I've picked some things up."

Zed snorted.

"Careful," Olivia warned, smiling at her. "If you get quiet the others might start thinking I'm infectious."

"Or maybe they'll think you're threatening me."

"I don't threaten," Olivia said, her smile twitching. "Tried that for a while. Just makes things worse. Do it or don't."

Nodding, Zed pointed back towards the others. "Come on. We shouldn't leave them too long. Bee might try to throttle Ty for trying to help her with stuff he doesn't get any more than she does."

Olivia laughed, pulled up her hood, and followed Zed back down the walled curve of the river.

With a running start, Bee launched herself up and forward and dove headlong into the stream. The lukewarm water rushed over her, tucked beneath a layer of cold that had settled along the surface. The rain had only just begun and it'd already tainted the river's warmth. Rising back through the cool, she sucked in a gulp of air, blinking away the downpour.

"Blessed be!" Bee crooned, raising her arms overhead.

The gesture stung, working muscles that'd suffered too much recently. Bee dropped them quickly, but the exuberance stayed. Closing her eyes, she leaned her head back and opened her mouth. Droplets fell onto her tongue and lips, colder than anything she'd had to drink in a week.

Bee froze, mouth agape.

More than a week.

It felt like so much longer. Strange to think that they'd only been here that long. Trippy, however cliché that sounded. The exercise didn't make things any better. After a life of avoiding sports, and athletes, for that matter, the whole fight-training thing was weird. She hadn't noticed it at first, but this was the third day and the moves were starting to feel smoother. Not very smooth, but better.

Bee sank till the surface was just beneath her nose. The beach was barely visible through the storm, but she could make out the others. Zed was dancing around, spinning and leaping, while Nat and Ty and Joey were huddled under an overhang.

Breaking off the routine because of the rain had been perfectly timed. All the running had made Bee's legs hurt. Just as they'd begun to feel better, Zed had started in on punching drills. Now all the limbs could hurt together, Bee groused to herself. Yippee!

It hadn't helped that 'Small Unit Tactics' had been cancelled. Zed's decision, that blank looks and incomprehension deserved more exercise, not more breaks, had sucked. Honestly though, it hadn't been a bad idea. Bee certainly hadn't understood why they were learning it. Zed's plans were all gun related, and they were distinctly gun-less.

Someone got up from under the overhang and walked towards the stream. Once they were about halfway, Bee could make out Nat's dark skin and wide hips.

Bee rubbed her scalp. Her hair was barely an inch long, even a week after the cutting. She'd started biting her nails to keep them short. Good thing she hadn't polished them before the kidnapping. Chipping polish was annoying.

Bee waved. "Hey, Nat!"

"Hey," Nat returned, splashing into the stream. She sighed and eased down into the warmer depths. She sank till only her head was visible, slowly making her way over to Bee. "How's it going?"

"Thank the gods for the break," Bee chuckled. "I think my legs were about to break off."

"Right?" Nat laughed. "I've done some of this stuff before, but she's working our asses off."

"No shit. At least it's for a good reason."

"So, gods? You're a polytheist?" Nat queried, her head tipping slightly to one side.

Bee nodded. "Yeah. Decided the whole Christianity thing didn't do it for me back in high school. I'm still feeling around though, trying to find a patron."

"Oh, is that how that works?" Nat asked, her brows knitting with confusion. "Gotta admit, I've never gotten the whole spiel."

"It varies a lot," Bee admitted, smiling. She liked explaining it, as long as the listener wasn't going to go Spanish Inquisition on her afterwards. "Some people pick out a pantheon that they like, some stick to a single Mother Goddess, some believe in them all and then pick one that they relate to or feel connected with or whatever. There are a lot of others too."

"And you're still picking?"

"Yup," Bee said. "I kept finding old gods that seemed right, but nothing really fit. I used to do Tarot cards, palm reading, a lot of that kind of thing. I wasn't very good at it. Ugh, I had this one friend, right? She could read someone's Tarot and straight up blow their mind. I watched her solve someone's relationship issues in five minutes flat."

Nat was frowning, incredulity clear.

"Don't say it," Bee warned, waving a hand above the water to shush the doubts. "Believe what you want, but Tarot is one of the things I believe in. Never been a big Zodiac person though, so feel free to trash talk that."

"Just new to the whole thing," Nat chuckled, raising her palms just above the water. "My parents were atheists. There'd have been some serious conversations if I went religious. You said yours were Christian?"

"Could never remember the flavor, but yeah. Not the church on Sunday's types, but they had a cross in the house and prayed before meals. My sister didn't really buy into it, but she went through the motions. Pissed them off when I didn't."

120

"I bet," Nat laughed. "Sister?"

"Older. We stopped getting along about the time I started rebelling. She saved up her rebellion for college. Don't know where she ended up."

"Sorry you had to go through that," Nat said, her smile gone.

"Is what it is," Bee returned, running one hand across her scalp. She winked, trying to lighten the mood. "So, girls or guys or both?"

"What? What do you mean?" Nat spluttered, turning in a slow circle. Between the rain and the movement, her face was pretty much hidden.

Bee smirked. Nat had talked plenty about herself over the last week, when she had the breath to do so. She was good about only doing it when no one else wanted to talk, but she had shared a lot. Siblings, parents, extended family, anecdotes about picnics, barbecues, reunions, school events, and sibling escapades; all retold for general entertainment, or at least to relieve the boredom. She wasn't a great storyteller, but it was usually funny.

Now, Bee raised an eyebrow and enjoyed seeing the woman speechless.

"Guys," Nat finally admitted.

Damn.

"Too bad," Bee sighed.

"Girls?" Nat guessed, half-grinning at her wistfulness.

"Yup," Bee affirmed, nodding. "Makes my romantic activities a lot easier than yours right now."

Nat winced. "Yeah. Even without STDs as a factor, pregnancy would be awful out here. Our diets aren't varied enough, Current could have an effect on in-utero developments, and UTIs…"

"Yeah… Better the girl on girl action than risk all of that," Bee chuckled. "Sucks to be you."

"Gee thanks," Nat laughed, splashing her.

Bee wiped the water from her eyes and smirked. "To be fair, it's not like it helps me much. Statistically, I'm probably the only one without a dick that likes girls here. Even if that weren't true, Zed and Stabby?"

"Zed's… athletic," Nat defended, trying to find other things to add to the list of positive features.

"And hot," Bee agreed, holding back the urge to laugh at the other woman's discomfort. "But she'd probably start counting beats or try to teach me a new move. And don't even get me started on Stabby!"

Nat's cheeks turned red and she burst out coughing.

"I mean, I could point out that part of the whole 'lesbian' thing is not getting 'stabbed,' but that's not entirely accurate," Bee added, barely stifling her own laughter. Too much fun.

That'd been the trick of attending a women's college. Lesbian jokes had been super hit or miss, and after a while she'd just avoided them. Except when drunk. Or high. Then it'd been worth it just to amuse herself.

Eventually, the laughter eased. They both sat in the rain, the water around them slowly cooling as the downpour dragged on. For once, Nat didn't try to fill it. The rain was enough.

"Can you do it?" Nat asked.

Well, the rain had been enough for a few minutes.

"Do what?" Bee replied.

"Kill."

"Would've killed that damn Kaskan if I could've," Bee grumbled, still angry at the overgrown iguana. "Teach it to interrupt a nice night."

"And a person?"

Bee hummed, thinking. Buying time really. She didn't want to say yes, that'd make her sound like a psycho, but no would make her a risk. "Did you take the oath thingy that doctors have?" she asked.

"The Hippocratic Oath? Sort of. Most pre-meds take one when they graduate, but it's not what Hippocrates wrote. 'Do no harm' is big, but there's a bunch of other things too."

"But you haven't graduated, so you've never taken it, right?"

Nat shook her head. "Nope."

"Can you do it?"

"I asked first," Nat countered.

"I don't know," Bee admitted, lifting her hand under the water and flicking the surface. Droplets lifted upwards, flying a few feet towards the beach. "I don't think we'll have a choice."

"There's always a choice," Nat said, frowning. "We could tie them up. Knock them out. Leave before they wake up."

"Seven or eight foot tall stickmen don't sound easy to knock out, and what would we use for rope to tie them?"

The frown on Nat's face grew.

"Zed said the less lethal we are, the more likely they are to get us," Bee said, coming to a decision as she spoke. "If one of them tries to surrender, sweet, but otherwise I think we need to focus on surviving."

"Us or them," Nat said, looking down at the water. "My dad said that a lot. He was American. After he served, he moved to Canada to be near my mom. He used to take me hunting for rabbits, raccoons; stuff like that.”

This was new. For all the talking, Nat hadn’t mentioned her dad being a soldier, or dying. “When did he pass?” Bee queried, not sure what else to say. She’d never lost a family member, let alone a parent.

“In two-thousand. Easy to remember. Cancer. He never could stop smoking.” Silence stretched for a moment, then Nat said, “They’ll probably declare us dead in another month or so, depending on how long we were out.”

“Out?” Bee muttered, confused by the sudden switch.

“Space travel,” Nat explained, waving around. “We can’t have gotten here instantly, so how long did they keep us unconscious?”

“I guess that’s true,” Bee admitted. “Goldilocks Zone planets are a big deal. They get splashed all over the web every time one shows up. I’ve never seen any shots of one that looks like this.”

“Goldilocks?” Nat asked.

“Not too warm and not too cold for living on,” Bee said.

“So, a long way even in space terms.” Nat nodded. “And it takes months to get around just our solar system…”

“Let’s not go here,” Bee said, trying not to think about what was coming.

“Oh come on!” Nat complained. “We need to think about it. We’ve all been ignoring it for a week. We’re light-years from Earth. Years. Even with some kind of super-alien engine to go at light-speed, we might be already be officially dead.”

“Or everyone we knew might be. It could be a thousand years since we were there,” Bee returned. “Thanks for the happy thoughts.”

“It matters,” Nat threw back, sadness coating her face like rain.

Bee nodded. “Yup. It means that not pissing off the aliens is even more important. If that much time has passed, we need them to keep us alive. If they got us here faster than light-speed, we need to get them to send us back.”

“Basically, we do what they say,” Nat sighed. “It’d be a lot easier if we knew why.”

“Would it?” Bee wondered. “At this point, I don’t think I want to know.”

“Everyone’s different I guess,” Nat threw out, a half-hearted chuckle on its heels. “Who knows what’ll happen. It’s a good thing we’ve got Zed though, she’d done a great job whipping us into shape.”

With a smile, Bee said, "Shush! Don't use the 'W' word or she might go make one!"

"Fair point," Nat laughed, the tension easing.

Lowering herself in the water, Bee opened her mouth and drank it in. Cold now, but the sun would warm it up again once the rain stopped.

"Are you ready?" Zed asked, catching Olivia's eye.

Olivia nodded. She'd already agreed to it, so she wasn't sure why Zed was asking. Maybe she thought Olivia might've changed her mind at some point during the walking. Or the running. Three days of walking, with running breaks and exercises at night. Yesterday had been all walking and only light evening workouts, so the soreness and ache was gone. Just like coaches did before games. Plenty of time for thinking, but she'd been preoccupied with practicing magic. Copping out of the plan hadn't come up.

"Ok, go get 'em," Zed said, visibly stifling an urge to pat Olivia on the back.

Without a backwards look, Olivia climbed down the wall and set off down the beach. It was about half a kilometer to the enemy camp, but she didn't need to rush. The others needed time to get in position. Their route was a bit shorter, but the woods were rougher going.

Eyeing the water, Olivia thought about her experiments. Magic, Current, whatever. She'd been getting better. Healing still didn't click, but she'd gotten better at easing her own pains. Making things was better. Anything sharp and she had it covered. The walk had given her time to mess with the process, make it less exhausting. She'd found out three things.

One, that making water from air was harder than using the already wet stuff.

Two, distance was a problem. The farther away the wet was, the more likely it would be that making stuff from air would be easier.

Three, shaping things by hand saved energy. So did physically throwing things instead of pushing or pulling with Current.

In a way, it sort of made sense. It took heat to condense water, and that was just another form of energy. Moving something from one place to another also took energy. Same for making something look a certain way. All just energy.

Or at least, that was Olivia's opinion. It'd been a few years since her last science class, and she'd only taken two years of the high school ones. If she had a chance, she'd ask Nat. As long as she could find a way to do it without sounding like a moron.

Moron.

The word echoed in her head in a dozen voices.

Rage welled up in Olivia's chest, heavy and brash. Brains. That was the first thing people went after when they saw a streeter. They thought a person had to be dumb to get stuck like that. Must make them feel safer. People who were one firing, one car accident, one robbery away from being in the same boat. Or some dead parents, in Olivia's case.

It was weird. Pimps and pervs hadn't been an issue for her in nearly two weeks. Probably a record, at least in the last four years. Or five. Ugh. When had she become a streeter? It didn't matter. Too long.

Not anymore.

Time to earn her ticket out.

A few minutes of walking later, the river began to bend sharply to her right.

The first alien was on the wall, looking down on her. Olivia almost missed it. She kept walking, strolling along the waterside, but it was there, at the corner of her eye.

Long, thin limbs hunched down, like interlocking bars extending from the thing's torso. Its head was nearly human, but it had big, dark eyes set into a pale face. A sleeve-like gray-green mottled suit hid everything below its chin, gently blending in with the woods beyond. If its head had been covered, she might not have seen it.

As Olivia came even with it, two fingers rose to its mouth. A shrill, carrying whistle followed.

Ahead, around a protruding boulder, Olivia saw their camp. A trio of tents, all made from the same gray-green mottle as the alien's suit. A small fire pit sat between them and the wall, some rocks and logs pulled close. The tents' flaps all faced the campfire.

Four more of the strangely stretched out humanoids sat by the fire. Clumps of cloth showed where they'd rolled up their suits, bare hands and feet held near the fire. They didn't move, but all four heads were turned her way. A fifth slipped out of a tent, scanned the wall, and stopped when it saw her.

Rock ground against rock, stray pebbles clacking as they fell. The guard moved behind her, preparing to block the beach. Didn't want her running.

Good thing Olivia didn't plan on running.

"You look lost," the one that'd risen from the tent said. Its voice was plain, almost calmingly normal. "Are you looking for someone? Maybe we can help." It walked towards her. "What's your name, little one?"

Olivia held down her rage. 'Little one' was right up there with 'pretty lady,' 'beautiful,' and 'love' when it came to pimp and perv red flags. She kept walking.

"Hello?" it went on, bending at the waist to peer under her hood. "Are you alright?"

Nothing. Olivia slowed to a stop. They were about ten meters apart. The four by the fire began to unroll their sleeves and leggings, sealing their hands and feet within. The one on the wall behind her made a soft thud as it jumped to the sand.

Interesting.

They were worried that she was a threat.

Olivia crossed her arms. It kept her from fidgeting. And from smiling.

"I'd really appreciate it if you'd talk to me," the alien went on, shooting her a tight-lipped grin. "Are you unable to speak? Deaf?" It gestured with its hands, pointing first at its mouth, then its ears.

Its ears looked pretty human, Olivia noted. Pretty sunburnt too. "I'm just fine, thanks."

It straightened, looking down at her from nearly eight feet. "Well, that's nice to know. I was starting to worry that you hadn't been given Translators. So, where are the others, little one?"

"What others?" Olivia returned, mentally filing 'Translators' under 'later.'

"The other of you," it replied, waving at her, "Humans, I believe? Is that right?"

Olivia nodded. No reason not to.

"I don't suppose you've run into any others, hmm?" it said, head ticking to one side. It was a tired look, and a disbelieving one.

"Nope, ran into a bunch back that way," Olivia said, thumbing over her shoulder. "Five, but they were assholes. I kept walking."

For a moment, the alien held still, then it burst out laughing. "Oh, you're a treasure! Uhle, take your shift. See if you can offer the other little ones some help."

One of the four by the fire nodded, looked at the other four, and took off at a jog. As they passed by, long strides making them seem graceful and quick, Olivia took in the knives they'd strapped to the small of their backs, and the short bows tied over their shoulders. The bows were strung, with handfuls of arrows latched to the arms. She didn't know much about bows, but they looked small for these guys. Like toys. The knives were only a little better, and the handles would be tricky.

"So, shall we step inside? I'm sure you're cold," the leader said, stepping closer. They were only a few meters apart, and the soft crunch of the guard crossing the sand behind her was getting closer.

Not much of a choice.

Olivia nodded.

"Clarify?" the alien requested.

"Yes," Olivia said, eyeing it. Apparently this type of alien didn't nod. Or it was rude.

"Wonderful." It swept to the side, gesturing for her to head into the tent in the center of the trio.

Doing as she was told, Olivia felt the guard and leader fall in behind her, one at each shoulder.

"What're you called?" Olivia queried, figuring she might as well find something to call them before she improvised.

"I'm Hune, and this is Fehel," the leader explained, his smile audible. "You?"

"Jane," Olivia returned. It'd been one of her early street names. One soup kitchen server had called her 'Quiet Jane' for a while. Even asked her to volunteer in exchange for extra food. She'd stabbed him when he'd tried to corner her in the pantry. Never found out if he lived. The name seemed appropriate right now.

"Jane," Hune repeated. "Welcome to our little home away from home."

Olivia paused. He'd said it just as she came within reach of the tend flap. The way he said it didn't sound good. Not for her at least.

"Check the river," Hune said, addressing Fehel.

"Can do," Fehel returned, giving off an odd, rolling chuckle as he made his way around the tent and over towards the water.

"Go on in," Hune urged, stepping closer behind her. Less than a step away now.

Ducking down, Olivia slipped into the dome-like tent. It was spacious, the bright sunlight seeping like liquid gold through the thin cloth. At the center, a single pole rose from the ground. A human sat with their back to it, facing Olivia, their hands tied. 'They' looked like a 'he,' with tanned skin and curly black hair that was a mess of blood. He looked up, exposing a split lip and long, thin cuts that ran across his cheeks and the bridge of his nose. His eyes were cloudy, unfocused.

There was another human on the sand to the right, face down. That one wasn't moving.

Long-fingered hands locked around Olivia's forearms. They were cold and hard to the touch, like digits made from steel wire.

"Jane, please understand, this is business," Hune stated, that serene neutrality like a suffocating blanket. "Vinna absolutely hate horn-hunters. You've probably spent your life thinking that space was a carpet right? You thought it was some kind of magical place where your ancestors go, or where an old enemy lurks. It's cruel to end your revelation so early, but I've never been a proponent of public education."

The hands drew her forearms behind her, then up and together. Olivia winced as her shoulders rolled, trying to keep her shoulders from dislocating as she rose to her tiptoes.

"Experimentation, that's how one learns," Hune continued, thoughtful. "For example: how long before your bones dislocate? If you scream first, I'll stop. We'll sit here and wait for the last two of you to come running."

Olivia almost laughed. She'd told him she'd seen five, and there were two here. He wanted the last two humans. Ten altogether. This piece of shit was-

Pain shot through Olivia's shoulders. Blood pounded in her ears. Things would pop out soon. She knew enough from swim team to know how far arms bent.

Screw this bait bullshit. Olivia wasn't screaming. She was going to end him.

Olivia willed two knives into existence. She could see them, jagged and hooked, and a fraction of a second later she felt their weight in her hands. They were cool, calming. She flicked her wrists, shoving the hooks at Hune's torso.

One wiry hand let go. It closed around her neck instead.

The hooks sank in. Olivia wrenched her hands outwards as hard as she could, willing the blades to cut and hurt. Something hot and wet splattered across her forearms and back.

Hune screamed.

The guy tied to the tent pole flinched and shrank back, eyes suddenly wide and focused.

Both alien hands let go and Olivia staggered, nearly falling forward. She spun, dropping low, knives raised. Hune was on his knees, his mottled suit torn open across the thighs, a familiar crimson pouring forth. His hands were clamped on the wounds but his eyes were on her, wide and dark and vicious. Spittle flew from his lips, ragged gasps shooting out.

"How many of you?" Olivia asked, straightening to stand just a tad taller than the alien. Good thing he'd lifted as he yanked on her arms, otherwise she'd have cut his knees. Much less damage. At least going by human anatomy. Maybe these things kept their brain in their knee.

"Ten," spat Hune, humiliation writ large in the contortion of his features. "Same as you."

"Where?"

"Shit fire!" he hissed. His hand shot to his back.

Olivia couldn't go close; he'd get her with the knife he was drawing.

Improvise.

Olivia slapped her knives together and willed them out, long and thin and straight.

Hune tried to turn away, but the meter-long spike shot through his neck. For a second, he hung there. Then he fell. His weight snapped the ice. He hit the sand. Blood pooled beneath him.

No time.

Olivia's heart was pounding, but the noise was gone. Everything felt slow, quiet, like the perfect rhythm of swimming.

But there was no time.

Stepping over his legs, Olivia took his knife and set about detaching his belt. It felt smooth and silky, with a sheath clipped in two places on the back. The buckle was simple. A hoop that the free end looped through and around. Undoing it, she put it on. The dangling end was too long. She cut it with the knife, but pocketed the spare bit.

Midway through stuffing the length of silken belt in her pocket, Olivia's eyes met Fehel's as he came through the flap.

"Shit!" Olivia hissed, willing two knives into her hands and launching herself forward.

Focused at first on the carnage, Fehel noticed the sudden trajectory of a small, knife bearing, screaming person and backpedaled. His feet dragged in the sand and he sagged backwards. One hand shot out and clutched at the upper lip of the tent's entrance. Planting a foot to hold himself up, his right leg punched at Olivia, long and whippy. Her right knife dragged across his ankle as his heel hit her diaphragm.

Momentum reversed, Olivia flipped backward and slammed into the sand. Fehel howled and dropped onto his ass, hands reaching for his ankle. Scrabbling in the sand, she shot to get her feet under her. The alien drew a knife, holding it low and close, glaring at her.

Olivia froze. She was crouched, knives out, same as with Hune. Same trick couldn't work twice, could it?

Rotating on his rear, Fehel pulled his legs back and out of the way. He planted one hand and shifted onto one knee. There was a wince as his leg came up to hold him.

Slapping her hands together, Olivia willed the ice into another thin spike. It flowed forward, shooting for the alien's chest.

Fehel smirked. His knife flicked out and slashed through the ice before it reached him. "Yeio, Hune's down!" he called, taking in the room.

No time. More problems coming. Olivia felt desperation rising, feeding her rage, bursting and rippling through her veins. Fehel was at her height, so going low wouldn't work, and he had better reach. Even if she could get close, that knife would hit her at least once. It was a big knife, nearly as long as a machete. She wouldn't survive that. Survival. That was the Goal. Always had been. Couldn't die here, not after everything.

Olivia wasn't dying here. Her teeth ground as her thoughts raced, fighting for an option.

Throwing knives was dumb. It wasn't as deadly as the movies made it, and if the throw was off then it would be about as helpful as throwing a stick.

But ice knives didn't work like regular knives.

A vicious grin curled Olivia's lips. For a moment, she saw the knife in her right hand flying at Fehel, punching into him. Then she flicked her wrist. Current flitted from her, guiding the blade.

Fehel keeled over backwards.

Two down, eight to go.

Olivia peered around the tent flap. No need to go rushing out, not when these sticks with assholes carried bows.

"Movement!" shouted a tall figure by the fire.

A fraction of a second later, an arrow hissed through the tent wall beside Olivia's face. It missed her, but not by much. Ducking low, she tried to see what was happening. There were two aliens back to back by the fire, both with their bows out. One faced her. The other aimed an arrow at the wall.

That was a problem.

Backing away from the flap, Olivia plucked the arrow from the sand and went to the back wall. The knife she'd taken from Hune cut cleanly through the cloth, giving her a nice quiet exit. The beach looked clear, but her eyes settled on the river. She had an idea.

For a moment, Olivia paused. She looked back at the man tied to the pole. He was unconscious. Probably still alive. She didn't have time to save him now. The choice stung, but it wasn't the first time she'd chosen to save herself.

Nonetheless, shame ran like ice down Olivia's spine as she slipped out and headed down to the water. She glanced back every few steps, adjusting her angle to keep the tent between her and the archers. At the river, she dunked the arrow, the knife, and then headed back. Circling the tent, she waited till she could just see the rocks around the fire pit. The archer was a few feet further. A couple more inches and she'd be seen.

One breath. Two.

Olivia's heart still pounded. The odd stillness still hung over her, the eerie sharpness of the world around made it almost surreal. It felt like minutes had passed since she'd gone into the tent, but it'd been less. Thirty seconds, maybe? Closer to fifteen, really, since Hune had grabbed her. Fights were like that. Adrenaline and time, sort of like alcohol and drugs; they did weird things to one another.

Third breath. Fourth.

Steady.

Goal: Survival. Rule: Hit first. Keep hitting until they can't hit back.

Taking a step back, Olivia bounced on the balls of her feet. Then she took off around the edge of the tent. The archer saw her sprinting at him, but she was faster. The arrow she'd doused in the river shot through the air, mirroring the image in her mind.

"Mo-" the archer began, but he gagged, sputtering as Olivia's arrow hit his neck. He collapsed, crumpling as his long limbs went directionless.

The other bowman spun and stared down at the body. They looked up and saw Olivia.

Too late.

Olivia chucked her semi-machete knife at the alien's chest.

The bow turned, twisting to knock away the blade.

Olivia ducked low and slammed her shoulder into one spindly knee. It broke like a stick. The sensation reverberated through her shoulder.

The alien screamed, falling on top of her.

Trapped under the alien's weight, Olivia grabbed for the place on their back where the knife was. Her hand caught the handle a split second before the alien's got there. Their other fist rocketed into her face, driving the back of her head into the sand. She held on to the knife. Her other hand found the arrow the alien had knocked and dropped alongside the bow.

The alien sat up, grinding its sharp butt bones against Olivia's ribs. The second punch came down like a falling rock, all bony knuckles.

Bursts of light and dull, throbbing blips blurred Olivia's vision. Her left hand loosened on the knife. The alien's long digits began to burrow and worm under hers. Then her right hand swung around, planting the arrow between some ribs and twisting.

They screamed, high and piercing.

That seemed to have worked. Olivia did it again. Pull, stab, twist. Another scream.

A third punch hit her, but the alien flopped to the side, screeching. The punches weakened.

Third stab, but this one scrapped on a rib. Olivia kept stabbing, faster and faster. The punches stopped at some point, but she had to be sure.

Memories were yanking at Olivia again, dragging at her psyche like a horde of ephemeral hands. She could smell garbage, sewage, and the moist damp of the afternoon rain. Distant cars honked, voices and chatter and shoes clicking on pavement. The solemn quiet of a thin alley surrounded her, like a tunnel, making the noise seem distant, and the stink thick and moldy.

Olivia stopped stabbing as the weight of the alien settled on her. She could feel the split of its legs against her belly, the hard cup of some kind of groin armor butting against her bottom rib. Too many memories.

Writhing, Olivia fought for a way out, gasping for air that didn't seem to come. Too hot, not enough air, too dark, too much pain.

Her leg got stuck.

Olivia contorted, yanking and kicking at the lump of meat that trapped her. Her fingers dragged at the sand, clawing up warm handfuls of golden grains and sending them flying. Another kick, timed with a twist of her hips, and she was free.

Air filled her lungs. The cool breeze ran across her face, sucking away the blistering, stinging, salty, sweaty heat. The pain stayed, but it was different. It was only skin deep now. Olivia knew what a split lip and some bruises felt like. She sat up, eyes wide, soaking in as much of reality as she could.

Sandy beach. Nice breeze. Sound of water. Rocky wall. Forest. That was real.

Alley. London. Not real. Not now.

"Not real. Not real," Olivia muttered, trying to convince herself. She stood. The knife she'd thrown was near her feet. She grabbed it.

"Stabby?" a voice called from the wall. There was even a head to go with it. Ty's actually, his eyes wide and shocked.

Olivia waved for him to come down.

"All clear," he called over his shoulder. Then he skipped down the wall and jogged over. The others were a few steps behind, taking the wall at a more sedate pace. Ty and Zed both had alien knives.

"What happened?" Nat asked, staring at the carnage.

"I got bored," Olivia said. Making her way over to the archer that she'd shot through the throat, she took the bow and arrows. Shooting was less likely to get her crushed, which would be nice.

"You got bored?" Nat demanded, waving at the archers. "What the hell!"

"You got the two on the wall?" Olivia said, ignoring the shock and focusing on Zed.

Zed nodded.

"The last four got sent out when I came in," Olivia said. "Hunting for you upriver."

"They'll be back soon," replied Zed, her jaw clenching. "Who knows how to shoot a bow?" she asked, her words terse, quick.

Joey's hand shot up, but that was it.

"Fuck," Zed growled. "Ok, Joey, take a bow and as many arrows as you can get. Nat, take that one's knife," she directed, jabbing at the alien that Olivia had water-arrowed. "Everyone else, back on the wall. We'll force them to come up at us."

Ty, Zed, and Bee took off running, headed back the way they'd come. Joey began to gather the fallen arrows.

Thinking, Olivia turned to look down the beach in the direction that the enemy would be coming from. There was a problem.

"You coming?" Joey asked, busily turning arrows to all sit in the same direction in his hand.

"There's a human in the tent," Olivia explained. "They might try to use him as a hostage."

Joey froze, staring at her.

"Zed would let him go," Olivia continued, glad that he understood the issue. "If she didn't, then Nat and Bee and Ty would force her."

"You don't think I'd let him go?" he asked.

Olivia nodded, her chest oddly tight. They couldn't trust the alien's prisoner. Stranger's were trouble in her book, and they didn't know how

Stockholm syndrome ridden he might be. Joey would let him go, but only because he preferred that risk to the loss of trust he'd get if he didn't. Olivia didn't see the scales the same way.

Joey nodded. "You guard the tent."

"You shoot them before they get there," Olivia agreed. "I've already had to take four of these stickmen."

"I'll do my best," he answered, shooting her a grin before he spun and sprinted for the wall. Zed was at the top, gesticulating for Olivia to follow suit.

Smiling, Olivia shook her head and returned to the tent. Back behind the mottled cloth's cover, she began to look over the bow. Might as well do something while she waited.

The guy tied to the pole mumbled something. Sleep talk, maybe.

"Sit tight," Olivia said, "Once the fight's over, we'll figure out how messed up you are."

Another mumble. Ok, maybe not sleep talk. Too bad.

"Don't worry, I don't think this bunch's the type to leave you behind," Olivia consoled him. "Well, most of them," she corrected. She'd consider it. Safer, really.

Then she froze.

Someone was whistling.

The bow wasn't bad. Short, maybe three and a half feet long, and made from a hard, dark wood. It felt like a forty-pound draw weight. Well within Joey's norm, though the others might have trouble learning with one. Practice took a lot of repeated shooting, and forty pounds wore down untrained muscles fast. Especially on someone Olivia's size. In contrast to the bow's wood, the arrows were clearly synthetic, made of a matte gray metal with hard feathering and a point all made of the same.

Joey settled behind a rock and waited. He wasn't kneeling; he just stood a little ways back from the wall's lip. It was far enough to be hidden from sight, but not so far as to be among the trees. Better to be standing and use the wall's obstruction to advantage.

The whistle came again.

They were likely looking for a response, but Joey didn't know the signal. He waited. The others were tucked behind the trees. If the aliens tried to climb up, they'd guard the lip, but the trees were their best cover if the aliens tried shooting first. Otherwise the aliens might just lob arrows at an angle to hit them from above. Arrows were nice that way.

Four figures rounded the beach in the distance. Three hundred yards, give or take. Not an easy shot, and impossible with an unknown bow.

The four were definitely Stickmen. Two had bows out, but the other two looked unconcerned.

Joey smiled. They weren't expecting to be ambushed.

When they were on the beach directly in front of Joey's section of wall, he released the first arrow. It wasn't what he expected. Instead of the normal twang, this one gave off a slight hum, less than the sound of a bee. The arrow went high, punching into sand. Joey ducked. One of the bowmen turned, weapon raised as it scanned the wall.

Stringing another arrow, Joey moved a few steps to the right. He rose and released in one fluid motion. The watching bowman staggered and fell. The fletching protruded from his chest. Not Joey's preferred target, but heads were tricky.

The shot bowman started shouting, curses and cries of pain mingling as he stared at the wound. The other three split. The second bowman aimed at Joey. The two with knives took off towards the wall at a dead sprint.

Joey fell back. He put his back to a tree as he strung another arrow. Seconds ticked by. He'd expected the thud of an arrow hitting the tree. It didn't come. The archer was waiting for him to come out. Damn.

Booted feet crunched on the wall. The aliens had begun their climb.

"Joey!" Zed hissed, drawing his attention. She was behind another tree, only a few steps away. "Two climbing?"

He nodded.

"One shooting?"

He nodded again. Faster than verbalizing.

"Can you hit the shooter?"

He shrugged.

Zed nodded. "You try it. Nat will stand by in case you get hit. Ty and I will take the two."

Joey nodded and spun around the tree. He took off down the wall towards the camp. Had to draw that shot. He stopped abruptly.

An arrow hissed through the air where his head would've been.

Joey grinned. Cheating death. It felt good.

Not as good as this would.

Joey took his own shot. It wasn't good, his footing was wrong, but the alien flinched. It ruined their next try. Kneeling, he glanced back at Nat. She was behind him, just inside the tree line. Ty and Zed were crouched behind the lip a dozen yards away.

The two climbers came into sight, knives drawn.

Ty's arm thrust his knife at one alien's face. It hit, but caught on bone. Screaming, grabbing at its own face, the alien bent back, teetering. The other had better luck, parrying Zed's stab. They slashed at her. She wove forward and kicked its face, knocking the Stickman out into open air. The sound of thin bones and minimal padding hitting the sand below was not a nice one.

The bowman had given up. It took off for the tents. Joey sent an arrow after it. Missed. Moving targets were worse than headshots. But he wasn't worried. Stabby could handle herself.

Ignoring the runner, Joey aimed his next arrow at the Stickman on the ground. It wasn't moving, so he switched to the one Ty had stabbed in the face. Blood was running now, and its blade had blood on it. Ty was on his back, clutching his arm.

Can't have that. Joey released. The alien went limp.

The one that'd headed for the tents screamed.

Zed stood, her eyes searching the trees. "Nat!"

The taller woman raced out of the woods and skidded to a stop next to Ty. She put both hands on his wound. Her face froze, eyes nearly closed with concentration.

"Bee?" Zed asked.

"Here," Bee replied, emerging from the woods.

"Joey?" Zed continued, looking at him.

"Down to one arrow," he noted, "But otherwise fine."

"Bee, get a knife, then go with Joey to get Olivia. I'll stay with Ty and Nat."

Joey nodded and set off down the wall. Bee got there first, sliding all the way on one smooth boulder. She snatched up a knife from the one with the damaged face, Joey grabbed the handful of arrows from the one Zed had kicked. Its spine had broken in the fall. Or its skull had. Either way, the arrows were fine.

They ran towards tent, but Stabby came out before they reached it. She had a bow in hand, arrow knocked.

"Three," Joey reported, coming to a stop.

"One," Stabby returned. "Ten dead. Everyone ok?"

"Ty got cut by one of them," Bee supplied, wide eyed, the words coming too fast. "Nat's taking care of him. What do we do? What happened? Ten?"

"Bee," Stabby said sharply, snatching the woman's attention. "Go check on the two guards you took out on the wall. Get their gear and bring it back here. Got it?"

"Got it!" Bee agreed. Then she sprinted off.

"Joey," Stabby said. "Start gathering the other gear. I'm going to check the tents."

"On it," he replied, heading for the two bodies by the fire.

Well. It'd gone pretty well. One injury wasn't bad. Lot better than he'd expected, honestly. Really, one death, maybe two, had been likely. Would've simplified things too. Fewer names to remember, for one thing. Better that they all made it though.

The exhilaration was over. Now came the hard part: the fallout.

For Zed, the fight was when the thrill hit the high bar, and coming down from that was hard. She could feel the rush of it still, but she had to hold back, had to keep her head on straight despite the urge to jump and dance and laugh.

Ty was going to be ok, Zed could tell from the way Nat was relaxing. Nat was tired, though.

After a few minutes, Nat stood. "I think he'll be fine."

The wound had been healed to the point of being closer to a cut, though he looked a bit pale. Blood loss maybe.

"He needs liquids," Nat said, confirming Zed's theory.

"Let's get to the tents," Zed offered, coming over to help Ty up. Over there was definitely more interesting than sitting here.

He stood on his own, but it was slow. Zed trailed him and Nat, waiting for them to make the slow descent from the wall. Zed would be last; otherwise she'd race ahead to see how the others were doing.

Damn it was good to be fighting again.

By the time Zed's feet hit sand, Joey was there, taking weapons and belts from the corpses.

"Everyone ok?" Zed asked, walking backwards to watch him as she followed Nat and Ty towards the tents.

"Yeah," he confirmed, unfazed.

Zed nearly socked him. 'Yeah.' What kind of answer was that? Where was his martial spirit?

"Hey, I'm going to check in on Olivia," Zed said, jogging past Ty and Nat. Screw being patient.

"Got it," Nat said, nodding.

Olivia was in the far tent, rifling through some blankets. "What?" she said after Zed pushed aside the flap.

"We need to move the camp or the bodies," Zed said. She wanted to ask about the map. She knew Olivia had it; there was no way she'd leave it lying around.

Standing, Olivia moved to the pole at the center of the tent. She tapped it with a finger. "They were looking for ten of us."

Zed nodded. "Makes sense. That's how many the Vinna dropped."

"There's a dead human in the middle tent," Olivia added.

Zed winced. "Ouch."

Every dead human made things harder. This Rite had been designed with a full team in mind, and they were down to nearly half that. Challenging was fun, suicide was not.

"Glad you lured the four away," Zed noted.

Olivia shrugged. "Lucky." She set her palm on the pole and slid it downwards. Around them, the tent walls rushed up and in, sucked back into the pole. The whole thing made a sound like a child sucking down a noodle.

Zed laughed, hovering on the border of amused and unnerved. Between vanishing tents and fighting aliens, she was all kinds of riled up. This wasn't the hunt she'd had in mind when she'd found the others more than a week ago, but it'd do.

"How?" Zed asked.

"Current in the pole," Olivia explained, rapping the pole with her knuckles. "They're Vinna made. Must've set them up for the Stickmen to make sure they didn't go anywhere."

"So, we're moving camp," Zed stated. "I'll let the others know."

Olivia grunted an affirmative. She tossed something at Zed.

Catching it, Zed felt the smoothness of a second sponge-map. "Thanks," she said, tucking it into a pocket.

"There's a survivor too, over in that one," Olivia said, nodding at the center tent.

Zed shot it a look, surprised. "What?"

"Nat looks tired, so we'll have to carry him until she has a chance to rest."

Zed nodded. Not much to add to that. She was right.

"I'll collapse the tents, then we'll get moving," Olivia said. She pulled up her hood to block the harsh noonday sun.

"We'll be ready," Zed replied. Orders. Simple and straightforward. Just the thing for a fight-happy brain. She glanced around, checking on where everyone was.

A stink swam by, just drifting on the breeze. The bodies were starting to shit themselves. Some things tensed up in rigor mortis, other things let go. It wasn't pretty. Thus the need to move either the tents or the bodies. Sleeping next to rotting flesh and fecal matter was generally suboptimal.

Zed didn't ask how Olivia knew all of that.

Jogging back towards the wall, Zed caught Joey on his return from the bodies by the wall. "We need to gear up and get going. Olivia's getting the tents."

"The two in the woods?" he asked.

"Bee's on it. I'll get whatever we need from the far tent, you take the near one."

"On it," he agreed, setting off towards the sucking slurping sound of another tent collapsing.

"What's the plan?" Nat called from the fire.

"The bodies will start stinking soon, so we're going to move camp," Zed explained, moving over to the fire pit. Ty looked a lot better. "They had a prisoner. Can you check on them?" She gestured back at the last tent. "We need to get moving, so you'll have to keep it quick."

"I'll do what I can," Nat said, stomping off in the direction of the tent.

"Don't use any Current," Zed warned.

Nat looked at her, stubborn determination in every inch of her.

Zed held her gaze. The Canadian wasn't the only stubborn one. "You can barely walk."

"I can carry them," Ty offered. "You can fix them up later."

"You sure you can handle it?" Zed queried, running a sarcastic eye up his towering height.

Ty laughed. He looked away, as though blushing.

"Nat, you're going to be carrying gear," Zed said. "Blankets, water bottles, food, anything that isn't ruined. If it's too much to carry, we'll figure out what to drop."

At that, Nat's dug in heels gave way. Limping along was one thing, but she knew they couldn't afford to abandon anything useful.

Nat nodded, conceding. "No Current."

"I'm going to find Bee," Zed said, shooting Ty a wink and taking off at a jog once again.

It didn't take long. The nearest stretch of wall had a few easy ascents. At the top of the nearest one, Zed heard sobbing. She followed the sound back into the trees. Bee was leaning against one a few meters in.

Zed didn't say anything. She came around the tree and sat, thigh-to-thigh with Bee. All slow, steady movements, she held out her hands to offer a hug.

A headshake answered. Bee pulled her knees up, the palms of her hands rubbing the worst of the tears from her cheeks. Her hair was less than an inch long and did nothing to hide the dark splotches.

"You're going to be ok," said Zed, resisting the urge to pat the girl's knee. Most people needed physical comfort, but some didn't. Bee had said no, so she didn't touch. She took a deep breath, trying to calm her excitement. It wouldn't help to be cheery now.

"This is the second test," Bee said after a few minutes, her voice breaking. "How many more?"

"I don't know," Zed confessed, "But we can do this. Together."

"Sure," Bee snorted, staring into the distance. A fresh tear ran down her cheek. "Six of us, fighting goddamn aliens while avoiding super-gators on a goddamn tropical hellhole! Sure! Sounds like Christmas!"

"I didn't say it'd be easy," Zed noted, trying to pull the darkness of Bee's mood into the joke. Bee's lips twitched, so it wasn't a total miss. "It's ok to be afraid of dying. That's healthy. It'll keep you-"

"That's not the problem," Bee interjected, her voice sharp, raw. "Before this fight, I was ready to kill those assholes. Five minutes ago, at the wall, I was about to start shooting ice at whichever of those two made it past you and Ty. Being afraid of dying isn't my problem, I'm worried about who we'll be when this is over."

Zed carefully held back the response that came to mind. Survivors. Themselves. Better. There were a lot of easy answers that wouldn't really be accurate. This fight had been easy, relatively speaking, but this was the first leg. By the end, they probably wouldn't even realize how different they'd become. Boot camp had been like that for a lot of people. Zed hadn't realized how much she'd changed, until she'd gotten out. Her old friends had noticed. Joked about it. The skin stayed the same, regardless of new muscles and scars, but the bit behind the eyes was different. Sharper, maybe.

Or maybe that was just ego talking. Maybe that had just been flattery and chatter.

"Tomorrow, sit down and list out what's important to you. Figure out who you are now, that way you'll know when you've changed," Zed said. It probably wouldn't work, but it'd make Bee feel better. Doing something always helped. She stood. "Come on, we need to pack up their camp."

"Why?" Bee said, wiping the last few tears away.

"We're moving," Zed explained, feeling the map in her pocket. "But first I need to figure out which way we're headed."

Olivia flopped down on the sand and sucked in massive gulps of air.

"Are you trying to," gasp, "Kill us?" Ty asked from somewhere to her right.

"Oh come on, we got a good night's sleep. Nothing like a good workout to start a new day!" Zed beamed, her audible smile adding another little twinge of hot annoyance to the day's rising heat.

The sun was just peeking out around the trees, but the air was thick and humid, adding unnecessary stickiness to Olivia's sweaty skin. It felt like a storm was coming, but that hadn't done anything to slake Zed's upbeat round of morning calisthenics. They were a few hundred meters upriver from the old camp. Far enough that anything going after the bodies wouldn't feel obliged to add live meat to the menu.

"Everyone, remember to hydrate!" Zed directed, calling out names as she tossed full bottles.

Catching hers, Olivia sat up on one elbow and sipped. Cold. Gloriously cold. She looked up at the sky again. The storm was coming. She could see the leading edge coming from down south, the same direction they'd marched up from.

Absently, Olivia rubbed her bare arm with the wrist of her bottle-holding hand. She was layer-less now. The day had been so hot that she'd opted out of her jacket, hoodie, and second shirt the minute she'd gotten outside. Just a shirt, underwear, and jeans. Felt weird not to have her armor. Like an itch. She'd barely had them off in two weeks, let alone the years before. Lying there, she could feel the sweaty damp that'd soaked into her shirt begin to cool.

Olivia stood and headed for the water. Cold sweat sucked, and she needed to refill her bottle anyway.

In a flash, Zed was beside her, all wide toothy smiles and big brown eyes.

"What?" Olivia said, deciding to just cut to the chase halfway to the water.

"You haven't asked about the map," returned Zed, smile going even wider.

"You haven't asked about the bag of clothes Joey found," Olivia replied.

Zed fought to frown down at her, but it didn't work.

"Watch out, your face might stick that way," Olivia deadpanned.

Zed sighed. "What clothes?"

"You first."

"I'll show you," Zed said, pulling the ball out and tossing it onto the water just before they stepped in. It settled and began to spin as they slid into the warm stream.

Olivia dove into the deeper water, luxuriating in the cool of the depths before surfacing and swimming back. The ball was emitting ribbons of light, unspooling.

"You're a good swimmer," Zed noted, watching her.

"Used to compete," Olivia said, short and simple. Enough to avoid further questions, hopefully.

Zed grunted, thoughtful. Then she pulled the map down to water level. A jab of her finger indicated the green dot. "Us." Another finger, this time at a red dot on the ocean's coast immediately to the right. "Them."

"Close," Olivia noted, frowning. The last target had been a week away, but the woods between the river and the ocean had taken less than a day to cross back when they'd landed. It was about as wide here as down south.

"How long do we wait?" Zed said, voicing the question that was already swirling through Olivia's head.

"The longer we wait, the more nervous we'll get," Olivia said, thinking it through. "Does it say anything about who we're fighting?"

Using her raised hand, Zed made a spinning motion. The map flattened and turned into a hex, then split in two. She tapped the second one.

"Shit," Olivia whispered.

The second file included pictures. Pictures of really big bugs. The Vinna had added human models for scale, just to make sure they got the point across. These insects looked about two meters long, standing on six rear limbs and exhibiting another four from their raised upper body. One image showed them flat, belly a half-meter off the ground, limbs mid-motion, like centipedes but bigger. Their backs and bellies were scaled, and pokey bits stuck out from their armored faces.

A blinking light popped up at the bottom corner of the collage of images. Zed tapped it and a box of text appeared.

"Talented earth controllers, they use magic to support their heavy exoskeletons," Zed read. "Clawed, fast, strong, but lacking in poison, toxins, or venom of any kind. Current will be neutralized on contact. Highly edible."

"Fuck," Olivia repeated, verbalizing the disgust on Zed's face.

"Well, glad we've got some knives and bows," Zed stated, visibly disheartened. "At least they warned us that Current doesn't work on them."

"I wish they'd give us a damn manual for how to use it," Olivia grumbled, running one hand through her hair. It was short, just like the others', but it still helped to feel her hand run across her scalp.

"It looks like there are gaps in their armor," Zed said, pointing at one of the pictures of the bugs. As her finger moved closer, the image shifted, pulled out and towards her fingertip. She jerked back, and it expanded, becoming a tiny 3D miniature the size of a finger.

"Well, that's cool," Olivia noted, impressed.

Leaning forward, Zed excitedly rotated the figure, looking at it from different angles. "Definite gaps in the armor. It covers the belly and back, but the strip along the side, where the legs come out, is mostly bare. If we can flank them, we'll get clean shots."

"If they get within knife range, we're fucked," Olivia said, trying to find a solution. Close up fighting would be bad, but they had to find a way to get these bugs to face away from the archers.

"We could make spears," Zed suggested, looking at the woods. "The wood here is really hard, so it might hold up to these things."

"Better that than a knife," Olivia agreed. "But there are still ten of them, and only seven of us."

"And that's if Nat can get our new addition to do better than eat, sleep, and breathe."

"We'll plan for six," Olivia decided. "We'll have to ambush them. Take them out one by one at the edge of their turf. Go for guards and lookouts until they're all gone."

"Were you ever in a gang?"

"Briefly," Olivia answered, allowing herself a tiny smile. It hadn't gone so well, but at least all the listening she'd then done was paying off.

"Great, you picked up basic tactics in gangster-land. Really makes me grateful for all those long days in cramped classrooms with loud Training Officers," Zed grumbled, rolling her eyes.

"Trade you," Olivia offered. "Any day," she added when Zed's eyes widened.

"I didn't mean to-"

"Stop," Olivia said, the word clipped, clear. "Leave it there. Do we need to plan anything else?"

Zed nodded, her expression softening. "Yeah, who does what and when to leave."

"You decide and tomorrow morning," Olivia answered. "And Joey found a bag of uniforms in human sizes in one of the cases. Ten of them. They're the same pattern as the ones the Stickmen had."

"Good camouflage around here," Zed said. She smiled, a gleam of humor in her eyes. "And it'll be good for us to change. Everyone's getting a little…"

Zed's eyes flicked down to the blood and sweat stains on Olivia's shirt. Zed had them too, but hers were smaller. A lot smaller. Getting trapped under that Stickman had stained all the way through Olivia's layers, and even a thorough washing hadn't gotten all the muddy brown discoloration out. Maybe if she had soap, but the Vinna hadn't provided any. Blankets, tents, bottles, knives, bows, arrows, uniforms, but no hygiene products.

Oh. That raised a good question.

"We've been out here a while," Olivia said, trying not to let on how awkward this felt. Streets weren't hygienic, nor kind to people who were hurting, so it hadn't come up unless it had to.

"Yeah?" Zed replied. Her brow rose, questioning.

"Uh, the Vinna, they didn't," Olivia fumbled. Each word made her surer that this would destroy whatever respect Zed felt for her.

"Didn't what?"

"Tampons," Olivia said, just going for it.

For a long moment, Zed stared at her. Then she burst out laughing, hooting and bubbling with amusement.

Feeling her cheeks heat, Olivia wished she had her hoodie. Blushing was bullshit. She wasn't a child! She punched Zed in the shoulder, hard.

"Ow!" Zed gasped, sputtering few more cackles.

Olivia cocked her fist for a second punch.

"Ok! Ok," Zed conceded, raising her hands and swallowing the last bits of laughter. "You're completely right. This is a dire and serious problem that we should think over with absolute seriousness."

It hung there for a moment.

A smile tugged at Olivia's lips. She couldn't help it.

Zed's mouth curved upwards. She winked.

They both burst out laughing.

Eventually, they both settled down again, at which point Zed said, "I haven't gotten my period since getting here, but they could've done something to us before the drop-off."

Olivia nodded, unscrewing her bottle and dipping it into the river. "Ask Nat and Bee? If it comes up, we can improvise something."

"We don't have any painkillers if cramps get bad," Zed pointed out.

"See if anyone usually gets painful ones. If someone does, I'll ask Joey what he gave Bee to make her forget that she had a broken ankle."

They both smirked at the memory of Nat's reaction to that. She'd ranted about it several times on the weeklong trek.

"We might need it if we run into an injury we can't heal quickly, and it might be handy for drugging bugs," Zed said.

"I'll ask," Olivia agreed, smiling at the thought of a giant bug tripping out. "Let's go day after tomorrow. Gives us time to make and practice with the spears, but not enough to get nervous."

"Aye-aye, captain," Zed agreed, shooting her an offhanded salute and doing her best to copy Bee's lazily sassy tone.

"Shut up," Olivia threw back, unable to bite back another smile.

Ty smashed the jagged point of his spear into the insect's face. It screeched; it's cry a high-pitched peal, like chalk on a chalkboard. Wincing, he shuffled back, carefully skimming over the roots and rocks that littered the forest floor.

Writhing, the giant bug contorted, coiling around itself to use its armored back as a shield. Its eyes loomed, dark specks glaring over the upper rim. It hissed, pain and anger steaming from its pincer lined mouth.

"Come on!" Ty shouted. He shifted one hand nearly to the base of his spear and lanced it out at the bug. The tip glanced off armored carapace, but it elicited another hiss. "Come on!" he shouted again. "Come get me, you overgrown cockroach!"

Silent, it frothed forward, its upper body sliding over its shielding lower, charging straight at him.

Planting his feet, Ty knelt, bracing the spear's butt against the ground. He aimed the tip at the bug's lower face, ready to drop. Sure enough, a second before impact, the bug ducked. He followed, fighting to keep the spearhead between them. The movement kept going, the bug's dodge turning into a flinch that turned its face away from him entirely.

From his right and left, Ty heard soft hums, like guitar strings.

The bug spasmed, its momentum barreling forward as its back flexed. It smashed into Ty's shoulder, sending him flying.

A tree trunk caught Ty across the ribs, knocking the breath from his lungs. He fell to the ground. Pain rolled through him, rushing outwards from his shoulder and back. Just as it started to pound to his heart's beat, something cold and numbing rushed through him.

Ty blinked, wiping tears from his eyes as he pulled himself into a kneeling position. Nat had her hands on his back. The cold washed out from her touch.

"Good?" Nat asked, moving around him to catch his eyes without breaking contact.

"Ready to go," Ty said, giving her thumbs up. Her hands vanished but the cold lingered, out of place on a tropically toasty day. He stood and checked on the bug.

Joey, Olivia, and Bee were retrieving arrows, yanking them from the meaty sides that the bug's carapace didn't cover. A leg twitched and Bee jumped, nearly falling over a root. A second later she was back, yanking her arrow out with a vengeful jerk.

"Jesus! Hell-spawn!" Bee grumbled, kicking the leg as she stepped back. "Set."

"Set," Joey agreed, moving back as well.

"Healed," Nat added.

"Move out," Olivia said, and a moment later they all took off at a jog.

It was the fourth bug in two days, so they'd figured out a rhythm. Archers in front, spears in back, just in case one of the bugs chased them down. Ty slowed to let the others get ahead. He ignored the dull throb in his shoulder. Nat had left the surface bruising. More economical that way, but it'd sting for a while.

Falling in beside him, Zed patted his uninjured shoulder. "You good?"

"I'm glad you hit that one," Ty shot back with a grin. "Just kidding. I'm fine."

Zed smirked. "Oh? Wincing as you stand up is pure reflex? I should've guessed."

"Shut up," Ty huffed back. She was right, but it wasn't that bad. He'd be ok. He was tough, and any Current that could be saved for the life threatening stuff would save lives. "Where were you while I was getting bug-bashed?"

"I was about two meters behind you, waiting for you to back your ass up!" Zed replied, smacking his shoulder again. "Not much point to having backup if you don't use them!"

"Wasn't a problem for the archers," Ty noted, heat rushing to his cheeks. At least she wasn't accusing him of trying to take it himself, which he had. The whole 'giant bug' thing had definitely done a number on remembering any part of the plan other than 'don't show your back' and 'get it to follow you.'

If Ty hadn't botched it, he'd have led the bug back to Zed. Her job was to be waiting behind a tree to jump out and stab the thing. Or, at least distract it. A surprised bug held still for a few seconds, which generally led to arrows hitting meat rather than armor. Most creatures didn't like surprises, and so far these bugs loved chasing spear-carrying humans, but got gun-shy when the number went to two.

But Ty had blanked. It'd been the fourth bug hunt, but the first time where he'd been on 'chase me, buggy,' duty. Before, he'd done the jumping. Zed had opted to trade after the last bug nearly got her.

"Next time," Zed warned, slapping his shoulder again, yanking him out of his thoughts, "Don't go solo. They're bigger, heavier, and better armored."

"Less hero, more team. Got it," Ty agreed wincing as a rock shifted and his heel landed lower than he'd thought. It'd jolted his shoulder.

Then his own words set in. Ty tried to digest what he'd said. Less hero. That was true. A hero wouldn't forget the plan. A hero might try to face down a giant bug all on his own, but he wouldn't get tossed like that.

A shiver ran down Ty's spine. Giant bugs seemed a lot more faceable in games and books.

"Crap," Ty muttered to himself, not quite able to bring himself to curse, despite his thoughts beginning to fray.

Maybe heroism wasn't all it was cracked up to be.

Ty glanced at Zed, then at the others ahead of them. Or maybe it just wasn't what he'd thought it was. He'd always wanted to be the leader, the main fighter, the guy who protected the beautiful woman, defeated the baddies. Perhaps not the guy at the top, but authoritative. Perhaps not the deadliest warrior, but a respected one. Perhaps not Paris protecting Helen, that hadn't gone well for Troy, or anyone else in that war, really, but certainly someone attractive. Perhaps not the one who killed Sauron, but definitely in the Fellowship.

That'd been the dream.

The Stickmen had made things seem a bit more challenging, for sure. Giant bugs were a lot more like the monsters he was used to seeing in games though. The lack of guns could be part of the disparity, but it still hurt to see reality. Shooting an unarmed bug wasn't exactly heroic, not unless there were a horde of them, and something told him these bugs were too smart to crowd together and be easy targets.

The dream was definitely not turning out as imagined.

Ty laughed darkly to himself, rubbing his face with one hand. Mysterious alien planet full of predators, and here he was realizing that he wasn't enough. For all the exercise, for all the planning and the simulation, the reading, the strategy games, he was just as screwed as everyone else.

Glancing at the others, Ty frowned. Not even. He was more screwed. At least some of them had something other than their size to offer. Something coiled in his chest, pulling tight, a burning weight in the bowels of his stomach.

Ahead, Stabby's hand rose and pointed left.

The frontrunners swung in that direction, curving around as she turned them back towards the bug camp.

Great. Disillusioned, bruised, and now off to hunt down a third bug. Ty sighed tiredly.

"Walk," Zed said, the words repeated up the line. A moment later, they slowed as Stabby and Nat reduced the pace from the front. "Better?" she said, nudging Ty.

Smiling at the misunderstanding, Ty nodded. She was trying. He was just preoccupied with figuring out what the - Nope. No cursing.

'Figuring out what he wanted.'

That one.

It'd help if any of them knew what'd happen after they finished the Vinna's Rite, but that hadn't been on Blue-Sight's list of handy tidbits.

A crack, sharp and grating, rocked through Ty's distracted mind.

"They're coming!" Zed barked. "Spread out!"

Ty stopped, digging his heels in, and turned. Beside him, Zed did the same. The spreading out part wasn't their job. That was for the archers. The shooters had to get around the flanks; otherwise it was all over.

Planting his spear, Ty leaned forward, bracing it with both hands. It was a lot harder to dodge two big pointy things.

A trio of bugs was visible between the trees, racing forward. They scraped and bumped into trees as they tried to maintain their breakneck pace. One wove right, breaking off from the other two.

"Eyes forward!" Zed reminded him.

Ty bent his knees, settling in. Two on two weren't good odds, but they were still coming. Last stands had always looked heroic, but this was ludicrous. There was no dramatic music, no one to remember if they died, nothing. They'd just be some meat to feed the bugs. He shivered, realizing that he wasn't sure if they'd end up feeding the little bugs or the big ones.

Familiar hums came from somewhere in the woods to his left and right. One bug bucked and slowed, several limbs losing their pounding rhythm.

Targets halved, the tips of Zed and Ty's spears moved closer. One charger. One enemy.

It reached them a second later. At the last second, it went low to avoid being skewered.

Ty adjusted, shifting with the drop.

Zed was a hair behind. Too later Her spear scraped across the bug's armored shell.

The usual abrupt crunch of bashed carapace didn't come. Ty's eyes widened, staring as the oncoming bug plunged down the spear, face first. The wood reverberated with a thick, molasses weight, dragging at his hands. Scattered throughout the sensation were pops and cracks and little snaps, vibrating down to his fingers as the spear plunged through organs and whatever else filled those shells.

Bile rose to the back of Ty's mouth, biting and harsh. He felt numb, but for the jerk of the spear against his fingers.

After less than a meter, the bug's armor caught on the uneven nobs of the spear. It jerked to a stop, nearly snapping the uneven hardwood.

Ty stood there, frozen, hands white with tension.

The other bug catapulted forward, recovered from its earlier shooting.

Zed shouted something.

Molasses again. This time it wasn't around the spear. It was around him.

Sluggish, that was the word. He was sluggish.

Funny, slugs were bugs, weren't they?

The speared bug shrieked. The sharp sounds came through the haze like ice water to a burn. It didn't fix it, but it was an anchor.

To Ty's left, Zed ran forward, stabbing her spear into the other bug's face. It flinched and scuttled back. She kept going, pinning it against a couple of tightly packed trees. An arrow flashed out, coming from somewhere to the right, and the bug slumped. The twitches started a breath later.

Nat and Joey burst from the trees to Ty's left and kept running. Seconds later, the third bug raced after them. It was smaller than the others, faster. An arrow protruded from one corner of its face, jiggling with the bumps and bounces of its pace.

Zed spun, shouting as the bog shot between her and Ty.

The bug kept going. It vanished into the trees to Ty's right.

Zed cursed, unhooked her bow from over her shoulder, and took off after it.

More shouts. A squeal. A shriek.

Ty vomited.

Another shriek.

More vomit.

Minutes ticked by. Ty kept trying to spit the bile out, but the taste stayed.

Hands settled on his shoulders. They were cold, cooling. The feeling spread, familiar by now.

Eventually, the nausea went away. It took a minute, maybe two. Hard to tell. Ty was sitting up. There was a sting to his knees, the kind that came from kneeling too long. He stood.

Nat was beside him, one hand on his shoulder. "You good?"

"Think so," Ty replied, carefully avoiding the sight of the bug a few steps from his feet.

"Bee, take Ty and Joey and start walking back," Zed said, her voice sharp as she came back through the trees. Her knife was bloody. The others trailed her.

Bee slipped from behind Zed and took Ty by an elbow. "Come on."

"I need to get my spear," Ty complained, but he didn't try to dislodge her. The contact was nice. Another anchor. And he didn't want to get the spear.

"Get going," Zed said, chuckling. "We'll grab the spear. Joey, make sure they don't get lost."

Ty nodded and followed Bee, who followed Joey. She kept her hand on his elbow, pulling him along as they headed off through the woods. They'd wandered a good bit today, but Joey knew the way back.

Slipping into the 'guys' tent, Nat took a moment to look at the seated figure leaning against the support pole. She'd gotten him to sleep in one of the blankets. He'd even joined them for some of the runs. But he kept coming back and sitting in that spot. It was the same position she'd untied him from. The cuts were gone, thankfully, as were the bruises. His mind was the issue.

Crouching, Nat tried to be as un-intimidating as possible as she made her way over to him. Unlike the rest of them, he hadn't traded his worn and bloodied clothes for a mottled suit. His jeans and shirt were tattered and damp with sweat, clinging to his long, lean limbs.

His eyes were focused on her, shifting as she moved. That was good.

Nat took a spot on the sand in front of him. Unclipping the bottle from her belt, she held it out for him.

A hand rose and took it. The other came up and unscrewed the top. Then he drank. Each motion was all slow, almost sleepy.

"Very nice," Nat said, smiling. "Been a hot day. Bet you're thirsty." She waited, trying to draw him into talking. He'd spoken before, mostly in monosyllables or one-word answers. Nothing helpful, but progress.

He grunted an affirmative.

Nat nearly rolled her eyes. She'd wanted to be a surgeon, not a psychiatrist. People were interesting, and she liked talking to them, or at them, if she was entirely honest, but she had no idea how to fix them. If she had, maybe she'd have gotten Olivia vocalizing a lot sooner.

"Ok, I've tried talking at you, talking near you, and I think I even talked a circle around you just in case, so I'm gonna try something new," Nat said, explaining her reasoning as fast as she came up with it. "Name. Yours. Share."

He was looking right in the eyes when he gave her the tiniest smile.

"Ok, big guns time," Nat decided. "Bee!" she called, "You 'round?"

A moment later, Bee stuck her head in the door. "Yup?"

"I can't get him to talk," Nat admitted. "Help?"

"Yeah, and you did such a good job with 'Stabby,' right?" Bee jabbed, chuckling.

"Help," Nat repeated, smothering the urge to toss something at her.

"Yo, butt-head, we're not going to hurt you, but if you don't work with my friend here, she's not gonna be the only one talking your ears off," Bee said, dropping her voice to comedy villain levels, "I'll help, and I've seen every Bond movie. Don't doubt my Monologue-Fu."

For a second, Nat weighed the objects nearby, trying to figure out which one to throw at her 'helper.' The blanket was too soft, but the bottle wasn't a bad idea. Maybe a shot to her shin-

Then their rescued gent burst out laughing. His humor was wild, bouncing and varying from one breath to the next. One of his hands fell from the bottle, slapping against his thigh.

"That's hilarious," he mumbled. Tears streamed from his eyes.

Nat stared. That was such bullshit! Intimidating a person with PTSD into reacting wasn't a thing!

"I'm gonna go and let you two chat," Bee said, backing out of the tent, "Before Nat starts throwing things." A single peal of her laughter carried across the beach in her wake as she disappeared from sight.

"Rude," Nat grumbled.

"Seems nice," he noted, smiling.

"Does that mean I get to know what your name is?"

"Seth, Seth Drake," he answered. "And you're Natalie Hyde, but you go by Nat."

"Guess I've kind of filled you in on everything already," Nat said, wincing at the realization that he'd actually been listening to it all. "Well, guess that means you're basically caught up."

"Pretty much," Seth agreed. "More baddies today, right?"

"We got the two we planned on, then three more chased us down," Nat explained. "Three left."

"Congrats," Seth muttered, his smile thinned, thoughtful.

"You're still watching how much you say," Nat observed.

Seth's smile darkened. "I keep wondering if it's really over, or if they'll come back when I wake up."

Nat poked him in the chest.

"Ow?" Seth deadpanned.

"No dream," Nat explained, poking him again. "You're stuck with us. Besides, if you were rude enough to make me up and give me the illusion of being real, the least you could do is live through the reality you've made me experience."

"I guess that's fair," Seth grumbled. He rolled his eyes. "So, what's next Dream Queen?"

"Well, it'd be handy to know if you have any useful skills," Nat said, thinking.

"Oh, standard rich boy stuff," Seth answered, with the faintest hint of a smile. "Chess, drawing, painting, horseback riding, fencing, archery."

Nat's brows knit. Fencing and archery sounded like exactly what they needed, but Seth's trauma was way too fresh.

"Give me time," Seth said, answering the unspoken. "I'll heal."

"Let's get you changed, and then you can tell me more about yourself," Nat said, changing the subject.

"Into one of those?" Seth guessed, looking at her mottled gray-green suit. "Pretty sure it won't fit."

"Guess again!" Nat said, knee-walking over to the clothes case in the corner. She popped it open and looked through the little stack of mottled suits. Checking the necks, she found one with 'SD' on it. Seth Drake. She tossed it at him. "Want me to step out?"

"It's fine," Seth replied, shaking his head as he caught the bundle. "Just… face the wall?"

Nat turned, staring at the cloth lining of the tent. "Where're you from?"

"Trying to avoid the awkward silence?" Seth joked, clothes rustling. "I'm from LA, but I'm in New York for college. Or, I was."

"Canada," Nat supplied, trying to distract him from his lost life.

"I remember," Seth said with a hint of sarcasm.

"Good! Now, I didn't think about this before, but you should probably wash before you climb into the suit," Nat said, wincing at her mistake. The rustling stopped.

Seth laughed. "Glad you said something before I put it on." More sounds of clothing moving around followed.

"Let's head out to the river," Nat suggested, standing and heading for the flapped entrance. "Meet you outside."

"Right behind you."

In the open, Nat stretched, reaching outwards as she drank in the sun's warmth. Despite the suits coverage, and the sun's touch, the heat didn't roast her. She felt pretty comfortable, actually. Maybe it was some kind of super alien fabric that adapted to maintain the wearer's temperature. That'd be impressive. Come to think of it, she hadn't gotten hot when they'd run through the forest. Suspicious, she looked down, plucking at a bit of the mottled material. It stretched, but not much. It fit, but it was tight, so she didn't have much to pull on.

All the suits were tight fits, which would've been a bit awkward if they weren't layered. The outer skin was just a touch looser, making it look less like a second-skin, even though it felt like one. Frankly, that they were heat regulating was less of a shock to Nat than finding out it stood in for her bra. For her, running usually took two, and finding out that this thing made them unnecessary was pretty impressive.

Seth emerged from the flap beside her, glancing down and catching sight of her examination. "Admiring?" he joked.

"Just trying to get a handle on alien fashion," Nat threw back, setting off towards the water. "So, you mind swimming near camp or should we head downriver?"

"What do you all do?"

"Usually we all swim in our clothes," Nat explained. "Clean everything off at once. But you need to change."

"I'll swim, then change in the tent," Seth decided.

Nat smiled. "Good plan. So, you're all caught up on us, but what about you?"

"Rich kid, grew up in LA, school in New York, skills as mentioned." Seth shrugged. "That's about it."

"Hey, if you don't want to talk, that's chill," Nat replied, oozing sarcasm. "I'm getting used to it at this point. Kind of the thing to do. I mean, we all know how healthy bottling up our emotions is, so it seems like brilliant idea to not talk to the nearest thing to a medical professional."

"Anyone ever mention that guilt tripping trauma victims is bad?" Seth shot back, smirking at her.

Nat blushed. What? Why the fuck was she blushing! Ok, so psych shit wasn't her thing, fair, and having it pointed out was embarrassing, also fair, but that wasn't the only cause of the blush. Part of it was that smirk. For a moment, Nat actually took in the guy she was talking to.

Seth was pretty. Really pretty. All over. Short, dark curls covered his head, accentuated by the rich walnut brown of his skin. Light stubble and a bold chin added to the effect, making his youthful face older, handsome in almost too-perfect way. The smirk made it all worse. It made his green eyes spark and shine, smile lines showing around his wide mouth and ivory teeth. What with the unfair amount of athletic litheness in the rest of his build, it was dangerous.

"Don't do that," Nat said, before she could actually think through the words.

"What?" he asked, one brow arching up, questioning.

"Don't do that either," Nat added, shivering at the oddity of seeing Stabby's trademark facial quirk on some not-Stabby hot dude.

"Now, that doesn't sound like any fun," Seth tossed back, his smirk coming out in full force.

"Just get in the water," Nat directed. She pointed at the river a few steps away.

Seth paused, eyeing the water, then her.

That smirk was trouble.

"Say please."

"No," Nat replied, indignant. He was the one who wanted to clean up. It wasn't her job to beg him to do it.

"Then tell me what I can't do and why," Seth retorted, crossing his arms and shifting a half step closer.

Casting around for some kind of rescue from a no-win scenario with an overly flirty trauma victim, Nat caught sight of Joey coming down the wall. "Hey!" she called, waving. He started walking over, but she waved again, hurrying him to a jog.

"Calling for help?" Seth queried, amusement dripping from each syllable as he turned to stand nearly shoulder-to-shoulder with her. He clicked his tongue, his head shaking sadly.

"What's up?" Joey asked, walking over.

"This is Seth. He needs to wash then put on his suit. Can you make sure he does it?" Nat asked, holding Joey's inquisitive gaze.

"Sure," Joey agreed, shrugging. "But-"

Nat panicked. The worry was that he would ask why she wasn't going to help Seth. So, she babbled. "I need to check on Ty and make sure that he's healed."

Joey's eyes flicked back and forth between them. "I was going to ask if you'd start a fire, but if you're busy…"

"A fire?" Seth asked.

"Bee caught a little croc around the bend," Joey said, thumbing back the way he'd come. "They're bringing it back now. I was sent ahead to get a fire started."

"I'll get started on the fire," Nat said, stepping past Joey and heading towards the fire pit. "Just make sure you get him cleaned and clothed."

"Are you sure?" Joey said. "He looks like he might pollute the river all on his own. I could take him out to the ocean and dunk him a few times instead."

"Less jokes, more swimming," Nat shouted over her shoulder. Goddamn blushing. Blurting. Goddamn smirk-faced asshole.

Worse, the acoustics of a stone lined flat, watery space meant that sound carried. Like, just for example, the sound of a hot, smirking asshole laughing.

Nat flinched, her shoulders tightening as she considered how feasible it would be to slip something foul into Seth's dinner. That might fall under abuse of her medical responsibilities, though. He probably needed all the nutrients and energy he could get. Maybe she could just foul up a bit of his meal. The first bit, that way there was no chance of him throwing up the whole thing.

The bouncing laughter ended rather suddenly with a loud splash.

Glancing back, Nat caught sight of Joey, knee deep in the water, one hand outstretched. Sputtering in the river, Seth looked indignant, not to mention comedically flattened. His dark curls flopped about his face, soaked.

"What the hell, dude?" Seth barked. He glared as he stood, knee deep.

"You were laughing at Nat," Joey explained. The words were flat and blank.

"So?" Seth demanded, arms tensing as a breeze cooled the water on his skin. "I'm allowed to laugh!"

"Not if she doesn't like it," Joey replied. He crossed his arms.

"It's a free country!" Seth shouted, waving a finger in Joey's face. "If you-"

Joey's hand flashed out, smacking Seth's cheek with a crack in a blink.

Waterlogged, red-cheeked, Seth stared.

"Incorrect," Joey informed him. "This is actually a rather un-free and un-fair world. The nations might be free, but we haven't seen any of them yet. Though, going by us being kidnapped and the aliens who're forced to fight us, I'm pretty sure freedom isn't a universal right."

"You can't just hit me!" Seth declared. He sloshed to the side, trying to circle around Joey.

"Why?" Joey returned, vaguely curious. "Because there are laws against it? Because you don't like it?"

"Because it's wrong."

"I disagree," Joey admitted, thoughtful. "She's a useful member of the team. You're not. You were laughing at her. She didn't like it. Simple. I could smack you again if that'd clarify the situation for you."

"That's…" Seth began, but he trailed off, grasping at his own thoughts. "That's insane!"

"Nat?" Joey called.

She jolted, her stunned trance broken. "Yeah?"

"How's the fire?" Joey asked.

"Just fine!" Nat threw back. Hurriedly, she set to blowing on the little pile of coals she'd dug out from the ash. She dribbled tinder on top of them, watching for the flames.

"See? She's being useful. Right now, you have negative usefulness. Should probably work on that," Joey explained to Seth. "Now, wash."

There was some muttering from the river, some splashing, but after that Seth seemed to capitulate.

Nat frowned, focusing on the coals. The fire caught, and grew as she added more twigs and wood. When Joey and Seth crossed the beach and went back into the 'guys' tent, she glanced up and watched them go. Seeing them next to each other made their difference in height clear. Joey was about Bee and Zed's height, but Seth was taller, around Nat's own six feet.

Joey was shorter, and thinner, but Seth had still taken the fall and the slap.

It made Nat wonder about Seth. Getting hurt so soon might've shaken him, feeding on his torture and fear.

Shaking her head, Nat tossed another stick on the flames. Nothing she could do now. Either she'd fucked up or she hadn't. Either way, Seth was up and moving. That was progress.

"You mind company?" Zed asked, looking up at the newcomer's perch on the wall.

Seth had found a spot a couple dozen meters from the tents, where the wall bowed and ran perpendicular to the rivers usual course. The view of the river was nice, but the moon's light made it enchanting. The moon was pale and cratered, familiar in a way that nothing else was. Its glow flickered on the water; a streak of white, like a line of snowy dancers gleaming and leaping.

"Would it matter if I said yes?" Seth replied, his voice tiny, hushed against the constant backdrop of the night's music.

"Course it would," Zed said, dragging her attention away from the sounds of the jungle at night, the trickle of the mountains, and the stream's chuckling gurgle. "You get a choice."

Seth grunted, dismissive. "Not much of one. Buck up and buckle in or die? Bullshit choice."

"Do you have a better plan?" Zed queried, watching him. When he didn't reply, she added, "Is this about Joey?"

"Nat told you," Seth guessed. His dangling legs bounced, heels tapping against the face of the boulder beneath him.

"Does it matter?" Zed pushed.

"That he got violent or that she told?" Seth returned.

"Either."

Seth shook his head, still staring at the water. "He's messed up."

"And good at what he does," Zed pointed out.

"That shouldn't give him the right to attack people."

"He didn't attack you," Zed said. Finally they'd gotten to the point. "If he'd attacked you, you'd be dead. He was carrying a bow and at least one knife. He could've done it. He didn't."

Seth snorted, derisive. "Is that supposed to make me feel better?"

"No, it's supposed to put it into perspective," Zed said, her patience waning. "We killed five giant insects today. Any of them could have killed all of us. We're already playing this game down three players. Four, before we found you. Joey has personally helped in every fight we've gotten into, and I know that he's taken out at least two of the things we've had to kill to get this far. He's good at following orders, he's smart, and I've never seen him hesitate. If you're planning something, don't. We need both of you, and he's not the one I'm worried about."

"So, I'm supposed to chill out and play nice with the team," Seth growled, his hands clenching. "I guess I don't have a fucking choice, so fine."

"Like I said, you can always walk away, but this place will kill you nearly as fast as these suicide missions we keep getting sent on."

"Let me guess, your job is pep-talks and shoving other people at the enemy, right?" Seth asked. "Bet your folks are real proud."

"They disowned me," Zed shot back. For a moment, she considered just how easy it'd be to climb up there and shove her fist through his face. "They didn't like me joining the army."

"Oh," Seth mumbled, his momentum gone. "I'm-"

"Shut up," Zed snapped. "I came over because I heard shit went down and I wanted to make sure it didn't happen again. I already talked to Joey. For future reference: he apologized for the trouble, you just dug yourself deeper. Get your head out of your ass. If you need to work through your trauma, talk to someone. Not Joey, obviously, and probably not Ty or me, but someone. If this is just you getting over the whole alien world thing, hurry the hell up, or we might all be dead. Clear?"

"Yes, ma'am."

"Good," Zed said. She rolled her shoulders, trying to ease the knots of tension. "I want you to be ok. I want all of us to get through this. Together. We can't do that if we're arguing, or if someone runs off and gets eaten by the wildlife."

"I got it," Seth said, his tone flat and toneless. "Go sleep."

"That's a great idea. You do the same. I'm upping the distance for the morning run." Zed set off towards the tents.

"Are you worried about the Kaskans?" Seth called after her.

"That's why we have lookout shifts. By the way, you've got the early-night shift with me tomorrow. Nat needs the extra rest after all the healing she's done."

He didn't reply, so Zed kept going. Tonight's lookouts, Bee and Olivia, were seated on the sand by the dead fire. One faced the wall, the other the river. As Zed passed, they both nodded at her, smiling as she went inside. Nat was already asleep, her snores a dull rumble, not unlike a diesel engine on a bad day.

Lying down in her bundle of blankets, Zed rolled the lip and settled it under her head, supported up by a small mound of sand. She wiggled for a few seconds, burrowing her shoulder and hip into the soft sand. The fabric was soft and warm, comfortable and comforting, shored up by the form fitting sand arrangement.

Zed had slept in far worse places, though none so far from home. She was asleep in under a minute, fighting to ignore the tears that trickled across her cheeks.

Bee collapsed onto the sand, bone-tired. Another long day.

"You alright?" Nat asked, one of her hands settling on Bee's shoulder.

"I feel like my bones were transmuted into cheese, grated, melted into a quesadilla, and then squeezed out into roughly shaped molds to be reinserted into my body," Bee explained, one sore hand fiddling with the lid of her half-empty bottle. "I'll be fine."

"Drills suck," Nat noted, smiling. Her hand stayed, emanating a cool numbness.

"But they'll keep us alive," Bee recited. She rolled her eyes. "You know, Zed should really say that more often, I might forget it someday."

"Maybe in another decade or three," Nat joked.

Bee rubbed her eyes. Her shoulders relaxed as the cooling sensation from Nat's hand flowed over her spine. "I can't complain about the extra healing, but don't you need to save up? We've got a fight tomorrow."

"As long as I get a decent night's sleep, I'm good to go," Nat said, hints of pride showing through.

"Really?" Bee asked, surprised. Current had been a pretty immediate drain when she'd tried it. Hell, she'd only just gotten to making a knife that'd last for more than a minute. Joey, Zed, and Stabby were miles ahead, but Nat didn't do the exercises, so Bee had no concept of how strong her Current was. At least Ty hadn't really improved. Not being alone at the bottom made her feel a bit better.

"How've you been sleeping?" Nat queried, hints of worry showing through in the way her brows twitched together.

"Fine." Bee shrugged the question off with a light smile. "Had a dream about walking naked through the suburbs and cussing out a bunch of fat toddlers. Perfectly normal."

Nat laughed. "If you say so. Let me know if you start having trouble sleeping?"

"Will do, nosy," Bee tossed back. She threw in a wink for good measure.

Nat moved on. Her hand went to Ty's shoulder next. The two of them chatted, voices low.

Bee ignored them. The day was dark, shadowy rain clouds scudding across the brilliant blues. Zed had said she didn't like running in the rain, thus the early workouts. Exercising in the tents hadn't been on the menu.

Now it was nearly noon and the storms were following the sun across the sky, chasing it from the ocean to the mountains.

It'd been a lie. Bee had lied to Nat. The sights weren't distracting enough to take the sting from that. She'd had nightmares last night. And the night before. Every night since the Stickmen. They weren't the obvious kind. No shaking, no tossing and turning, no talking in her sleep. If there had been, someone would've noticed. These were colder dreams, the kind that she woke from with her heart racing, cold sweat chilling her flesh, and dread locking her jaw.

Not the kind of thing Bee could share with Nat. Perfect, chatty, helpful, happy Nat. She didn't deserve to have that ruined by Bee's baggage. The nightmares would go away eventually. This wasn't her first rodeo.

"Penny for your thoughts?" Seth cut in, settling onto the sand beside her.

"Just wishing for a vodka or ten," Bee returned. She smiled, but it felt like a mask, a layer between her and everything.

Seth's face lit up with amusement. "Vodka? I was always more of a whiskey guy. Or bourbon."

"Nah, I'll stick to getting fucked up Russian style. Or some cheap cider if I actually feel like tasting something," Bee said, wistful at the memory. A cool, hard cider. That'd be so nice right now.

"Where you from?" Seth asked. His curls fell forward, half-hiding his eyes. One of his hands brushed at a little mound of sand, drawing gentle fingertips across the surface.

"Madison," Bee answered. "You?"

"L.A."

"Meh," Bee said, half-joking but a little annoyed. He'd said it with expectation, as though she was supposed to be impressed. Los Angeles. It was probably polluted and full of hipsters and strippers. Not that the strippers part was bad. She didn't have anything against strippers. Hipsters though, they could take their gentrifying, vegan asses elsewhere.

"Meh?" Seth repeated. His grin twisted, incredulous. "Not a fan of LA?"

"Not really," Bee said, shrugging. Leading questions and expectations tended to lower her opinion of places faster than the places themselves.

"I hear Madison's nice," he offered, spinning a finger in a soft circle around the pile of sand at his foot.

"It is," Bee agreed, smiling at the memories. "Lots of green, lots of students, most people have pulled the stick out of their collective ass. Pretty decent."

Seth laughed, but it felt thoughtful, like he was buying time to think. "Not a big fan of people, are you?"

"People? No. A person? No, most of the time."

"And if people proved you wrong?" Seth queried, his smirk slowly returning.

Bee rolled her eyes. "I'll let you know when it happens."

"What about these people?" Seth countered, gesturing at the others.

Bee glanced around, thinking about how to answer that. Nat had shifted from Ty to Joey, gently holding his shoulder as they talked. Well, he smiled and nodded, she talked. Ty had jumped in the river to cool off. Olivia and Zed were headed into the 'girls' tent.

Did they prove her wrong?

"No," Bee decided.

"Why?" Seth pushed, his voice rising with buoyant curiosity.

"Because we have these," Bee answered, tapping her forefinger on the bright, spiraling tattoo that covered her cheek. "We're in hell. What we do isn't normal; it isn't good; it's just necessary. It's what we have to do to get home."

"You sound like a soldier," Seth noted. His smirk was gone, replaced with something grimmer.

"I do?" Bee asked, genuinely surprised. She hadn't thought of it like that.

"My roommate at school had an older brother," Seth explained. He looked away, staring distantly at the mountainside. "He used to come around all the time. He was an officer. Served in Iraq. One time, we all got smashed at this club, right? And I get back from some party and he's sitting there. Just sitting. I ask him what's wrong. He starts talking about hell, about how you don't think about the reality; you make it something else. You focus on getting home, on winning, and try to forget the lives you take on the way."

Bee nodded. The story caught her, hook-like. It wasn't even that long, but there was a cold sadness to it, like tears on a snowy day.

"So, yeah, you sound kind of like that," Seth added, shrugging. "Not the same, but similar."

"Maybe finding you wasn't a total waste," Bee said, a small smile tugging at her lips. She was, and it was comforting.

"I think so," he agreed. He poked her with an elbow. "Becoming Slender Man lunch would've sucked."

"No shit?" Bee said, all sarcasm. "On a similar topic, don't elbow me."

"Whatcha gonna do? Eat me?" Seth joked, jostling his shoulder into hers.

Bee planted one hand and shoved him with the other. He was bigger, but he wasn't expecting it. He fell sideways, digging one arm into the sand to catch himself.

"I shove back," Bee informed him.

Seth laughed and sat up again. "Oh, really? I would never have guessed."

"And on that note, I'm gonna go get a drink, before you get any dumb ideas."

Bee stood and headed to the water. She'd refill her bottle and then go back to the tent. Shade would be nice, and it wouldn't be long till the rain kicked in. Hopefully Seth would back off. Either that or she'd shove him a few more times and then he'd leave her alone. Actually telling him she was lesbian wasn't an option. Guys never took that well. They either figured it was a lie, and therefore rude, or a challenge. Neither was good news, especially not in wilderness-land.

Maybe Nat could be convinced to distract him. Nat liked guys, and Seth was a guy. It'd be great. Or maybe Zed.

Bee cackled halfway through bending down to fill her bottle. She caught herself before she fell in, but it was close. The thought of Zed pushing Seth around was comedy gold.

"Ah, good shit," said Bee, wiping a tear from her eye as she stood and capped the bottle.

The first droplets began to fall from the clouds, splashing in the river and the pools beyond.

The rain had given the world a clean, salt-less scent, like the tang of the ocean and its breezes had been washed away by the night. Brightest greens and browns and rich grays stood out in the woods, leaves and roots and trunks and rocks creating a layered chorus of abundant color; fresh, rejuvenated.

When the ocean came into view through the trees, it was a mingling; an expanse of blue-green that seemed to flow from the leafy foliage. The shift was subtle, leaves and waves bouncing to a similar beat, given away by the sudden waft of salt. The breeze was thick, damp with spray and foam, almost sticky.

Peering down from the cap of a boulder that stood like a tower on the wall of stone that lined the beach, Olivia's eyes narrowed. The beach was thin here, only a couple dozen meters across. The far side was lined with rocks that shored the sand against the crash of the waves beyond. Spray flew over the lip from time to time, wetting the rocks as quick as the sun could dry them.

Olivia looked right and left. To her right, Ty and Bee crouched, watching the woods in that direction. To her left, Zed and Joey were in similar poses. Without looking, she knew that Nat and Seth were behind her, just as they had been for the last few minutes. They'd all been here for minutes now, waiting.

Waiting because Olivia didn't like it.

One hand outstretched, Olivia pulled a palm-full of water from the damp air. She dropped the map-orb in. It spun, but she caught the expanding display before it could rise like a sign saying 'we're here!' She held it down, keeping it to the size of a phone screen.

According to the super-helpful map, Olivia was standing on the enemy. Right now. So where the hell were they?

Yup. She didn't like this.

Not at all.

Bloody tricky bug-bastards.

With a sigh, Olivia flicked a rock towards Zed. The blonde turned away from the wood, eyes wide and focused, ready. Olivia pointed at her, at Joey, down the wall, and then curved her fingers along the beach.

Zed nodded, tapped Joey's shoulder, and headed off down the wall. She went further than Olivia had intended, but that was better than too close. Olivia didn't bother to ask Bee and Ty to do the same. They were improving, but they weren't as good. Joey was a better shot than any of them, and Zed had enough skill to make up for the size difference between her and Ty.

Plus, Olivia didn't want to trap the bugs. Traps made people fight harder. Better to get them running and chase. Chases were good. People got tired of running, but at different times, slowly wearing down until they give in and fight, one by one. Easy.

On the beach, thirty meters down-wall from Olivia, Zed stopped, waved, and pointed at the base of the boulder beneath Olivia's feet.

Shit.

Olivia pointed downwards, exaggerating her look of incredulous disbelief.

In response, Zed angled her hand and lowered it, as though descending a stair, or a ramp.

Or a tunnel.

A bloody tunnel.

The bugs had dug themselves a fort.

Olivia tossed a rock at Ty's shoulder. It bounced off, harmless, but he nearly fell over, eyes wide and nostrils flaring as he looked at her. She rolled her eyes, just so he got the point of 'wait to be called on' including 'don't get scared when you get called on,' and gestured for them to go down to the beach.

Catching Seth's curious eye, Olivia pointed at him, then at where she was crouched, then held up two fingers and panned across the trees. She waited for his nod before she moved on. He didn't look happy, but she didn't really care. He wasn't going into a fight until he got over the whole 'rich and sullen' thing and got a handle on not getting killed. And they really did need a lookout.

As Olivia stepped from rock to rock down the wall, she could hear Nat's boots crunch along behind her. A dozen meters over, Ty and Bee were already on the sand. Zed and Joey were still up on the big rock, watching the bottom of the boulder.

Coming around the edge of the gigantic block of stone, Olivia caught sight of the tunnel's mouth. It was thin, not quite tall enough to stand in, about a meter across at the widest. It was also dark, deep, and entirely foreboding.

A frown tugged at Olivia's lips. She circled around the slight rise that'd built up around the hole. The rise spread a few meters in every direction, totally encircling the hole. They must've just shoved the sand out and tamped it down coming and going.

So, one route in, one route out, and no way to know what the hell was in there.

Olivia's hold on her bow tightened, her fingers pressing tight against the grip. Everyone was in position. One spear and one bow on each side, her and Nat in the middle. The problem was that it only worked if the bugs came out. If they had to go in, it'd be one at a time and crawling. Neither of those was optimal for ultra-bug slaying.

A meter wide. It really was eerily tiny. Somehow that surprised her. The bugs were so long, their legs adding a half-meter of height, but they were probably less than a meter wide if they sort of squeezed it all in.

"I could try shooting Current at them?" Bee offered. A wave's crash rescued her voice from being akin to a shout in the silence.

Olivia raised an eyebrow.

Bee made shooting gestures with a finger guns.

Frankly, Olivia couldn't fault her logic. Maybe it'd scare them out. Worst case, what, they went further into the hole? Worth a try.

Olivia pointed at Zed and Ty, the spear holders, and waved them forward. There was a wait while Zed and Joey came down the wall. Once they were on the sand, Zed joined Ty and they headed in. Bee followed, palms raised. Nat, Joey, and Olivia waited, a bow-armed semi-circle.

A few seconds later, Bee launched a trio of pale, frosty spikes down the hole. They hissed through the air and disappeared into the shadowed hole.

Zed and Ty stayed spears up, while Bee fell back to Olivia's left, out of the archers' way.

Seconds ticked by.

Nothing.

Nearly a minute passed.

Then Olivia remembered that these assholes were immune to Current.

Ok, new plan. No more messing around. They needed to figure out what the hell was going on, and hand signals weren't cutting it. The bugs were in the hole, Zed and Ty had them covered; it would be fine.

"Bee," Olivia said, keeping her voice low, "Can you feel your spikes?"

"The spikes that these guys can't be hurt by? Yeah," Bee replied.

Olivia's teeth ground together. "How deep is the hole?"

"Oh!" Bee said, suddenly thinking that Olivia's plan had been to gauge the distance all along. "It's about twenty feet."

Internally, Olivia translated that into normal people measurement; a little over six meters, maybe? It might be a bend in the tunnel, or it might be where it spilled into a chamber. A room at the end of a chute would be easier to defend. If that were the case, the bugs would be coming from all sides at the other end.

"What's the plan?" Joey queried, looking to Olivia for direction.

"We could just wait," Nat suggested. She shifted nervously from one foot to the other. "Starve them out?"

Zed nodded. "That might be our best op-"

But Zed was cut off as three massive, ten-legged bugs burst from the sandy mound. They rose up, lashing out with their forelimbs. Loamy plating and dark chitin made them monstrous, shadowy beasts on the sunlit, golden beach.

Sand flew, spraying across Olivia's face, and something smashed into her, launching her through the air. She hit the ground, rolled, and fought to wipe the sand from her eyes.

Nat screamed.

Bee shouted, cursing unintelligibly.

A breath hissed between Olivia's lips. Rage roiled in her chest, beating at the sudden helplessness. She shook her head, trying to dislodge the sand. Blinking, she tried to see.

The stony lip of the beach was still behind her, the wall in front. The three bugs were upright, like insectile centaurs with too many arms and too much armor. The one on the right was chasing Joey. He dodged and wove, slashing at its limbs with his knife.

Hunched and scrabbling, the leftmost bug clawed at any icy dome the size of a bed. Through the crystalline lattice, Bee's face stared up, horror and determination writ large as frost poured from her palms.

The center one stood over Nat's prone body, one of its legs through her torso, another three fending off Zed and Ty's spears. The duo tried to flank it, fighting to pierce the meaty gap between front armor and back. The bug jerked and twitched, twisting to look one way then the other as its claws slashed at the gnarled, sharpened wood.

Bow raised, Olivia waited. Timing. All in the timing.

The center bug lunged, menacing Ty as he nearly scored a hit. It dragged Nat along, hooked in the crook of one segmented leg.

Olivia released.

The arrow was so fast. It appeared to sprout from the bug's side.

The bug turned, keening. Two claws poked at the shaft, confused.

Shouting, Zed charged in. She slammed her spear into the bug's blindside. It lashed out, trying to catch her. One limb hit and tossed her across the beach, clinging to her spear.

Ty dove forward, gripping his spear by the very butt as he went for the arrowed side. It thudded off chitin as the bug lurched backward. It yanked out the arrow and flung it away. It keened, a long fearful note that hung in the air, thick as the salt. Then it fell.

The other two bugs froze, and then spun towards their downed ally. The one attacking the ice-dome butted its massive armored body against it once more, then charged at Ty and Zed.

Joey's bug ignored him completely, opting to charge as well. A second later, it froze, quivering as Joey's arrow hit its left side and Olivia's its right. It sank, clawing at the sand. Joey kept shooting, but Olivia focused on the third bug.

Ty and Zed braced their spears, but the bug dropped its head, planted its forelimbs, and flipped. The thick, armor-plated weight of its lower body rose, and then fell like. The two dove out of the way, barely escaping the crashing weight of the meters long bug.

Or, nearly escaped. Spear-less, Zed crawled, pulling at the sand as her right leg hung, limp and eerily flat behind her.

The bug rolled to its feet again. Righted, the insect peered down at Zed, then at Ty, who still had his spear. Armed, but laying down on top of his spear's shaft, Ty looked distinctly like a wrong way up turtle.

Olivia breathed out as she released, just as they'd practiced. Her third arrow flashed towards the bug's face.

It twitched to the side. The arrow skittered off its shell.

Silent, deadly, and gigantic; the bug dropped onto all ten limbs and barreled towards Olivia. Casual, almost negligent, one insectoid arms flicked out and punched through Ty's leg with a sound like wet suction and chopped beef. He screamed, his mouth going wide as he stared at the spreading scarlet stain.

The bug hadn't slowed.

Goal: Survive.

Problem: giant bug, immune to Current.

Added issue: limited weaponry.

Olivia was screwed. The world was so quiet all of a sudden, so sedate. Her thoughts raced as her heart rose to her throat. The image of a rocket launcher came to mind, but that didn't do shit right now.

Solutions. There had to be a solution.

Joey missed, his arrow clacking off the thickly armored joint of an insectoid limb.

Wait, Current?

Current worked. The file had said it was neutralized on contact, but the dome had held. Bee's dome. Maybe it took time. The bugs could only damage so much at a time? Didn't help. She couldn't make a dome, and anything with an edge would liquidate too quickly on contact.

New plan, Olivia decided, releasing another arrow. It missed, but the bug flinched away to protect its face.

It flinched.

Plan.

Olivia drew, those pounding, claw tipped arms getting closer.

So close.

Meters away now.

Olivia tensed her legs, bent her knees, and released. The bug turned its face away again. The arrow skidded off again.

It was still coming, but it couldn't see Olivia. It couldn't see her bent knees springing forward, throwing her under. She landed on her back, knife drawn. The bug flew by overhead, close enough to touch.

Close enough to stab.

Olivia's right hand swung up and around, shoving the overgrown knife into the bug's unarmored side. The bug's momentum dragged against her grip, threatening to tear the blade away. She held on, willing her hand to hold. Current raced up her arm, cold and soothing as her muscles burned with effort. The knife didn't catch and she wasn't dragged, it just kept cutting as the bug fought to arrest its momentum.

A limb on the opposite side shot towards Olivia, narrowly missing her skull. Another, on the other side, sliced across the meat of her thigh.

The bug stopped, twisting to get a better shot at Olivia as she lay beneath it.

Desperate, every second stretching on and on, Olivia grabbed the lip of the bug's lower plating with her free hand and heaved herself up against its chitinous belly. She drove the knife deeper. Hot, wet guts and gore swallowed her hand up to the elbow.

The keening came again, desperate and afraid.

Olivia twisted the knife.

More bug arms slashed at Olivia. The bug's length coiled around her, fetal. It fell, collapsing onto its far side. The motion pulled her along, leaving her upright. The attacks became directionless, random twitches.

Breathless, Olivia pushed through the bright light and the constant throb of pain from her leg. No time. She pulled her arm free of the bug's innards. Her legs hadn't been caught when the bug fell, but her wounded left trembled.

One of the chaotic twitches jerked at her. It caught on her belt, throwing her back even as it punched through. It slid free as she fell back.

Olivia landed, clutching at the hole between her ribs. That wasn't where a hole should be. This wasn't the Goal. There were Rules against this. She'd screwed up, but she didn't want to die. Damn, she'd been doing ok so far. Even started trusting people, a little. Not much. Mostly Zed. Nat too, maybe.

Damn.

Olivia really didn't want to die.

Strange. Dying. Again. Wasn't Olivia's first time, but the others hadn't stuck. The whole gang thing had been the worst. Leaving a gang wasn't supposed to be a survivable experience, apparently. This dying didn't feel like it had then. Maybe it was because the hole was bigger this time. Olivia had gotten lucky back then. They'd missed the muscles she'd needed to swim. The bug might've missed her organs, somehow, but it didn't seem likely.

Olivia coughed. A red mist sprayed across the sand. Blood in her lungs. Bad.

Still not dead though.

Weird.

The painful, searing heat slowly faded. Cooling chills fluttered through Olivia's chest.

Chills.

Current?

Healing, maybe. Slow though, like someone was slowly dialing up the 'save Stabby's life' setting. Opening her eyes, Olivia tried to figure out how Nat had healed herself in time to get over here and help.

There was no one there.

Well, there was a very large bug a few steps away, but other than that…

More cold.

Goal: Survive.

Olivia focused on that, on living, on breathing and feeling and moving and being whole and well. She remembered the good moments, the thrill of racing across the sand, of swimming in the river, of how her back muscles flexed as she drew a bow.

The flutters turned into rushes, floods of Current that slammed against Olivia's wounds, pressing tight as the pain fled.

"Rule Five of Alien Tropics: When Dying, Decide Not To," Olivia whispered, a smile pulling at her mouth as she realized what had happened. Current followed will, so accepting death meant that it wouldn't try to heal anything. Fight death, and it'd keep you alive till there was nothing left.

Not for the first time, Olivia felt adrenaline and pride surge through her, doubling down on her Current's already heady rush. Current rocked.

"Hell yeah," Olivia declared, standing up. The pain was gone, and a cursory check told her that she was bloody, but otherwise fine.

The bug had left a thin corridor between its head and tail, so Olivia took it. She had a team to help after all. She could already hear the shouting.

Nat was down. Seth and Bee crouched over her, their hands pressed down on the massive hole in her chest. Zed was doing the same to Ty. Joey stood over the bug that'd attacked him, staring in Olivia's direction. For a moment, his slack confusion remained. Then the sight of her seemed to ravel his thoughts back together.

"Joey! That's all ten of them. Gather the arrows, then check the tunnel," Olivia barked. His posture shifted, straightening, snapping to attention, then he was off.

"Olivia?" Bee said, shock in her slack jaw and wide eyes.

"Olivia?" Zed asked, sounding as surprised as Bee looked. "What do I do?" she added, her gaze flicking down.

"He awake?" Olivia asked, heading towards Nat while advising her on Ty. If Olivia had to heal both of them she'd be out of juice.

"Yes," Zed replied, glancing down to check that his eyes were still open.

"Tell him to focus on wanting to live, and then focus on wanting him to live," Olivia ordered, fighting to keep her voice hard and stable. Her heart was bouncing, racing ahead, excited; exhilarated; thrilled at the revelation of her new Rule.

"Ok," Zed said. Her brow furrowed, her voice dropped, and she growled something that sounded like, 'You better fucking listen or I'm going to kill you for making me the one who got you killed on top of owing you my life.'

It sounded pretty serious, and Ty nodded quickly, so Olivia didn't worry about them. They'd last while she took care of Nat. She dropped to her knees beside Bee and opposite Seth, her hands settling on top of theirs.

"Move," Olivia ordered. Bee pulled back immediately, looking on expectantly.

"Why?" Seth demanded, the crack in his voice undermining the sullen rage.

Bee's hand rocketed out and clocked Seth in the chin. He sprawled across the sand, limp as much from shock as impact.

Without Seth, Olivia's hands pressed into a gaping hole in Nat's chest. The blood coated her fingers, hot and thick. Swallowing the surge of bile, Olivia poured Current from her palms. Something thrummed inside of Nat, then thudded. Her heart? It hadn't stopped. That was probably a good sign. Olivia could feel the wound filling. Current turned to muscle and vein and tendon, weaving fabric where tear had been. She could see Nat whole again; she could see her, hear her voice. Seconds ticked by. Current flowed round and round, a tide that drew the wound closer and closer to gone.

Eventually, Olivia felt skin close beneath her hands.

"Done," Olivia declared. She went to stand, but her limbs didn't move right. She stumbled, slumping back onto the sand.

"Olivia?" Bee demanded, helping her sit up. "You ok? What's wrong?"

Olivia's fingers tingled. So did her toes. She felt… hollow? Exhausted.

"What's wrong?" Bee repeated.

"Current," Olivia muttered, fighting back a yawn. "Tired."

"Can you take mine?" Bee offered, clamping her hand on Olivia's, as though that would magically do something.

Huh. None of them had tried that. It'd never come up. They'd all just done their own stuff. Olivia frowned, fighting back the urge to sleep. "Try."

Bee nodded. A second later, something butted against Olivia's hand. No, not butted. It was like Bee's touch had begun to vibrate. It hummed silently against Olivia's palm. Then the Current came flooding in, gates thrown wide.

Between one breath and the next, Olivia's eyes shot open, soaking in reality as color and sound and scent became all too detailed. Current roared in her veins, cool and quick.

"Ok, time to go," Olivia said, flung to her feet the minute she considered it.

"Wha-" Bee began.

"Doin' great. Good job. No worries. Got this," Olivia replied. She flew across the sand as her feet raced towards Ty and Zed. Ty was fine. Zed's leg was not, and she was already getting pale. Paler. Really, for someone that white, how come she didn't have a ton of sunburn yet? Zed was looking at her funny. Oh. She might've said that out loud. Oops.

Olivia's hands latched onto Zed's leg. The blonde's corresponding scream died halfway from her lips, replaced with a look of shock as her leg thickened, crushed bone reforming. It didn't even take all the Current Bee had given, but it did take the manic edge off.

"Shit, Bee," Olivia said, staggering at the dizzy rush that hit as she stood upright again. "How much Current do you have?"

"Not much?" Bee supplied, watching her with a look that hadn't yet decided on amusement or concern.

"Try somewhere between…" Olivia said. She trailed off as she tried to think of the words.

"Ouch and boing?" Bee guessed, smirking.

Olivia frowned. "No?"

"It's a movie thing," Bee said. She waved it off. "Glad to know I'm not the weakest though. Thanks."

"No worries," Olivia said, giving her a thumbs up. "Point is; you got Current."

"Thanks," Bee said, beaming.

"Thanks here too," Zed agreed. Her hands ran down her leg, tentative along once-flattened form.

"Can't have my backup boss getting de-legged on me," Olivia noted, raising one eyebrow in her direction.

Zed chuckled. "I think that means that I'm your Corporal."

"Funny?" Ty prompted, sitting up.

"I was a Corporal in the Army before this." Zed shook her head, rueful. "Took me nearly three weeks to work my way back up the ranks."

"And that makes her?" Ty asked, pointing at Olivia.

Zed stood and offered Ty her hand. "Sergeant, sort of. Not that it really matters."

"You can be the sergeant," Olivia offered. "I'll be Boss."

"Pretty sure that's not how that works," Zed muttered, but her smile widened.

"Works for me," Bee added.

Joey came around the bug that'd nearly killed Olivia, her knife in hand. "I like it."

"I'm in," Ty agreed, a slight smile baring his teeth. They shone in the sun, highlighting the darkness of his skin. He towered over Zed, despite the slight hunch to his shoulders.

"Second thought," Joey said, raising one finger to get their attention. "Are we going to talk about what just happened, or are we going to focus on healing, searching the cave, and getting back to our tents?"

"Second option," Bee voted, followed by a chorus of agreement.

"Joey and Bee, collect the rest of the weapons," Olivia said, taking her knife from Joey. "Ty, rest up, because you're carrying Nat if she doesn't wake up in a few minutes. Seth, stay. Zed, you and I are checking the cave."

Olivia didn't wait to see if any of them did what she'd said. They would. Maybe not Seth, but he couldn't mess it up that badly. Worst-case scenario was he'd injure himself on a bug.

Falling in beside Olivia as she neared the tunnel, Zed asked, "Light?"

Pulling the orb from a pocket, Olivia held it out and willed water to her palm. It began to spin and the hexes rose. Turning her hand, she held the water to her palm. The hexes shifted, acting like short-range torches. Workable.

Olivia crawled down into the hole. The sand was firm, packed in place between rounded stones. Three divots pocked the ground at the bottom, where Bee's spikes had landed. Just beyond, the tunnel opened up around them. Only a couple meters across, with walls lined in rocks of varying sizes, the room wasn't big. Nearly half the ceiling was one big mass of stone, the bases of the boulder they'd stood on before. A trio of cases sat at the center of the room. Similar to the stickmen's, they had rounded edges and smooth, blue-green metallic exteriors.

Careful, Olivia checked the mechanism on the left box. Her fingers sank into the spongy sphere that joined the lid to the bottom. It looked a lot like the map, but it felt softer. The lid flipped up, exposing a rack of five ovoid blocks. They hung from faint dents in the box's exterior, seemingly wedged in place.

"Those look like explosives," Zed noted, wary as she peered over Olivia's shoulder. She opened the case on the right. "And these look like… armor maybe?"

"Would've been handy to have earlier," Olivia grumbled. She checked the middle one. Its interior was lined with a spongy material, the pores so wide that it looked like holier Swiss cheese. Another map sat at the center. "We're going to have to start numbering these," she grouched, closing the case and lifting it by the small dips on the exterior.

Zed chuckled. "Take yours first, I'll get the armor."

With a nod, Olivia crawled ahead. She ignored the fact that her box was only half the size of Zed's. She was smaller. It was fine. At the top, they spilled out into the sun. The heat of the day blasted against her face, making her blink and tear up. Dropping her box, she slid out of Zed's way while she rubbed at her eyes.

"Wow," Zed mumbled, tearing up as well. "That's a lot."

"No shit," Olivia snorted. She looked out at the ocean to help her eyes get accustomed.

"I'll get the last one," Zed said, turning around to head back down. "Better to do it before I get used to the light."

"Ball?" Olivia said, offering her makeshift torch.

"I remember where it was," Zed said, already halfway in. "I'll try not to get lost."

Olivia grunted. "I'll send Ty in to rescue you if you're not back in five."

Zed's groan echoed from the tunnel's mouth.

Chuckling, Olivia checked on the others. Seth, Ty, and Nat were where she'd left them. Joey and Bee were down the beach a ways, washing the bug guts off of the spears and arrows. Thinking about her own gory mess, she glanced down at her right arm. She'd gone elbow deep, but there was no mess. Huh.

Curious, Olivia dug her hand into the sand. When she pulled it out, sand was caked on. Nothing happened.

Ok. So the suit didn't automatically magic away any mess. Good to know. Olivia thought about how annoying the sand was, giving her best mental Anakin impression. A little tingle raced along the sleeve of her suit, like a gentle breeze across her skin. The sand was swept away.

Olivia smiled. That was cool. So, super-suits came with built in cleaning, powered by Current. She checked where she'd been stabbed. And where her thigh had been slashed. The suit was fine in both cases. Add self-repairing to the list. She glanced at the others again. None of the others were sweating, despite the full-body suits on a hot day, and no one looked cold. Temperature regulating, self-repairing, easy-clean suits.

For the first time in years, Olivia felt a surge of pride at her threads. She'd never heard of anything this badass back on Earth, and they could be a lot worse. Mottled gray-green was perfect out here.

Opening the smaller case, Olivia plucked the next map from its setting. Current pooled in her hand. A moment later, she had the next target in full color. It was up in the mountains, perched somewhere on the near slope, North of their camp on the river. Close. Maybe a day's walk. Two.

"Anything interesting?" Ty asked. He looked over from his seat next to Nat. Seth copied the gesture, still sullen.

"Next enemy," Olivia said. "Looks like they're pretty close."

Olivia brought up the image option. Robots this time. They were only a meter tall, with four squat legs and four long, segmented limbs, each capped with eight multi-jointed fingers. One image showed one collapsed, segments of outer plating fitting together into a smooth ovoid. The one next to it was on a loop, limbs popping free, the upper third rising from the base to expose the arm ports. At the top of the oval, peaking the rising upper third, a small head appeared, an array of glowing blue sensors and retractable rods pointed in every direction.

Basically, Olivia summarized to herself, it looked like a nasty piece of shit. The new gear had better be pretty great.

Scraping, scratching sounds came from the hole, with Zed appearing at their heels. She dropped the last case on the sand and flopped down, lying on the mound at the tunnel's mouth. She took a deep, calming breath. "We won."

"We did," Olivia agreed. She shot the blonde a smile as she drained the Current from the map.

One thing at a time.

For now, they'd won.

They'd worry about the next fight later.

Olivia nodded. "Let's get going."

"Aye-aye, Boss," Zed said. She groaned as she rose to her feet.

Joey straightened, and nodded. He and Bee shook water from the last few arrows. Ty stood, heaving Nat up in his arms. Seth leapt up beside him, like a nervous shadow.

"Let's head out!" Zed directed. Her usual smile returned as she picked up a case and led the way up the wall. Joey and Bee took the others, waving Olivia off when she offered to hold onto hers.

Pausing as the case bearers went up the wall, Olivia glanced back. She took in the leaking corpses they were leaving behind. The first challenge had been the wildlife. Then Stickmen. Now bugs. Next was machines. She didn't know how many more there'd be, but they needed to get better at dealing with them. The bugs' trap had nearly been the end.

Lucky wasn't enough.

Olivia rubbed the handle of her long knife. She'd have to come up with some tricks to even the playing field, before a too-clever alien offed her and the others.

Zed kept walking right by the tents and into the stream. She dropped her case as she passed, but it was the water she focused on. Sweat, blood, and a thick, miasmic wrongness hung over her. She was too damn tired to do much about it other than sleep, or so she'd thought, right up until the river came into sight through the trees.

Plunging into the sun-warmed water, Zed brought her arms forward and out, stroking towards the center.

"You alright?" Bee said. Her voice was distant, muddled by water and distance. She must've followed Zed to the water.

After a few breaths, Zed said. "Not sure." She flipped over to drift on her back. A minute later, she righted herself. Bee was still there, capping her bottle.

"Have you nearly died before? When you were a soldier, I mean," Bee queried, hooking her bottle to her belt.

Zed planted her feet, knees bent to keep the water at her chin. "Yeah, but always from inside a tank."

"Scary?"

"It's a lot of trust," Zed admitted. "You have to trust your support. A tank is strong, it hits hard, but it's like a turtle. Once you have something that'll break its shell, you just have to hit it."

"How's being on the receiving end?"

"It's not…" Zed trailed off. Big, armored, hard hitting. Huh. Not far off. "Ok. It was… different."

"You hated it," Bee guessed, her mouth twisting into an unhappy smile.

Zed said nothing.

"Talk to Olivia. She's used to fighting tanks," Bee suggested. She turned and began to make her way back to the tents.

"How?" Zed asked, her voice soft, hollowed.

Bee looked back at her. The moonlight cascaded across her features, making her eyes into inky, empty depths. "You look like you can't get rid of the weight of that bug. Can't heal it off, can't walk it off, can't wash it off."

Watching her go, Zed realized she was right. That hard, scaled carapace had weighed her down, smashing bone and muscle into a paste. Somehow, even after the destruction was undone, the oozing slime that'd coated its shell remained. It was like oil between her fingers. She rubbed her arms, trying once again to banish the sensation.

Olivia, huh? Maybe. In the morning.

For now, Zed should sleep. They'd eaten this morning, but the trek had taken the rest of the day and late into the night. Lucky they made it back at all, really. If the moon weren't so bright, or if the tree's canopy were denser, they'd have broken a lot of toes and ankles along the way.

Zed remembered the way the trees had moved, the way birds had flitted overhead, racing through the leaves. She'd seen a few before, but never so many. Once, back when she'd been on her own, she'd found a nest with a half dozen little gray birds at the top of a tree. She'd taken one to eat. The others had woken, silent and still, watching her as she backed away. It'd been unearthly. What kind of world had quiet birds that flew at night? Zed smiled sadly and climbed out of the water. The answer was pretty easy. It was the kind of world that had mountains of tiered pools, Kaskans hunting the waterways, and aliens playing a weird team version of the Hunger Games in the backyard.

Stepping onto the beach, Zed sighed. Damn confusing suit. Her skin was already feeling dry. On the other hand, at least she wouldn't have to take it off before she went to sleep. Thinking it over as she headed back to her tent, she realized that everyone was sleeping in their suit. Nat and Bee hadn't the first night, but they'd collapsed into their blankets without changing on the second night.

Zed gave a mental shrug as she slipped into the 'girls' tent. Space aliens making super handy suits made sense. The suits had probably kept the Stickmen from freezing on the cold nights. They hadn't had enough fat to stay warm on their own.

Under her blankets, settled into her own little nest, Zed shivered. Suits, birds; the slime was still there. She'd talk to Olivia tomorrow. Maybe it'd help.

Zed ran a hand along her leg.

Still there. Good.

Just for a second, it hadn't been.

Nat woke with a start, her nerves on fire, except for a hollow in her chest.

There was nothing there.

Just… nothing.

Fear rolled through her.

Nat's eyes shot open. Her lungs heaved, fighting for oxygen.

Dark curls and green eyes greeted her. Two soft, warm hands came, cupping her face, thumbs grazing her cheekbones.

Blinking, Nat tried to fight through the mess. Heady with fear, breathless, some part of her missing, she grasped at a memory. Something huge, looming, limbs stabbing out. Then the feeling of hollowness. The emptiness throbbed, synching with the shadow of something huge and insectoid overhead. The two battered at Nat's senses, smashing like waves against her mind.

A forehead pressed against hers, warm and smooth. Soft whispers came next, hissed pleas and hummed comforts that sent warm breath washing across the lower half of Nat's face. The sound, the heat, and the touch pushed back at the emptiness.

A second later it came back.

Nat's right hand shot up, clamped down on Seth's left and pinned it in place. Her left went to the back of his neck, pulling him close.

There was too much emptiness, too much fear. Nat knew she was grasping at straws, her psyche clutching at the first comfort she could find, but she didn't care. Better to grasp than to do nothing.

Then his lips were on Nat's. Soft, delicate, and dancing sinuously, she ate them up, loving the way they filled her mind. Her arm tensed and pulled him closer when he tried to fall back. He pressed in, the hesitation gone, their dance suddenly feverous. The blanket lifted away, a cool breeze running up her suited torso. Even through the mottled cloth she could feel it. She shivered. A second later, heat replaced the breeze, another body pressing tight to hers as the blankets closed in around them.

Warmth flooded Nat, rushing through her veins. It shoved back the emptiness, blasting rivers of life through the void. Her breath became labored, fighting to bring in enough oxygen through her nose, not wanting to break their lip lock.

God, they were so soft! His lips danced on and on with Nat's, pushing and pulling. Her right hand on his neck rose, tangling in those curls. He pulled at her thigh, yanking it across his hip, drawing them even closer.

Nat hummed, happy, smiling with what parts of her face weren't occupied with kissing. There was so much sensation, a choir to drown out even the memory of silence.

His hand glided up her back, searching for something. It paused at the neck of her suit, feeling along the hem.

"The zipper," Nat explained, hissing out the words between kisses, "Fell off."

"How do you take it off?" Seth pulled away to meet her eyes. He was smirking again.

Nat felt dizzy for a moment, her eyes flicking from his face as a whole to his lips alone. The first was like art, almost unnerving up close. The second was a more visceral kind of beauty, one full of promise and memory and feelings. She tried to kiss him again.

That smirk widened as the hand on her cheek held her back.

"How?" he repeated.

The pause stretched, allowing thoughts to filter through Nat's haze. Her conversation with Bee came to mind. No condoms. No birth control. Nothing. Sex would be bad, and a full body suit was a very precipitous slope to slip down.

"No," Nat said simply, her smile becoming sad. "Isn't this enough?"

"Of course!" he agreed, coming in for another searing kiss.

Settling against him once again, Nat's tension fell away. She'd been worried for some reason, but whatever it'd been, it was gone now. No worries, no tension, just kisses and warmth.

Waking up was like standing between two big rocks that were both trying to roll downhill in opposite directions. Ty was pretty sure that being the meat-pulp in a rock-mash sandwich hadn't been the plan for today, but he was too groggy to be sure. After a few seconds, he was able to identify the metaphorical rocks.

One was his stomach, possessing the edge of a physical need unsatiated since yesterday morning.

The other, his bladder, was rather less long-suffering, but no less demanding.

Yet again, Ty's deep dislike of cursing butted against his inability to articulate how frustrating his current situation was. Not even because of the rocks. Frankly, both wouldn't be that hard to handle in short order, but his metaphorical feet were sunk deep into a swampy quagmire. It was a swamp identifiable as a combination of the deep need to sleep and the infinitely comfortable warmth of his mound of blankets.

Trapped by quagmire, wedged between the two rocks, in a fog of sleep, Ty's call to reality was when someone loudly declared, "Of course!"

Why they felt the need to say it so loudly, Ty had no idea.

Rolling onto his back, Ty began to rub at his eyes, preparing himself. He fully intended to tell off whatever jerk had woken him up. It felt like he'd barely slept at all!

Soft smacking sounds filtered through. Not like actual smacking, more the slightly wet, sucking, enthused smacks of a heavy oral interaction.

Ty's eyes shot wide.

This was atrociously awkward.

The smacking was close, only a meter or two away. Who slept…

Seth.

Who was Seth–

Some humming sounds accompanied a low moan.

Oh. Nat.

Well, now Ty would have to live with knowing that she was recognizable by moan. Either that or he was a talented moan identifier. Or everyone was identifiable by moan and no one had bothered to include that in any of the books, novellas, smutty short stories, or web-posted erotica he'd read.

Shifting uncomfortably, Ty coughed. Pointedly.

The smacking and slurping.

He coughed again.

A hissed whisper, then the aggressive make-out stopped.

Worried that they might think he was actually coughing, Ty faux-coughed a third time. And added a gravelly, throat clearing grunt. There, that should clarify-

They giggled. Seth made a shushing sound, and then giggled as well. That set Nat off again. After a few seconds, one of them rose, climbed out from under their blankets and headed for the door. The suffering groan of the remaining member of the duo made that one definitely Seth, with Nat as the departing figure.

Seth stood and followed her out.

To insure a maximum chance of avoiding any further awkwardness, Ty feigned sleep. His first choice would be to go back to bed, but there was sunlight outside. That meant he had slept through the night, and sleeping through the day would be bad.

Eventually Zed would decide it was workout time, and then being in bed would be Bad. Capital B. Ty took a moment to guess her likely response. Kicking him was one option. Dumping cold water on him was another. The first fit with her violent tendencies. The latter cost Current. It'd probably be the former.

"I'll pass," Ty said. He leveraged himself up and out from under his blankets.

Joey's nest was already empty, as usual, and Seth's a mess of outspread cloth.

Grumbling unintelligibly about his messy tent-mates, Ty rearranged his blankets into a neat square. Joey wasn't really that messy, but he certainly didn't fold properly. His attempt was more of a series of corners, flaps, and edges tossed back towards the middle.

Knife, bottle, bow, and arrows strapped on, Ty ducked under the flap and into the warmth of the sun. Wincing and blinking back he abundant light, he made out the sun nearly overhead. Noon-ish.

Wow.

How'd Zed managed not to reflexively kick, order, shout, or tell someone to do something yet?

Ty laughed at his own joke. Good not to vocalize it though. Not because he worried it'd hurt her, she was tough, but because it'd probably get him hurt. Self-preservation...

That thought trailed away. Ty's attention was snatched away by a whiff of something beyond delicious. Following it, his eyes settled on the circle of stones, the small fire at their center, and the meter-long baby-croc staked over it. Olivia sat nearby, slowly turning the spit that impaled the fish from nose to tail.

"Almost," Olivia noted, barely glancing at him.

"Perfect," Ty said, smiling widely as he sat down. He did his best not to drool, but he did wipe some excess moisture from his lower lip. He wasn't sure if she meant he'd almost gotten the Zed Treatment, or if he'd almost missed food, or almost had to hear far worse than some kissing.

"They wake you?" Olivia asked. She jerked her head to indicate something over her shoulder.

Ty looked.

Seth and Nat were in the water. There were a lot of nervous smiles, laughter, and teasing splashes.

Ty groaned, nodded, and opted not to speak lest his annoyance show.

Olivia grunted and turned the spit. "Problem?"

"Maybe," Ty said, considering that. He didn't like it. Them. It just… It didn't sit right. "I don't ship it."

"What?" Olivia asked. Her gray eyes sparked and a tiny smile tugged at her lips.

Ty rolled his eyes. Didn't they have the Internet in England? Or wherever it was she'd lived. England made sense with her accent, but it could've been anywhere. "It's web-speak. A 'ship' is when you want to characters in a story to be together."

Nodding, Olivia's smile widened.

"What?" Ty said, curious.

"Nothing."

"Oh please!" Ty groaned. "That was the completely not nothing. That was definitely a something!"

"What was a what?" Joey asked, coming around the tents. Zed was right behind him.

"Nothing," Ty said, shooting Olivia a look. She didn't say anything, but she kept smiling.

"Food nearly done?" Zed queried, squatting down to look at the fish.

Prodding it with a finger, Olivia nodded. "Ready."

Zed beamed. "Thanks for cooking!"

With that, Ty, Zed, and Joey cut slices from the fish.

It was odd, juggling hot fish between fingers and knife, but Ty moaned happily. He smiled up at the sun as his belly's aching eased.

"How'd you sleep?" Joey asked, bland.

Ty realized the question was for him. He swallowed and said, "Fine. Felt too short though. I'm glad we didn't put up a watch last night."

"We'll have one again tonight," Zed said, rolling her eyes. "We should've had one, but I forgot that I have to organize you babies to protect yourselves."

"We just beat the enemy!" Ty complained, waving a fishy hand at the woods. "We haven't even talked about what we're doing next. We're fine."

"Someone doesn't remember how mean Kaskans are," Joey stage whispered to Olivia. She smiled and nodded.

"Don't forget to leave some for the others," Zed noted. "Once Nat and Seth get done playing, they'll need to eat. Same for Bee."

Ty glanced around. "Where is Bee?"

"She went patrolling with us," Joey explained, jerking his chin at Zed. "We came back when we smelled food, but Bee said she wanted to do another sweep."

"Good for her," Ty said, not sure what else to say. It was good she was getting more competent though. That ice-ball yesterday had been incredible. Maybe she'd teach him how to do that.

"When did that start?" Zed inquired, watching Seth and Nat in the river.

"This morning," Ty said, checking for any bones in his next bit of fish. The pairing still didn't sit right, but he wasn't sure why. "Thoughts?"

"Hey, if it keeps her sane and makes him chill out, works for me," Zed said. She went for another strip of the croc. "I'm more concerned with how we're staying healthy on fish alone."

"Magic," Joey offered, wiggling the fingers of his free hand at her as though casting a spell.

"Current," Zed corrected.

"Could be different things," Ty said. "Maybe Current uses some kind of nanotech and isn't supernatural at all. Could've been implanted while we were in transit."

"That's a lot of ifs for something that looks like magic, walks like magic, quacks like magic, and magics like magic," Zed said, an amused smile taking the bite from her sarcastic tone. "They call it Current. This is their show. We call it that."

"Nice of us unwilling participants to stick to the assigned vocab," Joey joked, smiling up at the too blue sky.

"I guess it could be a subcategory," Ty said, thoughtful. "Like how specific breeds of dogs are still canines? It's still magic, it just gets a different name because it's a specific kind."

Zed rolled her eyes, her smile widening.

"Ty, what did you do back on earth again?" Joey asked, solemn.

"I was a student?" Ty said, looking back and forth between the duo.

"Academia," Joey said, nodding. "Good stuff. What kind?"

"I was a lit major."

Joey nodded again. "Lit. Lots of interesting classes, right?"

"Yeah," Ty said, wary of the joke he knew was coming. "This is a lot of lead up…"

"Don't worry, I'm not that funny," Joey said, waving his worries away. "I was just curious how many of those interesting classes were on identifying and classifying magic."

Zed burst out laughing, covering her mouth with an elbow as she cackled.

"Nat asked me that already," Ty pointed out, ignoring the redoubling of Zed's amusement.

A faint smile tugged at the solemnity of Joey's face. "Really? I guess I'm both not that funny and not that original."

Ty grinned, thinking of a good jab. "Could be worse."

"It could?"

"You could be stuck on an alien planet playing 'best killer' with aliens."

All three of them laughed at that. It was a dark humor, but it felt good to laugh.

"So, what's in the cases?" Ty asked as amusement faded to silence.

"Some kind of armor, I think," Zed answered, frowning. "Still need to test that theory. The other had ten rounded box-thingies."

"Explosives?" Joey guessed, scratching his chin.

Zed shrugged. "Our next targets look like some scary-ass robots, so I'd bet it's something that'll even the playing field."

"Great," Ty muttered. "Robots. Because things weren't tough enough."

"We've got this," Zed said. She punched him lightly in the shoulder. "We'll just have to train harder."

Ty moaned, theatrically mournful. "Not with the training! Couldn't we have a day off?"

Zed smirked. There was something evil sparkling in her eyes. "Yesterday was the day off."

"Worst day off ever," Joey chuckled. He set his knife against a stone, to keep the fishy blade off the sand.

"We can't start till everyone's fed. We could see what those boxes are though," Zed said, casual as could be.

"I'm in," Ty said quickly, a smile blossoming into existence on his face at the prospect. A puzzle sounded good. Really good, actually.

"Sounds interesting," Joey seconded.

Olivia raised a brow and stayed seated, but Ty and Joey stood and followed Zed to the 'girls' tent. Inside, Ty took his first look at how the girls had laid out their space. It was less empty feeling than the 'guys' one, which made sense considering the gender ratio. They'd set up near the center, all within arms reach, heads pointed outwards and feet near the post.

Then Zed was headed out again, brushing past him with one of the cases. Ty followed her, Joey beside him. At the base of the wall, a good two-dozen meters from the tents, she stopped and surveyed the spot.

"About here?" Zed queried. "Should work."

"Worried about blowing up a tent?" Joey said.

Zed laughed. "More than a little. We only have three. Losing one would still leave us plenty of room, but I'd hate to break something out of stupidity."

On the other hand, everyone sleeping in the same tent sounded pretty nice to Ty. Right up until he remembered the Nat-Seth situation. Never mind. Maybe he could convince Nat to set up the third tent for herself and green-eyes.

Popping open the case, Zed pulled one of the oval boxes from its groove. Hefting it, she bounced it in her hands. "Pretty light," she said, brows rising.

Ty copied her, nodding his agreement as he weighed one. It was light. Maybe two kilos. Like a laptop, except for being curvier, seamless, and lacking any visible ports or holes.

"No moving parts," Joey said, thoughtful as he held one to his ear and shook it. "Nothing."

"No loose parts," Zed corrected. "They're probably better made then the Earth equivalent."

"If there's an Earth equivalent," Ty added.

"They've given us suits, knives, bows, tents, bottles, blankets, and now armor," Joey listed, each word measured.

"Survivalist gear," Zed said, taking one ovoid between both hands and pulling it in different directions. She grunted unhappily and stopped after a few seconds.

"Except for the armor," Ty countered. He plucked a boxy ovoid from the case. To him, it sounded like a soldier's kit. Except for the bows. They didn't seem right, unless they were meant as intro weapons. If they were a way to prep for something bigger… "How did the tents open?" he asked, the words coming out vacant, distracted.

"Current," Zed replied, "Olivia just-"

"Wanted it," Ty finished, his smile painfully wide as both of their boxes began to move. He almost dropped it, surprised as cool Current ran from his fingers and into the box.

The box that was no longer a box.

The flattened ovoid gained new features as segments receded, whole stretches of its surface melting away. Ridges and dips became prominent, always gently rounded.

Seconds after the desire to see what the thing was had passed through Ty's head, he was holding a sinuous weapon. Around a quarter of a meter long, and less than half that in height, it rested easily in his arms. He slipped his thumb and forefinger through two holes near the bottom back corner, and his other fingers on a soft stretch of the lower edge. A grip, comfortable in his hand, and the edge beneath his forefinger flexed and clicked as he squeezed.

A trigger.

It was a gun.

Ty turned it over, wide-eyed as excitement shot through him.

There, on the bottom, was a round depression, centimeters deep, wedged between the grip and the butt. Ty's free hand ran across it, his fingertips feeling the edges. This had to be where the ammunition went.

"Well, I think we're ready for the robots," Joey said, his voice faint, his mind clearly on what he was holding.

"I can't find any magazines," Zed said, confused, rifling through the case's lining. It was empty, other than seven more guns.

No ammunition.

Ty felt the depression in the bottom again. It was like the magazine slot on normal rifles, though those weren't round. The Vinna wouldn't give them guns unless they wanted them to be used, so there had to be an answer they weren't seeing. These were alien guns, so they could fire lasers, or some other kind of missile.

Testing a theory, Ty pulsed magic through it again, but the gun just melted back into a smooth ovoid. Another pulse turned it back again. He tried sending a steady stream of Current into it, but the gun just cycled back and forth.

Frustrated, Ty growled. Today was turning out to really suck. First Seth and Nat, then the ribbing at the fire, and now guns that didn't work. Worse, there was a growing sense of helplessness in his gut. Nothing worked. Spearing bugs just got him stabbed, stickmen had to be shot off him, and now he couldn't even get some dumb Vinna puzzle.

Ty fumed, trapped and angry. The final straw was the gun, sitting useless in his hands. With a grunt of rage and effort, he threw it at the wall. A fraction of a second later, arm still outstretched, the gun hit the wall and shame came down on him like an avalanche. No wonder he wasn't the hero, or even a hero. Useless, temperamental, and now not even clever; of course he was the dumb jock.

"What the fuck?" Zed barked, glaring at him.

Her words were a wedge, slamming under the edge of Ty's shame, shoring it up and locking it in.

"Got it," Joey said, his calm oddly out of place as he wandered along the wall to where Ty's gun had fallen.

"Not now, Joey!" Zed declared. She waved him off as she moved towards Ty, one warning finger raised.

Ty could feel his ears burning. Zed was a lot whiter and a lot blonder than his mom had been, but she had the same look in her eyes.

Joey snagged the gun and checked it. "He didn't break it."

"It's a damn alien super-gun, how the hell can you be sure?" Zed retorted, spinning around to face him.

"Because it still does this," Joey replied. He tapped the gun's bottom against the wall. Then he pointed parallel to the wall and pulled the trigger. The gun thudded, less like the bang of a gun and more like a sandbag hitting the ground. A crack rang from a boulder a hundred meters down, broken bits of stone falling away from a divot in its face.

"See?" Joey said, bland as Ty's jaw dropped and Zed stared, wide eyed. "Works fine."

"One: what the fuck," Zed began, stunned. Then her face changed, a massive, vicious grin twisting the look of astonishment. "Two: do it again. And three: how?"

Joey caught Ty's eyes and nodded. "You're welcome." Looking back at Zed he pulled the trigger again. Several times. More thuds, more cracks, lots of broken stone falling into the sand. "And I figured that one of the big issues people have is running out of bullets, so what if aliens decided to make bullets from what's handy. Around here, that's rock."

"Why not wood?" Zed pointed out, her smile widening even more as her thoughts sped along.

"Because it'd degrade the wildlife habitat," Joey said. He glanced up the wall at his back. "And I didn't feel like climbing up to try it."

Ty laughed, his hands twitching from the cocktail of Zed's approach, the gun revelation, and his own rage. He wrung them, trying to pass it off as excitement. "How'd you get it to take in the stone?"

"It sort of vibrated when I rested it on a rock," Joey explained. "I figured that it warns you if things are compatible. When I gave it a burst of Current, it just ate the stone up."

"How many shots did you get?" Zed asked.

Shrugging, Joey kept shooting. Several thuds later, it stopped. "Twenty."

"Does it work with sand?" Zed wondered.

Kneeling, Joey set the gun on the ground and waited. After a second, he stood and the gun started thudding again. There was a low spot in the sand where he'd fed the gun. Another twenty shots and it stopped thudding again.

Zed beamed, bent down, and filled her own gun from the sand. When she stood, she shot one into the ground a few feet away. Darting after it, she used her free hand to dig up the slug. She held it up to the sun.

Ty came closer, squinting to make out the misty glass bullet. It certainly looked like a bullet. Round and maybe three centimeters long, it tapered to a sharp tip at one end.

"Guys, I think I'm a lot less worried about those robots now," Zed said. There was a thick, violent amusement that seeped into those words.

"That's so damn cool," Bee said from the wall's top.

Ty's jumped. "Geez, Bee," he grumbled, one hand over his heart. "You nearly gave me a heart attack!"

"You'll be fine," Bee told him, smiling. "You're cuter when you're scared anyway."

"You flirting with me?" Ty asked, confused.

"Just for fun," Bee said conspiratorially as she hopped down the wall. "Don't take it personally, sweet cheeks."

"Is there another way to take flirting?" Ty wondered, addressing Joey.

"Don't ask me," Joey warned him. He shook his head and gave Ty a small grin. "Flirting isn't my area."

"If it helps, you're not my type, so this is more like friendly banter," Bee explained. "So, Vinna guns?"

Zed was still studiously peering at her glass bullet. "How much did you catch?"

A smirk tugged at Bee's mouth. "Basically all of it. I wanted to see how long it'd take for you to notice me."

"Very high school," Ty said.

"Shut up, jock," Bee jabbed.

Smiling, Ty hid how much the term stung.

"Give it a try," Zed offered. She handed Bee her gun.

Bee took it and fired at the boulder Joey had shot. "That. Is. Fun," she said, punctuating each word with another thud.

Walking backwards to watch the shooting, Zed fetched another ovoid from the case and shifted it into a weapon.

"Gun?" Ty inquired, looking hopefully at Joey.

The guy smiled and tossed him back his gun. "Try not to throw it again."

"No shit," Ty laughed, glancing pointedly at Zed. They both smiled and started shooting.

After a few minutes, everyone paused; breathing a bit heavily after the storm of glass and stone bullets they'd blasted.

Ty could hear his pulse pounding in his ears.

Wow.

Ty had shot a hunting rifle before, and even a revolver once, but these things were totally different. These things were smaller, like an oversized and ovular pistol, but they had less blowback when fired, and the sound wasn't as loud. It was less stressful, but no less exciting.

It also helped that Ty kept seeing giant bugs coiled on the stone, writhing and twitching as they were riddled with bullets. The rage was still there, hot and heavy in his gut, but the helplessness was fading. He decided that he liked alien guns. A lot.

"Ok, we need to go over some basic firearm safety," Zed announced, her voice edged with the same tone she used when laying out the exercise plan.

"Fuck," Bee groaned.

Ty agreed with the sentiment, if not the word choice.

Bee dropped onto the sand beside Olivia with a wide grin. "How's it hanging?"

"Glad I have the suit," Olivia answered, watching the water. She sat cross-legged, her gun tapping the side of her shin to a mysterious beat. She had her hoodie on again, the stained and worn cloth long since more gray than black.

"You don't need the hood now," Bee pointed out, looking at the sliver of Olivia's face that showed around it. "We don't get sunburns."

Olivia sighed and pulled the cloth back. Her dark hair drifted in the breeze, a gentle mist wafting by like smoke.

Everything felt gray this morning, colorless beneath the thick clouds. Even the dawn's light hadn't shown itself yet, and it should've been beaming over the treetops by now. The trees whispered, the stream bubbled and trickled along, and the world felt hushed, hidden from something immense and frightening just beyond the clouds.

"I don't like it," Bee said, her voice loud, carrying across the water.

"Not getting sunburns?" Olivia threw back.

"Not that," Bee said, rolling her eyes. "The quiet. It feels wrong."

"City girl," Olivia stated.

"Like you're one to talk, Londoner," Bee said. She laughed, remembering. It'd been nearly three weeks, but she still recalled that night when she'd overheard Olivia and Zed's argument.

Olivia nodded. "Been a while."

"Accent's cute," Bee said.

Olivia blinked, a hint of surprise in the twitch of her lips. "Thanks."

"What do you think of the new toys?" Bee asked, gesturing at the gun in her hands. It took an effort of will not to look over her shoulder to make sure that Zed wasn't listening in. Getting told off for joking about deadly weapons would suck, and guns seemed to sap what little humor Zed seemed to have.

"I think the robots are going to be a problem," Olivia answered.

"Why?"

"We didn't get guns for the bugs, so why now?"

"Answering questions with questions is a bad habit."

Olivia smiled. "But I have a point."

"Yeah, no need to get a big head about it," Bee grumbled. "You got a plan?"

"Depends."

"On?"

"On why you're being chatty and sassy again."

"No idea what you're talking about," Bee said, staring up at the mountains.

"Comfortable or resigned?" Olivia pushed.

Out of the corner of her eye, Bee could see Olivia's eerie gaze linger on her. Those were two gray eyes that she didn't want to meet.

"Resigned," Olivia declared, nodding. "You've decided that you're going to die, so you might as well relax and enjoy."

"Stop," Bee said, half plea and half demand.

"It's good," Olivia said. "Relax. Enjoy. But you don't get to die."

"Shut up," Bee whispered, fighting through what felt like the tearing away of an immense scab.

"You don't deserve to die," Olivia said, her voice low, barely more than a whisper, but somehow full and inescapable. "We fight, we survive, and we keep going. That's the plan."

Bee shook her head, her throat too clogged to voice her disbelief. She didn't agree. She'd get them all killed, tucked under some ice-ball somewhere when she should've been helping. It'd happen eventually.

Something pounded into Bee's cheek, snapping her head to the side. Her eyes shot up, taking in Olivia's raised hand.

The shorter woman stood over Bee, one hand poised for a second slap. Those gray eyes were hard, her jaw set. The long fingers of her other hand curled tight, balled into a fist at her side.

Olivia bent low, her face inches from Bee's. "You. Don't. Die."

Staring, Bee felt the tears roll across her face. Their moisture stung as they streamed down her throbbing cheek. Her heart thrummed in her chest, pounding as instincts told her to run, to give in, to fight, or to do anything other than stay.

"You didn't fuck up," Olivia said, her voice as inexorable as gravity. "You stayed alive against something you couldn't hurt. That's called winning. Got it?"

Bee didn't say anything. Her breaths were fast now, hiccupping, damp with barely restrained sobs.

Another slap. It took Bee's breath away. When she turned back, Olivia was still there.

"Got it?" Olivia said a third time.

Bee nodded and looked down. There was too much certainty in those gray eyes. Too much certainty that Bee mattered, that she hadn't fucked up. It helped, but it stung worse than the slaps. Her eyes wandered away, down the beach.

Something moved, flying out of the water and charging onto the sands. Its legged whipped forward and back, droplets spraying wide.

"Croc!" Bee blurted. Numbed by old shock and fresh fear, her fingers scrabbled at the gun on the sand beside her.

Olivia spun, facing the oncoming lizard. Her gun lay beside Bee's.

It was close. Too close. Maybe a meter long, but ferocious and hungry.

Bee's fingers grasped her gun, but her fingers couldn't seem to find the holes. She yanked it into her lap, desperate to add her other hand to the search. She couldn't look down; her eyes were locked on the Croc.

With a grunt of effort, Olivia raised one fist and slammed it down on the oncoming Croc. She missed the head, catching it instead on its shoulders, but the punch kept going. The lizard's chest slammed into the ground, crunching and cracking with the impact.

Trembling, gun still not right in her hands, Bee sat, frozen.

The Croc twitched.

Bee squeaked.

Olivia stepped back. Her movement was jerky, exaggerated. Her feet staggered, as she drew in deep breaths.

"Current?" Bee asked, watching the croc. It looked really, really dead. Likely due to the massive pancake of broken everything that was all that remained of a four-inch wide chunk of its chest.

"I wanted to," Olivia admitted, her voice faint.

Bee nodded absently. "That'd do it."

"I guess we've got breakfast now."

"Yeah."

"It didn't feel like Current," Olivia mumbled.

"Then how…"

"No clue."

"Maybe we didn't just get the magic stuff," Bee suggested, her ragged breaths settling.

"Current," Olivia corrected.

"Whatever. It could be like Superman, ya know? Different sun equals superpowers."

"Three weeks in?"

Bee shook her head. "You're awfully complain-y for someone who doesn't have a better theory."

"You're awfully pretty for someone who's this annoying," Olivia tossed back, her voice strengthening again.

"You flirting with me, schoolgirl?"

"I'm older than you," Olivia reminded her.

Bee could hear the smirk. She was still watching the lizard. It could be faking.

After a second, Olivia added, "And maybe."

"Good to know."

"Don't take it personally," Olivia jabbed.

Bee smiled, recalling her shot at Ty. "Eavesdropper."

"Only when you're loud enough to hear a kilometer away."

"Careful, I'm a screamer."

"I've made gags before," Olivia countered.

"Little early on to be propositioning me."

"Adrenaline," Olivia said. "Think it's dead?"

"The fishy komodo dragon or our romance?"

"The croc."

Bee kicked it. In the face. Nothing. Well, the head got knocked to the side, but the eyes were glazed and the head seemed to be having little effect on the body.

"I think you broke its spine," Bee said, trying to decide between shock and amusement. She landed somewhere in the middle. She got to her feet. "Why don't you keep an eye on this guy while I go get Zed."

"Why?"

"So that she can carry it over to the fire pit."

"You can do that."

"What?" Bee squawked. Her stomach was somewhere around her ankles at the prospect.

"I killed it, you carry it, and I'll cook it."

Bee frowned, breaking her lock on the croc to express her ire in Olivia's direction. She didn't look impressed. "You're going to ask me to spit it too, aren't you?"

"You are bigger than me-"

"Are you calling me fat?"

"-But I can put the spit through it if you'd hold it right."

Bee rolled her eyes. "Of course you would, Stabby."

"We'd have breakfast ready just in time if we did it now."

"Of course we would," Bee groaned. She rolled her shoulders. Might as well just get it over with. After another careful kick, she hefted the meter long lizard and tossed it over her shoulder. Halfway to the fire, she noticed Olivia's smile. "What?"

"How much do you think that weighs?" Olivia said, nodding at the mini-Kaskan.

"Less than you."

Olivia snorted. "More than you could lift when we first got here."

"What?" Bee said, confused. "Really?" She didn't know. It was possible. "We've all been exercising a lot," she added halfheartedly.

"Just guessing, but it sounds plausible enough that you aren't denying the possibility," Olivia said, a small, cunning smile curling her lips.

"Fair point," Bee said, her thoughts racing. Was she stronger? As she shifted the lizard around so that Olivia could drive a spit through it, it dawned on her that she really was. Carrying something this big would've had her out of breath before. Their runs were more than she'd run before as well. A lot more.

"How long are we running in the evenings?" Bee asked. She took one end of the spit and set it on the Y shaped support on her side of the pit.

"Not sure. No clocks," Olivia replied. She set their guns aside on a rock and began to poke and prod the blackened sticks in the pit. There were a couple thicker logs mixed in, and as the ash fell away embers began to gleam and glow a hellish red. She tossed a couple sticks on, pressing them against the coals until the bark began to smolder and smoke. A few gentle puffs of air later, tongues of flame leapt and danced on old wood and new.

"Good thing we aren't starting fresh," Bee said, glancing up at the dense clouds.

"Finding the sun would suck," Olivia agreed.

It was small talk. They both knew it. Whatever the clouds, they could make a ball of water and refract the light into something that'd burn eventually. Joey had invented that trick ages ago, that way there'd be less demand for his glasses. Bee needed to think though, so she went through the motions.

Stronger. Faster too, going by Olivia's ability to punch crocs mid-charge. Current might be changing them, making them super-powered. Well, more super-powered than magic already accounted for.

Damn.

"You two get attacked?" Zed said quietly, emerging from the 'girls' tent.

Bee chuckled and flicked the lizard's tail. "A little."

"Both ok?" Zed asked, coming over to the pit.

"Yeah, but I could use a margarita and a masseuse," Bee said.

Zed stared at the massive flattened dent in the lizard's upper back. "What the hell…"

Bee pointed at Olivia. "She did it."

"With what?" Zed snorted, "A sledgehammer?"

"If you look close I bet you can see her knuckle-prints," Bee speculated. She liked the way Olivia's eyes rolled and twinkled at that.

Zed's eyes shot wide. She looked Olivia up and down. "You punched it?"

"It sounds dumber than it seemed at the time," Olivia said.

"I can't imagine why," said Zed, sarcasm oozing from every word. "I always punch giant carnivorous lizards, guns seem so last month."

"I was telling Bee to not give herself so much shit," Olivia explained. She rolled her eyes again at the drama. "My gun was on the ground. Getting to it would've taken too long."

"And you didn't use a Current knife why?"

Olivia's cheeks turned red. "Forgot."

"Dammit," Zed groaned, rubbing the bridge of her nose. "Ok, it's fine," she said with a forced smile. "It's fine. We'll just have to do more quick-draw drills. This is a great learning experience."

Olivia winced. "You're mad."

"Mad? Me? Why would I be mad, Boss? I can't imagine why you'd say that!" Zed said, calmly sarcastic again. It would've been convincing, but her tone kept fluctuating towards pissed. She also put a telling amount of emphasis on the 'Boss,' causing another wince.

"I'll work on it," Olivia said.

"Work on what?" Zed said. Her disingenuous smile didn't reach her eyes. "Probably best to focus on cooking, wouldn't want to have to send you out to punch another junior dino in submission just so we can have breakfast."

"I think she gets it," Bee said. She interjected partly because she felt bad for Olivia, and partly because she'd been the one who hadn't been able to pull the trigger on time, or spot the lizard coming.

"And what were you doing, other-person-who-had-a-gun?" Zed countered, her laser-hot beam of furious attention wheeling. "Or were you both standing around berating one another when croc-y came up and asked for the time?"

"I… fumbled…" Bee admitted, wilting.

"More drills," Zed decided, nodding. "Noted. Olivia fucking up is a bigger deal. Boss needs to lead by example, and that does not include punching lizards and leaving guns lying around."

"I've got it now," Olivia grumbled. She picked her gun from the ground and tucked it under her arm. The boxy shape sat awkwardly as she continued to turn the lizard's spit.

Silence hung in the air for a moment, wordless, but full of the rustling breeze and gurgling pools.

Zed rolled her eyes, still staring at Olivia. "I swear, the chance of you being the one who came out of that bug-fight un-traumatized has got to be smaller than the one for aliens kidnapping random humans."

"Been through worse," Olivia said, her voice soft, almost faint, a whisper in the morning mist.

"Remind me not to mess with you again," Zed said, rubbing her temples. "And sorry for the temper."

Olivia shrugged, conceding. "You were right. I need to get better. Drills will help, even if they suck."

"We need all of us, and we all need to be at our best," Zed agreed.

"Maybe next time we could charge in yelling 'All For One and One For All," Bee suggested, smiling.

"Sounds like a great way of warning the robots that we're coming," Zed threw back.

Bee shrugged. "War cries are a thing. Demoralizing, inspirational, all that shit."

"Except when the enemy is a 'bot," Olivia snorted.

"Still inspiring."

"You keep telling yourself that," Zed said with faux-kindness. She patted Bee's back. "We'll let you know when to 'demoralize them,' that way we can attack from the far side."

"I'm not playing decoy!" Bee declared, caught between wry amusement and genuine fear.

"You'll be fine," Zed disagreed. She added a mollifying wink a beat later.

"Armor?" Olivia suggested, a slim white blade solidifying in her hand as she went to poke the lizard.

"Try it while we're both here? Sure," Zed agreed, a bit surprised. She stood and brushed the sand from her backside nonetheless.

"Right now?" Bee queried, trying to catch up with the sudden shift. Not that she didn't appreciate a change in topic, but going from near-death dinner, to training plans, to checking out new toys was a lot of switching.

"Why didn't we break it out yesterday?" she added, trying to cover her mental whiplash.

"After we got the guns working yesterday, adding more new things would've been a mess," Zed said.

"One thing at a time," Olivia agreed, nodding. She peeled back a flap of lizard meat to check the color.

"Now that everyone has a feel for the handguns, we can see how the armor works," Zed finished, backing off towards the tent as she finished. She turned and vanished through the flap a few breaths later.

Bee pondered that. It was an interesting approach. Most army movies she'd seen just plunged the recruits in, handing them all their gear and throwing new things at them all the way. When she considered it though, that hadn't been true of everything. Uniforms, haircuts, marching, orders, getting yelled at, sure; but the guns and grenades and dangerous stuff had come later, in tightly controlled moments, usually with jokes to make the viewer more comfortable.

"I wonder what the endgame is," Bee muttered.

Olivia grunted a wordless request for the rest of that thought.

"It's like those teen franchises, right? It's a straightforward system that pushes people to the limit, but the goal varies. The Hunger Games was intended to keep citizens cowed; Maze Runner, Divergent, they were tests to see how genetics would work out. I don't know what the goal here is, but I'm pretty sure we aren't being sent home."

"Soldiers," Zed said, case in hand as she slipped from the tent. "What we're doing gets us ready to be some hellish guerillas. Guns that make ammo from anything, all purpose camo clothes, improvised weaponry from moisture, and medical support without supplies; all the ingredients for some insane mobile strike teams."

"Shit," Bee muttered, looking up at the sky. "And here we are proving that we can do the job in a super-gator littered tropical hell."

"That's the test," agreed Zed, the words heavy. "Most militaries work to train everyone capable of succeeding, but this speeds things along by killing off anyone who falls behind."

Bee frowned, pissed at the unfairness of that. "But what about the people who don't have survival skills?"

"Maybe it's meant to force people to team up," Zed said. "If the point is to work together, the aliens just need to make sure that certain skills are present in each group. Then anyone who dies is either a necessary loss or not a team player."

"Damn. If we end up needing anything from the two who died, we're screwed." Bee groaned. She rubbed her face, thinking. "Unless they put in a backup person for everything on the checklist."

Zed nodded. "It'd reduce the chance of bad luck fouling their test. Doubling up would make sense."

"Sort of like how both you and Joey know how to shoot," Olivia pointed out. She poked the lizard again.

"Or how I have basic first aid training and Nat's a med student," Zed added.

Bee shook her head. "They might've tripled up. I took first aid too, in high school, and I think Seth can shoot too," she said, nodding at Zed. "At least he looked like he had a handle on it yesterday."

"That's my read too," Zed said, smiling. "Makes sense to stack up the core skills for soldiers."

"Makes you wonder what else was on the alien army skills wish list," Bee muttered, thinking of the possibilities.

Zed popped the case and pulled out a flat oval of something like cloth. She turned it over, rubbing her thumb and forefinger against the varying gray splotches. "It's rough one way, smooth the other," she said, distracted. She leaned in, staring hard at the oval. "And it looks like it's some kind of scale?"

"Like skin?" Bee squeaked, confused.

Olivia came around the fire, plucking another patch from the box.

"Yeah, like a lizard skin," Zed confirmed. "Only on one side too."

"Sharks," Olivia declared, beaming.

Zed shot a questioning look at the shorter woman.

"These scales have spines that make them harder to break, and they overlap," Olivia explained, scratching a nail against her armored patch. "It looks a lot like shark scale, but harder."

"Well, that's comforting," muttered Bee. "If the Vinna are giving scales to us softies, maybe we've earned it. Like a coming of age or something."

Zed nodded. "They did say it was a rite."

Without warning, Olivia took the foot long ovoid and laid it across her shoulder. The soft patch fell flat against the slightly baggy exterior of the suit, hugging tight to the curve of her joint.

"Ok, that's cool," said Zed, her eyes nearly as wide as her sudden smile. She slapped her own patch over her knee, nearly hopping with excitement when it plastered itself to her suit, as though magnetized.

Olivia added another patch to her other shoulder. She rolled both arms, flexing and stretching to check if there was any change. "Nothing," she told Zed, smiling too now. "It's just as flexible as the suit."

"Try shooting it," Zed said, quickly tossing one of the scale patches on the sand.

"I'll do it," Bee volunteered. She wanted to be included, to help, but putting that stuff all over her made her stomach turn. Leveling her handgun, she fired a stone bullet at the patch of scales. A burst of sand flew up, obscuring the target.

Zed jogged over, plunged a hand into the cloud, and lifted the oval, her smile wide again. It was pristine. No dent, no discoloration, just a bit of sand.

"What?" Bee demanded, grabbing the patch and feeling it. Nothing.

"I'd bet that's Vinna body armor," Zed speculated, the words coming out in an excited rush. "Olivia, does it come off?"

Tugging at the patch on her left shoulder, Olivia nodded as one edge peeled. "It does, but only when I want it to. Current, probably. Like the guns."

"I bet it gets keyed into the wearer through the suit, that way it can vent excess heat and all the rest as well," Zed continued, hurriedly leafing through the patches in the box. "I wonder how many we're supposed to…"

Bee shook her head, dazed by the rush of excitement and the possibilities the armor represented. Guns, armor, tents, suits, Current; they were soldiers for sure. She thought back to how they'd started: a bunch of strangers. Other than Zed, they'd all changed a lot getting here. Hell, Zed too, at least as far as her personality. The rabid efficiency had eased off, in the same way that Ty's boyish heroics had calmed down.

They were the same people, but no one gets through hell unscathed.

A smile tugged and Bee's mouth, silent amusement at her own metaphor. She'd been so afraid of changing. Zed had talked her through it at the time. Now all Bee could think about was surviving. Bee didn't know if she'd accepted that she might not be able to recognize herself after all of this, or if she'd changed so much that she no longer cared.

Maybe it didn't matter.

"There're about a hundred patches," Zed said, bursting through Bee's bubble. "That seems like too few. Maybe they're not body armor?"

"Or maybe we've got to prioritize how we use it," Olivia suggested, adding more patches to her chest and right arm. After a few seconds, her arm was sheathed in splashes of gray, contrasting with green mottle of the suit. The armor stretched down and across her right side, shielding her from heel to throat on that side, though it took a score of the oval segments.

"Well, as long as you walk sideways at them, you'll be fine," Bee joked, trying to lighten the mood.

"We armor three, maybe four, send them in ready to shoot," Olivia explained, pointing her pistol to the right, so that anyone looking back from that direction would see only scales, gun, and head. "Smaller targets; maximize the armor."

"And everyone else attacks the flanks?" Zed queried, frowning.

"Sounds like it'd work," Bee said. It made sense to her, especially if she didn't have to be on the Bait Squad.

Zed snorted. "Weren't you mad at me for suggesting we use you as a decoy about three minutes ago?"

"Yeah, but this is Olivia being the decoy," Bee said, winking at their leader. "Totally different." She grinned, enjoying the way Olivia's cheeks flushed.

Olivia coughed, clearing her throat. "We should get everyone up."

Evil grin in full force, Zed nodded. "Once we've got armored fighters picked, we can do our morning run in full gear."

"Ha!" Bee blurted, cackling at the way Olivia's face fell.

"Do we have to?" Olivia queried. Her resigned expression made it a token complaint, but there was a hint of whine to the words.

"Hey, you're the Boss, but I'd rather know that everyone is ready for the fight tomorrow than sit around getting nervous," Zed explained.

"Tomorrow?" Bee asked, surprised again.

"Armor's light," Zed said. "That means it won't be hard to get used to. We'll do gun drills, maybe test out how resilient the patches are some more, and be ready by sunset. With a good night's rest, we can set out tomorrow. The robots are only a few miles down the river, so it won't take the full day to find them. Easy."

"Ugh," Bee groaned. Too soon. She felt almost nauseous at the thought.

"As the 'decoy,' I reserve the right to complain more than anyone else," Olivia noted, looking at Zed.

Zed shook her head. "Bad news. Officers don't get to complain down. If you did, you might look human. You only get to whine to other officers. Gotta watch out for that."

"But then I don't get to complain to anyone," Olivia grumbled, frowning.

"Yup."

"As the Boss, I'm making an executive decision regarding dumb rules about complaining."

"Can't."

"Why?"

"Because it's not a rule. It's just a thing."

"I'm un-thinging it."

"Can't."

"Why?"

"Because saying 'un-thinging' doesn't sound officer-ish," Zed explained, her tone that of one trying to project utmost patience while fighting not to burst out laughing.

"Do you mean official?" Olivia corrected, her slate-gray eyes flashing.

"Uh oh," Bee hummed.

"Touché," Zed conceded, frowning with comedic levels of exaggeration.

"You get to wake up Seth and Nat," Olivia told her, smirking.

"Now that? That sounds like the kind of vengeful ass-hat thing an officer would do," Zed sighed. Nonetheless, she turned and went to do it.

The rapid thump of bullets echoed across the tiered pools and mountainside falls.

A deep gorge gaped between streams of shimmering blue, almost staring up at the atrocious noise now enveloping its home.

Peeking around a wizened and weathered tree, Zed checked on how things were going. She was perched on the thin berm that rimmed one of the many pools, but down the slope other pools had far less human occupants.

Below, streams of water flowed like sinuous snakes, leaping from one pool to the next in gleaming ribbons of reflected sunlight. They dipped and dropped, falling all the way to the golden sands of the river at the bottom, maybe two hundred meters from Zed's tree.

Three figures stood on the boulder wall on the far side of that beach, their gray and green bodies blending into the mélange of trees and rocks. Olivia was at the center, with Joey on her right and Bee on her left. Each bore one of the curved handguns in their off hand, bent across their chest to put the sights just before their eyes, while their main arm curled into a shield to protect their heads. All three leaned forward, guns bucking lightly as thuds rang out.

Olivia, Joey, and Bee were after the four robotic shapes across from them, in the lowest pool. The foursome was clear at Zed's vantage, but from across the river they would be half hidden. They were the patrollers, guards for the rest. The two in the next pool back were the rear-guard, or that was Zed's guess. The last four were spread across the third pool back from the river. Those highest four were spread-eagled, or some mechanical equivalent. Their pale plating stretched out, sucking in sun like albino lily pads. Solar-powered space-'bots, or at least that was her guess.

That recharging foursome was Zed's target. Thus, her being about forty meters behind and above that third 'bot filled pool. It'd taken a long time to maneuver this far unseen, but she had, and she'd brought friends.

Bullets tore at the grass and cracked against the mountainside, but the robots didn't fire back. They were waiting, trying to draw Olivia and the others into crossing the water, where they would have a harder time fleeing from. Or maybe they were saving ammo. Whatever the plan, they'd expected a riverside attack and set up for it.

Of course, this particular semi-ex-military Current-wielding sort-of-sergeant was no amateur, she gleefully noted to herself. If the 'bots had been smart they'd have put the two in the center pool at the top instead, to keep a better watch and guard the back. But they hadn't. They'd left their recharging pals open.

Zed had never gotten to kick metal ass before. Her fingers clenched on the guns she held in both hands.

Lowering one weapon to the water by her right heel, Zed concentrated, and then flung it upwards. Water soared, a miniature geyser that stretched a dozen meters into the air.

That was the signal.

Zed took off at a spring along the lip of her pool.

Behind her, Seth's feet snapped branches and splashed as he followed.

On the lip of a nearly adjacent pool, Ty and Nat appeared from behind some grassy tufts and dove into the pool below.

At the same time, Zed turned and dove. She arced out into open air, the breeze fluttering through her short, blonde locks. A thought pulled the water's surface to her. She sank into the warm liquid, smooth and gentle. Another surge of Current jetted her forward, along the smooth ramp of the pool's tapered bottom.

Once again, Zed hung in the wind, but this time the four outstretched bots lay below her. A mist surrounded her, turning the light of the sun into a rainbow of color that seemed to hold her in its hand. Gleeful again, excitement in her very bones, she began to pull both triggers. Slugs made from the blue-green steel of the Vinna cases shot from both barrels.

Stone wouldn't tear steel, or whatever sci-fi stuff these things were made from, but the cases had been tough. From the look of it, betting on Vinna metal had paid off.

Massive holes opened in plating, limb, and sensor alike. Ivory armor bent and gave with a sound like punctured rubber, while the limbs shrieked as metal tore through metal.

Two shots from each hand. It'd have to be enough.

A fraction of a second, then another surge of warm water pulled Zed down. She raced along the bottom, eyes closed, focused on the Current. Her senses spread, like a cloud of awareness that filled the water around her even faster than she could move through it.

Then came the surface.

Out again, in the misty air, Zed flew. Her guns thudded as she passed the two 'bots in the middle pool. One shot from each hand this time.

Metal shrieked, but only once.

Then Zed was past them, falling into another pool. These four were turning. Each leveled their four sinuous limbs, like gun-tipped silver-snake arms.

Zed fired a fourth volley as she fell.

Nothing.

And she'd forgotten the landing.

Zed hit the surface with a sharp, hard splat. Shock rocked her inside and out. Force rolled across her body. Dizziness came next. She choked it back, swallowing vomit even as it spilled from her lips. She stood and fought for footing on the slope.

A brutal, desperate desire for solidity hardened the water around Zed's feet. She forced herself upright, fear roiling in her chest. A cough came, bile and puke sickening her stomach. Water rose around her, catching the others, but she didn't have time to count how many had made it. The pool was deep here, but Current held her only knee deep.

Raise, aim, squeeze. Zed fired.

One of the bots staggered, a divot torn in its ivory plating.

Something slammed into Zed's right shoulder. Current held her, her wet suit suddenly stiff and supporting. Water coated the wound, but her gun fell from limp fingers. She kept firing with the other.

It was a mess. Water sloughed and sprayed, 'bots and humans staggering and firing at point blank. Zed couldn't process it all, could barely see anything in the mess. The 'bots were cold and lifeless in the Current-flooded pool, like portly yoga balls mounted on three segmented legs, wielding four death-dealing arms. Current told her where the enemy stood, so she kept shooting.

Bits of metal and crystal blasted from the center robot. Its core billowed outwards, fragmented in a storm of slugs and the weight of its own limbs. The one that'd staggered, the one nearest Zed, righted itself and turned its guns on her.

Red blossomed from one of the liquid cocoons that surrounded her arriving friends. Current could catch bodies, but not bullets.

Zed fired, squeezing over and over as she fought to take out her bot before it ended her.

Another storm of bullets came, tearing apart the remaining center bot.

Two left. One on each side.

Zed shot a look to her side, at the others.

Hands wavering, shots flying wide, Nat hung on through pure will and water holding. Seth, beyond her, didn't miss.

Another bot fell. It squealed as exposed crystal innards shattered and crumbled.

One bot left. It was barely a dozen meters from Zed. Flashes blossomed at the tip of each arm. Four weapons for four humans.

Seth screamed and slumped. He sank into the water.

A fearful, stunned grunt erupted from Nat.

Something punched through Zed's belly, nearly bowling her over.

Another burst of slugs sprayed over the pool's lip, tearing apart the bot. It slumped, collapsing inwards as though its strings had been cut.

Olivia. Finally.

Splashes. Gasping. The creak of metal and the groan of pain. No thuds. No shots.

Maybe they'd won.

Pain throbbed through Zed's torso. Her muscles spasmed, almost giving out as Current-summoned solidity melted away. She couldn't hold it. Too much distraction. She sank till she was waist deep. The taste of bile sat on her tongue, and she was pretty sure she might've pissed herself. Thank God for magic suits and already warm water.

Olivia flew over the lip of the pool, a trail of water flowing like a shroud behind her. Scaled patches that festooned her left side and arm. She dropped to a crouch, gun on the pool above and behind Zed. Joey and Bee flanked her, though with somewhat less ease to their flight.

Coming short of the berm, Joey grabbed a handful of grass and dragged himself the last step.

Bee overshot and rolled as she hit the water.

Fresh thuds hit Zed's ears like stabs. She flinched.

Crashes and crunches from the pool behind her. The other bots.

Fueled by reflex and fright, Zed spun and added her own shots to the mix. She only saw one, peering over the muddy, waterlogged lip. She missed.

Bee screamed, rage and fury blaring across the mountainside as a spray of bullets tore the bot apart.

Quiet again. Ominous now.

Water still splashed, everything hurt, and time stretched for Zed. There was an empty, peaceful nothingness to that moment. It was something as indescribable as the sound of birds returning, or the bubble and burble one pool trickling into the next. It was wordless, yet pristine, and gone as a breath sent pain through every nerve in her body.

"Medic!" Zed called, knowing she wasn't the only one who needed help, but maybe it'd be handy to give Nat somewhere to start.

"Joey, Bee, heal 'em," Olivia's voice came back, followed by splashes as bodies ran through the water.

A deep, almost concussive boom rocked Zed. Her blinking eyes told her it was from Olivia's explosive upward departure, trailed again by delicate mist.

"Hey, where?" Joey demanded, his palm lightly tapping her cheek.

What, did he think she was fainting? Zed would've laughed, but it hurt too much. "Shoulder, belly," she listed. Minimum words. Still hurt. Would he hurry the hell up?

Cool Current washed over Zed. It flooded her shoulder, numbing it enough that she could actually feel Joey's hand resting there. It spread in and down to her belly, collecting there. The pain rolled back, receding like mist on a cold morning.

Zed coughed and spat as soon as she felt safe to move. She needed to get the taste of bile gone.

"Warn me next time," Joey joked, wry smile lighting his thin, tanned face as her eyes opened. The brownish mess she'd spat must've passed only inches from his chest, which was turned to avoid being hit.

"Don't get in the way next time," Zed shot back. She heaved in a deep breath. It took the edge out of her sarcasm, but it felt so good to breath easy.

"Hand over here!" Bee called.

Zed's head whipped around. Bee was with Seth, but she didn't look happy, and the red stain was spreading around them. Nat growled, something ferocious rearing as she saw the desperation in Bee's eyes.

Current rose around Nat, visibly propelling her forward as she added mind to muscle. Her front and back were all scarlet, two wounds in her chest leaking blood faster than the water could wash it away. Both appeared mostly healed. Mostly.

Zed patted Joey's shoulder and muttered, "Watch their backs."

"Aye-aye, sergeant," Joey said. He waded back and scanned their surroundings.

A thought pulled Zed's fallen gun back to her right hand. Her freshly healed shoulder felt stiff, but that'd fade. She rocketed upwards on a cone of Current. It took more than she'd expected. Damn. Healing, jetting, and the dive-catches had drained her. A lot.

Knees bent to take in the impact, Zed landed on the rim of the second pool. The water that'd carried her melted away, falling back into the pool below. The pair of bots sat like stacks of stones, hollow and lifeless.

More thuds from the next pool up, where the rechargers had been.

Zed launched herself up once more, teeth gritted as the strain hit her. She almost missed the lip, but she managed not to fall.

Knee deep, expressionless, Olivia waded from one mechanical mess to the next. Each ivory and chrome corpse got a bullet, or several.

Waiting, watching, Zed realized that the slugs weren't blue-green Vinna metal. They were white.

Another thud, another crunch, then the gun went empty.

Olivia bent and slapped the reload slot against a piece of bot-plate. When she stood again, she met Zed's eyes. She nodded at one of the four splayed robots. The others were still wide, unprepared. This one was mid-process, half rounded, ball-like, the other half disparate segments and sections, hanging here and there from spindly cobwebs of silvered steel. It slumped, tilted drunkenly on the uneven support of limp legs.

"It's harder to be sure they're dead when they're spread," Olivia explained.

"That rhymed," Zed noted.

"Not on purpose." Olivia took a long, deep breath. "You ok?"

Glancing down, Zed took herself in. The bile had washed away, but blood still lingered on her shoulder and belly. The holes in her suit were pretty large. Forty caliber, maybe fifty, by Earth standards. Those machines didn't play around.

"I'm good," Zed answered, straightening. "I couldn't heal solo, so Joey finished the job."

Olivia grunted. "Glad we asked Nat for the tutorial."

"Glad we figured out how to do the water landing-leaping thing on purpose," Zed returned, smiling. That'd been fun to learn. The broken bones hadn't been, but it'd given everyone a chance to try healing.

"We won," Olivia said, her voice oddly numb. She shook her head and waded onto to the grassy ledge, looking down at the others.

"Didn't think we would?" Zed said, curious.

"Cases are down there," Olivia non-answered, thumbing back at the water beneath the four dead bots.

Zed winced. Nausea and loathing pounded through her head at the thought of going to get them. Swimming around under those machines… No. She'd seen how bad they were when shooting, she was just glad she hadn't let one of them touch her. Maybe one of the others-

Wait.

"Where's Ty?" Zed asked. She spun in a circle, trying to spot him.

"Ty?" Olivia shouted, eyes wide.

Zed's fists clenched. "Ty!"

"Over here!" his voice came back. He sounded like he was a pool over from the one the others were in, two below Zed and Olivia's.

Olivia jetted, water scooping her up and shoving out and down.

Rolling her shoulders, Zed followed at a sedate pace. Better to watch from the rim while Olivia did the work. Olivia hadn't gotten shot, or done as much of the flying around, so she had the Current to spare anyway.

The big guy was on his back, propped against a tree on the rim of the pool to the side and above the one they'd been aiming for. Olivia planted her hands on his pecks, and then called up, "He's got some broken ribs, and a broken leg, but I've got it."

"Good!" Zed called back, not sure what they could've done if she didn't have it. Nat was probably drained, and Bee had sounded out trying to fix Seth, and Joey had healed Zed. They were all running on empty.

Still on watch over the others in the bot-filled bottom pool, Joey looked up at Zed and asked, "Cases?"

"Up here, under the ones that were recharging," Zed explained, thumbing over her shoulder.

"I'll swim down and get them if you'll carry them to the beach," he joked, his smile wide and teasing.

"Screw off," Zed fired back.

Joey gave a mocking salute, sunlight gleaming on his glasses. "Aye-aye."

"Insubordinate piece of shit," Zed grumbled, turning to face the wreckage.

Damn.

Someone had to fetch the cases, and Zed was already there. Might as well get it over with. She set her guns on the beach and dove. A tiny flash of Current told her where the boxes were in the murk. There were two, each about a meter long, and a half meter tall and wide. Doable, but her heart was beginning to pound, beating against her ribs as she fought to not look at the looming machinery overhead. A segmented limb hung before her, its eight sharp mandibles dug deep into the stone.

That was enough. Zed was done with this bull. Using the last of her Current, she reached out and pulled the two cases towards her, dragging them along as she swam back to the rim. Rising from the water, she met and smirked back at Joey's surprised expression. The two cases crunched as they crushed stray pebbles in their arrival beside her.

Then Zed was falling, her limbs tingling and numb as her last iota of Current drifted away.

Crap.
Too much.
Sleepy…

Everything was ok.

Everything was fine.

Nat breathed deep, sucking in the warm afternoon air as her adrenaline eased. Things hadn't gone quite as planned, but it had worked out. Everyone was alive, the robots were dead; it was over.

Robotic bits were strewn around, divots torn in the grass and stone by bullets and clawed limbs. Crystalline dust and cratered steel clung to ivory armor, like the waterlogged wreckage of miniature worlds. Mud and blood stained the pale robotics, drifting on the runoff of the pool's surface, slowly mixing, diluting thinner and thinner.

Pulling Seth a little higher on the berm, Nat straightened and caught Joey's eye.

A tiny smile curled the corners of his mouth. "Ready?"

"Yeah," Nat replied, a bit abashed at how much she'd tuned out while healing Seth.

"Cases are up there," Joey said, jerking his chin two pools up. "How much do you have left?"

Nat paused, considering. She was tired, but she wasn't done. "Close to empty, but I think I can carry a case down if I climb up the normal way."

"I'll take the other. There's only two," Joey said. "Bee?"

"On watch. Got it," Bee confirmed, already peering at the surrounding mountainside.

As Nat and Joey made their way over to the joint of their pool's rim and the lip of the one above it, she asked, "Where're Olivia and Ty? And Zed?"

"Up here," Olivia supplied. She appeared above them, glancing over the grassy tufts. "Ty's in the pool over there," she added, pointing to the side. "He needed a breather. Once you two have the cases, I'll take Zed down."

"Gotcha," Nat grunted as she began the climb. The slate-like layers of rock gave her easy footing, protruding like oddly angled shelves and ridges. Once on the grass above, she looked back and offered Joey a hand.

Surprised, he smiled and took it.

"Thanks," Joey said with a nod.

"Of course," Nat replied, heading over to the cases. Same size. Same shape. She hefted one. They even weighed the same. Sighing, she took her load and headed towards the berm.

"What's the plan?" Joey asked, right behind her.

"What, you all out of Current?" Nat joked, smirking back at him.

"Hey, I wasn't the one playing 'who can get shot more' with my boyfriend," Joey fired back, wry.

"Excuse you!" Nat said. Looking forward again, she paused, stunned for a breath. "I'm never going to get used to this, am I?" she asked no one in particular.

"The view or the Current?" Joey countered, coming to a stop beside her.

Glancing from the pool below to the world beyond, Nat genuinely didn't know which she'd meant. Current was strange, mind-bending, but this place was just gorgeous, however deadly its residents. Stark colors and bright light made it all glow, the whole thing seeming to breath through a thousand mouths as the forest swelled in the breeze, whitecaps just visible before they crashed on the far side.

"Hurry it up," Olivia growled from behind them, huffing and puffing beneath Zed's larger frame.

"Both," Nat admitted. Then she stepped forward and fell. Dropping feet first, she plummeted three meters before she shot forward, the water around her like fuel to her flame. She arced out towards the river. Catching herself left her exhausted. No more Current. She staggered, stumbled to the beach, and flopped down on the warm sand.

Joey was there, barely a step behind her, unfazed as he delicately set his box next to hers.

A breath later, Olivia descended, flutters of blue carrying her to the beach. She was dark, muted against Zed's pale skin and crop of bright blonde hair. The water fell away, leaving her to stride across the golden sands. She wobbled and nearly fell under Zed's weight.

Straightening, Olivia looked at Nat and Joey. One imperious eyebrow rising, she asked, "Waiting for something?"

"Nope," Nat said, smiling at the smaller woman's prickliness. Some things never changed. "Ty?"

"Coming!" he called. He started down the wall on the other side of the stream, slowly jumping from one ledge or block to the next. Further down, and directly opposite Nat, Seth and Bee did the same.

Olivia set Zed down, gently laying her on one side by the cases. "Joey, Nat, set up the tents," she ordered, arranging Zed's limbs so they wouldn't be stepped on. "Ty, Bee, and Seth will get the other cases once they're across."

"Got it," Joey said, setting off for the woods.

Walking backwards, Nat watched Olivia. "How're you doing?"

"I screwed up, but we made it," said Olivia, avoiding eye contact. "We'll talk it through later. Get the tents."

"Aye-aye," Nat said. She turned and jogged to catch up with Joey. Later sounded good. Maybe after a nap. Or in the morning.

It took a few minutes to find the red-barked tree where they'd hidden the gear, but Nat spotted it. Joey took one tent, Nat the other, and they left the six cases for the others. Five and a half really, considering the block of metal missing from one. They'd needed something that'd go through robot armor, and Vinna metal was the hardest thing they had.

They huffed and puffed their way back to the beach. Joey deployed his tent about a dozen meters from the wall. Sidling away, Nat made sure there was space enough that she wouldn't run into him, then stabbed her tent into the ground as well. A tiny flicker of Current and it blossomed, flowing outwards and enveloping the space around her.

Nat ducked out and stretched, popping tight muscles as Seth, Bee, and Ty passed by. At her stretch, they wandered a bit off course. Seth, in the lead, almost ran into the leading edge of Nat's tent, and Bee nearly hit Joey's a second later. Ty slowed almost to a stop, wide eyed.

A smirk tugged at Nat's lips, but she hid the tiny flush that warmed her face as she lowered her arms. Ty had been accidental, Seth had been intentional, and Bee had been a surprise. Nat had forgotten that Bee liked girls. Oops. Kinda mean, teasing her. Teasing Seth was fun though. Nat liked the zingy warmth that shot up her spine when he looked at her. Especially when it brought back memories. It was nice to have good memories out here. As long as he didn't piss anyone off, they'd keep making good memories. She sighed, remembering Seth's attempts to avoid the fight with the robots. She'd talked him out of it before he went to Zed or Olivia, which was good. If they didn't berate or beat him into cooperation, Joey might've gone Terminator on him. Again.

The memory of Joey's abrupt aggression made Nat frown. She forgot about that when she talked to him. He was smiley, not exactly friendly, but approachable in a calm, casual way. It made it easy to forget that day in he'd shot stickmen, or dueled a giant centipede, or charged head on at a bunch of battle-robots. Or beat up Seth. She looked over at Joey, curiosity sparking. Was he more than he appeared?

Joey noticed and frowned. "Everything alright?"

"Yeah," Nat said, shaking her head. Must be her imagination. Besides, he was weird, but she had fun memories to linger on. If Joey were an issue, Zed would figure him out. Or Olivia. It wasn't Nat's job.

"Glad Seth made it," Joey said, slowing as the other two hurried on towards the wall.

"Yeah," Nat said, smiling at her own success. She'd saved him. "Near thing though."

"Practice will help," said Joey, frowning slightly as he thought. "We're all getting better."

For a moment, Nat processed that. They were. A week ago, they'd have died. No question. They were learning. Growing. There was something amazing in that, soul healing, and at the same time cold and fearsome.

"And next time won't be a shit-show," Olivia called over as she opened one of the new cases.

"What'd we get?" Nat asked, focusing on the loot. She didn't want to push whatever issues Olivia was trying to deal with. The fight hadn't gone as badly as it could've, not by a long shot, but she wouldn't believe Nat on that. Zed was the expert, so it'd have to wait till she was up again.

"Hats?" Olivia mumbled, holding up one of whatever they were.

It was rounded at the back, like a biker's helmet, but the front was bladed, prow-like. The lower portion of the face tapered back, ending near the wearer's chin, while the upper stretched forward about six inches, like a horn. It was all the same dappled green-gray as the suits.

"Looks like head protection to me!" Joey said, his excitement bubbling through as he jogged over and pulled another from the open case. "Five a box?"

"One for everyone who could've made it," Nat guessed, following him. The thought made her sad. The woman the Stickmen had killed, the one Olivia had found, and some other who'd died in this paradise, unfound; they'd never known why they were here.

"Bit loose," Olivia said, settling her helm onto her shoulders.

Joey tapped a few letters at the back of the one he'd picked up. Initialed, like the suits.

"Oh," Olivia said, abashed as she lifted the helmet off again.

"This one…" Nat mumbled, picking up the smallest one and checking the tag, "Is… I.W.'s?"

"Must be one of the one's who didn't make it," Joey guessed.

"Here's yours," Olivia said, offering Nat a helm with the initials N.H. inside.

Taking it, Nat lowered it over her head. For a few seconds, it was dark, and then the world around her grew bright. From the way the interior had felt in her hands, she knew it was rounded and padded, but the beach snapped into focus around her. Colors and depth fluctuated for a breath, then it was as if there were nothing between her and the world.

Mouth agape, Nat reached out and poked Joey's shoulder.

"Yeah?" Joey said, looking up from his search of the other box. "Oh! How is it?"

"I can see everything!" Nat gasped.

"Well, that's handy," laughed Joey, continuing his search.

"No!" Nat said, annoyed. "Like it doesn't obstruct anything. I think it must have a screen on the inside or something."

"That's definitely handy," said Joey, thoughtful as he checked the last helmet. He smiled. "Always the last one." He slipped it on. "Whoa."

"Right?" Nat said, bouncing a bit in excitement. "It's incredible."

"Yeah," Joey mumbled, his helmet turning this way and that. "I wonder if…"

"It does thermal too," Olivia said, half-laughing as she whipped around. "Just give it a pulse and want it."

"Nice!" Joey said. "Convenient that the Vinna gear is all keyed to work the same way."

"Simple, easy; I'm a fan," Olivia agreed. "I also like that these things would give a mean head-butt."

"The angles are good too," Joey said, his hands running across the exterior of his helm. "Most things should just glance off, at least if they come from the front."

"Not getting shot in the head sounds really good," Nat agreed, nodding. Light and snug, her helm moved easily with her head, but there was no breeze. "Guys!" Nat blurted, feeling around her neck. Her collar had connected to the helmet. "They seal!"

Joey and Olivia copied her, feeling the smooth transition of the high necks of the suits into the lower edges of the helmets.

"How're we breathing?" Joey asked, oddly calm.

"Alien tech, alien air-filters?" Olivia answered.

A few seconds later, Olivia figured it out and tugged her helmet off. She beamed victoriously at them.

Joey tilted his helmeted head. "What's the trick?"

Olivia raised one sarcastic brow. "Pulse and want it."

"Oh," Joey grumbled. A second later, his collar separated from the helm and he pulled it off. "Right…"

"Should've thought of that," Nat laughed, rueful.

Olivia shook her head, waving at them, and dismissed the mistake without a word. She sighed, prodding the bottom of the crate. "Wish they'd given us more of the patches too."

"Did they give us another map?" Nat wondered.

Joey pulled another orb from an indentation at the bottom of the second case. Cupping it, he pulled water to his palms. Color flowed forth, unfurling into a map. There they were, a gently pulsing spot of green. A red dot was south of them. Maybe two days downriver, back the way they'd come. Pretty close to where they'd been camping before coming to get the robots, actually.

And then the blip moved. Not far, but just enough to be noticeable.

Joey grunted, his eyes suddenly wide.

Olivia leaned in, staring.

It moved again, slowly sliding a tiny bit closer as it pulsed again.

They waited, silent, and it pulsed closer, following a bend in the river.

"Looks like this bunch is coming to us," Olivia whispered.

Once again Joey smiled, relishing the smoky pungencies of the local meat. Kaskan, this time. Not as good as beef. It lacked the tenderness and fat, but the lean muscle tasted like a cross between trout and veal. He liked the new wood, too. Smokier than the other trees he'd tried. He'd been testing a few different branches the last few weeks, and this one, the red-barked kind, gave the food a peppery aftertaste.

The others were quiet, arrayed like stones around the fire. They smoldered, anger and fear hidden beneath silent exteriors. Arguments had kicked off when Olivia had told them the next fight was coming to them. The shouting had only died out when food had been handed around. Hunger was more of a motivator than fear; at least when the food smelled good and the terrors were days away.

Thank goodness.

Joey's belly had been about to collapse into a black hole. Fighting, Current, sneaking. It'd been a long day.

Munching away, Joey pondered his own fear. What little he had. There was no way to know what was coming, but at least they knew it was coming. Would've been nice to know what kind of alien they were killing next, for tactical reasons. Maybe these ones would have wings. Winged aliens could be fun. Tricky to hit, but in the woods they'd be forced to come down and get shot, like everything else.

Ugh. Hopefully these wouldn't be burrowers, like the bugs. That'd been a mess. Joey's nose wrinkled; distaste nearly spoiling his current mouthful of croc.

They'd gotten lucky that time, and one of the things Joey and Zed agreed on was that luck wasn't enough. Today had been better, but it'd been close. Those robots could've been able to hit them at any range, so getting in close had been their best chance.

Glancing down at his scaled patches, Joey smiled. At least he'd been on the better team. Less chance of dying was always better.

But they all needed to survive this. That was the other goal.

'Other' goal because Joey was still considering how to prioritize personal survival compared to group survival. Three weeks ago he'd wondered what eating Olivia would be like, but now the thought made him wince, and not just because he needed her to lead.

Which was… odd?

Joey was getting used to being part of a team, which was strange enough, but there was a sense of priority to them. Something that made saving them feel worth risking himself. Odd. It wasn't that he cared about them, no. Respect? Maybe.

Respect was new. So was risking himself for others. The two jumbled in his head, interwoven yet distinct, oddities in their own right.

Pivoting from that mess, Joey focused on the now. Survival. Patches were the best armor they had. More armored patches would be helpful no matter what. It'd be handy if they could just make them, but that would be a flaw in the aliens' methods. If all of this was a test, it didn't make sense to provide a reproducible tool that would solve the problem.

Not unless the point was to see if the rat in the maze thought to try…

Just to be sure, Joey delicately ran a tendril of Current around his shoulder patch, feeling it out. The water soaked in, wetting the space between the scales, the hard ridges and spines that reinforced each jagged disc. No magic though.

Shrugging to himself, Joey let the water slip from his grip. Good to be sure.

Bee stood, abruptly rising from her seat to declare, "Ok, we need to talk this shit through."

"Inevitable," Joey muttered. He took another bite of his portion of croc. At least he was mostly done. If he had to throw aside his food it'd get all sandy. Wasteful, but better that than let someone waste Current on an ally.

Bee ignored him. "So, the first thing-"

"What is there to talk through?" Seth asked, bursting in like a fist through paper. "They're coming, we run. Eventually, they'll stop chasing us."

"Big assumption," Zed noted. Her expression was deadpan, but there was a tic to her foot, an annoyed tap.

"So is thinking that we can take them head on," Seth countered, louder, heated.

"If we stay, we can dig in, give ourselves a chance to see them coming rather than showing our backs," Zed retorted. "It gives us more control over where this fight happens. If we run, the time we have to prepare will only decrease."

"Yesterday, we ran for hours. Not jog. Ran," declared Seth, his voice low as he shot to his feet. His right hand pointed decisively at each of them in turn. "You've all thought about it. I know you have. Magic, Current, this planet, whatever; we aren't normal anymore. We run faster, we run further, we fight harder, and we jump higher. We can outrun whatever new monsters the aliens are throwing at us."

"Vinna," Ty corrected.

Seth frowned, confused. "What?"

"Vinna," Ty repeated, scratching his chin. "That's what they call themselves."

"And they wouldn't have sent whatever these things are after us if we couldn't handle them," Zed threw in. "Right, Joey?"

"We've been able to take everything so far," agreed Joey, tentative. It was a not-so subtle warning. Zed was reminding Seth of whom he was shouting at. Joey knew that Zed had given Seth a talking to, and he fondly remembered shoving Seth in the river. And Olivia… If she got pissed, Nat might have to do some more repair work on her boy toy before they had their fun times tonight.

"You think we're meant to survive this?" Seth demanded, wide eyed and incredulous.

"Fingers crossed," Joey said, deadpan. Seth's volume had dropped, less of a near shout and more emphatic. He wasn't pointing either. Zed had taken the wind from his sails.

Nat hugged her knees to her chest and shifting closer to the fire. "The bugs almost wiped us out. I'm not so sure we're supposed to survive. Not all of us."

"The fewer of us there are, the harder it would be for any of us to make it," Zed said, her voice even, reasoning. "If this is a tool for making soldiers of us, they'd need to bond us, make us into unit. On the way, it's sink or swim. Hell, I'd bet the things we're fighting now are close to what they want us to fight later. The whole point is for us to make it through."

"That's if they want soldiers," Nat returned. "Maybe it's like a game-show. They keep knocking us down and laughing until they get bored and end the season."

"That sounds more like what asshole aliens would do than recruiting for their army," Seth agreed, nodding. "How could they trust us after this?"

"They could promise to take us home," Bee said, her voice quiet, almost a whisper.

Ty nodded. "That'd make sense. Roman legionnaires were given land after they finished their term. A new home for their labors. Other peoples did that on Earth. Think how hard a person would fight to get back home."

"Why would a space faring race that could not only get to Earth, but not be spotted on the way, kidnap a bunch of random people for its military?" Seth said, spreading his arms as though begging them to see reason. "We aren't special. We aren't the Chosen Ones. We're, what, a wilderness expert," he gestured at Joey, "A med student," Nat, "A single soldier from an army that shoots unarmed protestors," Zed, "A lit student," Ty, "An American liberal arts brat," Bee, "A rich kid," himself, "And some homeless person from yee olde London towne," he finished with a mocking wave at Olivia.

"Watch it," Zed said, the words like the glint of steel from the shadows.

Joey quirked his head, curious. Seth wasn't strong enough to really start a fight, but verbal stuff, leadership stuff, that sort of thing was Olivia's job. How she handled it would be interesting. Or would she leave it to Zed?

"Seth," Nat began, worried.

"No," Seth said, waving her off. "I'm right. We aren't special, yet you all think they need us for something. We don't know anything about them, but you think you understand why they traveled through space, from further away than our oldest probes can even see? Maybe they just wanted to make sure we worth hunting, or maybe they've been fattening us up to eat, or they've decided we're worth dissecting, or maybe they just like watching us freak out and nothing's even coming."

It was noise. None of it was actually helping anyone make a decision. Joey focused on Olivia, waiting.

At some point, Olivia slipped her hand to Zed's shoulder, keeping her seated. From the look on Zed's face, she was ready to stand up and give Seth a nice, public chewing.

But Olivia stood up instead.

Scanning the others, Joey took in the different expressions, the different reactions. Zed had a small, pleased smile. Bee was tired, but curious. Ty smirked. Nat frowned, worried. And Seth's teeth ground, his jaw set. He wasn't backing down.

This was going to be good. None of them had seen Olivia step up and lead yet, at least not outside of combat. The closest had been ages ago, when she'd stabbed Zed with a fishbone.

Joey wished he had some popcorn. Maybe a big foam finger with 'Stabby is #1' on it.

The silence stretched for a moment. Olivia was shorter than Seth, by more than a foot. Her sharp, gaunt features had filled out in the last few weeks. They still had an edge, but she looked stronger, fuller, and those steel gray eyes glowed, bold against her tanned skin and dark hair.

"You're scared," Olivia said. There was nothing but surety behind the words, like stones thudding into a hole.

"You-" Seth began, his features twisting. There was fear there, embarrassment, wrath, too.

Olivia's right hand shot out and pounded into Seth's gut. He bent double, gasping as the air vanished from his lungs. Abruptly, her torso spun the other way. Her left leg snapped up and out, smacking brutally against Seth's thigh.

Seth didn't have the air to cry out, but his gasp was desperate, wheezing. He dropped to his knees, clutching the newly abused muscle.

Joey winced. Getting hit like that wouldn't do lasting injury, but it'd hurt like hell. Lots of twitching and stinging.

"You're scared," Olivia repeated, standing over Seth. Her words lingered between the cool, calm range of the unworried and the vaguest hints of empathy's fervor. "We all are. That's ok. That's normal. I've been scared as long as I can remember. But when we have to decide how we're going to survive, or how we die, you don't give in." Her eyes went around the fire, locking with everyone in turn.

Seth sat up, his jaw tight, each breath long and ragged.

Olivia squatted down. It put her head below his, cocked to one side as she studied him. "Being scared and getting us killed are different. You can be scared. That's good. Healthy. Getting us killed isn't. We need a plan. Suggestions were made, but you were too busy being afraid to think. Think. If the Vinna don't want us to survive, we won't. That simple. We plan on it being possible to win, otherwise there's no point. If you can't handle that, then go. Those of us who're staying need to get some rest."

Olivia stood and met one set of watchful eyes after another. "That goes for everyone. Run now or fight tomorrow."

"Tomorrow?" Ty blurted. "That soon?"

"I think that was metaphorical," Bee answered in a stage whisper.

"Shush, Boss is doing a heroic speech," Zed added.

"Really? Seemed a bit dark to me," Bee said.

Joey snorted. "I liked it."

"Like I said, bit dark," Bee repeated.

"She's learning," Zed said, patting Bee comfortingly on the shoulder.

"Thanks guys," Olivia grumbled. She returned to her seat by Zed. "Really feeling the support."

"You had it covered." Zed shrugged. "Croc?" she offered, waving at what remained of the carcass over the coals.

Olivia nodded. "Might as well. It'll just rot if we don't finish it."

Joey let his eyes glaze, watching it all.

Chattering lightly of weather and the food, Bee and Ty went for more food. Nat joined in too, but Seth took the time to think. Every now and then he'd frown, his leg twitching. It seemed like he wanted to storm off, to vanish somewhere and fester, but he couldn't walk. Not yet.

Eventually, after the hubbub had lost any remnant of awkwardness, Seth's expression changed, bit of a smile cracking through as the banter came faster and faster. When the ice broke and he rejoined the conversation, no one mentioned the showdown.

The decision had been made.

Seven humans would use whatever they had, in whatever time they had left, to get ready for whatever was coming for them.

Joey felt oddly proud of the choice.

Flexing his right hand, Ty rubbed the palm with his left. The joints popped and cracked. The muscles were tight and strained after long hours of repetition. He glared at the culprits behind the pain: one battered, distant tree and the ovoid handgun on the stone beside him. The soreness was already fading, washed away by a soft wave of cooling Current, but he'd had to think about it. He was tired enough that he had to work to keep going.

On the other hand, the timing was pretty damn impressive. Ty smirked to himself, glancing over his shoulder. The sun was halfway behind the mountaintop, its gleaming gold light cascading down the tiered pools, turning trees and outcroppings into shadowy wisps.

After the morning run, stretching, and then lifting rocks, Zed had told them all to find a spot on the lowest tier of pools and start shooting. She'd also said that they should keep an eye out for Kaskans. Seated on the berms of murky pools to fire at the beachside tree line, the big lizards would be able to sneak up from behind.

That'd been this morning.

After most of a day of shooting, slowly burning away Current and attention, that ominous darkness at Ty's back was looming large.

"Enough to make you paranoid," Ty grumbled.

Spread about twenty meters apart, the Ty and five other shooters sat along the rim of one very wide pool. The seventh, Zed, was teaching, which apparently meant hovering over slackers. For now, she was adjusting Bee's aim a couple pools to his left. Between Zed and the lizards that could pop up and eat someone at any moment, paranoia seemed justified.

With a groan, Ty picked up his gun, slapped the bottom against a stone for a reload, and got ready to start again. Rock crunched as it vanished into the gun. A trickle of water was beginning to leak into the rough-hewn bowl that'd been left behind. Others like it lay scattered around him. He'd shot a lot of rock today.

Ty took his time with the first shot.

Smooth breath in, long one out, both eyes open.

After the first bullet, Ty kept them flying nearly as fast as his finger could pull. He gave himself a blink between each to make sure his aim was right. It usually was. The tree across the river was lower than he was, but not by much, and the spot he'd designated the 'Bull's-eye' was becoming one big divot in its dense gnarls.

Twenty shots later, Ty slapped the intake against the stone and did it again. His eyes never left the target, but there was no hurry in the motion, no rush. Zed had slapped him in the back of the head the first time she'd caught him hurrying, and she'd had plenty of time to reinforce the lesson long before they went after the robots.

It was starting to feel natural. A single fluid cycle: aim, shoot, reload. Ty had stopped counting his shots. He knew how many were left. Some part of him knew to remember.

But Ty wasn't the best. He knew that, and he'd made his peace with it. He was good, and that was enough. Bee… Bee was the best. He hadn't been sure of it till today. Over the first few hours her shots had shifted deeper and deeper into the trees, till he was sure she had to be hitting one twice as far as anyone else's.

Ty smiled. Good for her. She could have the 'top shooter' title; he just wished he could figure out how she did that ice-ball trick. They were still the worst at making knives or swords, but Bee could wave a hand and build an igloo or a bridge. She couldn't hold it as long, but she could go big. He was jealous of that, and he knew why. It wasn't even a competition thing anymore. Or a hero thing. It was that what she did looked like magic, like something from a book or a movie or a comic. It was magical, in the most ephemeral and childlike sense of the word. There was so much color, so much majesty, like the laws of reality had suddenly dropped to their knees and begged to help. It made ice knives and shooting look a bit paltry.

But of the three, the paltry ones lasted longer, and had a greater chance of keeping them alive in a fight. Olivia had proven that with the bugs. Bows, arrows, and a knife had worked better than all Bee could create. So, it was good that she could shoot too.

Ty would keep trying though. He'd keep making things, big and small, and he'd keep shooting. The enemy was coming, and when they got here he'd-

A sound hit Ty's senses like a jackhammer. It was odd, like a sudden incarnation of that looming presence at his back. His finger froze, his gun still half full.

This was going to be bad.

Ty tried to dodge, his feet digging into the grass. Teeth clamped down on his shoulder, like a pneumatic vice. At least it hadn't been his head.

Then Ty saw the blood smeared tusk pushing between his ribs. He screamed. Blinking, he tried to disprove his eyes.

One of its eyes was waiting, watching him from centimeters away. A black film flicked down. A humming rumble vibrated through Ty's very bones. Then it began to toss him, flicking him back and forth like a ragdoll.

Ty screamed again. Fighting to breathe through the pain, Ty choked, coughing as something wet and thick filled his throat. He shoved his gun over his shoulder and squeezed. The gun thudded. The Kaskan grunted, but it didn't stop. It dove back into the pool, water splashing around its massive, churning limbs as they submerged.

Rage and fear and frustration roiled in Ty's chest, rising above the pain and shock. He dropped the gun, willed something cold and sharp into existence, and slammed the pointy end into the Kaskan's black-lidded eye.

The eye burst, erupting a cloud of milky white liquid. The Kaskan thrashed, dragging Ty back and forth through the water. Something snapped in his chest, the sudden sound reverberating down his spine.

Screaming, his eyes clenched shut at the pain, Ty stabbed again and again, trying to dig further into the space behind the dead eye. Blade met bone and lost, skidding off and finding only leathery scale.

Red mist filled the water, billowing with every jerk and toss and shove. A thicker cloud wove through it, a pristine white that glowed in the sunlight.

Another rib snapped.

Ty's lungs chest felt at once collapsing, empty and airless, and expanding, punctured and spreading from the yank of tooth and tusk. He gasped fighting to breathe as stars spotted his vision. A cough, a spewing of blood and bile and water, then Ty sucked in a mouthful of fresh water.

The whole world shifted.

It was as though everything took an abrupt left turn, spun in a circle, and then sat back down where it had started, and now Ty was left dizzy. He was suddenly, painfully, aware of the long Kaskan's body stretching out behind him, of the rocking and jolting plant-life that rose from the depths of the pool, of the outer rim, where little waves lapped and splashed at the stone and roots. He could feel the spill of the pool above, the flow of warm water coming down, and he could feel the pool beyond.

Most importantly, Ty sensed the Kaskan's body double over like a coiling spring. It was going to flip. It was going to flip and slam Ty back down onto the surface. It'd break his neck, but barely faze the larger predator.

So Ty pulled. He tugged at that massive tail that coiled below him with a tendril of Current, and the Kaskan's doubling motion became a roll.

It froze, stiffening at the grasp. Ty stabbed at the empty eye socket again, pressing his will, his Current, into the blade. It crunched and dug deep somewhere near the base of the skull.

The Kaskan's jaw shot open. A clawed forelimb shoved Ty towards the bottom. He twisted to face the lizard and stared.

Ty had felt it, he'd felt the way its body stretched through the water, but he hadn't seen it.

It was massive. Ten meters long, at least. Bigger than the first one they'd killed. One empty eye socket oozed milk. Its remaining eye was lidded in black, almost invisible among the green-gray lattice of scales that left it a near shadow. Without the sunset's gold light behind it, he'd never have spotted it. That huge tail flicked, its body undulating as it surged towards the shallows.

Then it stopped.

Its head lowered, peering at him.

One clawed forelimb reached out, clamped webbed digits on either side of Ty's relatively minuscule knife, and pulled. The Kaskan flicked its wrist and the blade spun into the shadows at the bottom of the pool. Water churned again as its limbs shoved backward. Then it was gone, vanishing over the lip in an explosion of bubbles.

Ty stared. There'd been intelligence in those eyes, more than a lizard's cunning or the menace of hunger and predation. The way it'd removed the knife…

Abruptly, abashedly, Ty remembered the rather large knife on his belt. It was nice to know Current was becoming instinctual, but damn. He could've just used the real thing.

Speaking of… Ty focused. Current flowed from him. His gun came a second later, gently plowing through the water. He tucked the ovoid weapon in his belt and pushed off the bottom.

As his face broke the water's surface, Ty sucked in the clean, fresh, sweet oxygen. Or tried to. Opening his mouth reminded him just how much water, blood, and who knew what else had flooded his lungs. A surge of liquid shot up his throat and splattered before him, adding more red to the maroon murk.

Gasping, wincing at the burn of bile at the back of his throat, Ty breathed deep and tried not to think about how he'd just survived without air for quite a bit longer than was normal.

Yup. Definitely not thinking about it. Not thinking about that deep drink of water that'd somehow oxygenated him.

Nope.

A view of his surroundings provided a good distraction pretty quickly.

Specifically, the sight of Zed, Bee, and Nat. Zed and Bee stood at the lip of the pool, firing at something in the river beyond. Nat splashed through the water, racing towards Ty.

"You ok?" Nat queried, slowing as their eyes met. Her frown was concerned, but tempered with a violent kind of anger that made her lips draw tight.

"Fine," Ty replied. He swam into the shallows till he could touch the bottom and walk, all too aware of the bloody mess in the water around him.

"Good," Nat said, her tense features easing slightly. "We were worried you were in over your head."

"Only literally," Ty joked, forcing a smile. The pain was gone, but he felt tired. His hands weren't sore anymore.

Nat's tight lips curved into a nervous grin. "What, did it want to play patty-cake and you missed and hit its eye instead?"

"Something like that," Ty replied, rolling his eyes.

"Don't mention that to Zed," Nat advised, wincing. "She might give you more practice."

Ty smiled. Fighting off a Kaskan felt pretty badass, but the banter felt better. It was one thing to get flattered for pulling something off, but the oddly comfortable jokes were just the right amount of calm and supporting.

Snagging Ty's arm as he came even with her, Nat shot a rush of cold through him. She was checking, just in case he'd missed something.

"Thanks," Ty muttered, comforted as much by her concern as her banter.

"What was that about practice?" Zed asked, pointing her dual pistols at the ground as she turned to glare at them.

"Nothing, Sergeant," Ty said, snapping her what he figured was close to a salute.

"Don't do that," Zed warned, frowning.

Ty froze. "What?"

"Uh oh," Nat chuckled. She released her grip on him, satisfied that he was ok.

Zed's frown didn't change one iota. "Salute."

"Don't salute?" Ty asked, confused.

"Got there eventually, shit-for-brains," said Zed, so dry that her voice reminded him of cracking potato chips. "If you can even call that a salute."

"Sorry?" Ty offered.

"Don't let me see you doing it again."

Ty frowned. He'd never been a soldier, how was he supposed to know that he'd been doing it wrong?

"And why weren't you watching the water?" Zed added, spinning full around and pacing angrily towards him. Water sloshed and splashed around her feet, sounding as unhappy as her face looked.

"I was," Ty said, trying to think through the muddle of exhaustion and banter and Zed's glare. "It came in too fast. I didn't have a chance to turn around before it hit me."

"Which means?" Zed prompted. She stopped with her nose inches from Ty's. Her pale skin glowed with shades of orange and pink; locks of her cropped blonde hair dancing in the evening breeze, almost red in the sunset light.

"I should work on being aware," supplied Ty, glad that he couldn't blush. He should've led with the suggestion, instead of waiting to be told. Dumb.

"And your helmet?" Zed said.

Ty winced. "I should keep it on?"

Zed punched him in the shoulder. "Next time, don't scare me."

"Ow," Ty grumbled, rubbing the spot as she turned and headed back to the pool's dry rim. His helmet was still there, high and dry.

"It's a good lesson for all of us," Nat added, offering a small smile.

"Yeah," Ty agreed, smiling back. They'd been scared for him. That was... actually really nice. Heartwarming. "Just wish there'd been a less painful way to learn it."

"Nat!" Seth shouted, echoing across the tiers.

Seth knelt at the rim on the other end of the massive pool, his gun pointed at the river below. At the edge of the pool above, Joey stood, watchful of the water beyond.

The cause for the call had been Olivia. She was waist deep, her helmed head hidden by a Kaskan maw. Her gun was black with blood and Current, so dark that it seemed to consume the very light, its muzzle jammed against a massive mess of ruined flesh near the base of the Kaskan's throat. Her other hand clutched a dagger that protruded from the side of the Kaskans mouth, barely missing her own head. The Kaskan was still, glassy eyed, visible only where rock held it above the water.

There was blood. A lot of blood.

"Fuck," Nat hissed, her whole body rising up and out of the water as a coil of blue unfurled, launching her in Olivia's direction. Bee and Zed followed her, flitting on bursts of spray and mist that hung in their wake.

Both exhausted and drained, Ty swam. It was only thirty meters or so. Swimming was fine.

"Some help here!" Olivia demanded, her voice clear as crystal despite monster and helm.

Rolling his eyes, Ty sped along, slicing through the warm blue. Thinking as he swam, Ty decided that there were three reasons he wasn't more freaked out right now.

One, Olivia's helm hadn't looked damaged. Not even a scratch where those massive teeth had clamped.

Two, Olivia's voice had sounded peeved, not scared.

And finally, Ty was just too tired to feel much of anything, besides exhaustion and pain.

Oh, and bonus factor, compared to all the other hell they'd been through, this just didn't seem too bad.

Four reasons.

Huh. Reason four was alarming. Maybe he should be freaked out by that.

Then Ty's leading hand slapped into something scaled and leathery. He recoiled, jerking upright, his eyes wide. One big Kaskan, dead ahead. One trapped Asian woman, helmet clutched by rows of death-locked teeth, to the right.

Zed was already working, her knife drawn and hacking into the joint of the jaw. Nat held Olivia's shoulders, eyes closed in concentration.

Clambering onto a shallower stone, Ty stepped up between them. He hesitated, looking at the thing's massive, toothy jaw with distaste.

"Getting bored," Olivia growled. Her knife melted away, dribbling fresh water into the crimson mess. She waved for someone to hurry up and free her.

"I can lever the lower jaw down," Zed said, catching Ty's eye. "You got the upper?"

"Yeah, sure," he agreed, eyeing the row of teeth that he'd have to find a way to grip. Suboptimal.

"Better use your knife, in case you slip," Zed ordered.

Ty nodded, drew his knife, and wedged the blade under the upper jaw's front edge. With one hand on the handle, the other on the blunt back of the blade's tip, it was a lot less nerve-wracking. Thank goodness Zed's brain wasn't Current-fried.

"One, two, three, lift," Zed counted off.

At once, Ty went up as Zed levered down. Muscles groaned all down his back. The body twitched, but Nat got Olivia out and helped her stand. Once they were clear, Ty slipped his knife free. He flinched at the sharp clicks of teeth meeting.

"She seems ok," Nat supplied, not letting go of Olivia's shoulder.

"I'm fine," Olivia declared, audibly rolling her eyes. "This thing is great." She knocked the side of the helm with her knuckles. "I got distracted by how it interacts with the gun. Dropped my water-sense. That thing showed up about five seconds later."

Silence hung for a long moment.

Then Zed let out a low whistle. "Either that's an amazing coincidence…"

"Or they can use Current," Ty finished. He blinked as thoughts scudded through his cloudy brain. Why couldn't this stuff all happen when he was capable of dealing with it?

"It also means that it's possible to feel when someone is using Current," Olivia added, removing her helmet. With her inky hair cut short and the dry-seal on the helm, she looked untouched by her near miss with a dino's belly. "Detecting Current. Handy."

"No shit," Zed said, nodding, brows knit with thought. "If we can do it. Maybe it's just Kaskans."

Ty cleared his throat, realizing that he actually had something to add. "When the other one dragged me under, something happened. My sense of the pool skyrocketed all of a sudden."

Olivia raised one questioning eyebrow. Nat rolled her eyes at his pause.

"It happened right after I sucked in a mouthful of water," Ty explained, trying to remember exactly how it'd happened. The broken ribs and scraping teeth part of the memory were a bit distracting.

"Were you worn out before?" Nat asked, frowning.

"Very," Ty said, nodding ruefully. "It can't have just been me."

"It's not the water, we've been drinking it for weeks," Olivia grumbled, tugging at her ear.

"There was a lot of blood in the water," Ty added, thinking. Ugh. Disgusting.

Nat winced and Zed turned in a slow circle.

Olivia's hand froze mid-tug. "Seriously? We're vampires now?"

"I've never heard of a vampire that used water magic and dueled pool-diving super-gators to get their aquatic radar," Ty replied. He'd been trying for sarcastic, but he barely had the energy to pull off dry.

"He's gotcha there, boss," Nat chuckled.

Zed smiled. "Magic blood. Alien gators that sense Current. This place just keeps getting better."

"We get tired when we use Current," Ty said, words dropping quickly from his tongue as his thoughts began to regain quickness. "Maybe it's a type of energy? If so, the Kaskan's might use it to navigate the pools, avoid getting into fights, find mates, et cetera. If they run into another Kaskan's sphere of energy, they know to stay away, or come closer. Ours probably felt different, which is why they waited and watched us. Curiosity."

"Or they were just hungry," Olivia countered, glancing at the mound of dead lizard a few steps away.

Ty shook his head, frowning now. "The one that attacked me gave me a look before it left. It didn't look dumb, and it didn't look scared."

"Pretty sure reading alien reptiles' emotions via eye contact isn't on the list of available superpowers," Bee called over her shoulder, still watching the neighboring pool. "Hate to break it to you."

"Either way, they can sense Current, which means maybe we can too," Zed said, cutting off Ty's retort.

"If they even use Current," Nat added.

"If it isn't Current, we know it can pick up on us and that Ty used it," Seth pointed out, his voice carrying across the pool's still, sun dappled water.

"It's worth trying," Olivia decided. She turned and bent over the lizard's corpse.

"I, uh," Ty mumbled, suddenly feeling a bit worried. If she got some kind of alien blood disease because of this, it would be his fault. "What about–"

"Your idea," Zed said, pointing a warning finger at him.

That didn't make Ty feel any better.

The hole where Olivia had blasted the creature's neck oozed, dribbling thick red liquid into the clear water. Not clear anymore. A black, inky murk spread from the drip. Olivia leaned in, dipping her forefinger into the stream. Then she stood and licked the fingertip.

It took a few seconds for Ty to realize he was holding his breath.

Olivia shook her head. "Nothing."

"Where did you stab it?" Zed asked. "And don't think I've forgotten the part where you dropped your gun."

"I did that on purpose," said Ty, defensive.

Not looking at him, Nat leaned in and stage-whispered, "Not helping."

Zed's lips twitched but she didn't laugh.

"I stabbed it in the eye," Ty answered, giving up on his pride with a soft sigh.

"Did it bleed white?" Olivia asked, her eyes narrowing as thoughts turned, clicking and rolling like steel cogs behind those two gray irises.

"Yeah," Ty confirmed, nodding as he remembered the cloud of milky liquid that'd spread amongst the crimson.

Grunting, Olivia turned and squatted down next to the beast's face. In the time it took to blink, a piece of delicate, white fishbone was in her palm, thin and needle-like.

"Seriously?" Ty asked, trapped between revulsion at what he'd drunk and nausea at what Olivia was about to do.

Zed watched, unmoved, but added, "Boss, I'd like to request the 'dangerous magic alien liquid tasting' job."

"Jealous?" Olivia tossed back, poised.

"I don't care who it is, I have no idea how to heal poisoning, not to mention whatever bacteria or viral horror you might be chugging," Nat said, looking as ill as Ty felt. "Why don't we pass on the alien vampire tryouts?"

"Alien vampire tryouts?" Bee said, interest writ large in every word.

"You don't want to know," Ty answered, rubbing his face with both hands.

Bee groaned. "Now I really want to know!"

At that moment, while Bee's voice still bounced across the pool and rebounded from the stone, Olivia poked a tiny hole in the dark, murky eye. A single drop of pale white dribbled forth.

"You really, really don't," Nat said, watching with horrified fascination.

Ty grunted, his gut rolling, spinning like a top as the pale, thick liquid slid down the black eye, landing on the tip of Olivia's finger. The rotation stopped when her finger vanished into her mouth, but that only made the nausea worse. He burped, a surge of sickening acid and fumes coating his throat.

"Next time, don't share with the class," Zed coughed, waving her hand in his direction, fanning away the whiff she must've gotten.

"Sorry," Ty mumbled, trying to breathe through his nose.

A slow, small smile flowed across Olivia's features, her thin lips bending like a bow. There was something lethal in that smile that matched her eyes, glimmering like bits of cloudy ice. The smile, those eyes; they held silent a storm of unspoken screams and moans and the horrified spluttering of shock and disbelief and fear.

Cold rolled up Ty's spine. He shivered, but at the same time something heady filled his mind, some dark anger uncoiled, feeling the storm behind the silence. Anger, burning away the fear, sending a warm rush through his veins. It didn't boil, instead simmering as it mingled with curiosity and pride and a greedy want for the violence that hunkered, promising, behind Olivia's expression.

Ty couldn't tell if the shiver was instinct reacting to what he saw, or his body's surprise at the sudden rush. He saw Zed's smile, sharper, more like the stubborn, darkly immutable steel and shadow of a gun's barrel. Nat's frown held the same hunger, the want for Olivia's cold certainty, but the fear was still there, the worry.

They all wanted to live, but along the way they'd all gained a dark wish to hurt those that'd thrust them into this mess. Hell for hell, blood for blood.

And then it was gone, the moment passing as one breath became the next. Olivia's face smoothed, her usual smile back, filled with a pleased amusement, and a spark of glittering curiosity.

"I can feel the water a dozen pools up," Olivia explained, checking her finger for any remnants of the liquid. "It's not…" she trailed off. Bending at the waist, she plucked another drop from the thin stream that flowed from the eye.

Nat grumbled, all unintelligible incredulity.

Olivia tasted again. She nodded. "It's Current. Or at least it's got Current in it. But it's not…" She frowned. Streamers of water flew to her hand, congealing into a blue blade with a handle that flowed and curled around and between her fingers. "I can use it for other things, but if I do the sense goes away."

"It's Current with a plan?" Ty said, taking a shot at what she was trying to get across. It sounded right.

Olivia grunted the affirmative.

"That'll be useful," said Zed, her smile waning as thoughts flashed through her head.

"Yeah," Olivia muttered. Then she shook her head. "Joey, bottle this stuff for later," she snapped, her voice rising, pitched to carry to the others at the edge of the pool. "We're heading back to camp." She paused, glancing at Ty, lingering on his legs just as his calves began to tremble. "Zed, help Ty back, before he falls over. Bee, Seth, Nat, watch the water."

There was no silent moment, no breath when the words just hung in the air. Even to Ty's fast fading, exhausted mind; there was snap to the command, a sense of alacrity. He noticed Zed's spine straighten, her right arm twitching before she stepped over, tucking his arm over her shoulders.

"Thanks, sergeant," Ty said, smiling. Whatever pride he had left after that fight, at least now he wouldn't lose it by collapsing. The tents were close. Close, down the pool's hem, across the stream, and on the other side of the beach, close. On second thought, it sounded a lot less close now than he'd expected.

"You'll be fine," Zed told him. "I've got enough to lower us down and get across the stream." She guided him forward, heading towards on of the gently fountaining creases in the pool's edge.

"I wonder why some people have more Current," Ty grumbled, the idea rankling, his brow furrowed at the unfairness of it.

"You know, my old sergeant used to have an opinion on things like that," Zed said, humor warming her voice.

"Yeah?" Ty prompted, shuffling along through the water.

Zed chuckled. "Yeah, he used to say 'if you don't know and your sergeant can't tell you, it ain't your business'."

"And you wanna be just like him," Ty returned, rolling his eyes.

"Nah," Zed laughed, "But I think it's a decent solution to a question we can't answer."

"I don't like it," Ty complained, his frown returning.

"You're a big boy," Zed retorted, patting his broad shoulder with her free hand, "You'll live."

Flopping down on the warm sand, Seth groaned. Too much Current, not enough rest. Zed had always shown up when he slowed down, probably following any hint of slowing in the rhythmic thuds from the guns. She hunted the weakening drumbeats, pulling them back into line with a single reprimanding look, or a warning grunt. For some reason, her looks worked on him. After a dozen different schools in half that many years, a few lockups, a rehab center or three, and one military academy that'd lost its dining hall in a mysterious fire, the fact that Zed's looks affected him at all was surprising.

Ruffling his short, dark curls, Seth stretched, deepening the depression that cushioned and couched his back. It wasn't his first time on a beach. This one reminded him of Florida, sort of. There were more bugs there, more beaches, fewer mountains, and the pools were the chlorinated kind.

Home.

A long way from here.

Breath whistling through Seth's nose as he released a long sigh. The sun had vanished before they'd gotten back across the river to camp. The heat was still fading, lingering only in the water and the sand. Grains warmed his back as cool winds began to whip and dance through the night air.

Then Seth made a decision. It was time to look. He'd avoided it before the Stickmen, and he'd avoided it afterwards. There'd been enough to process, enough to survive. It was time to start working through this one.

So he looked at the sky, starry and bright. There was no moon, no breathtaking, shining sphere of pale light. The stars stole his breath instead. It was as though the bright white light of a full moon had broken, shattering into a chaos of glittering fragments, scattered across the blackness of infinity. Between the shards were mists and wisps, streams of dust-like particles that wove clusters of moon-bits together. They spiraled and streaked the sky, immovable, impassable, and bright.

A cloud scudded by, drifting on the wind, its pale, grayish form outlined in white wisps of starlight.

The sight of it all was like a judge's gavel. It rocked Seth, cementing the new reality. He wasn't Toto, and this wasn't Oz, but a slim hope had remained for some ruby slippers.

"Hey, Nat?" he queried, knowing she was somewhere in the tent behind him. He suddenly missed the warmth of her, the feeling of closeness and connection. There was too much emptiness, too much vastness among the stars that transfixed him.

"She's asleep," Joey's calm, even voice replied, only steps away.

Seth would've flinched, maybe shot the man a withering look, but he couldn't look away. The stars held him. "Oh," was all he said.

"You looked up," Joey noted, appearing at the corner of Seth's vision as he sat down beside him. "First time?"

"Yeah," Seth breathed, his eyes wandering along the magnificent, expansive billow of a glimmering cloak of light that hung halfway above the horizon.

"Fascinating, isn't it?" Joey hummed. "How does it make you feel?"

Seth snorted. "You my new shrink?"

"No, I'm curious," answered Joey. "I don't know what to make of it. I want to know if it makes you afraid, if all you see is the beauty of it, or if it's something else altogether."

"Uh," Seth mumbled, buying time. "And why would I tell you?"

"Because we're on the same side," Joey replied, still calm. "We had our problem, but that was a week ago."

"You shoved me," Seth noted, his gaze half on Joey's profile now.

"You were a dick," Joey returned, shrugging. "You were a dick again last night." His head turned, his eyes shifting to Seth. "I'm moving past it and trying to strike up a rapport."

"Yeah, right," Seth grumbled. "You probably just want Nat and think this is the best way to break us up."

"Not interested," Joey said, smiling bemusedly. "She's pretty, but she's so emotional. Nearly as emotional as you." He paused for a moment. "Well, maybe."

"What, too much humanity in her for you, robo-boy?" Seth shot back, a flush of anger and embarrassment rising to his cheeks.

"Spoiled brat," Joey threw back.

"Backwoods asshole."

"I prefer 'wilderness survivalist'," Joey corrected.

Seth laughed. "I bet you do."

The moment stretched. Wind rustled the trees, water splashed from the pools, a gentle gurgle of water across the beach under it all.

"Feel better?" Joey queried.

"Yeah. You?"

"You got your head on straight?"

Seth rolled his eyes. He did. It'd taken Zed's talk nearly a week ago to make him get that he needed to be part of the team, and it'd taken Olivia's last night to really drive the point home. He wasn't sure if he'd gotten the message they intended, but he had an idea. It was a team, and he was on it or he was out, but this team didn't have the option of losing. Somewhere between Olivia, the Kaskans, and the stars, it'd sunk in.

"Yeah," Seth replied, nodded. "I got it."

"Good, because-"

"Hey, Joey," Bee said, jogging over from the tents. "Do you have any of that plant you gave me?"

"That was nearly three weeks ago," Joey noted.

"Well, can you tell me where to find it?" Bee pushed, heated now.

"No need, I still have it," Joey said. He plucked a leaf from under the cuff of his suit.

Bee snatched it, glaring at him. "Why didn't you say so?"

"Curiosity."

"Why do you still have it?"

"It seemed to work pretty well. Never know when a painkiller might be handy."

"Oh. Well, thanks," Bee said. She spun and headed back towards the tents.

"Welcome," Joey muttered, wry amusement in his eyes as his attention returned to the stars.

"What was that about?" Seth prodded, wondering if Joey's annoying curiosity was infectious. He corrected the wonder a moment later. He'd always been plenty curious all on his own, no backwoods runt-Rambo needed.

"Painkiller," Joey stated.

"Duh," Seth grunted. "Why did she need it?"

"Are you telepathic?"

"No?" Seth said, confused. Had there been something unsaid that he'd missed?

"Oh good," Joey replied, grinning down at him. "Neither am I."

Seth smiled and rolled his eyes. "Fine. We're both clueless."

"Now you're catching on."

"Then why give it to her?"

"Because I can always find more?" Joey offered.

Seth chuckled. "Or maybe because you're afraid of her?"

This time, Joey didn't look away from the stars as he said, "Aren't you?"

"Maybe a little," Seth admitted.

"Good," Joey said, nodding to himself. "Some of the best friendships start that way."

For a second, Seth wanted to argue with that, but the longer he thought about it the more true it became. Fear of rejection, fear of exclusion, fear of loneliness, usually, but there was almost always something fearful in anything that lasted. At least at the beginning.

Hopefully that wouldn't be true of their time on this world.

They were so screwed.

That was all Olivia could think as she sat in the river, water up to her waist, ball and map before her.

Running had never been an option. Olivia had known that right at the start. The Vinna had driven them to fight, kill, and move on. Running in any direction but at the enemy was a waste of time. In this case, it wouldn't even be that much time. This round, the enemy was coming, and coming fast. Yesterday, the red blip had been near where they'd camped before heading north, hunting robots. Two days away. Tonight, they'd crossed more than two thirds of the remaining distance.

Too fast to outrun.

Better to wait and rest.

So here they were, but Olivia didn't feel very rested. She felt stretched, strained at the constant effort of the day. The Kaskan hadn't exactly been relaxing. She'd been so tired she'd asked for help. That'd stung. Some leader. Some boss. To hell with the overgrown geckos.

If only she had a plan.

A plan would help. For one thing, it'd make her feel like less of a fake.

That last fight… It'd nearly gone worse than the bug-fight. All this preaching about needing everyone, and yet Olivia had thrown them against the enemy, wildly hoping that something would work.

Relying on luck would get them all killed.

But Olivia had no ideas. She was a lump of useless bullshit, wallowing in fear and loathing and the utter helplessness that was all she could muster. The night was all the darker for the glow of the map bouncing across the river's surface, like tiny, weaving dunes.

"Useless," Olivia muttered, hollowed by it all. Her mind wandered, the glow hazing, weaving into flashes of memory.

There was no sense to the images, no logic, just feeling.

That first Kaskan loomed across the sand, huge and quick, its eye oozing pale liquid in the starlight.

Fear.

A bug was next, its legs glistening, its carapace gleaming in the sun. Behind it, Zed lay on the sand, her leg flattened and her mouth open in a silent scream. Nat lay on her side beyond, eyes vacant, the sand on the other side visible through the hole in her chest.

Olivia had put them there. Her mistake.

Helplessness.

Then the robots came, their curved bulks spewing arms and armament and death. Olivia stood there, watching as they shot her friends. Zed. Nat. Ty. Bee. Joey. Even Seth. And she just stood there, hiding behind armor patches.

Self-loathing.

Olivia couldn't remember why she'd wanted to be in charge. She couldn't even remember if she'd ever wanted to be in charge. Now, she couldn't let go. They'd all die. Zed didn't want to lead. Ty wanted it too much. Bee would want it just because. Nat? No. Joey? No. Seth? Hell no.

Her friends.

Olivia couldn't stop, but if she kept going, it'd be her fault when this next horror murdered all of them. There had to be someone better, someone who could…

But no. That'd been the point. Olivia had gotten the job because there wasn't someone like that. In the quiet emptiness of the river, she could admit to herself that it wasn't the fault that she feared. If hell was real, she already had her ticket. If hell was real, she'd already lived it once or twice. She was afraid of losing this. This was the closest she'd been to happiness in… a long time.

The Goal had always been to stay alive. Always. Since before she'd found her mother in the bathroom, hunched over a bottle of pills for the first time. Since before her coach had started giving her looks. Since before her first beating on the street.

Now, the Goal was to keep them all alive.

It was a radical change, a complete warping of something deep in Olivia's mind. Little things, that's what had done it. Little jokes, sideways smiles, the chuckling, shoving rush of running together, and sitting in silence after a long day was done.

Now it was too late to change back, and too late to save them. Olivia was going to fail.

Fear. Helplessness. Self-loathing.

The red blip had stopped for the night, but they were close. Just a few bends away. They'd be here in the morning. Fall upon their human prey when there was light enough to make sure no one got away.

That's what Olivia would've done.

Olivia couldn't run. She couldn't hide. These things were hunting them the same way Olivia had hunted the Stickmen, the Robots, and the… the Bugs…

No. It couldn't be that simple.

Plucking the ball from the water, Olivia stared at it. No goddamn way. She wracked her memory. She'd checked the map a dozen times when they'd gone after the bugs. Another dozen times as she'd stood on that boulder. Her ball had tracked their ball, not their actual bodies.

The orbs found each other. They tracked each other, nothing else.

It was so damn simple.

Olivia shot up, sprinting back to the tents. She ignored Seth's querying look. She ignored the grumbles of sleepers in her tent. Yanking open the boxes, she found all of the various balls. The Kaskan's, the Stickmen's, and the Bugs' little metal orbs soon joined the Robots' in her hand. She went back to the water and dunked them all. Menus sprang up on all but the latest, but she flicked to the maps. All of them showed green and red blips. One of each. And all but the last red blip was stacked in the exact. Same. Place.

Simple.

The balls tracked one another, nothing else.

A slow, harsh grin tugged at Olivia's lips. Maybe it'd work, maybe it wouldn't, but either way it'd wreck these bastards' day.

There hadn't been enough time to fortify, really, and no point without knowing their opponent. Running hadn't been an option. Fighting fair would get them killed. Now, there was a fourth option: a trap, with a little metal ball as the yummy bait.

It was palpable. The nerves, that was. Seth's. The sweat gave it away. None of them really sweat any more, not unless they'd been running for a while. Hell if he knew where the heat went. Maybe their bodies ate it up and burped it back out as bonus Current. That'd be a cool trick.

Ha.

Cool. Sweat. Heat.

At least the sun was out of sight. It'd fallen behind a particularly obliging block of clouds just after dawn. Everyone had already been awake, rubbing away the restless night. No, not restless, if there hadn't been any rest, they wouldn't have recharged their Current. Anxious night? Worried night?

Whatever.

Now they were here, and they were all nervous. The ones Seth could see, at least. They'd split up again. It'd worked on the robots, so Zed had pushed to do it again. Olivia had taken Joey and Bee and the armor patches and stayed in the woods. Zed had led Nat, Ty, and Seth across the river. The four of them sat within the lowest pool, submerged completely, thanks to their helms. Only Zed could see anything of the beach or the stream, and that was due to her face being in close proximity to a small gash in the grassy rim. The water was clear as glass, giving her a pristine view.

Seth imagined what she saw, what lay across the stream. They'd done nothing to hide their camp. The tracks that led across the stream, those had bee wiped away with a sweep of Current. One tent was still on the sands, empty, but for a metal ball buried in the ground below its center. The other had been packed up and hidden in one of the upper pools, along with the cases. Everyone knew where to look when this was over, but till then it was out of the way. Until then, all they had was what they carried. In Seth's group, that meant a gun, a knife, a suit, and a helmet. In Olivia's, it was two guns, two knives, armor patches, suit, and helm. The spare helms had seemed less than helpful to double up on, so they'd been left in the box.

A flickering memory surfaced, a flash of a face, of screaming and blood, bubbling up in Seth's mind. He shoved it back down, swallowing the rush of bile and impotence that'd come with it. That woman had died back with the Stickmen. Nothing he could do for her then, nothing he could do now. He hadn't even known her name. One of those three spare helms had her initials, but he had no idea which.

Seth had sunk below the surface of the pool an hour ago, maybe less. It felt longer. It felt like forever. He kept wondering if he'd actually loaded his gun. If his knife was still in its sheath. If his helm was properly sealed. Once, he'd even wondered if he was still awake, but that'd been wishful thinking. He was too nervous to fall asleep. There was too much that could go wrong.

The wait forced Seth to think. He was still mad at Olivia, that bossy twerp, but he'd seen her face last night, in the starlight, when she thought he wasn't looking. There'd been so many unspoken worries there. That she was smart enough to be the boss had been driven home during their showdown, but that expression had proven to him that she didn't want it. Or, at least that it wasn't something he'd want.

Worry had never been Seth's strong point.

Perhaps that was why this waiting was particularly grueling.

If Seth were prone to worrying, which he reminded himself that he wasn't, he would likely think of home. He'd exhausted the local things, after all. The boss was the boss, the enemy was coming, he was as ready as he could be, and there was nothing he could do about anything until he got the signal. Thinking of far away problems, of things that he missed, or might never see again, was a worry that only a worrier would resort to.

And Seth wasn't a worrier.

But Seth was greedy. His parents had said it first, mixing in a liberal sprinkling of 'ambitious' and 'clever'. The 'greedy' had proven more accurate than many of the others. No shame in it. For a man of no particular religion, Seth had a remarkable grasp of sin. Lust, envy, sloth, greed, wrath, gluttony, and pride; shit, his freshman year he'd made a checklist just to make sure he didn't skip any of them.

Freshman year of high school, of course. By college…

Well, he'd learned to manage his time.

And now, the greed that Seth's parents had seen and fed was a bit directionless. There wasn't much to be greedy for here. Olivia was boss, Zed was sergeant, and he wished for neither gig. Home though…

Better not to think about it.

Too much of that line of thought and Seth might very well miss Zed's signal entirely. That'd either result in her punching him or everyone dying. Both of those options were terrible.

So Seth waited, trying his best not to-

Zed's fingers clamped around his bicep. Despite only barely being able to see her camouflaged shape, he could still feel that grip. It shifted, four fingers pressing against the inside of his arm. The countdown.

Hurriedly, Seth snatched for Nat's arm, mirroring Zed's four-fingered touch. She stiffened, jerking slightly as she grabbed Ty.

One finger disappeared from Seth's bicep. Three. He passed it along.

Then only two.

Then one.

Then Seth was rising, pushing upwards. The water was thick, goopy with Current, clinging to him as he went up. There would be no drips, no splashes. It was Ty's trick, to give them a few more seconds of surprise.

There were the treetops, a verdant green sea that obscured the ocean beyond. Then the trunks of the nearest stands, the wizened and gnarled bodies that capped of the rocky rise. Then the rocks themselves, a messy cascade held together by massive chunks of stone. Then came the beach, rich and golden, with a single mottled tent and ten figures on it.

Ten. Of course.

They wore suits, but theirs were tight, like second skins, and colored a muddy reddish maroon. Bared heads and hands showed coats of blue-green scales. Long, clawed fingers held guns or overlong knives. Lips peeled back as they neared the tent, exposing teeth so long and white that they were visible from a hundred yards away. The snarling faces, the raised weapons, and the curling horns that rose from their foreheads, curling back and then forward to end near their chins, gave them a sense of vicious implacability, of violence under the barest hint of leash.

It was at that moment, when Seth gulped, trying to swallow his fear along with the bile, that he noticed their tails, longer than a leg and thicker, and their cloven, hooved feet.

The fear didn't go away.

None of them were looking this way. None of them had noticed.

Seth could still hide. Just drop back into the water, sit, and wait for it all to be over. Maybe these monsters wouldn't find him. Maybe they'd ignore him.

To his right, Zed's gun rose, settling comfortably in front of her helmet. Her helm slowly turned, looking at him.

The fear suddenly got complicated. It shocked him, but the irrational fear of the monsters met his fear of Zed and Olivia and dying and sputtered. He wanted to see home. He didn't want to piss them off. And, though he'd never admit it, he didn't want to disappoint Nat.

There was no tremble in Seth's hands when he raised his gun. In his mind, he pulled a taut string of Current from the gun to his helm.

Instantly, a glowing V appeared on the helm's interior, rising and falling with each breath. Beside him, the others were doing the same. It'd taken a couple tries to learn, but it didn't take much Current. Easy.

Seth's V-shaped sight settled on a figure at the center-right of the group that fanned across the sand. It crept forward, glancing sideways at one of the others. The leading monster neared the tent. They were all leaned forward, low and stealthy. The only sound was the splash of falling water.

The thud of Zed's gun was quiet, but it rang through Seth's skull, like a hammer striking a bell. One of the lizards, tall and broad and carrying two guns, staggered as a tiny pucker appeared on his back.

Nat and Ty started shooting.

The other lizards were crouching, firing back.

Zed's target still stood, both guns thudding.

Seth's first shot sent up a puff of sand. His second hit a smaller lizard's shoulder. It didn't spin and fall dramatically. It didn't fall at all. A divot appeared in its suit, and a spasm shot across its features, but it didn't stop shooting. Seth kept his V on that one. Kept adding divot after divot. Eventually, this thing had to die. His heart pounded in his ears, faster than the storm of thudding shots.

Bullets were whizzing by now, hissing like angry cats as they careened overhead. The pool's lip began to spit, cracks ringing out as missiles smashed the stone. Shards flew, clicking and crunching against helms and guns. Seth could feel little pokes and jabs as they flew into his suit. A little bit of Current and the holes sealed, the cuts stopped bleeding. Bending down, he slapped the base of his gun against the stone at his feet. A flicker of Current and he was loaded again. He returned to his target. He'd hit the lizard at least five or six times now, why wasn't it dead?

Near the far side of the group of lizards, the one nearest the tent ducked behind it. Another followed. Then a third.

On the wall beyond, Olivia, Bee, and Joey were visible, lying on the ground behind the top of a particularly large boulder.

As a fourth and fifth lizard darted behind the tent, Zed's arm rose. Her next shot hit the boulder's upper edge with a sharp crack. That was the signal for Olivia's team to go to work.

To Seth's left, Nat staggered, scarlet liquid splattering across the water's surface behind her. He wanted to help, he wanted to check on her, but he kept shooting. He could hear her breathing, could see her hand clenched over the wound. She was the healer. She'd be fine. The best thing he could do was keep shooting. A drumming, pounding beat echoed in his ears. His shots began to synch with the sound, thuds mirroring the drums.

Across the river, on the far side of the beach, Olivia, Bee, and Joey opened up on the lizards behind the tent. For the first time since it all began, someone spoke. The verbal silence shattered, broken by an outraged scream. The tent collapsed, crushed as two lizards scrambled and tore their way through it. The third went backwards, firing up at the trio on the wall. On the sand where they'd stood, the fourth lizard lay, motionless.

Something smacked into Seth's helmet, shoving him back. Steadying himself, he kept shooting, glad for the padding that'd absorbed most of the impact. Good to know the helms weren't just pretty decoration.

"Brassbrains!" shouted one lizard, grabbing one of the two tent-smashers by the collar. "Charge!" It shoved the lizard back the way it'd come, nearly crashing it into the backwards-pacing shooter that'd followed behind.

The two tent-tramplers stared at each other. Then they stared at the shouting boss-lizard, who'd leveled its gun at them. In one smooth motion, they turned and charged the wall.

"You too!" added the boss-lizard, gesturing at two others. They didn't hesitate, they just ran. By then, the first two had already reached the wall. One went wide, trying to climb the rubble ramp, the other leapt, going straight up the boulder's face. The first made it, stumbling and nearly diving face first twice. The latter surged upwards on a flurry of jetting water, but quickly buckled, toppling backwards as sprays of red fanned through the air behind it.

"Die!" ordered Olivia, leveling both guns on the boss-lizard. Joey moved back, tracking the rubble-climber, while Bee shot legs out from under the two remaining chargers.

"Everyone, with me!" the boss-lizard declared, drawing his knife. Divots appeared in its suit, bursts of red coloring the beach, but its expression didn't twitch. "Death or pardon!" he shouted, charging.

"Death or pardon!" the four crouched shooters echoed, turning and following him towards the wall.

Two possible dead, two at the base of the wall, one working around the side, and five more darting across the toppled tent. Things weren't looking good over there.

Seth put two more shots into his target's back, but it just kept going. He stopped when it found its stride. He couldn't hit a running target. Five shots left. Less than a second per shot. The fight had gone on half a minute, probably less.

The flanking lizard wove through the trees, heading for Olivia's back. Joey slid from behind a trunk and slammed his oversized knife into the lizard's skull. It fell, boneless. Using the gun in his other hand, Joey shot the reptile a few times.

On the wall, Bee's hands flew back and forth, spewing shots in multiple directions. Legs collapsed under chargers, knees bending as bone splintered.

Guns aimed together, Olivia kept pouring shots at the leader. It just kept coming, barreling forward, undaunted.

Seth blinked and everything changed. The tide of maroon bodies came together, crashing against the rock wall, claws grating against stone. Three figures in mottled suits flew forward, pillars of blue springing them out across the sands. They hit the ground and rolled, perfect copies of Zed, and came up at a dead sprint towards the river.

"Plan C!" Zed commanded, leaping backward.

Ty followed, Nat and Seth on his heels. Their feet slammed into the stone once, twice, then they dove down into the pool's depths. Seth sent out a flow of current, snatching up a cushion of water that billowed around him like a sail. The clear, pale blue surface rose around him as he shot upwards. Then he flew, climbing up and up until he passed the lip of the next pool.

Beside him, the others arced, springing from pool to pool as they climbed. Pain blazed a trail across Seth's calf, tearing through his thigh. He flinched, nearly slamming into the stone of a pool's lip, but kept going. Glancing down, he saw the ribbon of red that flowed into his trail, but no pursuers. One of them had gotten a last lucky shot. Damn lizards.

Olivia and the others would go downstream, or south. Seth's group would climb a good way up, and then head upstream, or north. They'd find each other once both were clear. Plan C had been less optimal than A or B. A had been all the enemy dying in the crossfire. B had been the enemy running away. C relied on balls and luck.

The flaw was the separation.

There were still eight of those lizards, and if they all went after one team…

The clouds were growing darker. Bee almost didn't notice. Being chased by carnivorous, humanoid, gun-toting lizards was pretty distracting. Or at least, in her experience that seemed to be the case. Considering she was probably one of the only three humans to ever undergo the experience, she felt very firm in her assessment. All the firmer for the way her companions sped forward, pouring every ounce of Current into it. Bee didn't go that far. She could go faster, and probably for longer as well. She just could. She had the Current for it. She didn't though. She wouldn't leave them behind. Part of her wanted to, part of her was so afraid, so terrified, that it begged to shoot ahead and never stop.

Every now and then, Bee caught herself starting to pull forward. She fell back every time, letting Olivia and Joey stay even with her. Bend after bend, river jetted past. Schools of fish, fronds and weeds, chunks of downed trees and fallen stone littered the stream's course.

With the helmets, Bee could only tell Olivia from Joey by build. And Olivia was slowing down.

Slower was bad. Twitching hands didn't seem like a good sign either. Bee reached for the woman, feeding her Current like she had after the fight with the bugs. Olivia surged forward, sucking down Bee's Current like fuel from a hose. Smiling, relieved, Bee kept feeding power through the line.

"Thanks," Olivia said, her voice somehow carrying to Bee's ears.

"What?" Bee squeaked.

"Helms," Olivia chuckled back, still knifing through the water, her course unchanged. "They connect to our guns. Got excited and wanted to say thanks, so I hooked mine to yours. Seems to work."

"I'll say," agreed Joey, bland.

"You had no idea if it'd work?" Bee demanded, oozing sarcasm.

"Pretty sure I just said that it was accidental…" Olivia returned. Joey snorted.

Bee rolled her eyes. "Next time, warn me before testing possibly catastrophic theories on my gear."

"That seems a bit harsh," Olivia noted, "But ok."

"So does splattering into one of those trees," Bee grumbled. "Unless being Current-high comes with a bonus package of cartoon physics."

"I'm not high," Olivia said, her voice oddly flat.

"Oh, and you've got so much experience with what that's like, I'm sure," Bee replied, once gain oozing exaggerated sarcasm from every syllable.

"You won't like how I answer that, so I won't," Olivia said, the flatness growing, giving her words an implacable, echoing, permanence.

Quiet hung for a long moment, their bodies gently bending to the right as they shot around a curve in the river.

"Sorry," Bee whispered.

"Accepted," Olivia answered back.

Joey stayed silent.

"So, how far do you-" Bee began, trying to change the subject, but she was cut off. Instead she shouted, "Shit!" and gritted her teeth as pain throbbed through her foot. Glancing down, she saw the hole through the ball of her foot. Beyond, she could see a lizard, beaming through the cloud of red she trailed.

"Lizards!" Joey barked, in case anyone had missed the fact.

"Got that, thanks," Olivia replied. "Number?"

"No idea," Bee answered, her attention stretched to its thinnest as she tried to heal her foot, keep moving forward, and keep feeding Olivia Current all at once. It was like juggling weights that kept getting heavier.

"Four," Joey replied.

"They can out-swim us," Olivia said, decisive. "We need to get into the woods. Bee, when you're good."

"Good," Bee hissed, sealing her suit over the freshly healed skin. The pain was almost gone. Upside to being the Energizer-Bunny around here, she got things done.

"Hard left on me," Olivia ordered, "Keep going till we're in the trees, then turn and fire."

"Check," Joey grunted.

"Good," Bee agreed.

"Go!" Olivia said, and they whipped around.

All three burst from the water, blasting across the sand as tendrils of liquid stretched further and further, flinging them on. Olivia dropped first, ducking and rolling as she hit the beach. A blink later, Joey did the same. Both ran for the rocky wall. Bee skipped the beach altogether, releasing burst of liquid like jets, boosting herself through the air. A little higher, a little to the left.

Perfect!

Then it dawned on Bee that she had to land too, and stone was less forgiving than sand. She tried to cushion herself with Current, willing a flurry of moisture into being to catch her. The droplets slowed her, fighting to maintain their place in the air even as her momentum pushed them down. She still hit hard, and the droplets kept her from rolling. The shock rolled up her legs, throbbing in every joint between her big toes and tailbone, but she didn't fall and nothing broke. At least not as far as she could tell.

"Up!" Olivia barked. Her long-fingered hand clamped around Bee's elbow and yanked her towards the trees.

Scrambling, Bee followed, trying to keep pace with the shorter woman. A low branch clipped her helm, knocking her sideways, but Olivia's grip yanked her back on course. A root nearly tripped her, but she staggered and kept on. Another root. Another branch, this one whipping back as Olivia released her grip on it.

Then it stopped. Olivia spun, dropping to one knee halfway behind a particularly broad tree. Bee hesitated, and then went for the tree behind it. Snipers at the back, just like Zed had said. She'd also said not to show your back to the enemy, but Bee didn't think Zed had considered this possibility at the time.

Latching onto a gnarled outcropping, Joey whipped around a tree, nearly smacking into its back. He curled into its lee as he slapped his gun against the gravelly ground. Bee copied the gesture.

A second later, two of the horned, humanoid lizards rushed up the rise. They froze, staring into the woods.

Bee didn't breathe. Didn't twitch. A branch pricked her shoulder. Her ass itched. Her right foot was at an uncomfortable angle. She didn't move.

The two lizards were tall, at least six feet, with tails nearly half-again the length of a leg. Their maroon suits stood out like dried blood, but their guns were familiar, their knives the same shape as the one at Bee's hip.

It clicked. The thought came as fast as a light bulb flicking on, with all the subtlety of an explosion. They didn't just have Vinna gear. These were Vinna. The first Vinna she'd seen since the recording in the Kaskan and the white-eyed one in the plane. For some reason, some mysterious blockage, they hadn't been the same till that moment.

"Screw you!" Bee screamed, her stillness vanishing as she drove Current into both guns. Rage, frustration, pain, fear; finally she had an outlet for it all. It poured from her, fleeing through her palms in washes of pulsing power. Both guns hammered away, bullets streaming forth. When they clicked empty, she allowed herself to inhale.

One of the lizards, the Vinna, was curled on the ground, much of its torso and head simply gone. The other slipped back down the wall, eyes wide and fearful.

"Shit," Joey muttered.

"Not her fault," Olivia returned, barely audible to Bee's ears. "Bee," she added, louder, sharper. "Reload. Then tell me how the hell you did that."

"Uh, yeah," Bee agreed, blinking, dazed. She twisted, putting her back against the hard, stable tree. She tapped her guns against the ground, breathing deep as they inhaled gravel.

"So?" Olivia asked.

"Lots of Current," Bee said, trying to think through how she'd gotten the guns to fire that fast. "I pulled the trigger, then pushed."

"Makes sense," Joey said, a fascinated, eager smile audible. "Triggers back on Earth were to set off a chemical reaction. These things are all Current-based, so it could be decorative."

"We'll figure that out later," Olivia said. "How much?"

Bee winced. "Not sure."

"Repeat that," Olivia growled.

"Not sure, boss," said Bee. "Bit stressed."

"Fine," Olivia gripped. "They're down to three, let's-"

Three Vinna barreled over the stone lip, guns pounding and knives drawn.

Bee was silent. Olivia and Joey were silent. There was no point now. Turn and run, and these things would be close enough to shoot them in the back. Hand to hand was suicide. The Vinna were built for that. Shooting as many as possible and hoping that those claws, those teeth, never tore human skin was the only option left.

This time, Bee wasn't the only one who poured stony bullets into the oncoming reptiles. Six guns, three reptiles, but still they came. The rightmost one staggered, falling as its upper and lower halves nearly separated.

A bullet scored Bee's shoulder, like a tongue of white-hot flame. She screamed, her vision hazing. The pain walked down, drawing down her limb as she crumbled to the foot of the tree. It stopped, but the echoes kept going, reverberating in her head. She blinked, fighting to see through the fog. Seconds ticked by.

Looking up again, Bee saw Olivia and Joey, blades drawn, dancing with the remaining two dinosaurs. Joey's suit was slashed, tatters hanging, fluttering like tassels as he darted forward and back. Holes peppered

Olivia's right leg and side, exit wounds like polka dots on her back. The duo danced, feet sure and quick across the rooted, stony ground. Clawed, scaly feet matched them, mirroring the steps as they fought for angle, for purchase, overlong, curved knives flickering out, like fragments of the cloudy sky above.

So much for not fighting hand to hand.

Seconds were so slow now. The fog rose and fell on every breath, a single moment of gasping desperation turning into an eternity. Bee knelt there, the fire that'd walked down her shoulder a burning outcry that rang in her skull.

Light and quick, Olivia darted in, her whole body rocketing at the lizard. Both knives flicked forward, ramming over and over into the Vinna's chest. A startled, belching croak came from its mouth, jaw dropping open as it frantically turned its blades on her. One drove through her unarmored side, the other skittered across armored patches.

Darting into Bee's view, Joey fell as his pursuer's blades blurred into a cascade of jabbing metal. He rolled, trying to use the stumble to gain distance. But walking was faster than rolling. The Vinna just kept coming, its tail whipping back and forth in the air. Joey rose again and chucked one knife at the lizard's face.

A negligent backhand knocked the blade away, but it bought the pause that Joey needed to draw a gun. The Vinna froze, eyes going wide. There was a helm masking his face, but Bee could imagine the calm grin.

The gun clicked.

Empty.

Snarling, gleeful, the lizard lunged. Vinna claws hit human flesh, splashing the trees and stones with blood. They fell together, disappearing from Bee's sight.

Olivia and her dance partner reappeared in the gap. The Vinna pinned her against a tree, its tail reaching around to wrap around the trunk. Olivia's feet kicked, slapping against scaled muscle. It'd dropped its knives and now grasped for her neck, but she held it by the wrists. They stayed that way, its claws inches from the joint of her helm and suit. It was like some horrible painting. The tips of her blades protruded from its back.

The clouds were so dark now, leaching the color from the world. It was all reds now, bloody reds and woody browns and stony grays. Even the leaves were hollowed, barren of brightness, left with only their rustle.

And there Bee lay, the agony in her arm barely eased. Perhaps it wasn't lessening at all, simply becoming easier to ignore. She could barely turn her head; barely hear her own thoughts through the clamor in her skull. Olivia was about to die. Joey might already be dead. The others were likely no better off.

So Bee poured Current out, willing it into a curling coil that flew from her. Bee nearly blacked out, fog rolling in again around her weeping eyes. The coil of Current lashed out, curling around the Vinna's throat, and yanked backwards, but it wasn't enough. The Vinna's head turned, glaring hatred her way.

Distracted.

From Olivia's hands came jagged shards of palest ice, vapor flying like steam as they burst through the Vinna's wrists. Its head swung back around, shocked and hurting. Olivia's helm jabbed forward, driving the horned face into his forehead. Something cracked, the lizard staggered, and Olivia tumbled to the ground. Its tail swung, batting Olivia off her feet and into a tree. She fell, gasping. The Vinna teetered, blood oozing from its slit nostrils, blinked, and fell.

In the distance, Bee could hear grunts and thuds. More fighting. Something wet splattered. More grunts. A groan.

Bee tried to breathe, willed herself past the urge to scream. Her arm was healing; she could feel a hellish itch as the flesh knit. It'd been the bone. She could feel it now. The impact had shattered the joint, but it was healing.

A figure staggered into her sight. Joey. Wounded, but standing. He went to Olivia first, dragging her to her feet. She wove, almost drunken, then steadied. Her blood-spattered helm jerked, nodding.

Jogging the few steps to Bee, Joey pulled her up by her good arm.

"Next time, try to get shot on the armored side," he joked, humorless desperation heady in every adrenaline-drunk word.

"Go to hell," Bee groaned, fighting to get her feet to do what she told them.

"No thanks," Joey returned, stretching her arm over his shoulder. "Boss, we need to go."

"Coming," Olivia said, her voice rough, hoarse.

A gun thudded.

Spinning, Joey brought Bee around.

Olivia was standing over the big lizard. Her gun was pointed at its head. Her finger plucked the trigger, strumming it like an instrument.

"No time!" Joey hissed. "Shooting them doesn't work!"

"Headshots do," Olivia said. "Run. I'm coming." She didn't move.

"Fuck!" Joey growled. He turned again, dragging Bee along with him, and ran. It was really more of a hobbling, hopping jog, with a few dodges to avoid low branches and high roots.

"Shit," Bee hissed, pain bursting like pressured pustules in her head as the jolts hit her arm.

"She damn well better follow," Joey grumbled, speeding up. "I signed up for 'Stabby the Badass', not 'Curly Boy and Medical Girl Play King and Queen'."

Nat had given up on figuring out where her oxygen was coming from. No, she knew where it came from; she just didn't like to think about it. She'd been the one to fall into the river and suck down water. By comparison, helmets with some kind of underwater breathing apparatus seem pretty normal.

Far less normal were any reliefs from the boredom. Long hours would pass in silence with nothing but the gentle tug of the water to break the monotony. No Kaskans, no Vinna. Every few hours, Zed would slowly rise to the surface. The water would go sludgy, thick and silent as she scanned the mountainside. She'd come down, shake her head, and they'd wait some more.

As Nat saw it, there were three issues.

One, they didn't know where the Vinna were.

Two, if they tried to run the Vinna might be close enough to ambush them.

And three, if the Vinna used Current to detect things, like the Kaskans, then there would be no way to know the Vinna were close by until it was too late. The Kaskans had already shown that stretching Current out wasn't enough warning the enemy had a better feel for the task, and the Vinna were probably better trained than the overgrown alligators.

On the other hand, thank God that no Kaskans had shown up. One of those monsters and this whole sneaky hiding until the Vinna passed would be-

A single, tennis ball sized orb of purest white appeared, hovering in the pool's murk. It hung there, like a ghost in the shadows, or a white moon among the kelp and weeds. Clouds wandered beyond it, like an upside down sea, waves of gray slowly rolling, on and on.

For a moment, Nat's heart stilled, stalling as her chest drew tight. It was behind her, further down the slope of the pool's bottom. It was eerie and all too familiar.

An inky blackness flowed across the orb's face. It reappeared a moment later, half-obscured. Another half-visible ball hung near it. The kelp broke Nat's trance. She could see the strands and stalks bending, bowing before the weight of something huge.

Zed had chosen a larger pool, something with space to hide in, if need be. None of them had considered what else might live in the depths.

Stillness. Nat fought so hard against every instinct to flee, fight, or freak. She had to stay still. Had to.

Beside her, Seth reached out, petting her arm.

Nat didn't move.

He kept petting her, gently brushing his suit-covered hand down her suited arm and shoulder. At least he didn't cop a feel. If he'd been that oblivious and ill timed she wouldn't be able to hold back manic laughter. And a punch.

The twin balls of white blinked again, stationary, staring at her. It felt like the thing could see right through her. Memories of the other Kaskans, of their size, of the tusks and fangs, of their brutal speed, rose like thick, tarry bubbles. The only reason they'd survived those attacks had been Current, and Nat was out. They all were. Drained nearly to unconsciousness. Otherwise they would've kept running.

In the midst of Nat's icy fear, the frozen tableau only broken by blinks and pets, a shadow passed overhead. It began behind Nat, at the shallow mountainside lip of the pool, and flowed across the center of the pool. Towards the eyes.

The white orbs twitched, glancing upwards. The plant-life billowed, blasted outwards as the Kaskan's massive body emerged. Its head was huge, its bulk lodged deep in the pool's depths. It shot forward, coiled on the bottom, and pushed off the bottom in an explosion of motion. In an instant it towered, upright and immense as in the sunlit sky. It had to be fifteen meters long, maybe twenty, and only the tip of its tail lingered in the water.

The crunching, meaty crack of the huge Kaskan's jaws closing was like thunder in the silence. A scream trailed after it, like the creaking, mournful outcry of a falling tree. The Kaskan's bulk descended to the tune, slowly crashing back into the pool.

Right at Nat.

She shoved off a stony protrusion, clawing, kicking at water, weed, and rock as she fought her way along the pool's hem. Beside her, Seth did the same, his sleeker build slicing through the murk. No time to check on the others. No time. That enormous length of leather, muscle, and teeth was coming.

A gasped breath later, the water surged around them, rising in a wave of force that blew outwards. Behind her, Nat could hear the grating scratch of claws on stone. The harsh, hateful sound vibrated through the water. Then the wave picked her up and drove her a dozen meters forward.

Flipping, Nat stared at the Kaskan. With a bloody, scrabbling body writhing in its jaws, it sat like a cat with a mouse. This mouse was horned, scaled, and wearing a maroon uniform.

The peak of the surge passed and Nat began to drop, falling towards where water level should've been. At the same time, water crashed in on the Kaskan and its prey. Twin nostrils at the end of the Kaskan's head exhaled, spraying foam into the air.

Nat's downward momentum carried her to the bottom, drifting away from the dinosaur and its Vinna prize. She was still rim-side of the beast, close enough that she might be able to make it. Getting out of the water that hid massive magical monsters seemed like the sane thing to do.

More shadows flew by.

Looking up, Nat saw three more Vinna, guns pointed towards the mess of blood and foam and torn weeds that coated where the Kaskan had landed. Thuds hummed through the water. Bullets left trails of white as they drilled into the depths. Two things happened to those bullets. Most simply slowed, their power stolen by the warm, watery thickness around them, but some ended with meaty thunks, blossoms of scarlet wafting from the dark mass they'd struck.

The three figures came down feet first, crashing into the water like the bullets that'd preceded them. Foam frothed from them, like steam. Their guns were already vanishing, swapped for knives. Two darted in, their bodies propelled by bursts of Current-fostered motion. The third landed right on top of the Kaskan. That one bent double, slamming its knife into the beast's back.

Once again, a patch of reality that Nat's mind had wishfully labeled 'stone' or perhaps just 'not a monster,' abruptly proved its appalling speed and power. The Kaskan's limbs flexed, shoving it up from the bottom. This left a void where its body had been, one that the pool fought to fill. The crashing rush of water pouring in yanked the two oncoming Vinna off course. One smacked shoulder-first into the Kaskan's side, the other dropped like a leaf on the wind, carried towards the bottom. The Vinna who'd stabbed the Kaskan's back skidded on kelp-slicked scales. It slid into the water on the far side from Nat.

It was all a mess, bubbles and smears of mud and plant matter drifting in the confused melee.

Then the Kaskan bent the other way, its upper and lower body rising from the water. This drove it's torso downward, a combination of Current and weight turning its broad belly into a falling anvil.

And it landed directly on top of the Vinna that'd been sucked down a moment before. The crunch of bone carried through the water. The Kaskan snapped back and forth, jerking the squirming Vinna in its jaws. Somehow, it was still alive and punching at the monster's teeth.

Helmet-less, armed with knives, the Vinna kept fighting. The one on the far side stabbed again and again. That one's mouth was open, bubbling forth a stream of trapped, watery screams. The Vinna nearest Nat paused, its hands disappearing as a shaft of curved ice materialized around them. It was inches thick, bulging where the Vinna's hands were embedded within, and tipped with a jagged, serrated harpoon. A second later, it punched the brutal spear into the Kaskan's side.

That massive tail moved first, whipping sharply around in the second before the roll began. When the Kaskan went, its whole body followed, twisting directly onto the spear-Vinna. The icy weapon snapped, joining the general crunch that filled Nat's ears.

The motion brought the Vinna on the far side to the fore, its blade still hilt-deep in thick hide. A cord of silver-blue spooled from its hands, shooting back, towards the bottom it was being carried further from. In one smooth twist of its wrist, the Vinna wrapped the cord around the handle, and then clutched the loose end. Nat's breath hitched as she saw the cord tighten.

Somehow, the cord had been anchored in the stone. The roll's force yanked the feet-long knife the wrong way. The Kaskan jerked, its jaws flying open as its eyes snapped shut. A long line of blood rose from the gash, a meter long now. It bloomed outwards, petals of red flowing into the water.

The Kaskan didn't stop. Its jaws snapped shut again, barely missing the bleeding, fleeing Vinna it'd caught initially. Those twin orbs blinked open again, looking for targets, but Nat could barely even see the whites through all the mud and blood and mess. That thing couldn't see any better. With another snort, streaming bubbles towards the surface, it shot forward, flying over the pool's lip without pause.

The Vinna who'd made the Current-cord fell away in the sudden maelstrom of swirling water. The two who'd been nearly flattened were still on the bottom, oozing scarlet clouds. The fourth, the one who'd been bitten, crawled towards the shallows.

The cord-maker dove, Current speeding it to the two wounded. It grabbed one by the arm and dragged it to the other. It held both of them, cold blue light pulsing between its hands and their… wounds. They quaked, shivering and shaking as bone and flesh knit.

Nat sat there, hovering in the murk, watching. The Kaskan's absence was like a black hole in her mind, sucking away thought. Things like that couldn't move that fast, couldn't disappear like that, or shouldn't. This one had.

And now the Vinna, the one fixing its buddies, was looking at her.

Shit. With all the damn camo on the gear, Nat hadn't really worried about wrapping herself in weeds or something.

Shit.

The Vinna didn't move. Light kept pulsing from its hands. The mangled messes beside it began to look more humanoid, regaining recognizable limbs and chest cavities.

Nat waged an internal war, caught between sinking out of sight and shooting. No Current was bad, but all four Vinna looked like they were out as well. If the two squished ones could've healed on their own, they probably would've by now. Looking more closely at them, Nat marveled that they were still alive. How… It couldn't just be Current. Energy alone couldn't keep someone alive, that made no sense. Their bones had been smashed, organs punctured…

Oh.

Their heads.

Both of the semi-pancaked Vinna looked bad, but their heads were basically fine. If they'd used Current to shield their heads from the Kaskan's weight, maybe that was why they were still alive to be healed. Either that or those curled horns were as good as a helmet.

So, heads were the key?

That was stupidly simple. It couldn't be that simple.

But then, why else would the helmets be the last piece of gear? It had to be the most important. Everything had gone in order of usefulness. They'd been forced to earn their survival, so it made sense not to give the most lifesaving piece of gear until the end.

Flaw: why then send in Vinna without that piece of equipment?

It didn't make any sense.

Distracted by her internal debate, Nat almost missed the Vinna's departure. They exited the pool the same way they'd come, the same direction the Kaskan had gone. All four were battered and visibly not using Current.

At the last moment, after the three others had gone over the lip, the one that'd made the cord, the healer, turned and shot Nat a look. It'd seen her, and it wanted her to know that.

And then it left.

Once again, silence fell in the pool.

The uphill end was even deeper than it had been, a gaping wound in the weeds marking where the Kaskan had lain. Torn chunks floated, accompanied by slowly diluting swirls and swaths of blood and mud.

After several long minutes, a suited, helmeted figure rose on the far end. Two more followed. Nat pushed off the bottom, beaming.

They'd survived.

Now if only they knew why heads kept Vinna alive and how to tell where super-Kaskans were.

Bloody tired, that's what Olivia was. Bloody tired of all this damned running. Her legs shook, making her weave drunkenly as she dodged between the trees. So far she hadn't crashed into any of them. She was rapidly coming to the conclusion that it was only a matter of time. It'd been a bad day, but ending it with a concussion or a broken skull would be moronic.

"Stop," Olivia said, hissing the word out between deep breathes. She planted her feet, stretching up and back to relieve the knotted muscles along her spine. They went off in a series of ghastly, rattling pops.

Joey and Bee dropped to the ground, their chests heaving with effort. The night was already dark and cold around them, the sunset's last warmth long gone. Olivia didn't bother to look up. She didn't need the gut-wrenching reminder of how far from Earth they were. There was no reason to look up anyway. No moon to tell the time from. And this wasn't London, with nice, convenient clock towers parked all over the fucking place. Damn.

It was late. And they were tired. That's all she really needed to know.

Joey yanked off his helmet. It dropped to the ground. He looked exhausted, barely holding back the inexorable draw of dreams. "Sleep?"

"Sleep," Olivia agreed, pulling her helm off as well. She turned, put her back to a tree, and slid down. Her butt hit roots and stone and complained. Didn't matter. Her legs were still pissed over the running, and they were a lot louder with their unhappiness. Wincing, she shifted around, moving her knife's sheath off her lap.

"How far?" Bee muttered, lying down on the ground near Olivia's feet. She deposited her helm on a rocky protrusion.

"Since morning?" Olivia replied, fighting to think. It'd been… morning? Morning when they'd ambushed the Vinna. A few hours after dawn. Maybe eight or nine hours from then to sunset, then about three or four till now. Call it five miles every hour. "Sixty miles."

Bee grunted, surprised.

"Thanks for the help," Olivia offered, thinking of the thin stream of Current that'd fueled her through the afternoon and evening's nonstop slogging jog.

"No problem," Bee said, waving it off with a listless flop of her near hand. "Stupid not to."

"Done stupider," Olivia admitted.

"You callin' me names, shorty?" Bee shot back, her head rolling around to half-heartedly glare up at Olivia.

Amused, Olivia snorted. "Talking about myself, dumbass."

"Now you're definitely calling me names," Bee grumbled, looking up at the stars.

"You started it."

"Baby."

"Brat."

"That's Boss Brat to you," Olivia noted.

"What, you gonna spank me if I don't?"

"Maybe. Current might make for a nice whip."

Bee yawned. "Always preferred riding crops."

"Shucks," Olivia grunted. "Left mine in my dungeon."

Bee chuckled. "You wish you were cool enough to have a dungeon."

Olivia sighed, fighting to find a way to keep the conversation light. Nothing came to mind. She just kept thinking of London, of how everything had fallen apart. A dungeon. Dungeons meant a house, or some kind of home at least. Something better than the shitty places she'd lived. 'Lived.'

"Sorry," Bee gently whispered. The word sliced through Olivia's fog like a cool breeze.

"Not your fault," Olivia said, not sure what else to say.

"Do you want to talk about it?"

In the dark, Olivia could see Joey's chest rise and fall in long, slow breaths. He was out cold. That was better. It would be hard enough to talk about it with one person, but two would be... too much. She'd learned the hard way that talking didn't help. Thus, Rule Fourteen: Don't Tell People the Fucked Up Stuff, Stick to the Sad, Especially Fictional Sad.

Olivia had added Rule Fourteen after a man at a soup kitchen called the cops on her. She'd never found out which bit he'd decided was cop-worthy. She hadn't gone back there. That'd been two weeks after being shoved onto the streets.

The sad bits earned sympathy more often than not, but the horrifying parts, the fucked up shit, people rejected. It was too much reality for their happy little bubble. Making up sad bits made them hurt less, it made the pity feel distant, impersonal.

"You don't-" Bee began.

"Maybe it'll help," Olivia grunted, shifting to put her back more flush with the tree. "You told Zed to come talk to me after the bugs. Seemed to help her."

"Or you're just so tired that you you've lost the ability to withstand my chatty charms," Bee deadpanned.

Olivia snorted. "Or that."

"So?"

"Give me a sec," Olivia grumbled.

"Oh yeah, take your time." Bee nodded sagely. "Nothing to worry about out here. No rush. Let my secretary know when you're ready."

"Like you'd ever have a secretary."

Bee chuckled. "Probably would've helped a lot to have one freshman year."

"I wouldn't know," Olivia sighed, finally letting some of her stinging, biting resentment to leak through. It wasn't Bee's fault, they both knew that, but that didn't change it.

"Tell me," Bee said, turning away from the stars. She watched Olivia, her face calmly interested, the short shock of hair on her head still bright, bold green, strands and locks of blue and black streaking through.

"How much did you hear that first night, when I talked to Zed?"

"Uh," Bee said, eyes narrowed with thought. "Not much. That feels like years ago. I think I only caught the fight at the end, and I don't really remember that. You two got over it pretty fast."

"True," Olivia agreed, nodding. It was almost enough to bring a smile to her face, but not quite. Not right now. Maybe she was too tired. She let it all go. The words came in a tumble, like water from a burst damn. "My parents are dead. No money. I was homeless in London for… a long time. Not sure if I ever technically graduated high school. I was on track to be an Olympian. Swimming. Diving. I was good in the water."

"Aren't you a little short for an Olympic swimmer?" Bee asked, curiosity driving her to cut through the flood.

Olivia nodded. "By more than a head. No idea how much is malnutrition and how much is genetic. Might never have made the cut anyway."

"You still deserved to try."

Olivia snorted. "No shit."

"You missed the joke," Bee added.

Olivia grunted.

"A little short? Like in Star… Never mind. Bad time."

Olivia grunted again.

"I'm not good at this."

"Ha," Olivia huffed. "Is anyone?"

"Therapists?" Bee offered.

"Pretty sure they'd just shove me in a padded room with a straight jacket."

"You really don't like people, do you?" Bee queried, blinking up at her.

"Why should I?" Olivia returned, her teeth gritted, hands flexing. "People have screwed me over one way or another for my whole life."

"We haven't."

"I know," Olivia admitted, unclenching her teeth. She flexed her jaw, trying to release the tension. "Still working on how to deal with that."

"If we get home," Bee said, wiggling to get comfier, "You're coming to live with me."

Olivia didn't breathe.

"Or, uh, you can, if you want to. You know, it's an option," Bee added, looking away. "Just wanted to put it out there."

"If," Olivia repeated. It was the safest option. Her heart was pounding, adrenaline rushing through her.

"If," Bee repeated, still watching her.

"Gotta survive this first," Olivia noted.

"At least we figured out the bad guys' weakness."

Olivia raised one eyebrow.

"Getting shot in the head," Bee supplied.

Frowning, Olivia nodded. It had worked better than anything else. "Fair point."

"Thanks," Bee said, giving her a soft smile. "Doesn't help us figure out how close they are, but it's something."

"I've got an idea about that," Olivia said, a tiny, uncontrollable curl twisting her lips into a smirk.

Bee chuckled. "Not sure whether to be happy or deeply concerned."

"They've got two balls. The one they used to find us, and the one we left for them…"

"And you have the rest?" Bee asked, the words slow as realization dawned.

Olivia nodded. "Except for one. Zed had the second to last one we found, the bugs'."

"So she can find us because we have the robots' ball," Bee said, beaming now. "And the Vinna have a ball that leads to you too."

"They have the Kaskan ball, from back at the beginning," Olivia explained. "It'll lead them to the next ball we got, the Stickman one. The problem is that we can't use that one for a trap."

Bee's eyes went a bit wide, her smile waning. "Because then the Vinna would use it to find Zed and the others."

"Kaskan leads to Stickmen, Stickmen to bugs, bugs to robots, robots to Vinna, Vinna to Kaskan," Olivia said, verbalizing the circular puzzle the Vinna had forced them to use. "Without them, we can't find Zed. With them, its only a matter of time till the Vinna find us."

"But as long as we have the Stickman, the Vinna can't find Zed."

"We either hold on until Zed finds us and we can lay a trap, or until the Vinna get so close that we can't hold onto it any longer," Olivia said, enjoying the quick, bouncing rapport of the logic. It was complicated, and if it weren't life threatening it'd be a fascinating puzzle. "But Zed can't come rushing in or she might be caught by a Vinna ambush, if they take our ball before she arrives."

"Shit."

"Yup," Olivia agreed, smiling.

Bee hummed for a moment. Then she asked, "So, what's the plan, boss?"

"Sleep," Olivia answered. "I've had as much heart-to-heart as I can stand, and we need as much Current as we can get. Tomorrow, we'll walk. No Current. When they get close, we'll drop the ball and ambush them. If we're lucky, there'll only be two or three of them."

Bee groaned.

"What?"

"You had to go and jinx it," Bee grumbled.

Olivia laughed. "Shut up and sleep."

It took about a minute for Bee to start snoring. Olivia wasn't far behind. In the distance, just out of sight, she thought she heard the clicking, scratching of insects, but she couldn't see any. She'd heard it before, on the nights back at the start when she'd slept in the trees. Never on the beach though. Never any bugs there, or anything more than the sound of them here. Weird.

Olivia hoped that she didn't dream of bugs. That'd suck.

The dream had been of chocolate and beds. There'd been warmth, the comforting weight of blanket and body, and the hazy, musky scent of deodorant and sweat.

Basically, it'd been of the good old days. Days now long gone, a realization made harsher by the stinging, itching pain that ran across Bee's cheek. Frozen, flat on her back, her eyes shot open.

And shot closed again.

Waking up at the best of times could be rough, but waking up from the best of times to find horrors waiting? That was enough to disturb anyone. In Bee's opinion, the fact that what she had seen didn't make her scream seemed like the icing on a cake that was probably poisoned.

Scratch that, definitely poisoned.

Moving beyond disgust at it all, and revulsion at how much of Bee's old self this place had erased, she actually took in more than a first impression.

The sun was up. That was good.

Trees were still there. Few clouds overhead. Lots of blue. A rock poked her back.

Oh, and there was a big asshat of a lizard holding a knife to her cheek.

Bee could feel blood running down her face, dribbling across her ear. Flat on her back, she could see all but its feet looming over her. It crouched, thick knees and bulging thighs spread to support his elbows. The curved two-foot knife hung almost delicately from scaled fingers capped with ivory. Blue-green scales ran up each hand, vanishing into the muddy maroon suit, reappearing at its neck, where the wash of color seemed to flow up, pouring into its thin mouth and flattened nose, fading ever smaller at the roots of two spiraling horns. Those twin curves of bone rose from its brow, bending back as they circled each side of its head, ending in spikes near its earlobes.

"Don't scream?" the lizard said, ending in a hopeful uptick.

Bee nearly growled, unable to hold back a stormy frown. Besides mentally cussing the shit out of this asshole, her brain was heavily preoccupied with the fact that it had sharp, fang-like teeth. A lot of them. Not long ones, but enough to bring a T-Rex to mind.

"Good," it sighed, patting her shoulder with its free hand. "Thanks. Can't tell you how much I hate screaming. Nearly put me off the whole sex thing-"

"Flat!" another Vinna voice barked, "What'd I say about hitting on dinner?" That one held Olivia against the tree, clawed hand around her throat. Olivia's feet could just touch the ground, but only just.

"Oh, come on," 'Flat' groaned, rolling its eyes. "This one's obviously a female, and she's totally into me!"

"No means no!" the other one repeated, tinged with disgust now. "You don't know what you could catch from some alien. Especially these ones."

"Whaddaya mean?" a deeper, thoughtful voice queried.

Bee couldn't fully see the one giving orders, just it and Olivia's upper bodies, but the third Vinna was closer. It was also tall. Really tall, even though it was sitting on Joey. Even with the height reduction, its head was at least four, maybe five feet up, with shoulders to match.

"I mean that these particular ones eat meat," the bossy one explained, grumbling and annoyed at being forced to spell it out. "Just look at their teeth! Can't even properly pick one way or another, no. Bunch of omnivores. Bit of this, bit of that, like some kind of scavenger." Bossy added a hacking cough, imitating a puking sound.

"Oh, don't do that, Desert! You know I've got a delicate stomach," whined a fourth, stepping out from behind one of the trees. This one was thinner, with horns that barely reached the back of its head.

"And I told you not to call me that!" hissed the bossy one, baring fangs at the newcomer. "I'm Blood!"

"Like you'd have a name like that," Flat grumbled, scratching the base of a horn. It peered down at Bee. "Does he look like a Blood?"

"Why're you asking it about names?" the deep-voiced one boomed, confused.

"I wasn't!" Flat returned. "Listen, Long-Arm, you really need to get the whole sarcasm thing working for you. Maybe you can get your Translator to give you subtitles or something."

"You calling me dumb?" Long-Arm boomed, jerking to its trunk-like feet. Joey gasped and coughed at the sudden absence of pressure on his chest.

"I told you not to get up!" Desert barked, waving at Joey.

"What? Oh," Long-Arm muttered, looking down. "I… forgot…"

"Of course she did," Desert hissed, waving its arms in the air.

His, Bee corrected herself. Desert was male, Long-Arm female, others unknown. Not that any of that helped.

"Maybe I could watch it," the whiny one offered, wandering around Joey in a slow circle. It didn't look up, just stared at his chest. "It looks easy."

"No eating, Beige!" Desert ordered, pointing her knife at him. "We don't eat any of them till we're sure we've won. We don't know if the others caught the ones that went up-mountain."

"But there aren't any birds here," Beige whined back, not looking up. "And the Kaskans are all jumpy. Can't get a decent meal for miles! And it's so plump…" Beige licked its lips.

"No eating!" Desert repeated.

"I agree," Flat added, nodding. "We gotta be sure. These ones got us good on the beach. I don't want to chase them all over the Range, I just want my pardon."

"This isn't a democracy!" Desert shouted, glaring at Flat.

Long-Arm rubbed her belly and whined, "I'm hungry."

"Maybe just a bit," Beige wheedled. "This one looks overweight. See, its got all kinds of extra danglies." Beige toed Joey's arm.

"That's an arm," Flat pointed out. "I think they need those."

"They definitely need those," Desert declared.

"Does it really though?" Beige pondered, pausing. It glanced at Desert. "What's an arm, really? It's for swimming, working stuff, and these things probably don't know about any of that. I bet they don't even swim!"

"I swim," Bee stated.

Silence.

"Well, now we know they have Translators," Flat declared, looking at Desert. Going by tone, Bee figured it was smiling. Vinna smiles actually looked a lot like human ones, though with substantially fewer visible teeth. "That means they got cleaned…" Flat added.

"No sexing the dinner!" Desert growled.

"So they are dinner!" Beige said, hopping on the balls of its feet.

"That's it, Beige!" Desert howled, straightening to his fullest height. It wasn't even close to Long-Arms, but it was more than Beige's. "You're gonna be dinner if you don't shut up and wait!"

"Come on," Beige whined, wilting. "It'll be hours before the others show up. They got absolutely dried yesterday. I bet they wouldn't complain if we left them some limbs. A leg or two? That one's haunches look plump," Beige gestured at Bee, "More than enough to make up for lost opportunity."

"It's not even about that," Desert said. "It's about finding the rest of these aliens, because they could vanish into the pools for weeks if the others lost them. If we kill these ones, we lose our bait. And information. We need to wait to eat them until we start torturing them, at the very least!"

"I could go for some torture right about now," Long-Arm mumbled, his voice echoing through the trees.

"What she said!" Beige agreed, beaming and stabbing a claw towards Long-Arm's broad chest.

"Why are we even talking about this?" Desert hissed, wiping one hand slowly across his face.

"Because you kept us up all night walking, after fighting that beast of a Kaskan, so now we don't have Current to cannibalize instead of food?" Flat offered.

Desert hissed angrily. He spun and snatched Flat's nearest horn. Wrenching them away from Bee, Desert shouted in their face, spittle flying, "What'd I tell you about keeping your mouth shut in front of the-"

Two things came to a head in the moment of silence that followed.

One, the Vinna realized that they'd let go of all three humans.

And two, all three humans realized they'd been let go of.

Bee's hand shot up. She pushed Current out as fast as she could, pouring it into a circle of ice that radiated from her palm. The disc of white grew, hungrily expanding outwards at the upright Vinna. Flat took the blow full force in the thighs and flipped forward, legs flying back and up. Beige gaped, then flipped as well, howling with pain as something snapped. Long-Arm and Desert were equidistant, but neither were hit. Desert dug a clawed hand into a tree and raised himself above the ice. Long-Arm smashed one meaty hand down and smashed the circled before it touched him.

Olivia was up before the broken chunks of ice hit the ground. A blur of blue-green suit and icy-white knives, she shot around a trunk and smashed into Desert from behind.

A shriek roared from Desert's mouth, fangs spread wide as he snapped his jaws closed over and over. One clawed hand pinned to the wood by an ice-knife, he used the other to hold back Olivia's other blade as it hovered a hair from his chest. The duo hung there, suspending in the air, Desert by his claw and Olivia by a strand of Current that wound from her torso to the tree's branches.

Then Bee's was attention torn away by the long, curved knife Beige stabbed into her arm. She hissed at the pain, spittle flying between clenched teeth. She rolled, far hand rising and falling like a crashing wave. In her mind she saw a mace there, a handle and a chain of crystal and a ball of brutal, jagged white. The ball smashed into Beige's chest, drawing a bellowing scream from its lungs. The sound cutoff suddenly, replaced by a gagging cough, blood splattering across its lips and the nearby stone. Bee felt drops land on her face.

Pushing herself up, Bee backpedaled from the coughing, bleeding Beige. She clutched at her mental image of the mace, of the spiked head, and reshaped it. She drove those edges, those spikes forward and into Beige. Flickers of white punched through the Vinna's back.

Bee let go of the ice. It dissolved, condensation flying as it melted away. There was a hole in Beige's chest, but Bee didn't want to see the mess that was inside it. She didn't want to see the tears pouring from Beige's eyes. Flat was on his ass a few steps beyond Beige, staring.

The moment broke with Long-Arms bellowed howl. The massive Vinna was behind Bee now. That was bad. She lunged, fighting to gain distance, but a massive hand snatched her up. Long, thick digits encircled her neck like the limbs of a steel vice.

"You killed Beige!" accused Long-Arm, shaking Bee like a toy.

Knife still protruding from her bicep, whipped back and forth like a dog toy, Bee decided that today sucked. The motion disoriented her, pain from the wound in her arm adding insult to injury. She didn't know where to throw her Current, let alone think of what to do with it when it got there.

"Long-Arm!" a far smaller, sharper voice cut in.

The jerking stopped.

Dizzy, the world hazy around her, Bee blinked, frantically fighting to regain her senses. Long-Arm was still, staring past her at the scene strewed before them.

Joey sprawled at their feet, almost below Bee. He was heaving, arms wrapped around a chest that looked disturbingly more concave than human chests were meant to be. At the center of the clearing lay Beige, hollowed and bloody. Flat sat on the far side, still as stone and wide-eyed, staring at Olivia and Desert. The duo stood on the root strewn forest floor. Olivia had a saw-edged length of ice in her hand, its blue, oozing handle showing, putty-like, between her fingers. The blade was against Desert's neck, little trails of blood showing where the teeth had dragged.

"Let's talk," Olivia said, the bruising on her neck fading.

"Let go of him!" Long-Arm demanded. She bared a dizzying number of large fangs.

"No," Olivia stated, stony.

Long-Arm frowned.

"She's got a point," Flat noted, nodding.

"Shut u-!" Desert began, but he cut himself off as Olivia's blade dragged another inch down his neck.

"She has a point?" Long-Arm asked, peering curiously at Flat.

"Well, we were talking about eating them," Flat explained.

"You wanted to screw 'em," Long-Arm said.

Flat winced. "So glad you reminded them of that."

"You calling me dumb?" Long-Arm boomed.

"Oh no," Flat said, ostentatiously derisive, "I'd never insult a big-blood. Never consider it. Especially not criminal ones, that'd be silly!"

"I'm gonna break you, Flat!" Long-Arm growled, the boom suddenly deeper, grating. Her claws dug in, slicing deeper into Bee's suit and skin.

"Please," Flat groaned, rolling both eyes skyward. "You're a big-blood with a bad temper, Desert's trapped, and I'm on my ass. You're too stupid to figure out how this goes. Get on with it already."

Desert's mouth shot open, but Long-Arm's name didn't survive the journey from his brain and his lips. Olivia slashed his neck.

The massive paw Long-Arm had around Bee's throat clamped tight. Those claws grated against Bee's bones.

Hardening Current into a burst of ice, Bee flared it from her throat like a bladed frill. Wetness splattered across her head and shoulders. Long-Arm's grip vanished as her fingers fell to the ground. Bee dropped to the ground barely missing Joey he rolled away.

Then Long-Arm screamed. It was huge. The booming depth of her voice transformed into the body of a piercing, echoing resonance. There was no warble, no trilling, just a rocketing shock of noise.

Rising to one knee, Joey snatched the gun from Beige's belt. He leveled the weapon and fired.

The scream stopped. Long-Arm stared.

Joey kept firing until the gun stopped responding. It'd had a full clip.

Long-Arm teetered and fell like a bag of bricks. Dust and rubble rose in her wake, clouding the clearing.

Upright, Bee moved away from the body. It'd nearly fallen on her, but not quite. The lack of an arm's balancing weight had sent it more to the side. Joey crouched, gun reloaded and pointed at Flat.

"Wait," Olivia ordered, her saw-blade dribbling from her hand.

"What'd it look like I was doing?" Joey returned.

Olivia grunted. "Bee; helms and weapons?"

Nodding, Bee spun in a slow circle looking for where their gear had been thrown.

"Over there," Flat supplied, gesturing behind the tree Joey had been leaning against last night.

"Thanks," Bee said absently, making her way past Long-Arm and around the tree. Sure enough, three helms, six knives, and six guns waited on the other side. "Got it!" she called, bending down to collect the first load.

"By the six, you people are efficient," Flat sighed. "Nice trap on the beach, by the way. The Ritualists will be so pleased."

"Really?" Olivia queried, oozing disbelief and sarcasm.

Flat nodded, his mouth curling into a smile while his teeth remained hidden. "Oh yeah. A bunch of them bet on your species getting at least one team through the Rite."

Olivia grunted, noncommittal. "And I care about that because…"

"No reason," Flat admitted with a shrug. "Just saying. I kind of babble when I'm nervous. Or excited. It's just a thing I do."

"Along with getting your team killed?" Joey demanded.

"Hive-mind, or no?" Flat shot back, looking back and forth between Joey and Olivia. "You look different, but you both make me nervous. Makes it hard to tell."

"Not," Olivia said.

"Glad you got the right impression though," Joey added.

"Anytime," Flat said, still smiling, but Bee caught the gulp that bobbed their scaled Adam's apple.

"Guns," Bee said, offering Olivia her pair.

"Thanks," Olivia said, taking them and reattaching them to her belt. "How far out are the rest?" she asked Flat, glancing over at them.

"Hours?" Flat offered, shrugging in a nonchalant and entirely unhelpful fashion. "You hit them pretty hard during that chase. Only reason we caught you was because you turned north again after fleeing south." Flat frowned, mock-thoughtful, one claw tapping their lips. "Maybe not the best plan?" they offered, sardonic.

"I hate when the cannibal's right, but…" Joey trailed off.

"Meet many cannibals?" Bee countered, already on her way back with their knives.

"He's not a cannibal," Olivia grumbled. "They said they'd eat us. That's not cannibalism."

"Do you eat each other too?" Joey asked, looking at Flat.

Flat half-nodded. "More or less."

Joey smirked at Olivia. "Told you."

"Shut up," Olivia shot back. She took her knives from Bee and strapped them on.

"That scream probably got them running, if they weren't already," Bee noted.

"Ball problem," Olivia reminded her, shifting her knives and guns more comfortably about her hips. "Trap or escape?"

"Trap," Joey voted. "This bunch weren't bad. We-"

"Point of order," Flat interrupted.

"Yes?" Olivia prompted after a pause.

"We got left to go hunting through Kaskan-pools while the others went down the nice quiet river; which part of that makes you think we were the big, boss ones?"

"You're the runts," Joey said, groaning.

"Hey, now that's not what I said!" Flat griped, shooting Joey a venomous look. "I'm just saying that we weren't the really criminal criminals. We just sort of tagged along."

"Criminals," Olivia repeated, her eyes narrowing.

"Yeah," Flat said, nodding. "Penance through service. You must do it too, right? We serve our people to make up for our wrongs. Do enough and you get to go home."

"Our version doesn't include hunting aliens in dangerous wildernesses," Bee explained, coming back with helms for the others. Hers was already on.

"Weird," Flat deadpanned. "Anyway, the assholes were in the other group. Career Ritual-grinders."

"Explain that," Olivia said, shaking her head.

"Ritual-grinder?" Flat clarified. "They're the ones that commit bad enough crimes that they're sentenced to life as Ritual fodder. The ones that get good at it are nicknamed grinders because they make so many aliens into meat."

"So you four committed lesser crimes," Bee said, getting it. Trying to. The sickening image of lizards turning humans into 'meat' was making her stomach turn.

"Desert had anger issues and refused to work them out. Ended up hitting a child. Long-Arm attacked a Holy for implying she was dumb. Beige stole someone's Kaskan-milk stash. I might've, maybe, slept with the wrong alien."

"Wrong alien?" Joey repeated.

"Well, I thought she was the alien that'd been flirting with me the night before, but in the dark things get so confusing…"

"What'd the other group do?" Bee pushed, clamping down on the urge to shoot the rapist cannibal.

"Couple of murderers and a rapist, I think," Flat said. "Never really saw the file on them, you know, but word gets around when someone goes criminal. Doesn't happen often. Juicy gossip."

"What makes the other one a rapist and not you?" Olivia queried, her voice even, neutral.

"Oh, I slept with an alien, not a Vinna," Flat answered, smiling with just the faintest hint of teeth. "Totally diff-"

Bee shot him first. She'd seen Olivia's hand move to her gun. Bee had already drawn hers. Joey lowered his and stood up.

"So, Joey muttered, thinking as he went around and shot each Vinna in the head. "I got one in the head on the beach, and now these four. When we left the river, how many headshots?"

"Two," Olivia said.

That meant three more baddies. With a tracker ball. Damn.

Joey nodded. "We should get going."

"Let's," Olivia agreed, taking off at a loping jog. Bee and Joey fell in behind her.

Ten steps later, a thud echoed through the trees. Olivia hissed and dove behind a tree trunk. Blood rolled down her arm, seeping from a fresh hole in her shoulder.

Left shoulder. Enemies on the left.

More thuds. Shards of something whistled through the air.

Bee dropped into a crouch and put her back against a convenient tree. Behind her, Joey thumped against another trunk.

Silence.

Looking past Olivia, Bee could see the mountains looming. They were close. Really close. They must've wandered west, towards the range as they ran north last night.

"Bee, can you see them?" Olivia's voice queried.

For a moment, Bee couldn't understand why Olivia was giving away where they were to the Vinna, then she remembered the helms. She wasn't giving them away; she'd just reconnected them.

Ducking around the tree, Bee tried to get a quick look. A stony bullet shattered against her helm, spinning her back behind the trunk.

"Nope," Bee answered. She ran a flicker of Current across the helm, looking for cracks. Nothing. Good.

"I see them," Joey announced.

Glancing over at him, Bee beamed. Damn clever bastard. He'd made a mirror from Current and stuck it out to see the enemy's reflection.

Joey grunted. "I see two, about thirty meters off. One gun each."

"Where's the third?" Bee wondered, nervous. Shooting looks at the surrounding woods, she tried to find the missing one. The trees were too dense; it could've gotten around behind them. Could be sneaking up behind them. Fuck. Her heart pounded, adrenaline rushing.

"Breathe," Olivia ordered, still even but with just a hint of sharpness. "Joey, can you get a shot?"

"Not from this far with this many trees," Joey replied.

"Go right on my mark," Olivia said. "Ready?"

"Ready," Joey returned.

"Go!" Olivia blurted, bending at the waist to fire around her tree. Thuds carried among the branches, stone bullets whispering along with the leaves. Stray shots hit wood and sent splinters raining out with deep, shaking thumps and cracks.

Kneeling, Bee copied Olivia. She couldn't see the Vinna, so she shot in the general direction and hoped that got the point across. Twenty shots didn't last long. She switched guns and added another twenty. Empty again, she shifted behind the tree to reload. Back to the trunk again, she looked up and met the eyes of a big damn lizard.

"It's-" Bee shouted, but the words were cut off.

A knife slammed into her chest like a sledgehammer. It plucked her from her feet, pummeling her against the tree, but it didn't go through. Gasping, she fell back as the knife withdrew.

Pitching forward on stiffened legs, Bee blasted Current at the lizard. This time it wasn't controlled, just raw force barreling from her core.

The Vinna snarled, leaning into the torrent of blue. Scales chipped and flew, patches of the maroon suit tore and dragged, but its hooves didn't even shift. Amidst the pain, the stunning breathlessness, and the shock of the Vinna's ambush, Bee didn't see the knife coming. This time it didn't catch on her patches. It went straight through, just under her ribcage, and thunked into the tree.

Bee gaped; the torrent of blue that'd filled her vision waned. It was surreal. It was… wrong.

Hissing, lips curled upwards into a sneered facsimile of a smile, the Vinna released its knife and plucked one of Bee's from her belt. It shoved that one through her belly, inches below the first.

Its eyes never left hers.

The second blade vibrated as it hit a knot in the tree. Bee flinched, rocked by another wave of pain. The movement made the first knife throb.

The Vinna winced as a bullet burst through its shoulder, splattering Bee's helm with blood. For a breath, the liquid hung in her vision, levitating in the air inches from her eyes. Then faded into nothingness.

Snatching Bee's other knife, the Vinna drove it through her belly. Even lower than the first two, it barely missed her pelvis. Apparently Bee looked pretty dead, because the scaled monster spun and took off towards Joey. Halfway there, the Vinna stepped around a large root, shifting just far enough to the side that Bee could see Joey. With the mottled suit, helm, and two guns, he looked like something from another world.

Both of Joey's guns began to thud. Bullets slammed into the Vinna over and over, peppering its head and shoulders. The lizard staggered, weaving drunkenly, arms raised to block what it could. Swaths of ice appeared, veiling its forearms as it covered the last few steps.

A tendril of Current rose from the earth; it wove around Joey's feet and carried him back, flitting through the trees. He didn't stop shooting, and the Vinna didn't stop following. Every time the tendril reached more than a few yards, it slowed, dropping Joey, only to be replaced by another as soon as his feet touched the ground. It happened two, three times in a dozen seconds.

Bee couldn't summon the courage to move, it hurt enough just holding herself in place. Even breathing hurt, every gentle motion of muscle and organ grating her innards against the knives. Current flowed into those holes like water through a sieve, replacing blood and flesh just quickly enough to keep her alive.

Hurtling above the trees, Ty heard the thuds again, directly below now. With a thought, he banished the Current that spread, paper-thin, from his arms. The expansive wings of his glider disappeared, leaving him hurtling towards the treetops.

"Oh crap!" Ty screeched, realizing quite how far up he was only as he began to fall.

Imagining an icy umbrella, Ty tried to concentrate through the pounding beat of his heart and the rush of adrenaline. Blue-white blossomed from his hand, flowing out into a snowy bowl that slowed his descent as much from magic as aerodynamics.

Seconds later, Ty descended through the canopy. His legs quivered, desperate for ground and wired with adrenaline and stress from his sudden fall.

The Vinna were right in front of Ty. Two of them. One was turned the wrong way, shooting at something out of sight. The other snarled and spun to shoot at him. Both wore the maroon and carried guns. No injuries. Yet.

Ty ground his teeth and banished the umbrella. He dropped to the forest floor, surefooted, gun raised. Badass. Time to end some lizards.

The Vinna shot first. Bullets smacked into Ty's torso. Pain tore through his nerves, lighting up like fireworks behind his eyes. Hissing through his clenched teeth, he fired back, taking a second between each shot to put bullet after bullet in the thing's head. It didn't try to dodge. Instead, its head disappeared behind a darkly hazy bubble of Current. His shots hit, but they only crunched, creating spidery cracks that quickly receded.

Ty dropped to one knee and leaned forward, hoping to use his helm as a bit of a shield. It felt wrong, but Nat had been right so far.

The others broke through canopy overhead, guns drawn and shooting.

Ty frowned. He'd gotten too far ahead. And he'd forgotten how high he was. Next time, more planning, less cowboy.

The second Vinna turned at the added noise. After a momentary double take, it scrabbled around to the other side of the tree. Bullets reddened its fleeing back. It pitched forward, but Current rushed out to form a blue shell in its wake.

Advancing at a walk, Zed and Seth moved towards the runner. They staggered their shots, each giving the other time to aim without easing their fire. Zed had spent hours getting them all to do that right.

Nat was already moving, too. Ty leapt to join her, hop-skipping to catch up. He'd forgotten the whole 'get close all together and overwhelm them' plan. Definitely less cowboy next time. His steps were longer, so he slowed once he was even with Nat. Going for the first Vinna's head, Ty sent bullet after bullet into that bubble of magic, but Nat went for its chest. She varied, looking for organs and sensitive spots. Red blossomed over where a human sternum would be. The lizard crumpled, slumping to the ground. The bubble melted away.

Dancing around a low branch and some roots, Ty slammed his gun's base into a trunk. Reloaded, he poured wooden bullets into the Vinna's head.

"One target!" Zed said, drawing him away from the corpse. She and the others were still a few paces back, blasting the other lizard's shield.

Skipping around the tree that was in the way, Ty realized that he could nearly see around the edge of the blue barrier. He circled further, trying to get a clear shot. He was almost opposite Zed and the others when he realized the Vinna was rotating the shield as he moved.

Quelling the urge to curse, Ty gave up on being clever. He started shooting the shield. The Vinna couldn't hold it forever.

Seconds later, Zed vaulted up and over the wall's far lip.

Ty whooped, impressed as she rose up and over in one graceful flight. She was grinning, knife in each hand.

Then Ty noticed the thuds coming from further into the woods. He hadn't caught them before, not with the mess of gunshots going on, but now they were the only ones. Zed had the second Vinna, but there could be more. More who might be killing his friends right now.

Spinning, Ty charged off towards the noise. A dozen strides later, someone groaned to his right. His head whipped around, his feet still rocketing on.

A human was pinned to a tree by three knives. Not tall, so not Joey. Not short and slight, so not Olivia. Had to be Bee. She was a mess of fresh and congealed blood. He kept running, feet on autopilot, as he stared. Was she-

Something hard clotheslined Ty, smacking into his upper chest with all the subtlety of a battering ram. He flipped, his helm slamming into the rocky ground. Through some miracle, nothing broke. A clawed hand snatched his collar and heaved him against a tree. Gasping at bruising impacts, Ty glared into the eyes of a Vinna. It was huge, broad shouldered and ripped, rows of pearly daggers flashing. It smiled at him for a fraction of a second, then its gun began to thud.

Ty felt the bullets tear through his chest. He wished he didn't. He poured Current into the wounds, trying to stifle the pain, but it didn't stop.

The gun clicked.

"Heal that, weakling," the Vinna spat. It dropped him, letting his body contort at the base of the tree. Between its feet, Ty could see a slight figure, icy daggers in each hand. Olivia. She flashed across the ground, her feet graceful as a dancer's.

Bending down, the Vinna plucked Ty's gun from the ground. Then it froze.

Olivia was so close now. Ty could see her feet through the gap between the lizard's ass and the dirt.

The lizard spun, falling backwards on top of Ty. He couldn't see anything, but he felt the jabbing pains of knifepoints. They peppered his chest, faster than the bullets but only an inch or so deep.

Long seconds passed, but no thuds came. The Vinna's taut muscles relaxed, slumping into dead weight. After what felt like a century, it was rolled off of him. Olivia waited on the other side. Her helm was still on, but he could feel the determined smile behind it.

"You ok?" Olivia queried.

"Need Nat," Ty grunted. The pain was gone, but the discomforting emptiness of those bullet holes was very present. It gave him odd, ghostly reminders of the wounds the robots had given him, though these were smaller. He chuckled. Then he coughed as something wet filled his mouth.

"I've got you," said Olivia, distant, her voice never rising. Her hand rested on Ty's chest. He felt the holes healing, their entrances and exits gently sealing. "Medic!" she called.

"Thanks," he muttered, trying to clear his throat. "Bee's in a bad way too," he added. Something dribbled down the corner of his mouth. Didn't taste like bile. Was he drooling? No, it was metallic. Thick. Yuck.

"She's a big girl, lots of Current, she'll be fine," Olivia said, her voice quickening, as though trying to convince herself as much as him.

"Yer a good boss, boss," Ty said, patting her shoulder. Wow. The motion made the world bob and weave disconcertingly. Crazy. Getting shot hadn't done that last time.

"Thanks," Olivia replied, distracted, her helm rotating as she scanned the trees. The cool rush from her hand was slowing to a trickle.

"Don't give me all of it," Ty said. He gently lifted her hand from his chest. "Might need that."

Her head jerked around, staring at him. "How many are left?"

"Not like that," Ty replied, groaning as he shifted to a more comfortable spot on the tree's roots. "Think we got em all. Still might need it though."

"How many did you get and where?" Olivia pushed.

"Two when we landed, one here," he answered, blinking. His eyelids felt really heavy.

Olivia sighed, audibly smiling. "That's all of them, then."

"You should go find the ball-thingy," Ty said, working to get the thoughts out. Talking was hard too. Weird.

"In a minute," Olivia said, shifting her squat to a seat on a large rock. "Gotta make sure you're not gonna get in trouble first."

"Ha! Right, because I'm such a troublemaker," Ty retorted. He chuckled, but it rolled into a hacking cough. More wetness slipped from his mouth. He ignored it. Maybe if he didn't think about it the problem would go away.

"Hey! Ty!" Olivia said. She punched his shoulder. "Keep talking to me, ok? All this quiet out here makes me nervous."

"Quiet makes you nervous?" Ty said, chuckling again. It became another wet cough. "After everything, I thought it took more to mess with you. Like maybe a dragon or a plague of locusts or maybe a divine intervention."

"Maybe it's the whole alien planet part," Olivia replied.

Ty tried to nod, but his head felt heavy. His chin slid forward, stopping only when his helm landed on his chest. "Alien. Yeah, that'd do it," he agreed.

"Hey, Ty! Ty! Keep talking," Olivia said, punching his shoulder again. He didn't feel the punch, but he guessed there'd been one. His eyelids were so heavy.

Everything was just... heavy.

"Talk about what?" Ty asked. He was slurring his words. Had he been doing that before? He didn't remember. Bit out of breath too. Weird.

"I dunno," Olivia said, an odd desperation slipping through. "What's your favorite color?"

"Easy, boss," Ty said, smiling. "Blue," he added, but it didn't come out right. He felt flat, emptied, and there was a lot of liquid in his mouth. He coughed again.

"Ok, what's your favorite song?" Olivia went on.

Ty didn't answer. It wasn't important. His eyelids were so heavy.

"Ty!" Olivia said.

Silence.

"Ty!"

Nothing.

It was late. Far later than Zed should've stayed up, but she couldn't sleep. Today have been… a lot. If they'd come an hour later, even a minute later…

So, Zed sat by the fire and added twigs. Minutes later, tongues of flame lavished their attention along every stick she cared to give them. She kept it small, less than a foot. The smoke wouldn't be visible at night, but too much light would be. They didn't know where the next enemy was yet. Yet.

The little fire slowly chewed away at the large root that it leaned against. She couldn't tell which tree belonged to the root, but hopefully it didn't cause too much damage. Lean-to fires had always been easier for her. Little stack of sticks against something larger, bit of burning something and tinder underneath, and you had fire. Easy.

Easy.

God, it'd been a day.

Rubbing her eyes with both hands, Zed almost missed Olivia emerging from the tent. She was facing the water, watching for Crocs and Kaskans, but she heard the light, padded steps. Glancing over her shoulder, she watched the shorter woman come closer. The sand was bright with starlight, making the muddy colors of the suit stand out. Olivia had ditched her helm, leaving her black hair to dangle, lifeless in the windless night.

Turning away, Zed ran her eyes across the river and the pools beyond. The water trickled, almost loud in the emptiness. This spot didn't seem to splash as much as past campsites. The pools were shallower, cleft here and there to flow in thin streams, without noisy fuss. Other than that, it seemed the same. It made her wonder though. How many days would they spend out here before they could tell the difference? After two months, maybe she'd be able to spot different peaks or bends. After six, maybe the woods would start feeling comfortable, less like the clueless mystery it was now. She'd find some bit of moss or a particular type of branch that only grew on the south side of the trees, something to relieve the enigma.

Olivia sat, settling softly onto the ground. She inched forward, hands going out to bathe in the fire's meager warmth. Not that it mattered. Neither of them was cold. If Olivia rolled her sleeves down even her fingertips would be fine.

But that wasn't the point. Zed looked at her own bare hand. Flexing her wrist, she popped the joint. Then she added her hands next to Olivia's. It wasn't about being warm. The fire felt comforting, safe.

There hadn't been much of that in a long time.

Silence. Comfortable silence, the kind that seemed to weigh down the tongue like a finger to the lips, whispering of quiet joys.

Zed shifted around to stretch her legs. She sighed, relieved. For a second, she'd wondered.

Doctors had called it Ghosting. The feeling when amputees felt missing limbs. She didn't know what they'd call someone feeling the echoes of a limb's loss. Ghosting still, or maybe something else. Probably somebody's name. Henry's Echo or something dumb like that. Or a syndrome. Doctors.

A shiver ran down Zed's spine. She pulled back from the fire, rubbing her hands together. How long it would take for her phantom wound to fade was another question she wished she didn't have.

Another series of soft steps came from the tent.

Olivia looked first. Zed copied her.

The figure was tall, broad shouldered, and bald, with a face darker than the shadows of the trees beyond. Ty.

They turned back to the fire. Zed returned her hands to the flame's heat. Olivia just stared at the mountains.

Ty sat on Olivia's other side. For a moment, it looked like he had something to say. Then his jaw closed. He shook his head and gazed at the rivers gleaming silver surface. He looked better than he had this morning, but that wasn't exactly a hard thing. Nat had gotten him patched up, barely. She'd collapsed afterwards. Fainted. It'd taken a few hours to get them to the beach, a few more for the adrenaline to wear off. No one had wanted to sleep while the sun was up. They'd all wandered around, listless and armed with paranoia and exhaustion.

It'd taken until nearly sunset for anyone to bring up finding the tent. They'd managed it, but only because Joey had recognized a particular stand of trees halfway up the mountainside. Well after dark, he and Seth had come back, armed with the tent and nothing else. No one asked. They were all tired. They must've taken turns to carry that much.

More patting from the tent, with some dragging, scuffing sounds mixed in.

This time, Ty was the only one to look. He smiled, but it was the sad, regretful kind.

A minute later, Joey sat down on Zed's left. Bee went beside him. Zed didn't look at them until they'd both settled in. Once they were, she caught Bee's eyes and smiled. She tried to make it comforting, but the warmth couldn't quite break the sad ice around her eyes. Bee smiled back, stiff but trying. Trying was enough.

Zed returned to the fire. She used her warm palms to scare the chill from her ears.

From the tent, a thumping, slapping sound puffed and huffed its way across the beach.

Goddamn horn-dogs, Zed cursed internally, rolling her eyes. It wasn't quite real though, more an obligatory derision than actual dislike or discomfort. There was something comforting to the sound, to the humanity of it. Like laughter, but less G-rated.

With a deep breath, Zed straightened her back and peered up at the boundless star-scape that filled the sky. It was like one of those spinning spiral things, the one that were supposed to make you dizzy, or hypnotize you or whatever. It wasn't the shape that did it though; it was just so damn beautiful.

Long minutes passed. No one spoke. The tent noises just kept going. Someone was having a good time.

Eventually, they stopped.

A few minutes later, more footsteps came. No one looked this time.

Nat and Seth sat on the open side of the fire, their backs to the river. Maybe they trusted the others to watch their backs, or maybe they were still a bit high from their fun.

"I couldn't sleep," Nat said, filling the silence with an almost reflexive quickness. "I guess we all had… a bit of a day."

Joey snorted. Zed smiled. Ty shook his head, rueful.

"It'll be nice to move on to the next one," Bee said.

"Here's to that," Ty agreed.

There was a general murmur of agreement. They were all still a bit stunned to have the option.

Zed leaned forward, her hands near the fire again. "Do we look tonight, or wait?"

There was a pause, and then Seth said, "Better to know."

"What he said," Joey agreed.

Zed looked to Olivia. Out of the corner of her eye, she saw the others do the same.

Olivia nodded. "We're all up anyway." Reaching down the collar of her suit, she pulled a thin chain. The ball emerged, metallic and the same as the others. "Who's got Current?" she queried.

"Me," Zed said, offering her hand. She filled her palm with clear water. Olivia dropped the ball in. It spun.

And spun.

And spun.

And spun.

And nothing else happened.

"Is it broken?" Seth asked.

"How would we know?" Ty countered.

"That seems like a pretty good hint," Nat pointed out, thumbing at the spinning ball's lightless surface.

"Well, only if you're impatient," a voice said from behind Zed's back. It was silken, nearly sibilant.

They all drew. Zed and Olivia didn't bother trying to get back; they just spun and leveled their guns.

"Oh good," the Vinna said, eyeing them critically. "Good start. Good start for sure, but you'll have to work on that one. Remember, if you spread out it'll decrease the effectiveness of most ordinances. Though, if your enemy gets this close there won't be much point in worrying about explosives." Another Vinna stood at their shoulder, but they were alone, as far as Zed could tell.

"You're Blue-Sight, the one who left us the message in the Kaskan," Olivia said, nodding at the speaker. "And you're the one that shoved us out of the plane," she continued, shifting her aim to the quiet one.

"Feather," the quiet one added, nodding. He gave them a close-lipped smile. "Good memory."

"Hard to forget," Olivia growled.

"You'd be surprised," Feather said, glancing back at the tent. "Seems like you've done pretty well for yourselves."

"Nearly seven," Blue-Sight added, nodding happily. "Pretty high mark, so far."

"That's a compliment, in case you missed it," Feather explained. "Your species seems a bit… fragile. You're scoring pretty low in your Rites."

Zed swallowed, trying to get rid of the lump in her throat. She didn't want to know how many people had been put through this hell. She really didn't. Speaking also seemed like a bad idea. She was too mad. Not shooting them was taking almost all of her attention.

"But now you've passed!" Blue-Sight added, raising both hands towards them. "The Rite is over. Congratulations on your victory!"

Silence.

Shock rolled through Zed's very bones, layered with relief and disbelief and utter confusion. It was over? How… Why… Over. Finally over.

"Thank God," Zed whispered.

"Seriously?" Bee said.

"No way," Ty mumbled, numb.

"What?" Joey hissed.

"Finally!" whispered Seth.

"It's over," Nat muttered, repeating it over and over again under her breath.

Olivia didn't say a word.

"Did pretty passably too," Feather agreed, nodding. "I do have some thoughts and suggestions, but we'll get to that. For now, we should get you to a warm meal and some beds."

Jaws dropped.

"Shut up," and "Damn," came from several mouths, but Zed couldn't tell whose. She was too distracted by the very thought of a real meal, let alone a real, soft, sand-less bed.

"So, everyone take one of these and we'll get going," Blue-Sight said, reaching one hand around to procure what looked like a half-dozen cloth binders.

After a few breaths, Olivia made her way over and took the packets. She frowned, half-turned back towards Zed and the others. "There are only six," she said, shooting Blue-Sight and Feather a withering look. "Didn't think we'd all make it?"

"Oh no," Feather said, adding an emphatic headshake. "We brought one Waterwing for everyone who may leave."

Silence.

"Who can't leave?" Ty asked, fear making his voice quaver, dancing like fire before a withering wind.

"The dark female," Feather declared, nodding towards Bee.

Shifting as if to block their sight, Zed bared her teeth. What the hell were they trying to pull? She shot a look over her shoulder. Bee sat, gun in hand and wide eyed. The gun wandered, drooping from nerveless fingers as her eyes pooled with glistening, starlit tears. They all knew what made her different. It was the same thing that'd caused her to scrape and scuff across the beach. No matter what Nat had tried, Bee's legs still didn't work. One of the knives had severed her spine. Apparently Current couldn't heal that.

"What…" Seth trailed off.

Nat growled, full of all of the desperation and futility and rage that Zed felt.

"Fuck that," Joey said.

"She passed," said Olivia, her back straightening, decisive.

"She may not leave," Feather countered.

Olivia shook her head. "You're wrong."

"If you refuse to accept my ruling, you will all be in the same boat," Feather warned.

Olivia turned to look at the rest of them. "We either abandon her, leave her out here alone, or we all have to stay with her."

Silence.

An almost inaudible sob came from behind Zed, from Bee.

"I know this isn't a democracy, but I think we need to vote," Seth said, each word grating in the fearful, stunned quiet.

Olivia looked at Zed. Numb, Zed nodded. She wanted to shoot so badly, but the lizards would just heal, and then they'd all be screwed. A vote. She didn't wasn't even sure of her own choice yet, what would the others say?

"Vote," Olivia said.

"I vote we stay," Seth replied, barely waiting for her to finish.

Olivia's eyes went a bit wider, the whites gleaming with starlight.

"Seconded," Nat added. "We don't leave friends behind."

"Stay," agreed Ty.

"Stay," Joey said.

Zed nodded, a rush of warmth running through her core. God, she was proud of them. "Stay."

Silence hung for a moment, full of cold foreboding and the heated looks of friends accepting their fate. Olivia smiled, bitter and pleased.

"We're staying with her," Olivia told Blue-Sight, turning back to face him. She offered him the cloth packets.

"You're sure?" Blue-Sight said. "Understand, you're agreeing to something that will likely consume the rest of your lives."

"Never thought I'd live long anyways," Olivia answered. "Might as well spend my time with friends."

"A consensus?" Blue-Sight asked, stepping slowly to one side, then to the other, meeting every human eye in turn.

"Screw leaving," Zed muttered. It hurt, but it'd hurt more to live with leaving Bee. She'd trained her, she'd hunted with her, slept with her, stood watch with her, listened to her snore, heard her whine, fought with her, and nearly died with her over and over. Leaving had never really been an option.

"Fuck off," Bee agreed, crawling forward to sit next to Zed, gun leveled again. She grunted at the effort, pulling herself along one-handed, but no one interfered. Joey slid out of the way, but didn't say a word. They knew her well enough to know she didn't have want help, not then. Not in front of the enemy, and not after all they'd just given up for her.

Out of the corner of her eye, Zed could see the tear-streaks that ran down Bee's cheeks. They still ran, but there was a bitter clench to her jaw, a buoyed resolve in her eyes.

With a calm, graceful shrug, Blue-Sight back away, stopping just behind Feather.

Feather moved closer, looming over Olivia. Bending at the waist, nearly eye to eye with her, Feather said, "Congratulations again."

Silence hung in the air like the toll of an enormous bell, deafening and long.

"You've chosen to protect your comrade. You're showing compassion and loyalty. That's exactly what we're looking for," Feather said, his lips splitting into a beaming, toothy smile.

With a deep breath, Zed asked what they were all wondering. "Why?"

Feather shifted to look at her, dark lids flicking over his white eyes. "Because this Rite is one of recruitment. Loyalty is vital in good soldiers, and I have every hope that your team will be very effective."

"Soldiers," Olivia repeated, the word soft, numb.

"Welcome," Feather said, arms sweeping wide, "To the Third Range, home of the Second Legion of Forlorn Hope."

The End

Acknowledgements

There are so very many people who helped me get this far. I am so very grateful to my parents, siblings, and family, of all sorts. You are part of this, always. Georgia, my heroine, read every page along the way and made sure that I never gave up, no matter how doubtful I was that this would ever be printed. Ariel, my dear friend, took one look at it and found the good and the bad.

To all those who've pushed me to tell this tale, thank you.

About the Author

William McDonald-Newman grew up on an island, reading Greek myths and Arthurian legends. Along the way, a lot of home schooling and a bit of public school launched him into Beloit College, where he received a bachelor's degree in Anthropology and History. Currently, he has trouble deciding between Hufflepuff and Slytherin, but why choose when you can have both? Waterborn is his first novel.